THE PROMISE

THE PROMISE

THE FOUNDATION CHRONICLES

TERRENCE L. ROTERING

XULON PRESS

Xulon Press
555 Winderley Pl, Suite 225
Maitland, FL 32751
407.339.4217
www.xulonpress.com

NOVELS BY TERRENCE L. ROTERING
Available from Xulon Press
THE FAITHFUL (2024)
STAND (2024)
FOREVER (2024)
THE CHRONICLES OF TRINIAN (2024)
www.xulonpress.com

Paperback ISBN-13: 979-8-86850-405-1
Hard Cover ISBN-13: 979-8-86850-406-8
Ebook ISBN-13: 979-8-86850-407-5

†††

This book is dedicated to:

God, The Father, The Almighty, Maker of Heaven and Earth,
of all that is, seen and unseen.

Our Lord and Savior, Jesus Christ, The Redeemer, The Lion of Judah,
The Lamb of God, The Good Shepherd, The Prince of Peace,
The King of Kings and the Lord of Lords!

The Holy Spirit, The Counselor, The Comforter, The Spirit of Truth,
The Spirit of Wisdom, The Spirit of Knowledge and Understanding,
The Spirit of Counsel and of Power, The Spirit of Holiness,
The Spirit of Grace, The Spirit of Life.

†††

"The Lord has established his throne in Heaven and his kingdom rules over all. Praise the Lord you his angels, you mighty ones who do his bidding, who obey his word. Praise the Lord all his heavenly hosts, you his servants who do his will.
Praise the Lord, all his works everywhere in his dominion.
Praise the Lord, O my soul."
(Psalm 103:19-22)

"The Lord reigns, let the nations tremble;
He sits enthroned between the cherubim, let the earth shake.
Great is the Lord in Zion; he is exalted over all the nations.
Let them praise your great and awesome name — He is holy."
(Psalm 99:1-3)

"Now faith is being sure of what we hope for
and certain of what we do not see.
This is what the ancients were commended for."
(Hebrews 11:1-2)

†††

"For the Lord loves the just and will not forsake his faithful ones.
They will be protected forever,
but the offspring of the wicked will be cut off."
(Psalm 37:28)

AKNOWLEDGEMENTS

†††

Thank you Mom and Dad for loving me and raising me to know my God — this is the greatest gift a parent can give their child.

To my pastors and teachers; thank you for teaching me of God's justice, God's love, and the truth of God's plan for our salvation through Jesus Christ, our Lord and Savior.

To Theresa, my wonderful wife, my best friend, and my partner on this so temporary walk upon the earth; thank you for loving me despite my many imperfections, for keeping me on the straight and narrow, and for constantly reminding me of the eternal retirement we have waiting for us in Heaven. I will love you always.

To my two noble sons, Tanner and Thomas, godly men and sure to be my lifelong best friends; I am so honored to be called your father. Run a good race and may the Lord always bless you and keep you in his loving care.

To my magnificent daughter-in-law, Shannon, a godly woman and a wonderful addition to our family; we are so blessed to have you in our lives. May the Lord always be with you and bless you in everything you do.

To Grandbaby! I can't wait until you get here. Already, I love you with all my heart. I hope you find enjoyment and faith in these books and a bit of your Grandfather Terry.

To all my extended family, friends and fellow Christians; God has richly blessed me to have you in my life. You inspire me, comfort me, bring me great happiness, and sweeten my hope of eternity in Heaven with the Lord.

Finally, and most importantly, thank you, God, for creating me, saving me, and bringing me to faith in you. Thank you for all the blessings you have given to me in this life and prepared for me in the next.

Thank you for bringing this book — this story — to completion. May it always bring honor to your name and accomplish that which you have prepared for it to accomplish. If just one soul comes to know you through these books, all the effort will have been eternally worth it. Who can put a value on eternity?

"Just one soul is the goal!"

THE FAITHFUL STAND FOREVER!
THE PROMISE TIME REDEEMED

†††

PROLOGUE

†††

The faithful stand forever. It's an excellent motto, and it is true from the viewpoint of God's faithfulness to us in helping us withstand evil's temptations and guaranteeing us the eventual victory. However, it does not mean that we always do the right thing, that we always trust God's promises, or that we do not suffer the consequences of sin in this world. God has told us we will face trials and tribulations in the race we run upon this earth — right until we leave this temporary home and go to our forever home that he has prepared for us with him in Heaven.

A great cloud of witnesses surrounds us, giving us strength when we remember that many have come before us on this walk in his-story and many are with us now throughout the world, struggling against the same enemies in both the physical and spiritual realms. We are often so introspective that we focus solely on our own challenges and discomforts, failing to see those around us who are hurting and need help more than we do. This results from sin in the world — for as we all have heard, at the center of sin is "I".

It is here that we continue the story of the founding of Trinian. There is much remaining to reveal in her foundation story; many faithful to acclaim and warnings to pass down to future generations. Those who do not know of evil's tactics in the past are at significant risk of falling prey to them in the future.

Rarely in man's walk through time is there a golden age when he does not face-off against evil. The faithful that had been called out of Tophet had much yet to endure — much tempering of their faith to forge the steel required to serve as the foundation for a new country. In this age, a day of survival simply meant a man or woman had lived to fight another day. There was only one given, one absolute. With God on their side, **The Faithful Stand Forever!**

Now let us explore **The Promise Time Redeemed!**

"From one man, he made every nation of men that they should inhabit the whole earth; and he determined the times set for them and the exact places where they should live. For in him we live and move and have our being."
(Acts 17:26, 28)

"For no one can lay any foundation other than the one we already have — Jesus Christ."
(1 Corinthians 3:11)

"We believe in one God, the Father almighty, Maker of Heaven and earth, of all things visible and invisible.

†

"We believe in one Lord, Jesus Christ, the only Son of God, eternally begotten of the Father, God from God, Light from Light, true God from true God, begotten, not made, of one being with the Father. Through him all things were made. For us and for our salvation, he came down from Heaven, was incarnate of the Holy Spirit and the Virgin Mary, and became fully human. For our sake he was crucified under Pontius Pilate. He suffered death and was buried. On the third day he rose again in accordance with the Scriptures. He ascended into Heaven and is seated at the right hand of the Father. He will come again in glory to judge the living and the dead, and his kingdom will have no end.

†

"We believe in the Holy Spirit, the Lord, the giver of life, who proceeds from the Father and the Son, who in unity with the Father and the Son is worshiped and glorified, who has spoken through the prophets. We believe in one holy Christian and Apostolic Church. We acknowledge one baptism for the forgiveness of sins. We look for the resurrection of the dead and the life of the world to come. Amen." (Nicene Creed)

†

"If you love me, you will obey what I command. And I will ask the Father, and he will give you another counselor to be with you forever — the Spirit of Truth. The world cannot accept him, because it neither sees him nor knows him. But you know him, for he lives with you and will be in you." (John 14:15-17)

"I believe in the Holy Ghost; the holy Christian Church; the communion of saints; the forgiveness of sins; the resurrection of the body; and the life everlasting. Amen.

†

"I believe that I cannot by my own reason or strength believe in Jesus Christ, my Lord, nor come to Him; But the Holy Ghost has called me by the Gospels, enlightened me with His gifts, sanctified and kept me in the one true faith; In like manner as He calls, gathers, enlightens, and sanctifies the whole Christian Church on earth, and keeps it with Jesus Christ in the one true faith; In which Christian Church He daily and richly forgives all sins to me and all believers; And will at the last day raise up me and all the dead; And give unto me and all believers in Christ eternal life."

"This is most certainly true."
(The Third Article, Doctor Martin Luther's Small Catechism)

"If you love me, keep my commands. And I will ask the Father, and he will give you another advocate to help you and be with you forever — the Spirit of truth. The world cannot accept him, because it neither sees him nor knows him. But you know him, for he lives with you and will be in you. I will not leave you as orphans; I will come to you. Before long, the world will not see me anymore, but you will see me. Because I live, you also will live. On that day you will realize that I am in my Father, and you are in me, and I am in you. Whoever has my commands and keeps them is the one who loves me. The one who loves me will be loved by my Father, and I too will love them and show myself to them…

"Anyone who loves me will obey my teaching. My Father will love them, and we will come to them and make our home with them. Anyone who does not love me will not obey my teaching. These words you hear are not my own; they belong to the Father who sent me.

"All this I have spoken while still with you. But the Advocate, the Holy Spirit, whom the Father will send in my name, will teach you all things and will remind you of everything I have said to you. Peace I leave with you; my peace I give you. I do not give to you as the world gives. Do not let your hearts be troubled and do not be afraid." (John 14:15-27)

†

"And you also were included in Christ when you heard the message of truth, the gospel of your salvation. Having believed, you were marked in him with a seal, the promised Holy Spirit, who is a deposit guaranteeing our inheritance until the redemption of those who are God's possession — to the praise of his glory." (Ephesians 1:13-14)

†††

"I am sending you out like sheep among wolves. Therefore be as shrewd as snakes and as innocent as doves. Be on your guard; you will be handed over to the local councils and be flogged in the synagogues. On my account you will be brought before governors and kings as witnesses to them and to the Gentiles. But when they arrest you, do not worry about what to say or how to say it. At that time you will be given what to say, for it will not be you speaking, but the Spirit of your Father speaking through you.

"Brother will betray brother to death, and a father his child; children will rebel against their parents and have them put to death. You will be hated by everyone because of me, but the one who stands firm to the end will be saved…

"The student is not above the teacher, nor a servant above his master. It is enough for students to be like their teachers, and servants like their masters. If the head of the house has been called Beelzebub, how much more the members of his household!

"So do not be afraid of them, for there is nothing concealed that will not be disclosed, or hidden that will not be made known. What I tell you in the dark, speak in the daylight; what is whispered in your ear, proclaim from the roofs. Do not be afraid of those who kill the body but cannot kill the soul. Rather, be afraid of the One who can destroy both soul and body in hell. Are not two sparrows sold for a penny? Yet not one of them will fall to the ground outside your Father's care. And even the very hairs of your head are all numbered. So don't be afraid; you are worth more than many sparrows.

"Whoever acknowledges me before others, I will also acknowledge before my Father in Heaven. But whoever disowns me before others, I will disown before my Father in Heaven...

†††

"Anyone who loves their father or mother more than me is not worthy of me; anyone who loves their son or daughter more than me is not worthy of me. Whoever does not take up their cross and follow me is not worthy of me. Whoever finds their life will lose it, and whoever loses their life for my sake will find it.

"Anyone who welcomes you welcomes me, and anyone who welcomes me welcomes the one who sent me. Whoever welcomes a prophet as a prophet will receive a prophet's reward, and whoever welcomes a righteous person as a righteous person will receive a righteous person's reward. And if anyone gives even a cup of cold water to one of these little ones who is my disciple, truly I tell you, that person will certainly not lose their reward." (Matthew 10:16-42)

†††

"Do you not know that in a race all the runners run, but only one gets the prize? Run in such a way as to get the prize. Everyone who competes in the games goes into strict training. They do it to get a crown that will not last, but we do it to get a crown that will last forever. Therefore I do not run like someone running aimlessly; I do not fight like a boxer beating the air. No, I strike a blow to my body and make it my slave so that after I have preached to others, I myself will not be disqualified for the prize." (1 Corinthians 9:24-27)

"However, I consider my life worth nothing to me; my only aim is to finish the race and complete the task the Lord Jesus has given me — the task of testifying to the good news of God's grace." (Acts 20:24)

"But the fruit of the Spirit is love, joy, peace, patience, kindness, goodness, faithfulness, gentleness, and self-control." (Galatians 5:22-23)

"A thousand years in your sight are like a day that has just gone by, or like a watch in the night." (Psalm 90:4)

"What once was, as well as what will someday be, are not limited by what currently is; and none are limited by man's limited ability to understand." (The Faithful)

For the Spirit ALWAYS points to the Son!

TIMELINE

†††

Creation and Fall	
|	
8000 years	
|	
Tophet	**Tophet**
|	
Parlantis	**The Promise**
|	
Heath	
|	
Omentia	
|	
The GreatAwakening	**The Faithful**
|	
The Great Struggle II	**Stand**
|	
A Long Time	
|	
The Great Unraveling	**Forever**

CONTENTS

†††

THE PROMISE

Chapters:

TOPHET

Part 5: Deliverance

THE PROMISE
Part 6: Darkness

Part 7: Opportunity

Part 8: Preparation

Part 9: Another Time

Part 10. Darkness

Part 11. The Players

Part 12. Somewhere in Time

Part 13. The Plan

Part 14. Complicated

Part 15. Battle

PREFACE

†††

Promises — there are several referenced in this story. Promises are made, believed, and trusted. Sometimes they are kept and sometimes they are broken. The fate of a promise very often depends on who is making it.

Men make promises. Very often, men are not in control of whether they can keep their promises. Sometimes they are kept and sometimes they are not. Men simply do not have the power to guarantee the fulfillment of their promises.

But God is in control of his promises. He has the power to ensure his promises happen. He has never broken a promise and he never will. Very often, the only factor up for debate relating to God's promises is time — when will the promise be fulfilled?

The Foundation Chronicles begin with Tophet. Even though Tophet was first included in *Stand*, the second book of the Chronicles of Trinian, it also begins *The Promise*, as it is critical to the Foundation Chronicles.

I have to mention one additional note related to Tophet that I still find amazing. I came up with the names of the five historical land masses in both the Chronicles of Trinian and the Foundation Chronicles over a twenty-year period. Back in 2005, *Stand* introduced the lands of Trinian and Dexilia. In 2010, *The Faithful* updated Dexilia to Omentia, and added the lands of Parlantis and Heath. Then, in 2024, *Forever* introduced the land of El Tigre.

These names were random and completely pulled out of a hat, with no rhyme or reason. When writing *Forever*, I realized I had one remaining unnamed landmass on the map. I made this landmass the geographical location where the worshippers of Molech had originated from at the very beginning of the story. However, since I didn't have a name for it, I took the first letter of each of the places I already had on the map, in the order introduced, to see if that could give me a useable name. So, for Trinian, Omentia, Parlantis, Heath, and El Tigre, it spelled, "Tophet." I thought it had a nice ring to it.

A couple of days later, I googled the name to see if it might be an actual place. I didn't think it would be, but out of curiosity, I looked. To my amazement, and an overabundance of shivers down the back of my neck, Google read, "Tophet… a location in the Valley of Hinnom where worshippers engaged in a ritual involving 'passing a child through the fire, most likely child sacrifice… ascribed to a god named Moloch.'"

The Faithful, the first book in the Chronicles of Trinian, had introduced a fire-demon named Molech. His worshippers sacrificed children to him in the fire. How the first letters of the above land masses, randomly named over twenty years, could spell out the name of this place, matching my story — I have no answer. What are the odds of this happening by chance?

This question, having been asked, let us begin the Foundation Chronicles.

The Faithful Stand Forever!
The Promise Time Redeemed.

TOPHET

Part I:
Borrowed Time

Chapter 1

Discovery

†††

As the sun rose over the Dark Sea, its bright glow illuminated the top of the dormant volcano and cascaded down its enormous dome. The volcano, known by the people of Tophet as Ashtar, was the first thing the sun focused on every morning as the light made its way down to the bustling city of Tophet that thrived at its base. The early morning focal point reminded all those living below that in the distant past, the mighty mountain had breathed, resulting in the obliteration of everything within a five-hundred mile range. But that was then. This day, the mountain named Ashtar was simply a beautiful part of the eastern landscape to all that lived below and a major part of Tophet's culture.

At the southwestern base of the volcano, a team of scientists continued their study of a recently discovered labyrinth of tunnels.

"Down here!" Gatesh yelled as he held the lantern up to a nearby wall in a newly discovered tunnel of the caverns.

His team scrambled to his location as quickly as possible without stumbling over any of the many stalagmites of the cavern; their lanterns chaotically tossing light in every direction of the cave as they ran.

"Look! Look!" Gatesh pointed to the wall in front of him. The painting on the wall clearly illustrated some sort of cube-shaped or block-shaped starship, several stones of various colors, and what seemed to be a map of the stars.

“This proves it!” Gatesh said to his partner, Mika'el, who had arrived with the team. “What else could this mean?”

Mika'el's area of specialty was more on the technical side of things. This was the first time he had actually accompanied Gatesh to the caverns. Mika'el studied the ancient painting. It was the latest of several cave paintings that Gatesh's team had discovered in this section of the caverns on the southern slope of the great volcano's dome. There was little chance the paintings were fake, as it took months of excavation for the team to reach the tunnels.

“I agree. This implies that the stones are crucial for someone's journey, and their journey definitely originates from — somewhere else.” Mika'el was much more serious than celebratory, contemplating the many astronomical implications of the discovery.

“Yes! If they can do it, we can do it. Time travel. It is possible.” Gatesh had spent several months exploring the underground cavern of the volcano and its ancient tunnel system, ever since a pair of students who were spending the day spelunking found the first wall paintings depicting the ancient travelers and their devices.

“It definitely appears so.” Mika'el continued to study the drawing. He had harbored reservations about the cave paintings and their apparent suggestion of using a sequence of colored stones for time travel, but the more corroborating evidence they found in the ancient tunnels, the more his resistance to the idea was breaking down.

“What is this?” Mika'el asked as he moved his lantern a couple of feet to the right, exposing another area of the wall that the uneven curvature of the rock had shadowed.

Gatesh joined Mika'el at the wall, staring at the additional drawing. “It looks like — a door?”

“Or maybe a portal?”

They stared at each other and said the words together. “Or maybe a time portal?”

“No way! Do you think it is possible?” Gatesh had a look of wonder on his face.

"Well, I wouldn't have thought anything else depicted here would have been possible, so I don't see how your question has any relevance to this particular subject. All of this is simply beyond our current level of understanding, but that in itself doesn't make it impossible. Do any of the other paintings include or refer to a portal of any kind?"

"That is an excellent question. I don't remember them including a door or portal, but we should go look. The closest tunnel is this way."

Gatesh headed off down the cavern to an adjoining tunnel, with Mika'el right behind him. After a couple minutes, he turned abruptly to his right to enter a tunnel that had a wall painting discovered just a week prior.

"Whoa!" Gatesh's lantern was the first thing to hit the wall, followed immediately by Gatesh. Mika'el barely stopped before plowing into him.

"What in the world?" Gatesh said as he adjusted his glasses.

Mika'el helped Gatesh off the ground. "Looks like your map is wrong."

Gatesh was in shock. He had been in charge of the excavation of this tunnel himself. How could there not be a tunnel, especially if he had annotated it on the cavern plans? "No, this is just the where I remember the entrance being! Where is the tunnel?" He looked down at the plans. "This is all wrong!"

About that time, the rest of Gatesh's excavation team caught up and joined Gatesh in his struggle to understand what was going on. They were all dumbfounded.

"It's like this tunnel never existed! Where did it go?"

Mika'el asked, "What about the other tunnels? Weren't there another three?"

"Yes, that is correct. Gatesh looked at the plans. This way."

The team headed off down a tunnel to their left, turned a corner, and found another surprise. Where there should have been another tunnel to the left, instead, there were two to the right.

"Ok, there is something strange going on here!"

Everyone was suddenly very uneasy. They stood in the dark with their lanterns looking at each other apprehensively.

Mika'el broke the silence with a suggestion he immediately found had unanimous support. "Maybe we should find some sunlight and sort this all out before we find we can't make our way out of this maze."

"Right!" Gatesh agreed and headed out with everyone close behind. They backtracked and found their way to the cavern entrance. Though they all put on their game faces as soon as they hit sunlight, it was obvious everyone was relieved they had made it out.

Chapter 2

Sisters

†††

"Shan!" Mirah shouted as she saw her best friend arrive for a visit.

"Mir!" Shannon shouted in reply.

The girls ran and greeted each other with a hug. Then they immediately ran around the cottage to play in the backyard. Mirah's twin sister, Tarah, followed the girls with less enthusiasm.

Shannon's mother, Sandrah, and the twins' mother, Mia, smiled as they watched the girls run away to play.

"They sure look forward to seeing each other, don't they?" Sandrah said.

"They sure do. I am so glad they found each other. Tarah isn't there yet, but she is coming along."

"Oh sure. I don't even begin to understand the bond between identical twins. If they didn't wear their hair differently, I wouldn't be able to tell them apart."

"There are days I can't tell them apart after twelve, almost thirteen years. And I'm their mom!"

"Wow! Well, you have done a wonderful job raising them. We just love them both."

"Thank you so much. Would you like to come in for something to drink?"

"Sure, that would be great."

Sandrah and Mia went into the house to relax and chat while the girls played in the backyard.

†††

"Aren't they beautiful?" Mirah asked Shannon as they looked at the drawings of the fashionable celebrities of Tophet.

"Gorgeous," Shannon replied.

Tarah looked over their shoulder. "Beauty can be powerful, but power itself, that is what you want!"

Shannon and Mirah looked at each other and then laughed. Tarah did not take kindly to their response and left them to their silly dreaming of fashion and beauty. Tarah wandered back to the workshop to see what her father, Travork, was working on.

Travork was an academic philosopher. As such, he really didn't have an opinion on much of anything. He just taught what he was told was the truth, and what Tophet's powerful elite demanded he teach was simple: worship Molech and revere time. In Tophet, these were the only things that the people held in reverence; the only things they could hold in high esteem — at least publically.

Travork was good friends with a scientist named Gatesh, who worked studying time. Gatesh was about ten years younger than Travork. They had met at a conference that brought various disciplines together to discuss the concept of time from their respective viewpoints.

"Hello father."

"Hello child."

"Hello Gatesh." Tarah smiled longingly as she looked up at Gatesh.

"Hello Tarah."

Tarah had a crush on Gatesh and everyone in the family knew it. Tarah had even stated in front of them all that someday she and Gatesh would be together. The family found it cute. Gatesh told Tarah that he was way too busy at his work to consider a relationship, and also that Tarah was simply too young to be thinking about such things.

"What are you working on, Father?"

"I am painting a picture of the temple for the upcoming festival."

"Another painting? Why?"

"It was a suggestion."

Tarah rolled her eyes. She was both annoyed by and envied how the powerful people in Tophet could manipulate everyone by just making suggestions. "Someday, I will be a suggestion maker."

"If that is what you want, that is your choice."

Tarah could not understand how her father could be so malleable and complacent. It was like he didn't have a unique thought or personal desire in the world. He just did what he was told — with a smile. Tarah felt sorry for him and was embarrassed to call him her father. Tarah respected power, and as such, did not respect her father. But she loved him.

Someday, I will be powerful and stand up for him, since he can't stand up for himself.

Someday.

†††

Deep within the bowels of the cauldron beneath the massive volcano that towered over Tophet came the mighty roar of Potentus, the demon of power.

"What do we have here? This little one desires power. I can give her power!"

Bellatate, the demon of beauty, desire, and envy, joined Potentus on the rocky ledge of the pit. "Her sister desires to be beautiful. I can make her beautiful beyond imagination! I can make it so every man wants her so badly, they will do anything to have her."

Without warning, the fiery coals of the cauldron exploded as a blazing red dragon emerged from the molten lava of the pit and sprayed rock, ash, and magma in every direction.

The explosion of matter from Satan's arrival pinned Potentus and Bellatate against the rock wall and burned them mercilessly. They shrieked in agony.

The dragon spoke. "I have plans for them both! You will get them to volunteer their allegiance to me by tempting them with their deepest desires. They do not know it yet, but they will do anything to get what they want most — beauty and power!"

"Yes, master." Both the demons laughed in devilish delight at their assignments. Satan extended his enormous wings and, with a flip of his tail, dove back into the fires of hell. As he did so, his tail knocked both of the demons off the ledge and into the flames, where they screamed again in misery.

Chapter 3

Offerings

†††

While smiling fiendishly at the flames in anticipation, he meticulously aligned the stones on the altar of Molech.

Soros, the High Priest of Molech, was also the keeper of the sacred stones. Soros became the high priest at thirteen, after the previous high priest of fifty years ascended to the spirit world by fire. As the High Priest of Molech, he would spend most of his life, with a few exceptions, on temple grounds.

The stone pyramid at the center of Tophet rose three hundred feet into the sky. An enormous altar surrounded a fire-pit at the top of the pyramid. Massive mirrors surrounded the entire altar, focusing the sun's powerful rays into the center of the fire-pit. The fire at the center of the altar burned incessantly under the intense heat generated by the sun during the day and by rising magma from vents underground that bubbled up from deep within the volcano to the altar of the temple pyramid.

Without compromising the integrity of the structure, the ancients ingeniously constructed the temple pyramid over a boiling magma vent and successfully channeled the molten rock upwards through the center of the pyramid. The ancient builders had insulated the center of the pyramid structure with a special type of rock they had found and harvested in other dormant magma vents within Ashtar itself. As the magma flowed up through the center of the pyramid, it oozed out various vents the designers had constructed on the sides of the pyramid.

The seeping magma flowed down the sides of the pyramid and cooled, sealing the exterior of the pyramid in igneous rock. It was a marvel to all. Many people believed the ancients had help from the stars in constructing the temple pyramid, as they did not fully understand how mortals could have accomplished the feat on their own.

Soros aligned the organs upon the altar, as the high priests had always done. In Tophet's tradition, the people would pay homage to Molech each week by burning all the internal organs of those who had died within the city that week. The temple staff of several hundred would spend their days disemboweling the dead and returning their sewn up, eviscerated bodies to loved ones for burial.

According to their ancient high priests, this practice would appease Molech and protect Tophet from both Ashtar's wrath and the wrath of the dragons that were believed to long inhabit the caverns within the mountain.

When Soros had meticulously arranged the organs as instructed by the ancient texts, he summoned the fire-beast, known to all in Tophet as Molech, using the words of remembrance. Moments later, the beast rose from the flames that burned atop the floating ash of the molten lava. Soros thought himself as close to being a god as any. He alone spoke directly to the master of the flames and he alone kept Tophet from its would-be destruction.

The massive fire-beast rose out of the blazing flames. Its crimson eyes locked onto the small man before it. Soros loved the feeling of impending doom that this moment gave him. On the one hand he felt special, but on the other hand, he was as close to death as anyone could be.

The beast slowly moved its jaws forward to the meat sacrifice prepared for it and then surged forward, grabbing the organs with its teeth and devouring every piece. The meat hung from its teeth as its massive wings tensed in satisfaction — its body quivering in ecstasy.

Soros was relieved that his master seemed satisfied with the offering. He grinned and bowed to the creature.

The fire-beast looked down on the man and it hated him as much as it hated all the human creation. Someday it would remake them all in its image, but for now, this man served a purpose.

"Master, I hope you are pleased with Tophet's offering."

The fire-beast looked down on Soros and snarled at him. "If I were not pleased, you would feel the flames!"

Soros instantly realized he had been careless with his words. He cowered before the fire-beast, bowing. "Forgive me, master. Your humble servant forgot his place."

The fire-beast drew close to the puny man before him, towering over him. It looked down on Soros and putrid drool poured from between its teeth and out of its mouth.

Soros could feel the breath coming from the great crimson dragon's nostrils, and he wondered whether it would be his last moment of life. The not knowing brought a terrified excitement to Soros. It was a dance he had with the beast often.

"I still have a use for you." The dragon withdrew back to the center of the fire.

Soros rose. "What would you have me do, Master?"

"I demand more from my subjects than their leftovers, the putrid pieces remaining after they have lived out their lives."

Soros' face lost its color as he considered what the fire-beast was saying.

"I demand they give me that which they care about the most — that which they love the most. In so doing, I will know it is for me they hold the highest reverence and love in their hearts."

Soros was not sure what the beast wanted, but also didn't want to ask for fear of getting it wrong. He just stared up at his master, silent and petrified.

"What, Soros, would you say they love the most?"

Soros' mind raced. He wasn't ready for this, but he knew he had to say something. "Their gold and gems, master?"

The fire-beast rose out of the magma and the flames soared into the air. "No! I didn't ask what you care most about! I asked what they care most about; what they love most!"

Soros was terrified! This was it. One chance left.

What do the people care about most?

A fiendish grin crossed Soros' face as the thought entered his mind — as the answer poured from his lips. "Their children."

"Yes, their children! On the last day of every month, you shall bring me six children from the city of Tophet. Three of them should be new, from the age of one month to the age of one year. Three should be in their prime, an age between that of twelve to thirteen suns. If you do not, I will unleash Ashtar's fury upon you and the city of Tophet!"

"How will I know which children you demand from those groups?"

The dragon whispered, "I will leave that choice up to you."

Soros smiled. "Yes, master."

CHAPTER 4

WITNESS

†††

Kissami had always wondered what the purpose of his life was to be. The answer to that question came one day as he was taking a walk in his native land.

Kissami lived in a very arid area surrounded by rocky terrain and rugged mountains. He was a young man and really had given little thought to his place in the world. Where most of the young men in his land had a trade or a family business to tend to, Kissami was adrift. His parents had passed years earlier, and he didn't know what would become of him. That was all about to change.

Kissami was daydreaming as he was walking from a nearby village back to his home. Suddenly, an enormous lion confronted him out of nowhere. He froze.

Surely, I am a dead man.

He cried out to the God he had rarely considered. "Almighty God, have mercy on me?"

The lion advanced.

Kissami realized he had nowhere to run. He dropped to his knees and raised his hands to the heavens, begging the God of his fathers for help! "Please, God in Heaven, maker of the universe, ruler of all the kingdoms, save me?"

The magnificent beast charged Kissami and lunged into the air, intent on devouring him. At that instant, there was an explosion of light and a mighty clap of thunder! A mighty angel appeared in front of Kissami and engaged the lion head on, repelling the beast and throwing it the opposite direction into a rocky cliff some twenty feet away. The lion rose to its feet and darted off in the opposite direction.

The mighty angel turned toward Kissami. His eyes glowed a brilliant gold and his tunic was that of a bright alabaster. His hair was white with streaks of silver.

Kissami bowed to the angel in intense fear — falling with his face to the ground.

"Do not bow before me! I am but a servant of the most high and a messenger! Rise to your feet, Kissami!"

Kissami stood, though still petrified in fear for what was happening.

"You have wondered all your life what your calling is. I am here to tell you. You too will be a messenger of the Lord your God to the peoples of the west — to the peoples he will show you."

"But who am I that I should be a messenger for the most high? I am but a lowly man, not well-spoken; I have no talents of speech or ability."

"It is not about you. It is not your story, it is His-story. He will show his power through your weaknesses. You will endure much, but no weapon formed against you will prosper."

"I am the Lord's servant, and I will do his will in my life."

From that day forward, Kissami had a mission.

†††

Kissami sat in the shade beneath the patch of trees on the river's edge. After a long journey, Kissami found himself in this place and he didn't know why he was there. But it wasn't for him to know why. He had been told where to go and to be ready to give testimony to his faith and the faithfulness of his God.

To all passers-by it would have appeared that he was alone in this place, but he had learned ever since the day with the lion that he was never alone. The day before, an old friend with a silver streak in his hair had greeted him and told him to remain in this place. He wasn't told why, but was joyful that his journey had purpose, and he was eager to find out what that purpose was.

As he prayed for guidance, he heard the family approaching.

Thank you, almighty God. Please give me the words that I should speak.

Chapter 5

Family

†††

"Look at that one!" Shannon pointed to a shiny silver stone about thirty feet out into the river that flowed by them. "Look how bright it is!"

"And that one over there! It is gold!" Jacob, Shannon's older brother by a year, pointed to another stone beneath the water. "This place is awesome!"

Mika'el and Sandrah stood behind their children, smiling. It was a good day for a walk along the Ashtar River. It was a beautiful morning; the skies were blue, and the temperature was a perfect sixty-two. The family walked along the river, seeing if they could spot any beautiful stones they could reach to add to their collection.

Ever since Jacob and Shannon were old enough to walk, Mika'el and Sandrah had enjoyed bringing them down to the river. Throwing rocks into the river was all the rage when they were younger. Now the activity of interest was pulling special stones out of the river.

The Ashtar River flowed out from the southern region of the mighty volcano, Ashtar, which towered over Tophet like a giant sentry. Legend had it that Tophet's ancestors had named the volcano after the ancient warrior, Ashtar, who had jumped into the crater to appease it and keep it from erupting.

Because of its dominant presence over Tophet, Ashtar had become one of the central focal points of Tophet's social structure. The leaders of Tophet for hundreds of years taught all citizens from childhood to worship Molech, the fire-beast of the volcano. According to the High Priests of the temple, Molech was the only one who could keep Ashtar from erupting, and the only one who could keep the fire-breaths that lived within her at bay.

"Oh, look at that one!" Sandrah pointed at an enormous emerald green boulder in the center of the river. The fluorite rock appeared fluorescent as it glowed bright green below the water, sharing its color with all the other rocks around it on the riverbed.

"Nice! And look over there. There is a purple one!" Mika'el was really enjoying the walk along the river and spending quality time with his family. Family was everything to him. He enjoyed working with Gatesh, trying to decipher the mysteries of time, but he would never trade his work for the people he loved. His people were everything!

Mika'el, Sandrah, Shan Shan and Jacob walked along the river for an hour, exploring and enjoying each other's company. They came upon a bend in the river and realized it was time to have their picnic lunch.

"See that patch of trees up there?" Mika'el pointed. "Let's stop under those trees and have our lunch. The shade from the trees will keep it nice and cool."

Everyone headed for the trees. When they were almost to the trees, Jacob noticed there was a man sitting under the trees and pointed. "Dad? There is a man under the trees."

Mika'el studied the stranger as he approached. It wasn't terribly dangerous around Tophet in the middle of the day, but things did occasionally happen. When it came to family, it was wise to use caution when meeting strangers, especially in remote areas.

Mika'el motioned for everyone to stay behind him as they approached the man. It looked like the stranger was resting from the heat in the shade of the trees. He was sitting with his back up against one tree with his head bowed down.

Is he sleeping?

Mika'el and family stopped about twenty feet from the man. He had gray, shoulder length hair, which was the first telling sign he wasn't from Tophet — the men of Tophet kept their hair cut short. He wore a tattered tunic and sandals, and there was a leather pouch by his side, next to the tree.

"Hello, friend." Mika'el said.

The stranger slowly opened his eyes, saw the family, and smiled. "Hello."

"We are sorry for waking you. We were just coming over to have something to eat in the shade of the trees."

The man rose to his feet. "No worries. Come on over. There is plenty of shade for everyone. You didn't wake me. I was praying. Please, join me."

Mika'el and his family were all a little surprised that the man was praying. They only prayed at the temple under the direction of Soros. They walked over and joined the man.

"This is my family; my wife, Sandrah, our son, Jacob, and Shannon, our daughter. My name is Mika'el." Each extended their hand, in-turn, and greeted the stranger.

"I am very glad to meet each of you. My name is Kissami."

They all sat in the shade of the trees. Sandrah pulled out the lunches she had prepared for everyone that morning. She noticed the campfire and a fish on a stick. It looked like it was about ready to eat. "Is that your lunch?" she asked.

"Yes, it is. You are all more than welcomed to have some."

"That is very generous of you." She replied. "We have some bread, apples, and corn we can share."

"That is very kind of you. Thank you very much."

Mika'el asked, "Are you from Tophet?"

"Oh no. I am from a faraway land. Far across the sea."

Jacob asked, "You said you were praying. Were you praying to Molech?"

"Molech, no. I don't know who that is."

Mika'el and the members of his family all looked at each other in confusion. Mika'el asked, "Well, who then? Who else is there besides Molech?"

With a smile, Kissami proclaimed, "There is only one true God. He is God, the Father, the Almighty, the Maker of the heavens and the earth, of all that is whether or not we can see it. If you do not mind me asking, why do you worship this, Molech?"

They had never thought about it. It was just what everyone expected and required of them. None of them had an answer.

Then Shannon said, "We worship Molech of the mountain, the keeper of Ashtar and the dragons."

"Hmm. I see." Kissami broke the fish he had caught into pieces and gave each of his new friends a portion. As they were eating, Kissami noticed the medallion that Shannon was wearing around her neck. He asked Mika'el, "Has your family always lived in this region?"

"Actually, no. My grandfather grew up somewhere faraway. When he was but a child, slave traders captured him and brought him here. He used to tell me stories. He always wished to return to his home, but didn't have any idea where that home might be. So he stayed here and started a family. The rest is history. Why do you ask?"

Kissami glanced over at Shannon's pendant. "The pendant."

Mika'el explained. "The pendant was my grandfather's. He gave it to me before he died, and I gave it to Shannon. Do you recognize something about it?"

"Yes, I do." He smiled. "Apparently, our meeting today was not by chance." Kissami pulled the medallion he wore around his neck out from under his tunic. It was identical to Shannon's. He instantly had everyone's attention. "The letters on the medallion are the name of the one true God. We are of the same family. Let me tell you about our family."

Part 2: The Tunnels

Chapter 6

Open Sesame

†††

Gatesh went over it again and again. There was simply no way he could have annotated his diagrams of the tunnels inaccurately, especially not all the tunnel diagrams. There had to be another explanation, and there was only one other possibility — the underground labyrinth of tunnels was changing.

But how could that be happening?

Gatesh went down to the tunnel entrance by himself. He needed time to sit and think about the problem.

Could the changing tunnels have anything to do with the information we have gathered from the cave paintings? The paintings show us someone used stones to travel vast distances through space. What does that have to do with the changing tunnel system?

Gatesh entered the enormous cavern that was the central hub for the maze of tunnels that branched out from it in all directions. To Gatesh's amazement, the tunnels had all changed again! Not one of them was where it was the day before.

How can this be? I might understand this happening over a tremendous amount of time, but overnight?

Gatesh moved into the cavern and stood next to the first tunnel.

Maybe if I stay here and watch, I can see something change.

Gatesh stood at the tunnel entrance and watched for any change. He didn't notice a thing.

What could be the connection between space travel and these tunnels changing over time? What do tunnels, time, and travel over great distances have in common?

Gatesh stood at the entrance of the tunnel for hours, trying to understand the connection.

If the travelers that left these maps on the cave walls couldn't travel tremendous speeds, but had to travel tremendous distances, they must have used some other means or they would have been dead before they ever reached their distant destinations. What if these ancient travelers used tunnels in space to travel from one place to another, like the tunnels of this cave system?

He stared at the tunnels that had changed.

Time, distance, and speed. Without traveling at a higher speed or being unable to change the distance, what remains? Just time. This tunnel is changing over time. Time. It's time! Somehow, they had tunnels through space that affected time!

Gatesh realized the cave wall paintings were actually maps.

Tunnels in space. What do they have to do with these tunnels? What if the maps showed the hubs or locations of the hubs that connected these space time tunnels? But why put them here, in these tunnels? Wait. What if the paintings on the cave walls were not maps for the tunnels in space but maps of these cave tunnels and where they lead? Where they lead — in time?

Gatesh had been standing in front of the tunnel for so long that he lost track of time. His lantern sitting on the ground next to him flickered and then went out.

"Great!"

Gatesh turned around and realized it was dark — very dark.

Ok. That is another fine predicament you have gotten yourself into!

Gatesh stood in the dark, wondering what to do next. He was stuck deep within the cavern with no light source, and he hadn't bothered to tell anyone where he was going. About the time he reached maximum frustration, the unexpected and inexplicable happened. The space map on the cave wall lit up. It wasn't the entire map, but just the multicolored dots on the map.

Gatesh carefully walked into the tunnel and over the map. It was beautiful!

How does this work?

As soon as he spoke the words out loud, twelve different colored lights lit up on the tunnel's walls. The lights were being emanated from various glowing stones embedded within the walls of the cave tunnel, and they corresponded to the colors on the tunnel diagram.

I never noticed those before. Of course, I have never stood in the dark and asked how it all works before, either.

Gatesh walked over to the rocks in the cave wall. They were beautiful! There was emerald, sapphire, topaz, amethyst, beryl, sardonyx, jasper, chalcedony, sardius, chrysolite, chrysoprases, and jacinth. Gatesh reached out and touched the emerald stone. As if it controlled all the emerald stones in the tunnel wall, hundreds of the emerald stones lit up, marking a route through the cave tunnel — begging Gatesh to follow. He did.

As Gatesh walked deeper and deeper into the emerald tunnel, it seemed to transform before his eyes, curving and flowing to the left and right as he passed through it. Gatesh stopped, suddenly realizing that he had been blindly following the lights.

Wait. What is happening here? Where am I going? This is amazing, but I don't really know the ramifications of what I am doing.

Gatesh turned around.

Oh no.

When Gatesh turned around, he realized that there weren't any lights behind him.

How do I get back to where I started?

Gatesh walked back down the tunnel from where he came. After about one step, he hit a wall.

What? This is bad. Changing tunnels. Right.

Gatesh turned around again.

Well, I guess I don't have a choice. Forward it is.

Gatesh followed the emerald lights through the ever-changing tunnel. After about five minutes, the lights brought him to a stone archway. Next to the archway was a glowing emerald stone, much larger that the stones in the walls. It was sitting atop a pedestal.

Now what?

It was decision time for Gatesh. Gatesh wasn't married and didn't have a family. He was a scientist, and what he was experiencing was the most amazing thing he had ever discovered in his lifetime — granted, he was only thirty-two years old. But to his knowledge, no one had ever reported anything like this before. It was simply miraculous!

I have to walk through that door. I have to know what is there.

Gatesh took a deep breath and stepped through the archway.

†††

Gatesh was in shock. It was all he could do to remain standing. He just stood frozen on the battlefield. All around Gatesh lay the charred bodies of an army of men — men now no more. Thousands of enormous black birds were devouring their bodies. The stench and destruction almost made Gatesh be sick.

Gatesh had just watched the sun rise in the east.

How does the sun rise from the opposite direction?

A few others stood next to him on the battlefield amidst the carcasses of the dead. Facing Gatesh and the others was another army under the banner of a golden lion upon a white background. The others walked slowly towards this army.

No. I don't think so.

Gatesh backed up. A split second later, he was once again standing before the emerald archway.

What was that? This must be a portal to another place, or another time, or both!

Once Gatesh realized he was safe, his anxiety levels returned to a light panic, and he looked around for some kind of idea of how to get home — back to his time and place.

After looking around the emerald portal, he found another cave painting. It depicted a different constellation of colored stones.

I do not know how to pick the right colored stone to navigate me back to where I live. Nothing in this painting looks familiar!

Panic set in again. Gatesh sat on the floor of the cave.

Ok, get it together. I have to control my breathing and my thinking.

After a moment, Gatesh got his breathing under control and he felt better. He stood and looked at the cave wall painting.

Ok. I followed the emerald green light to get here. Let's take a scientific approach to this problem. What colors make up green? Blue and yellow make up green.

Gatesh noticed an amethyst colored stone on the cave wall map.

Amethyst is blueish. Let's give that a go.

Gatesh touched the amethyst stone on the wall next to him and a series of amethyst lights lit up the cave walls. Gatesh followed the amethyst lights to another archway with a large amethyst stone next to it on a pedestal.

Here goes nothing!

Gatesh stepped through the archway and crashed to the cave floor. There wasn't any light but that of a lit lantern sitting on the ground next to him.

A lit lantern? Ok. At least I don't see a thousand charred, decaying bodies littering a bloody battlefield. I'll take it! But where did the lit lantern come from?

Gatesh had a thought. After checking that there was still fuel in the lantern and that he had his flint with him, he blew out the flame of the lit lantern. A moment after he did, a map lit up on the wall of the cave. Gatesh checked the map. It looked familiar.

This looks like the map on the wall from where I started. Could it be?

He struck the flint and lit the lantern. The glowing rocks once again disappeared under the direct light.

Ok, let's walk out of here and see if we are home.

Gatesh walked toward the cavern entrance. Sunlight soon penetrated the cavern, and he could see that he was indeed home. As he exited the cavern entrance, he dropped to his hands and knees and kissed the sandy dirt.

Praise Molech the merciful!

About that time, two men arrived from the town. They ran to where Gatesh was on his knees. "Gatesh, is that you? It's Gatesh! Are you ok?"

The men from Gatesh's excavation team lifted Gatesh to his feet and hugged him like a long-lost friend. "I can't believe it is you!" one man yelled. "We thought you were dead!" exclaimed the other.

"What are you guys saying? It has only been a few hours. I'm fine. My lantern just went out in the cave and I got a little lost."

The men looked at each other, confused. "Um, actually, you have been gone for three weeks."

"What?"

"You have been missing for three weeks. We were taking turns searching the caves. Because of the constantly shifting tunnels, we could only place the lantern a little way into the cavern, but we left it there, lit, to help guide you back to the entrance. We were about to give up all hope!"

Gatesh felt amazed and confused. He kept silent about what he had discovered.

Three weeks? I'm not even hungry.

Chapter 7

New Life

†††

Sitting next to the stream that day, Kissami had revealed the truth to them, and they had all listened intently. The hours passed, the Spirit moved, and the encounter changed Mika'el's, Sandrah's, Jacob's and Shannon's lives in the most fundamental of ways. It was a seismic event, and it forever altered their understanding of the world they lived in; as well as their place within it. Spiritual sight had given them knowledge of their Creator, the love he had for his creation, and the promise of a savior for all. Gone forever was the spiritual blindness that allowed for the worship of any false god. The Spirit had opened their eyes, the seed of faith had sprouted, and there was simply no going back. The truth had given them a new joy and freedom that completely eclipsed any semblance of happiness and contentment they thought they had possessed before. They were a new creation.

Mika'el had tried to convince Kissami to return with them to their home. Kissami had thanked them sincerely for their kind invitation, but had said that there was still much work for him to do and that he had to continue on his journey. They had parted ways as the sun set, thankful for having met alongside the river that day, and amazed at how God had brought them together.

Mika'el and his family returned home — changed forever. Shannon could not wait to tell her dearest friend, Mirah, the truth of her loving God and all the things he had done in the world, along with the loving promises he had made to those who believe in him. She could barely sleep.

Mika'el and Sandrah sat by candlelight, revisiting the day's events. The children had gone to bed, though they doubted if they would get any sleep after the momentous revelations of the day.

Mika'el held Sandrah's hands as they sat together on their porch, looking at the stars twinkling overhead. "For so long I have wondered where it all came from — why the God of the universe had not revealed himself to us. I thought there had to be more than the worship of a mountain and a god that kept the dragons away. That was so small compared to everything we see around us; the sun, the moon, the stars. Now we know the truth. How wonderful to know the truth!"

"Isn't it amazing how much the one true God of the universe cares for us — such insignificant creatures — that he sent Kissami on such a long journey just to let us know the truth? That he orchestrated our meeting with him along the river?"

"That is amazing. It shows what a loving and merciful God he is — not a god of anger and hate like Molech. How could we have ever been so blind as to think Molech was who we should worship? He is such a small, false god."

"I'm just so thankful Jacob and Shannon know the truth. Can you imagine if they had lived out there lives believing in a false god? What would have happened to them — to all of us someday when we passed from this world to the next? I shudder to think about it."

"Indeed. We have been so blessed to know the truth. This changes everything. Now I understand why the things we are studying in the lab exist. Why everything is so ordered? It didn't just happen by chance. A loving God set up the natural laws that govern our existence. He holds everything together for our benefit. Science isn't god, rather, it is the study of his creation."

"I don't think I will ever be able to sleep. This is so overwhelming, isn't it?"

"It is. It truly is."

†††

Kissami watched the family depart. They were so excited to know the truth that they were all trying to talk to each other at the same time. The kids were jumping up and down as they spoke. The adults were smiling and wiping tears out of their eyes. It was quite the sight to behold and Kissami was so grateful to the God of the heavens for giving him a place in the spreading of the truth. It had been a dangerous journey reaching this place, but it had been worth it.

Kissami wondered what purpose the Father had in ensuring these children knew the truth, what God had planned for them, and how those plans would someday unfold. God's purpose could be just for the salvation of these four souls, or his purpose might be much more extensive. Only God knew what good works he had prepared for these souls to accomplish and where those works might lead.

Who can put a value on just one eternity, or four eternities? And how might these four impact the world? The future? God is so big! His plans are so unfathomable!

The God of the heavens had told Kissami that his work in this place was complete, but that there were many others in faraway lands waiting to learn the truth.

If no one goes, who will tell them?

Kissami packed up his belongings to make an early start the next morning. For the time being, he would just stare up into the night sky and adore the creation of his Father in Heaven.

Look at all the stars. So are his children upon the earth. Those lost in the darkness must be told the truth. Thank you, Father, for letting me be a part of that mission!

Kissami carefully poured the handful of multicolored stones into a leather pouch, pulled the drawstring tight to seal the pouch and placed it into a pocket of his backpack. Then he closed his eyes and dreamed.

Chapter 8

The Unbelievable

†††

Gatesh sat in his lab thinking about what had happened. He contemplated what to do with the knowledge he had gained.

First, the capabilities existed in the cave tunnels to travel either through time or through space — Gatesh was unsure of the time question — he had definitely traveled through space.

I do not know where or when that was, but it was not Tophet. And the sun rose from the opposite direction. Was it even our planet?

Second, the time that passed within and without the tunnels was not equivalent, but far from it. It was as if the tunnels were train stations where people could get off one time-train and transfer to another. While at the station, time stood still. Time didn't start again until one got on another time-train. It was like exiting the time dimension for a period and then re-entering time somewhere or sometime else. Compared to people on a time-train, less time expired for the person who spent time in the station (the tunnel). So all the time Gatesh spent in the tunnel, he didn't age at all compared to people on time-trains who aged significantly.

Third, if the place he had traveled to was on his planet, somewhere and sometime, the rotation of the planet would change to cause the sun to rise from the opposite direction; unless he had traveled to the past and the change had already taken place.

Fourth, there was interaction and correlation between the different colored stones and the resulting destinations of the tunnel navigation. In addition, the system was stable and not random, since he could find his way back using rational thought. Some rational being had designed the system to operate that way.

And finally, based on the tunnel maps, peoples from off planet constructed or at least used all the time or space travel tunnels; perhaps to assist them in traveling across space via time loops, to alter the relative passage of time using time loops, or to affect events on the planet in the future.

This is complicated stuff, but very intriguing! Just figuring it out is overwhelming! Who could have designed this and implemented the design?

Gatesh wondered who would believe him about these matters — he wasn't sure if he even believed what had happened. He decided he would tell Mika'el.

Mika'el will believe me and help me figure out what all this means. If he doesn't think I am crazy, that is.

†††

Mika'el sat alone. Sandrah had gone to bed to get a couple of hours of sleep.

I can't keep this a secret. I have to tell Gatesh, if he ever comes back to the lab! He's my best friend. He is resistant to believing in any god because of his faith in science, but I have to at least try to tell him about the God who created everything! His eternity depends on it.

†††

Mika'el arrived at the lab just after sunrise. Gatesh was there, working at the large board in the front of the room. He had drawn on the board what looked like a map similar to the cave drawings and paintings within the caverns. There were several colors annotated with each of the tunnels depicted. In addition, he had several observations annotated below the illustrations.

"Good morning Gatesh. It is great to see you!"

"Good morning Mika'el!"

The two rushed to the center of the lab and gave each other a brotherly hug.

"Where have you been the last three weeks? I know you sometimes take off for on extended research projects now and again, but you usually tell someone how long you will be gone. You had everyone quite concerned this time."

"Well, about that, you will not believe what I have to tell you, but I'm going to tell you, anyway!"

"Funny you should say that, because that is exactly what I was about to say."

The two walked to the front of the lab and the big board that Gatesh had been working on all night. They leaned against the desk that was directly in front of the board.

"Now Mika'el, before I get started, I want you to keep an open mind. This will not be easy to accept, let alone understand — I don't yet understand it myself. I am just going to tell you what happened and what I witnessed, ok? I haven't decided on what to make of it all — I'm hoping you can help me with that part."

"Got it. Fire away!"

"In my reality, I was only gone for about an hour, not three weeks."

"In your reality? What does that mean?"

"Mika'el, trust me on this. We will get much further if you try to save the questions until I give you most of the information."

"Ok. I'll try, but that was a bit of a zinger, you know?"

"I know. There are a lot more zingers where that came from. I will try to give you the condensed version."

"Ok, go ahead. I'll keep my mouth closed until you finish."

"Again, I was only gone for about an hour. I was in the cavern and my lantern went out — no source whatsoever of light. Basically, trapped until someone else showed up. Suddenly, there was a glowing stone. I touched it and a chain of glowing stones in the cave tunnel walls lit a route for me to follow, so I did.

"At one point, I decided it might not be such a good idea, and I turned around, only to discover the tunnel behind me was gone. On top of that, the tunnel in front of me was changing before my eyes as I walked down it. It was like I was inside of a worm or snake that was slithering through space to some other place.

"The tunnel led me to an archway. I step through it and I'm in another place, or time, or both! I'm standing in the middle of a bloody battlefield amongst thousands of charred, dead warriors. Some giant birds are ravaging the bodies of the dead. There is another army of men in front of me. To top it off, the sun is rising in the east! I panic and I step back through the archway. I am immediately back on the other side of the portal.

"So again, I'm stuck. I look around. There are no tunnels out of there, and I am not going back through that portal! Then I think of how the journey started, and I look at the cave painting near the portal. To find my way back, I must choose a color and hope it presents me with the correct tunnel. I pick one and it leads me back out to the place I started. I find the lantern burning in the cavern and exit."

Mika'el remained still, quietly taking it all in. He had known Gatesh for a long time, and although he could be emotional occasionally, he was much more animated than Mika'el had ever seen him. In Mika'el's estimation, Gatesh truly seemed to believe that what he was saying was what had actually happened.

Gatesh was done, at least for the moment. He sat silently, looking at Mika'el and waiting for a reaction.

"So, you think the cave drawings in the cavern are actually maps for navigating the tunnels and not maps of the stars?"

"Yes, exactly. Or maybe both. I don't know. Does this mean you believe me?"

"My friend, based on the last day, I am of the persuasion to believe the unbelievable. Yes, I believe you."

"I knew I could confide in you, Mikaël!"

"How did you know what color of tunnel to pick to get back to our place and time?"

"Well, I didn't. I took a wild stab at a primary color relationship and luckily it worked out. Otherwise, I might have been stuck bouncing around the universe for years, only to show up back here, long after you are all dead."

"Scary thought, right?"

"Yes indeed, but at the same time, exhilarating! I mean, isn't this an amazing discovery? I'm not sure if the tunnels lead to a different place or a different time, but either way, it changes everything we know about our reality, what we can discover, and where we can go!"

"Yeah. Do you think whoever made the cave paintings used the tunnels to travel great distances across space or used them to traverse time itself?"

"I don't know. That is still a mystery. I know time in the tunnels passes much slower than time on the outside. I found it hard to believe that my one hour of traveling in the tunnel was the equivalent of three weeks to you and everyone on the outside."

Mikaël put on his thinking hat. "I guess the tunnels could be used to either transport travelers across great distances of space using different portals or be used to slow down time itself for the travelers to witness the future — a future they would never have lived long enough to experience in the normal length of their lifetimes."

"Right. Right! So, the travelers could have a long sequence of these time loops across space that they travel to and use as rest stops, where they basically let time speed up past them while spending minimal time within. They exit the tunnels and continue on their journey, effectively traveling further and further into the future with every additional rest stop they visit. They get to their destination, wherever that may be, and they are visiting a place way into their futures. Or, they return to the place they started, like I did, to see a future they would have died way before ever experiencing."

"That blows my mind!"

"I know, right! In a way, it is a kind of immortality. The time ratio of one hour inside the tunnels to the three weeks that passed for you is 504 to one. So, if I spent my days within the tunnels and exited, I would live maybe 500 times longer than you. Every ten years would be the equivalent of over five thousand years. I could meet my great — great — great grandchildren as far into the future as I wanted."

"But what a lonely existence it would be."

"Unless you brought someone with you, that is."

"True."

"Do you think they could travel the other way? Back in time?"

"I don't know. I was only in one tunnel. But, even in that tunnel, time slowed way down on the outside compared to the inside. So if I travel through space to some faraway land that it would have taken hundreds of years to get to by some other space traveling means, I would then experience a time I could never have seen; relative to the conventional traveler, a time in the past."

They sat reflecting on all of it as they stared at the board in the front of the lab.

"True. Hey, speaking of immortality, I have something incredible to share with you as well. How about we take a break from this mind-blowing stuff and think about other mind-blowing stuff?"

"Sure, fire away."

"Remember, just like with your story, please, keep an open mind? This is a day of mind altering revelations."

"You got it Mika'el, it is the least I can do. Go!"

"Ok. Here goes. So the family and I go out to the Ashtar River for a picnic and we run into this guy sitting in the shade under the trees. Nice guy. Obviously not from around here. He invites us to eat with him. We are all talking and he notices Shannon's medallion — the one my dad gave her. If you'll remember, my dad never knew where he grew up — where he came from. He says the medallion bears the name of the one true God and that my father was in his family; and therefore, the rest of us are part of his family, too. He pulls out a medallion identical to Shannon's from around his neck! All these years, I thought there was only one medallion. He claims God sent him to find us and reveal to us the truth. He spends the next several hours explaining the history of everything to us. It is amazing, and it all makes sense!"

Gatesh looked at Mika'el in disbelief. "What did he want from you?"

"He wanted nothing. He said that he had fulfilled his mission in finding us and he would be on his way with the morning light. "

"Seems a little crazy, don't you think?"

"Seriously? My story is a little crazy?"

"Mika'el, please don't take offense. I'm just saying, my story is all, well, science. Yours requires a blind faith in something. Words. There is no proof that anything the man said is true."

"What about knowing what the medallion said, having an identical medallion, and being sent to find us and running into us on the river? What are the probabilities of all that just happening?"

"He could have been lying about all of it, just a superb storyteller."

"I have to tell you the rest. It is amazing—"

"Look, I'm more of a fact guy. Stuff I can see with my eyes and touch with my hands. We have to figure these tunnels out. I'll come over one of these nights and we can sit down and you can tell me everything. But for now, I have to focus on time."

"Ok, let's talk about the tunnels. Where did they come from? Who made them? Someone made them. Doesn't this all go back to God?"

"I don't know, maybe the space travelers made the tunnels."

"Then who made the space travelers?"

"Look, Mika'el, I am just not that interested right now, ok? I am a little distracted to be that interested in the stories the stranger told you. Now, are you going to help me figure these tunnels out?"

"Sure, ok. But you will see that this is all related, somehow."

"Ok, buddy. But first, let's figure out what to do next with the time tunnels. If we figure out the time tunnels, we will have all the time in the world later to figure out God."

"What is this?" The red dragon whispered from the darkness.

"What is it that the flesh speaks of from Tophet? Time? Time tunnels? Interesting."

Chapter 9

Homage

†††

The entire city of Tophet congregated beneath the Temple of Molech as it towered above them in the shadow of Ashtar. They complied as instructed by Soros, the High Priest of Molech, like they always did. Their compliance resulted primarily from their upbringing; there simply was no other option but to conform.

Soros spoke to the people from the top of the pyramid. The flames of the altar rose high into the sky behind him.

Hundreds of the Temple Guard were visibly present throughout the crowd to ensure there was no dissent. If there was dissent, the Temple Guard would escort dissidents to reeducation sites on the outskirts of Tophet. There, they would learn in a variety of ways the errors of their thinking.

"People of Tophet. Greetings from your protector and provider, the great Molech of the Mountain."

The people, at the direction of the Temple Guard, cheered in acknowledgement and salutation to the god of Tophet.

"As you all know, Molech has kept our city and our people safe from both Ashtar and the fire-breathers within for hundreds of years. We owe Molech our reverence and tribute for our safety and very existence."

The people cheered, and with each of Soros' pronouncements, the flames behind him burst forth with more fury.

"Without Molech, we would have nothing! Without Molech, the mountain and the dragons would have rained fire down upon us and consumed us."

The people cheered louder.

"We owe Molech everything!"

The flames exploded skyward, and the cheers grew to a deafening level. Suddenly, the flames died down, and the crowd hushed.

"But lately, Molech has felt like you no longer appreciate his care for you. He feels as if you have found other objects for your affections."

The crowd grew nervous. The people whispered to each other. This was not a good sign.

"Molech requires that his people show their esteem for him in a more visible way. He needs to know that he holds the top position of affection and service in your hearts. There can be no one higher than Molech!"

The whispering stopped as everyone held their breath, wondering what Soros would say next.

After a brief pause, Soros said the words. "Molech requires that Tophet dedicate six children to him on the full moon of every month. We will all assemble like we are tonight, and I will sacrifice the children to him for us, here, at the fire of the altar."

The people gasped. A few people screamed their objection and the Temple Guard quickly whisked them away.

"I will contact the parents of the children chosen in the coming days. What an honor to be chosen to represent your people in a rite of reverence to your god."

The tears flowed quietly in the crowd as all the parents hugged their children and prayed for mercy. They didn't see the opportunity to sacrifice their children in the fire in quite the same way as Soros did.

High above the people on the top of the temple pyramid, Soros smiled. It was a glorious night. *Now, who should we choose?*

Chapter 10

Temptation

†††

Molech had given Soros discretion in deciding which children would willingly sacrifice themselves in the fire for their people. However, there were requirements. The children had to be between the ages of one month and thirteen years. In addition, Molech had specifically designated the children of one family to be in the first set of those chosen to enter the flames. Soros made it a priority to visit this family immediately.

There was a knock on the door of the small home. Mia rushed to the door and opened it. She was shocked to see Soros and three of the Temple Guard on her doorstep. Bowing, she invited them in.

Soros signaled two of the guards to stay at the door on the outside of the dwelling, while one stayed with Soros as he entered.

"Your Excellency, my husband is not home. What an honor it is to have you visit our humble family. Of what do we owe the honor?"

"I was hoping to speak with your daughters, if that would be acceptable to you."

"Oh, of course, I will call them. They are just playing in the back."

"Perfect."

Mia went out the back door and returned moments later with her twin daughters. "This is Tarah, and this is Mirah."

"Wow, they are identical, aren't they?"

"They sure are. I can barely tell them apart after twelve years. They will have their thirteenth birthday next month."

"Will they now?" Soros smiled warmly and addressed the girls. "I have never met more beautiful girls."

"Thank you." The girls said together.

"Oh, they are darling, aren't they? May I speak to them for a few minutes?"

"Of course, Excellency. Of course."

Mia remained in the room.

"Alone please."

"Oh, I see. I will just be in the back room. Please call me when you are done." Mia exited through a back door. Soros nodded to the guard accompanying him, and the guard assumed his post at the back door of the room.

"Hello girls. Sit down. Let's have a chat, ok?"

The girls sat on the chairs in the room and listened to Soros, the High Priest of Molech. They were awestruck by his beautiful robe filled with jewels and the power that he projected by his mere presence.

"I will get right to the point. What is it you girls desire the most?"

Tarah answered first. "Power, I want power."

"Power. Yes, that is a wise choice. And you, Mirah, what do you desire?"

Mirah stared at the jewels of Soros' robe. "Beauty, I want to be beautiful."

"Beauty. Yes, another wise choice. With power and beauty, a woman can get anything else she desires, can't she?"

The girls both nodded in agreement. They stared into Soros' eyes like star-struck children.

"I can give you these things. Tarah, I can give you power. Mirah, I can give you beauty. Would you like that?"

They both nodded yes.

"Very good. Come with me to the temple."

Both of the girls followed Soros out the front door without thinking twice. Visions of power and beauty filled their minds as they were about to be granted their deepest desires. The guard posted at the back door of the house followed them out as they left.

A few minutes later, Mia opened the back door to see if everything was going alright. To her surprise, no one was in the room. She walked to the table where everyone had been just a few minutes earlier. Glancing down on the table, she noticed two red rubies.

Sitting down and smiling, she picked up the rubies and held them in her hands.

These must be worth a fortune! What an honor to serve our people.

Chapter 11

Dreams

†††

Mika'el was alone in the candlelight of a solitary candle. He kneeled at the window of their small home and looked out at the stars. For the first time in his life, the identity of the Creator was now known to him.

Mika'el looked up into the night sky and prayed. "Almighty God, maker of the heavens and the earth, I, your humble servant, Mika'el, come before you. Please forgive me and my family for all the things we have thought, said, and done in offense to you and your truth. Forgive us for worshipping a false god. Thank you for sending a messenger to tell us who you are and all the mighty acts you have done, as well as the promises you have made to those who love you. We love you, God, and call upon you now to keep those promises to us. We honor you by asking this?

"We now know that we live in a land that is hostile to you. It is a land that worships a false god, if not a demon from hell itself. This demon now requires our people to sacrifice our children to it upon an altar of fire! I fear for my children and call upon you, the one true God, to save them.

"We go to sleep tonight, resting in the assurance that our faith in you is not misguided superstition, as my friend Gatesh tells me, but a genuine belief given to us by your Spirit. Please protect your people,

Oh God, for without you, we are defenseless. However, with you, no weapon formed against us will prosper. So shall it be."

Mika'el returned to the bed and joined his wife Sandrah in a restful sleep, confident that their God would not forsake them.

†††

Jacob and Shannon were fast asleep in their beds when the wolves began their night songs. Shannon rose from her bed and walked to the front door of their home. She left through the door and walked down the front hill to the trees below. Beyond the trees was a pasture. Shannon saw a solitary lamb walking in the pasture and followed it. The lamb led her to a peaceful stream where she sat down, cradling the lamb in her arms. Moonlight reflected on the gentle waters of the stream.

†††

The voice spoke into the void, "She is important in His-story. She must not survive. Kill her."

†††

A pack of wolves slowly crept across the pasture and crouched behind Shannon as she sat by the edge of the stream. They were inside ten feet and ready to strike. Shannon did not know they were there.

A dome of golden light slowly grew from the ground where Shannon sat until it surrounded her with its aura, six feet in every direction. She took no notice of the light. The wolves, however, took notice. They could see the mighty angel that stood guard behind the girl and the flaming golden sword it held within its hands. They rolled over on their backs, instinctually terrified and frozen in submission.

Shannon turned her head and saw a young man in a white robe with a silver streak in his hair sitting beside her at the edge of the stream. "Hello."

The young man smiled. "Hello."

He looked like he was just a little older than she was. His voice was soft, like the waters flowing over the smooth stones of the stream.

"Do you come here often?"

"Whenever someone wants to meet me here, I enjoy sitting beside the peaceful waters and visiting with them."

They sat for a few moments, just watching the water run over the stones.

"My name is Shannon."

"Hi Shannon. My name is Engel."

†††

The six demons fought savagely with the mighty angel sent to protect the girl. He was holding his own against them, but they were landing serious blows. The angel needed to hold off the demons and those they would use in the physical world to kill the girl. Failure was not an option.

†††

Shannon spoke her mind as she watched the peaceful waters flow down the stream. "My family just learned about the one true God. Everyone around us still worships Molech, although I don't think they really want to. I think they are just afraid of what might happen if they say they won't worship him anymore. They are afraid of the Temple Guard, Ashtar, and the dragons."

"Are you afraid?"

Shannon thought about that for a moment as she watched the waters of the stream flow peacefully over the stones. "I think so. A little. But the stranger who taught us about the one true God told us that God would send his angels to guard us and help us face the enemy. He said that having God on your side was to always have more than the enemy has on its side."

"Do you believe his words?"

Shannon turned her head and looked directly into the young man's eyes. "I do."

"Good. You and your family are very special to God. He loves you all very much, and he has important plans for you."

"He does?"

"Yes, he does. You can call on him whenever you are in trouble. Rest assured, he will help you."

"Will he send you to help us?"

"Sometimes. Sometimes he will help you directly. It just depends, but he is always near."

Shannon thought about what her new friend said and smiled. "Thank you, Engel. That makes me happy."

"I'm very glad, Shannon."

†††

Mika'el and Sandrah awoke to the panicked voice of Jacob yelling at the side of their bed. "Mom, Dad, wake up! Wake up!"

"What is it?" Mika'el asked, instantly awake.

"Shannon is gone, and the front door is open."

"What?" Mika'el jumped out of bed, slipped into his shoes and darted out the front door, with Sandrah and Jacob close behind.

They looked around frantically in the moonlight, but didn't see Shannon anywhere.

"Ok, split up. I'll head toward the barn. Jacob, you head down toward the pasture. Honey, check the house again and make sure we didn't miss anything."

†††

The fighting was epic and brutal. Although the mighty silver angel with the golden sword had already taken care of the weakest four demons, two remained, and they were intent on reaching the girl. They attacked the angel relentlessly!

†††

"I want to tell you a psalm that will remind you of what we talked about today. It is one of my favorites."

"Ok."

"The LORD is my shepherd, I lack nothing. He makes me lie down in green pastures, he leads me beside quiet waters, he refreshes my soul. He guides me along the right paths for his name's sake. Even though I walk through the darkest valley, I will fear no evil, for you are with me; your rod and your staff, they comfort me. You prepare a table before me in the presence of my enemies. You anoint my head with oil; my cup overflows. Surely your goodness and love will follow me all the days of my life, and I will dwell in the house of the LORD forever."

"That is beautiful."

"It is."

Shannon looked at the young man. "Will I see you again?"

"I will be around. I'm sure we will meet again. Just remember — fear not, have faith, God is nigh."

"I will."

†††

Jacob ran down through the trees to the pasture. He looked toward the stream and couldn't believe what he saw. Shannon looked like she was asleep beside the stream. One of their lambs was asleep next to her. That wasn't the shocking part — there were six wolves on the ground behind her. Strangely, they were on their backs.

Jacob was going to try calling to Shannon to wake her up, but he didn't want to startle the wolves. Instead, he walked as calmly and softly as he could over to Shannon and the wolves. If the wolves woke up, the plan was to grab Shannon and jump into the stream, hoping the wolves would think twice about going in the water. It wasn't a good plan, but it was the only plan he had.

As Jacob carefully stepped over a wolf to get to Shannon, the largest of the wolves opened its eyes and tracked Jacob's movements. Jacob made eye contact with the wolf, and as he did, all the wolves' eyes opened and looked at Jacob. That totally freaked him out, but he held it together.

†††

Both demons attacked the mighty angel at once in a head-on charge. At that moment, the angel's wings exploded in color, its eyes blazed brilliant gold and its powerful sword swung across the demon's path. The demons flew right into the angel's sword, and it decapitated them both instantly. The angel slowly raised the golden sword again above its head as its eyes darted in all directions, searching for further threats.

†††

Mika'el came running from the pasture just in time to see Jacob stand Shannon up. Jacob and Shannon then stood at the edge of the stream. Suddenly, six wolves that had been on the ground next to them rolled over and sprung to their feet.

What can I do against six wolves? Doesn't matter. Charge!

As Mika'el began his questionable charge to defend his children against six wolves, the largest of the wolves took off for the trees and the rest followed. Mika'el joined his children at the stream.

"Outstanding Dad!" Jacob said. "Very impressive!"

"Well, you know. Sometimes you just have to do what you have to do."

That is when Shannon woke up. "Why are we out here?" She looked at Jacob and then at her dad. "Why did you guys bring me down here in the middle of the night?" Annoyed, Shannon turned and walked hastily toward the house.

Relieved at the outcome of the event, Jacob and Mika'el just looked at each other and laughed.

Shannon stopped, turned, and shouted, "Really!" Then she turned again angrily and headed up the hill.

Mika'el and Jacob chuckled quietly as they followed.

She won't believe this in the morning.

Part 3:
Darkness Descends

Chapter 12

Fire

†††

Shannon was up bright and early the next day and couldn't believe the story her family told her at breakfast about the night before. They had decided that the middle of the night was not the time to tell her about the sleepwalking adventure she had survived. She remembered it all, just in a little different way, and she shared her details with Jacob and her parents. It had seemed like a dream, but obviously it wasn't. Discussing everyone's experience, the family concluded that something supernatural had taken place, though they weren't exactly sure what. Even Mika'el didn't believe the wolves had scattered because of his courageous charge, though everyone agreed it was courageous.

"Got to go!" Shannon said as she pushed away from the table.

"Where are you off to in such a hurry? There is no school today." Sandrah asked as Mika'el and Jacob also showed some concern about Shannon leaving so soon after the wolf encounter.

"I have to tell Mirah about everything that has happened in the last couple of days — the stranger, my pendant, my dream or — maybe not the dream."

"Ok, but remember to be home before lunchtime. You can bring Mirah over for lunch, but I want you to check in, ok?"

"Ok, Mom, I will. Bye everyone!"

Everyone said goodbye as Shannon ran out the door on her way to Mirah's house. She couldn't wait to tell her best friend all the interesting things that had been happening, and of the God of love!

†††

Shannon knocked on the door of Mirah's house, and Mirah's mom answered the door.

"Good morning, Ma'am. Can Mirah come out and play?"

"Oh, Shannon. I am sorry. Mirah isn't home."

"Oh. Do you know when she'll be back? I can come back later if that will be ok."

"Well, actually, Mirah won't be coming home."

"She won't be coming home? Where did she go?"

"She went with the High Priest of Molech to the temple."

"Why did she do that? Why won't she be coming home?"

"I'm sorry Shannon. Have a nice day and say hi to your mom for me." Mia closed the door.

Shannon turned away from the house, confused. She began her walk back home.

Why would Mirah go to the temple? Why wouldn't she be coming back home?

As Shannon walked, she remembered what they had seen at the temple pyramid a few days earlier. She remembered what Soros had said about the six children and the next full moon.

No. She wouldn't. It can't be!

Shannon ran home in tears.

†††

Bursting through the door of her house, Shannon found Jacob and her parents still sitting at the table, finishing their breakfast. Shannon was crying.

"They have taken Mirah to the temple!"

Sandrah jumped up and rushed to Shannon, throwing her arms around her in a big hug. "Honey, settle down, it's ok."

Sandrah brought Shannon to the table and sat her down. Mika'el and Jacob listened closely, concerned.

"I went to Mirah's house and her mom said Mirah had gone to the temple with Soros!"

Jacob tried to comfort Shannon. "That doesn't mean the — worst-case scenario. Maybe they are just talking about something." Jacob didn't even sound like he believed what he was saying.

"Her mom said that she wasn't coming home!"

Mika'el looked at Sandrah in shock. "What? She said Mirah wasn't coming home?"

"That is what she said."

Everyone tried unsuccessfully to console Shannon as they wondered if it was the worst-case scenario.

Mika'el and Sandrah moved to the other side of the room.

"We better go over and see what is going on," Mika'el suggested.

"I'll go get my walking shoes."

†††

Mika'el and Sandrah stood outside the door of Mia's and Travork's house. Mika'el knocked on the door. Travork answered the door.

"Hi Travork."

"Oh, hello Mika'el, Sandrah. What can I do for you?"

"Well, we were hoping we could sit down with you for a few minutes and talk. Shannon was over earlier and said Mia told her Mirah wouldn't be coming home. We know that can't be true, so—"

"Actually, that is true. Both Mirah and Tarah went to the temple. We don't expect they will be returning. Now if you'll excuse me." Travork started to close the door.

"Wait, Travork." Mika'el put his hand on the door and stopped it from closing. "That is it? Your girls are just gone and you are ok with it."

"Look. You do with your kids as you want, and we will do with ours as we want! Now, if you will kindly remove your hand from my door. Have a nice day."

Mika'el dropped his hand from the door, and Travork closed the door in their faces.

Mika'el looked at Sandrah and found her as shocked as he felt. "Do with your kids as you want?"

†††

Everyone gathered below the Temple of Molech at sunset, as Soros had directed. The colors of the sky were deep orange and red behind Ashtar as the full moon shone its light on the volcano's cone. The Temple of Molech towered high above the people as its flames erupted skyward into the night.

"People of Tophet!" Soros welcomed the people to the dark ceremonial sacrifice. He stood next to the altar, hooded in a crimson robe. "Molech welcomes you to the Ritual of Consumption and Conciliation."

†††

At the direction of two of Satan's lieutenants, Deceiptus and Obaminous, thousands of demons swarmed the crowd and filled their hearts with anger, hate and an intense desire for blood. Their souls, empty of truth, there was no resistance to the occupation of their hearts and minds by evil. What they moments before recognized as the most vile suddenly became the object of their most intense desire.

The spectacle of fire and moonlight mesmerized the people below. As the ritual progressed, their state of mind transformed from one of empathy for the families losing their children to one of blood-lust. They abandoned their rational thought and joined in a madness of many with Soros, their director. Soros couldn't wait to see the children they had just empathized with — enter the flames.

The families of those being offered as sacrifice joined on a platform of special recognition. Travork and Mia, both wearing rubies as pendants, watched the tower with pride, knowing their daughters were giving their lives for their people. Next to them stood four other pairs of parents, their children also being offered as reverence and appeasement to their god. The parents of the infants being offered hoped their babies would have wanted this fate as they obviously didn't have any choice in the matter. They also wore jewels around their necks. Little did they understand the jewels were but milestones around their necks that they could never remove.

†††

Mika'el, Sandrah, Shannon, and Jacob watched in horror as the hooded children walked to the edge of the flames. They did not join in the crowd's sudden delirium. The change of the sorrowful atmosphere around them to one of rage and insanity shocked them.

"What is happening here?" Mika'el looked at his friends and neighbors and did not recognize them. Sandra, Shannon, and Jacob drew in close behind Mika'el in a futile attempt to escape the madness of the surrounding crowd.

"We gather here today to show our love and fealty to our master, Molech!" Soros lead the crowd and the crowd followed willingly.

"Molech!"

"Molech!"

"Molech!"

Mika'el, Sandrah, Shannon, and Jacob were very uncomfortable. They knew they shouldn't be in this crowd, because they didn't have love for Molech or loyalty to him. They also thought the crowd of lunatics would realize they were different at any moment and there was no telling what they might do. Fortunately for them, the crowd focused on the altar and didn't care about their lack of interest.

The flames erupted more violently into the night sky as those being sacrificed walked to the fire's edge. All the human sacrifices wore crimson hooded robes — even the infants who were being held by Soro's servants, standing on either side of him.

Standing next to what Shannon thought were Tarah and Mirah were two smaller children, old enough to stand but half the height of her friends. Unlike Tarah and Mirah, the smaller children were not there of their own free will, but were being coerced to stand next to the blazing flames of the altar. At Soros' direction, the servant's holding the infants stepped forward and stood next to Tarah and Mirah.

"What's happening?" Shannon asked her parents. "They aren't really going to walk into the flames of the altar, are they?"

Sandrah could not believe what she was seeing. "I don't know, honey. Close your eyes."

But Shannon could not look away. None of them could.

Then the even more unthinkable happened. The servants of Soros placed the babies into the outstretched hands of Mirah and Tarah, who held them out in front of them as they turned back toward the fire.

The crowd was in a frenzy — screaming, cheering, and chanting for the children to meet the flames. Scire or Deceiptus, as the demon of logical deception was known, drove the inhabitants of Tophet to insanity.

At Soros' nod, the hooded servants standing behind the smallest two children pushed them forward into the flames of the altar. The crowd cheered as the children danced around in the fire for a few seconds and then disappeared from sight amidst a sudden burst of sparks within the flames.

Sandrah screamed, "No!" and buried her head in Mika'el's shoulder.

Soros grinned and nodded again. A moment later, Mirah and Tarah walked forward into the blazing inferno with the babies held out in front of them. The babies burst into flames, fireballs in each girl's outstretched arms. Then the flames consumed the robed figures of Mirah and Tarah, who stood motionless in the flames for ten seconds and then dropped to their knees. After another ten seconds, they, too, disappeared from sight.

Sandrah wept, Shannon screamed, Jacob stared as if in a trance, and Mika'el boiled with righteous anger. The crowd continue to cheer their approval.

"Molech!"

"Molech!"

"Molech!"

To everyone's surprise, the fire-beast appeared, emerging from the flames and hovering over the altar. The flames altered their heavenward course and lashed out around the colossal beast as it beat its massive wings against them.

At first, the crowd was silent in awe and wonder of the creature, the object of their newfound worship and sacrifice. Then, as if seeing a long-lost love, they cheered at its arrival.

Mika'el and his family recoiled in revulsion at the sight of the monster. How their friends and neighbors could love such a beast, let alone not flee from it, was inconceivable.

Soros walked forward to the altar and held his arms up into the sky. The beast continued to hover over the altar, its blazing crimson eyes scanning the crowd of worshippers.

Then the inconceivable happened, as if anything that had happened was conceivable. Two figures rose within the flames. They looked from the distance like two human bodies, though they appeared to burn as blazing embers within the altar flames. A moment later, they walked from the flames and stood before all to see. They were featureless and glowing like they were still burning. Their faceless heads were smooth and bloodied; only their mouths remained — wide open in silent but endless screams. Slowly, their bodies cooled and took on form and feature.

The crowd became silent. Their mouths were agape as they stood in awe.

Soros' servants rushed to the figures and covered them with crimson robes. They stood the same height as Mirah and Tarah had stood, but there was no way to tell if it was them.

How could it be? How could it possibly be?

The two hooded figures walked from the altar and disappeared into the pyramid. Soros lowered his arms and the fire-beast plunged back into the molten flames of the temple altar. Fire and magma erupted, flowing over the edge of the altar. Soros turned to the crowd. "Now you have seen the power of your god!"

The crowd cheered!

Soros disappeared into the pyramid as the Temple Guard ushered away the crowd. The ceremonial offering was over.

But what had just happened?

Mika'el and Sandrah rushed to get Shannon and Jacob home. It had been the worst experience of their lives, and Mika'el shuddered to think of the ramifications that would result from it, both psychologically for each of them, and for the city of Tophet.

Will we ever recover from this? How can we continue to live here amongst this madness? What did we witness emerge from the fire tonight?

There would be much to discuss at breakfast tomorrow, though no one would sleep that night.

Chapter 13

Choose

†††

The family met at sunrise for breakfast. Sandrah thought that some level of normalcy might help keep the family sane after the ordeal the night before. It was a tall order. From the look on the children's faces, they got little sleep, if any. It was the same for Mika'el and Sandrah.

Mika'el started the talk no one really wanted to have. Still, it was important that the family discuss what had happened and what it meant for each of them. "We need to talk about what happened last night."

"Where do we even start?" Jacob asked.

"Well, I think we start with the big picture and go from there. Sound alright?"

Everyone nodded, though Shannon just stared down at her plate.

"Ok. I'll start. Obviously, there have been some really life-changing events happening lately. The timing of meeting the stranger at the river and Shannon having her dream with a pack of wolves, right before last night's nightmare, is not a mere coincidence. I don't believe in coincidences. I think everything happens for a reason."

Shannon asked, "So, what do you think those things had to do with last night?"

"Well, I think there is a battle being waged."

"Between good and evil?" Jacob asked.

"Between good and evil. And we are all right in the middle of it. I think we have to choose which side we are on."

They sat, reflecting on it, but not for long.

Sandrah said, "Well, I know what side I am not on. I am not on the side of killing babies and sacrificing my children in a fire to some monster!"

Mika'el and the children were a little surprised by Sandrah's sudden outburst, though they all agreed completely with her sentiment.

Mika'el said, "I think the stranger sent to find us and tell us about the one true God, as well as Shannon's dream and the event with the wolves by the stream, were all meant to prepare us for what was coming. I think it was the reason we could clearly see what was happening last night while evil overtook everyone around us. We didn't go looking for the truth, but the truth found us. We have been called to be different. I think we have changed."

Shannon said, "Tophet is not our family. It is not our home."

Sandrah put her arm around Shannon. "I don't think so, honey — not anymore."

Jacob asked, "Where will we go? We can't stay here."

Mika'el stood. "I think you are right, Jacob. We can't stay here. I don't have a plan yet, but I'm working on it."

Sandrah stood and motioned for them to all join in a group hug. As they all did, she said, "We'll figure it out. We have each other."

Shannon added, "And we are not alone."

†††

"What are we going to do, Mika'el? Where are we going to go?"

"I don't know, honey." Mika'el and Sandrah sat at the table alone as Shannon and Jacob worked on assignments in their rooms.

"Remember when I told you about the tunnels and the experience Gatesh had?"

"Yes, that was crazy. You don't think that really happened, do you?"

"I was skeptical, but now, considering everything else that has been happening, I think maybe the tunnels might play a part in what is going on. Maybe there is something to Gatesh's experience that might provide an answer to what we should do."

"Really? You think so?"

"I don't know. There are no coincidences. The strange tunnel anomalies happening right with everything else? I think I will give Gatesh the benefit of the doubt and see if I can help him figure out what is going on in the tunnels. Perhaps it is what I am meant to do right now."

"Ok, but be careful. If he is correct in what happened to him, it seems you could get lost in there."

"Don't worry. I am well aware of the danger and will be careful. I might be gone for a bit. Last time Gatesh was gone for three weeks."

"Please don't let that happen. Now is not a good time to be gone for three weeks."

Mika'el kissed Sandrah goodbye and left for the lab. He couldn't help but notice how much their lives had changed since the last time he left the house for the lab. He also had an increased awareness of how much his family meant to him.

Chapter 14

The Future

†††

"Ready?"

"Ready."

Gatesh and Mika'el stood with their lanterns at the tunnel map. They had planned extensively for the experiment and were ready to give it a go. They both shut off their lanterns. A moment later, the map lit up. Mika'el believed Gatesh, but still looked surprised when it happened.

Mika'el touched a purple stone and a long series of purple stones lit up along the tunnel walls, leading the men forward.

"Amazing!" Mika'el said as he followed Gatesh down the tunnel. Mika'el turned around and saw that the tunnel disappeared behind them with every step they took. There was no going back, at least not in the conventional way.

The men walked through what appeared to be an ever-changing or morphing tunnel. It turned many times before arriving at the archway. After about ten minutes, they arrived at the portal.

"Are you ready for this?" Gatesh asked.

"No, I don't think I am," Mika'el replied, "but it is why I am here, so let's roll."

Realizing every second inside the tunnel was the equivalent of eight minutes in Tophet time, they stepped through the archway. Instantly, they stood together in a crowd. The sun had just set, and reflections of many colors covered the terrain. They saw a beautiful person on a stage say "See." Suddenly, hundreds of beautiful creatures surrounded the crowd, their multicolored wings sparkling beneath the night sky.

Gatesh wanted to stay longer, but Mika'el, having promised Sandrah to minimize the time he was gone, pulled Gatesh back through the gateway.

"Why did you pull us back so quickly? That might have been who created the time tunnels. Those might have been the space travelers that made the maps!"

"I know, Gatesh, but we have to stay aware of the time. I promised Sandrah I would — hurry. It is what we agreed to when I agreed to come with you, remember?"

"I remember. Yes, of course."

Without delay, the two men proceeded to the tunnel map for the portal and chose blue once again; it and red being the primary colors that make purple, the stone that brought them to this portal.

A tunnel presented itself before them and they followed the blue stones through it, hoping it would once again lead them back home. After about five minutes, they arrived at another archway with a large amethyst stone on a pedestal.

"Here goes nothing," Gatesh said as he and Mika'el stepped through the archway and crashed to the ground next to the lantern they had left there. Gatesh had extinguished the lantern before they had stepped through the portal, so it still had plenty of fuel left. After lighting the lantern, Gatesh and Mika'el exited the tunnels.

"That was unbelievable!" Mika'el screamed, suddenly euphoric, realizing they had made it home.

"Right! Though I am still trying to get used to that step through the gateway."

"You could have warned me about that."

"Sorry. I forgot about it."

Mika'el looked around. "No obvious way to tell what day it is. I would guess we spent about fifteen minutes in there, so about five days. Wow!"

"Why do you suppose time slows down for us inside the tunnels?"

Mika'el thought for a moment. "Well, the tunnel that took us to whenever or wherever we just went must use a magnetic field to bend the space-time continuum. I have hypothesized about the effects of high magnetic fields on time, but never had a way of testing my theories. Apparently, someone else has not only tested their theories but has implemented ways to harness time with magnetic fields."

"What did we just see? Do you think we might have just met the people who created the tunnels, or at least made the maps?"

"I don't know, but maybe we can use these tunnels to get out of Tophet, after-all."

"Careful what you wish for — we do not know how to control the where or the when of the tunnel destination."

"Those are just details. Let's talk about it back at the lab. I have to go see my family and find out what has been going on and how long we have been gone."

†††

The voice whispered in the void of the pit. "What is this they have discovered, and how can I use it?"

Chapter 15

Mystery

†††

"Dad! Dad's home!"

Everyone came running when Mika'el entered the house.

"Where have you been? We were so worried!" Shannon said as she wrapped Mika'el up in a hug.

"I have been away at work."

"For five days! Where are your bags? You are wearing the same clothes as when you left."

"I'll explain later."

Sandrah gave Mika'el a big hug and whispered in his ear, "Five days?"

Mika'el whispered back, "Fifteen minutes."

After hugs, Sandrah asked Shannon and Jacob to let her and their dad talk for a while. The children gave their dad another hug and then went to their rooms to continue their studies. Sandrah and Mika'el sat down at the table with his lunch to catch up.

"How was it?" Sandrah asked. "Was it like Gatesh said it was?"

"It was unbelievable! I don't know how to explain it. We went somewhere or sometime — I don't even know which. It could be a way for us to leave and escape the growing madness in Tophet. We would all be together, but we wouldn't know the where or the when of our destination. So there would be some risk involved."

"Looks like there would be risk either way, whether we stay or go."

"What has happened here for the last five days?"

"Oh, where do I start?"

"Really? In five days?"

"Oh, yeah. The day after you left, Mirah and Tarah left the temple grounds."

"So it was the twins that came back out of the fire?"

"Yes. Although critics say that there is really no way to know that the twins were the ones that entered the altar fire, since no one could see their hooded faces from so far away."

"Good point."

"Still, if it was them, how could they survive what we saw?"

"I don't know. Yet, there has been a lot happening that I can't explain. It appears we have been living in ignorance of truly amazing things going on around us all our lives. Really mind-blowing stuff. So, who can say, right?"

"Anyway, Shannon was so relieved that her best friend had survived, that when she heard a rumor that Mirah had gone back to her house, she went right over to see her. When she arrived, the Temple Guard was there and wouldn't let her go inside. But she saw Mirah leaving and called out to her. Mirah stopped, looked right at Shannon and said she didn't know her. It broke Shannon's heart."

"Oh no. Poor thing. That is terrible."

"She cried all night. I talked to her the next morning about it for hours. She is doing better now, but it is very hard for her. Mirah was so important to her."

"I know. It must be terrible. She lost a major source of stability in her life."

"We all have. Everything is changing all around us."

"We need to take it to the one true God and ask for his help. He needs to be our solid ground now."

"I am glad you said that. We were so worried about you when you were gone. We started praying together to the one true God every evening. Then we sang his praises. Shannon and Jacob wrote some songs. It was very comforting for all of us to give our worries and troubles to

God in prayer and to sing his praise. I really noticed the difference it made for Shannon."

"Excellent! That is wonderful. I can't wait to join you tonight."

†††

She sat in her room in the temple.

Shannon looked so hurt when I told her I didn't know her. I remembered her and all the times we had together, but I felt nothing. Those feelings are gone. I am changed. I have a new name.

She stood and walked to the reflecting glass. She looked at her image in the glass. The reflection showed a face that was charred, bloody, and burned beyond any recognition. She closed her eyes for a moment and concentrated. When she opened her eyes again, her face was beautiful, with a complexion that was new and without blemish.

My name is Mirare, and I am beautiful.

†††

She sat in her room in the temple. She and her twin sister had made a deal with Molech.

They had given Molech their flesh, and he had given them gifts in return. She got up and walked to the reflecting glass and looked at herself. She saw a monster.

My name is Thalia, and I am beautiful.

As she looked into the reflecting glass, her burns healed, her flesh regenerated, and she was without blemish. Then she smiled, and raising her hands up into the air, she levitated above the marble floor of her room.

And I am powerful!

†††

Soros summoned the people to gather around the temple pyramid for a special daytime announcement.

Soros addressed the crowd. "People of Tophet, I have summoned you here today to witness the power of Molech, whom you serve."

The people looked upon the altar platform from which Soros spoke. Beside him were two hooded figures.

"As you all saw a week ago at the Ritual of Consumption and Conciliation, twin girls walked into the cleansing fires of Molech. After the flames had consumed them, they emerged once again. They were once girls named Tarah and Mirah. Molech has appointed them his high priestesses, giving them new names. I present to you, Thalia and Mirare."

Thalia and Mirare amazed the crowd as they stepped forward and revealed their beautiful faces; faces that many in the crowd had known for years and recognized as the children of Mia and Travork. Those standing next to Mia and Travork congratulated them on their daughters' new positions as High Priestesses, totally forgetting that the week prior they had given their daughters over to sacrifice in the flames.

"As you can see, Molech can do as he pleases. If he finds you bring your children out of a pure heart of worshipping him and that they are worthy, he can return them to us as special servants in his kingdom."

The people nodded in agreement, still in awe of the girls' beauty.

"Do you think your children are worthy? Do you bring them for sacrifice to him willingly, out of love for him? If you do, this is what Molech can do!"

The crowd cheered and shouted their devotion to their god of the fire! In the days to come, the people would offer thousands of their children for sacrifice, many more than Soros requested for the next ritual. None of these children would survive the fire that was coming.

Chapter 16

Found

†††

Pieraj, Soros' Chief of Information, gave his daily report on the state of Tophet's compliance. Through Pieraj, Soros dealt with any subversion of the control of Molech, either through word or deed, with an iron fist.

"Overall, the people are compliant and eager to serve Molech and the Temple. There are a few small gatherings of sceptics and potential dissidents we are keeping our eyes on or actively engaging. One report of note was from about ten days ago. A local angler was fishing on the river that afternoon and oversaw a stranger speaking to a family under a patch of trees. He thought it was odd in that it looked like the stranger was teaching them. Also, after a while, it looked like they were praying. While they were praying, he drew in close to them, behind the trees. He overheard the stranger talking about the one true God."

Soros turned suddenly. "The one true God?"

"Yes, sir, that is what he said."

"Go! Find this teacher and the family. Dispose of the teacher. Dispose of the fisherman too and make it discrete. And I want to know who the family is. I will deal with them myself, in a way that is — appropriate."

"Yes, sir!"

†††

"There! There he is! Get him!"

Kissami had spent the last week praying, visiting with a few other families, and awaiting spiritual direction. He had been told that there was still one other to share the truth with before he departed. He had set up camp in the rocky foothills of the great volcano. Without warning, several guards were rushing him from the south. "I guess the Lord wants me to go north."

Kissami grabbed his pouch and ran for the field of large boulders close to his camp, the guards from the temple in hot pursuit. Kissami entered the boulder field, and the guards entered right behind them. What the temple guards did not yet understand was that the boulder field was a natural maze, and few that entered ever exited.

At every turn, the guard commander split some of his command off in one direction and some in another. Before long, the commander found himself alone, hunting Kissami while attempting to navigate the rocky maze. Before long, he realized he had lost his way.

The commander leaned against a boulder and shouted out to his men. "Hello, can anyone hear me? Hello!"

"Can I help?" Kissami said as he stepped out from behind a boulder.

The commander spun around and raised his sword. "You, hands up!"

"Absolutely."

"You are now my prisoner!"

"Ok. If you say so."

"Don't move!"

"Alright."

The commander called out to his guards, "Over here! I've got him!" There was no response. Again, the commander called out, "Temple guards! Over here!" Still, nothing. After calling out for a few more minutes, the commander stopped trying. He decided he would walk out of the rocky boulder maze with the prisoner on his own. "Move! That way."

"Ok. Are you sure?"

"Move!"

"Alright."

Kissami started walking, and the commander guided him in choosing the right way every time they encountered multiple options. The problem was that the sequence of right ways never led them to the exit of the maze. The commander tried to use the sky above and the sun's position to guide him to the exit, but it seemed as if the sun's position kept changing.

After a couple of hours, the commander ordered Kissami to stop and sit down against a rock — he did the same.

The commander saw Kissami showed no signs of fatigue or frustration. The Commander asked his prisoner, "Any idea where we are going?"

"I know where I am going."

"What does that mean?"

"Exactly what it sounds like. I know where I am going. Do you know where you are going?"

The commander thought the question either ridiculous or obviously provocative. "Look, you are my prisoner. Answer my questions!"

"What would you like to know?"

"Am I on the right path?"

"No."

"Will you show me the right path?"

"Sure. I've been waiting for you to ask. First, why am I your prisoner?"

"You have been teaching a false religion and steering people in the wrong direction."

"And yet, you are now asking me for directions?"

"Stop playing games with me."

"Oh. No games. This is a deadly serious conversation."

They stared at each other for a few minutes.

Kissami broke the ice. "Aren't you curious why I am not worried about getting out of here?"

"I don't care."

"Ok."

A few more minutes went by.

"Ok, why aren't you concerned?"

"I know the one true God will take care of me."

"Oh, rubbish. That sounds like something my grandmother would say to me when I was a boy."

"I know."

"You know? How could you know?"

"That is why we are here together, sitting on the ground of this maze. Your grandmother was not from Tophet."

"How do you know that?"

"I know a lot about you. You're not married. You don't fit in with the rest of the guards. Someone killed your parents when you were just a baby, leaving you orphaned. Your grandmother raised you but died when you were very young. I know you have been searching for the truth, and I know you don't want to follow Molech."

Kissami completely overwhelmed the guard with his knowledge about the guard's life. No one knew this much about him, not even the temple leaders.

"I am here because the one true God knows you, Captos. He knows you by name. You thought you were looking for me, but it was I who was looking for you. I have been waiting for you. We have somewhere to go."

Captos was in shock. He didn't know what to make of this. Everything this prisoner said was true. How did this stranger know so much about him? How did he know his name?

"Why me? Of all the people in Tophet, why are you here for me? What have I done that the one true God would search me out?"

"You have done nothing. He will have mercy on whom he will have mercy."

"Tell me about him, the one true God. I want to know."

"I know you do. Come with me. You have nothing left here. I will take you to a place where you will learn about the one true God. You should get used to listening to your prisoners, Captos. Come."

Kissami stood, walked over to his guard and extended his hand. Captos took it.

Captos followed Kissami through the maze of boulders to a small cave opening. They entered the cave and found a tunnel. About one hundred feet into the tunnel, there was a map on the tunnel wall. Kissami reached into his pouch and pulled out an orange jasper stone. He placed the stone against the wall near the map and the tunnel lit up with dozens of orange jaspers embedded in the tunnel walls. They marked off a route for the men to follow through the tunnels.

"How? What?"

Kissami smiled. "Follow me. You ain't seen nothing yet."

Chapter 17

Targeted

†††

Pieraj reported the unacceptable news to Soros. "The stranger got away. We believe the Commander of the Temple Guard helped him escape."

"How can that be? Don't we even know our own? And the commander none the less?"

"Yes sir. Very troubling. But we found out who the family is that he was talking to by the stream."

"Who are they?"

"A man named Mika'el, his wife, and two children. He works in the time study laboratory."

"Time study, again! Those people are a thorn in my side. How old are his children?"

"Sir?"

"How old are his children?"

"He has a son thirteen, and a daughter twelve."

"Twelve? Good. Very good. Looks like I have my first volunteer for the next Ritual of Consumption and Conciliation. What about the fisherman?"

"Unfortunately, the fisherman met with an accidental drowning."

Soros grinned. "You would think a fisherman would know how to swim."

"Yes. You would think he would."

Part 4: Attack

Chapter 18

Run

†††

Mika'el looked out over the ocean as the sun rose. The waves of the ocean rocked the schooner and forced everyone aboard to hold tight to the railings. They watched as Ashtar released its fury, the dark clouds of ash and rock exploding skyward as the bright crimson magma flowed down through the city of Tophet to the sea. The eruption meant complete annihilation of their home. There would be no survivors in Tophet.

Sandrah cuddled up to Mika'el. She put her arm around his waist and pulled him in tight. "It's a good thing we didn't delay or we would have died there."

"I have to admit, I didn't really believe the signs." Mika'el turned his head to look at Sandrah.

Suddenly there was a blazing gold explosion of light on Mika'el's face! Sandrah was gone and a man in a white robe stood there and was speaking to him. His eyes shone like the sun. Silver streaked through his hair. "Do you believe it now? Take your family and leave immediately! Bring nothing with you, the Lord will provide! Just leave! Now! The city of Tophet will face destruction for its unbelief and worship of a false god!"

Mika'el closed his eyes, stumbled backwards, and fell to the deck of the schooner. He opened his eyes to find himself laying on the floor of his room with his feet still up on his bed.

"Are you ok?" Sandrah peered over the edge of the bed, looking down at Mika'el.

"What happened? One second I'm on the boat and the next, I am—"

"The boat? What boat?"

Mika'el pulled his feet down off the bed and stood up. "I could have sworn I was just on a boat. It seemed so real, but I must have been dreaming."

"What was the dream about?"

"We were on a boat looking back at the city at sunrise."

"How romantic!"

"No, not really. Ashtar was erupting and destroying everything. We barely made it out of there."

"Oh, how terrible!"

"It was terrible!"

Sandrah went to Mika'el and wrapped him up in a big hug. "It was just a dream."

Mika'el paused for a moment, wondering if he should tell Sandrah the rest of the dream. "I'm not so sure."

Sandrah looked up into Mikal's eyes. "What do you mean?"

"Well, in the dream, there was a man in a white robe with blazing gold eyes. He told me Tophet was facing destruction for its unbelief and worship of Molech."

"Oh, Mika'el."

"He told me to take my family and get out. Now."

They stood quietly; their minds raced over the information and what they thought it meant. Before either of them could say anything, they heard Jacob screaming from his room.

"Mom! Dad!"

Mika'el and Sandrah ran from their room and into Jacob's room. Shannon came running in right after them.

Jacob was lying on the floor like he had just fallen out of his bed. "You won't believe the dream I just had!"

Mika'el and Sandrah looked at each other. Sandrah said, "I think we will."

Shannon looked at Jacob, and then at her parents. "What?"

"Ok, everyone get dressed and splash some water on your face. Let's meet for breakfast in about five minutes. We will talk about it there."

Sandrah and Mika'el left for their room. Jacob rushed to his closet and started packing.

Shannon just stood where she was with her hands out. "What? What did I miss?"

†††

Everyone met at the breakfast table. Jacob carried a bag with him. Shannon could barely wait to ask. "Is someone going to tell me what is going on?"

Jacob couldn't wait to speak. "I had a dream Ashtar erupted and everything was being destroyed. I think your angel told us to leave here immediately!"

"My angel? Why do you think it was my angel?"

"He wore a white robe and had a streak of silver in his hair."

Shannon looked at Mika'el. "Dad, did you have a dream too?"

"Yes I did, Shannon. Same dream."

"Well, why didn't he tell me?" Shannon asked.

Jacob said, "Shan, big picture. That doesn't matter."

"Well, it matters to me!"

"Ok, kids," Mika'el said, "let's not argue. We have to figure out what we are going to do."

Sandrah said, "Well, this is a big step. We have to decide what to bring and—"

Mika'el and Jacob spoke at the same time. "He said to leave everything and just go."

Shannon looked at Jacob. "Then why did you pack a bag?"

Jacob thought for a second and just raise his hands out in front of him, palms to the ceiling. “I don’t know.”

As they were talking, there was an urgent knock on the door. Mika’el opened the door to find a young man in a white tunic standing there.

“It’s time to go.”

Everyone but Sandrah looked at the man like they were seeing a ghost. Sandrah looked at Mika’el, then the kids. “What is wrong with you all?” She walked over to the doorway and smiled at the young man. “Hello. Please, come in. How may we help you?”

The man looked young, but he was not small. He had very broad shoulders and was taller than Mika’el. He had a very fair complexion, like he had never seen the sun, and had blonde hair with a streak of silver. The man walked into the house and smiled calmly back at Sandrah. “Thank you, Sandrah.”

Shannon and Jacob just stood motionless with their mouths agape, staring at the young man.

Sandrah looked surprised. “I’m sorry. Have we met?”

Mika’el gently touched Sandrah on her arm to get her attention.

Sandrah held her smile and looked at Mika’el.

“Honey, this is Engel.”

Sandrah’s expression didn’t change as she processed the information. She just stared at Mika’el as if too nervous to look back at the young man.

“It is ok, Sandrah, I am a friend. It is nice to meet you.”

Sandrah turned back toward Engel. “Nice to meet you, too. I have heard a lot about you.”

Engel looked at Mika’el. “We really need to go now.”

“About that—”

“They are coming to take Shannon.”

“What?”

Shannon echoed her dad. “What?”

"Soros found out Kissami was speaking to your family by the river. He wants to punish you by sacrificing Shannon at the next ritual. They are coming to take her right now. We have to go!"

Sandrah turned around to grab something and Engel repeated, "Leave everything. Bring nothing. We must leave now!"

Shannon was the first one out the door. "Let's go!"

Chapter 19

The Temple

†††

Thalia and Mirare were at the temple altar, deep within the inner sanctum of the temple pyramid. This was the altar for the high priest and priestesses; no one else would ever see it.

The twins were admiring the stones that encircled the altar. There were twelve of them. There was topaz, amethyst, emerald, sapphire, chrysoprases, jasper, chalcedony, beryl, sardonyx, sardius, chrysolite, and jacinth. They were told they all had special properties — magical properties — and eventually they would be told what those magical properties were.

Soros was not with them. He was going with the Temple Guard to take a young girl into custody. Soros had accused her family of worshipping a false god, and she was to be the first of the six girls sacrificed in the Ritual of Consumption and Conciliation that evening.

The flames rose high into the air within the enormous cavernous room. Thalia burned frankincense to Molech. Mirare just stood and stared at her own reflection in a ruby.

Thalia looked over to Mirare and said, "I wonder how long we will have to serve Soros? Why does he think himself so special? Did he emerge from the fires? Surely we should be the ones who hold the power, not him!"

As she spoke the words that Potentus was laying upon her bitter heart, the flames soared! Both of the twins sensed the presence of the beast, as they were bound with it forever. They backed away from the altar, kneeled and bowed their heads. A moment later, the beast slowly rose from the boiling magma and ash that floated upon the blazing altar. Only its head emerged from the lava, its crimson eyes focusing on its servants.

"Rise and approach me."

The twins stood, showing no fear of the dragon, for they were all one. They approached the fire, too close for any other creatures of flesh to endure without bursting into flames. The entire altar room was a combustion chamber to any other beings on the planet, which was another reason that Soros was not in attendance. He had found that the chamber reached temperatures above his liking ever since the twins had arrived.

Within moments, the girls' robes burst into flames and fell to their feet, burning into ashes. They stood naked before the altar, glowing a crimson red like the embers of the fire. Neither of them showed any emotional or physical distress.

"You will serve Soros no longer. He has outlived his usefulness to me. I now have both of you, and you are very special. I have given you both special skills that I will use for my purposes throughout the ages to come until we reign together over the creation."

Both Thalia and Mirare answered as one. "Yes, master."

The fire-beast smiled. "Destruction is coming to Tophet. Take the stones from the altar — they too have a special purpose for another time. Go to the tunnels, then to the coast. Use the talents I have given you to find another land across the sea where you will build for me a new following."

"Yes, master."

The beast slowly submerged into the fiery inferno. The twins' bodies cooled, and they collected the stones from the altar. Then they left the altar chamber to do their master's bidding.

Chapter 20

The Tunnel

†††

Gatesh had waited for Mika'el to arrive for two hours. He couldn't wait any longer. The tunnels were calling. He left a note this time for Mika'el letting him know where he was going and that he might not be back "for a while." Mika'el would understand.

Gatesh grabbed his backpack and notes. He headed out. It was time for another experiment in the tunnels. Both of the previous times, the stones had taken him to a future place, at least he thought so. The first time, he wasn't sure, but the second time was definitely a future place. The things he and Mika'el saw there, even in the few seconds they had on the other side of the portal, were eye-opening. Thinking back over the event, he even thought he had glimpsed some sort of flying machines. Certainly, these machines were in the future. What else might one encounter in the future? As a scientist studying time, there was so much more to learn from the tunnels.

Gatesh understood that the impact of going into the tunnels was greater for Mika'el than for himself. The time discrepancy between inside and outside of the tunnels made it very difficult for Mika'el. Mika'el could not regain the time lost with Sandrah and the kids. So, realistically, Mika'el could not stay in the tunnels but for a few minutes, and this made investigation and study of the tunnel system very difficult. It was better for Gatesh to go by himself. He could stay longer, accomplish more, and have very little impact on anyone else, since he didn't have a family waiting for him. He would miss the time lost with Mika'el, his associate. Hopefully, the time discrepancy wouldn't be too great.

Gatesh entered the tunnel cavern and instantly noticed how significantly the tunnels had transformed since the last time he and Mika'el were there. He still didn't understand why this happened.

Does it occur when someone uses the tunnels? If so, are there others using the tunnels? They have definitely changed since we were last here.

Gatesh looked at the map on the cave wall. In order to determine if the tunnels were consistent, he needed to know if there was any other variable that had to be considered when traveling. Would using the same colored stone again take him to the same time and place as the previous time they used it, or would it be different for some yet undiscovered reason? He touched the purple stone and the colored stones appeared on the cave walls once again, leading him forward. He followed them to the portal, and without delay, he stepped through.

Gatesh could not believe what he saw. It was definitely not the same place that he and Mika'el had transported to the last time. Something else had changed. Some other variable was definitely at play.

Gatesh was standing in the middle of a sizeable village with buildings that rose high into the sky. People were everywhere! Strange carriages went by at speeds faster than horses could run. People walked with wolves on chains and talked to something they held up to their ears. But most distracting was the high number of women walking by him with little clothing.

Everything he was seeing instantly overwhelmed Gatesh. He went to step back through the portal when a large group of people rushed by him, apparently because some flashing light on a pole told them to move forward. As the group went by, they swept Gatesh away with them.

The people rushed across a flat hard surface and in front of several of the carriages that had stopped for them, leaving Gatesh alone in front of the carriages. Gatesh looked back to find the portal, but could not see it anywhere. He really didn't even know what to look for since all he had done in the past two times was step backwards to return through the gateway. There was so much in this place that looked different that he wasn't sure he would know the portal if he saw it.

Without warning, all the carriages started emitting loud noises. Gatesh did not know what to do. He stood still, holding his hands over his ears.

Suddenly, a very attractive woman with red hair rushed to his side and pulled him away from the carriages with her. After she had pulled him to the place where the crowd of people had gone, she stopped. She looked into his eyes. "Are you ok?"

"I don't know?"

"Are you new here?"

"I am. I think I'm lost."

She smiled warmly. "The big city can be quite overwhelming. Come with me. We will sit down and have something to eat. Everything will be just fine. You will see."

Gatesh didn't really have much of a choice. He didn't know where the portal was. He didn't know where he was or when, for that matter. So, he said, "Ok."

"You have some very interesting clothes on. What is your name?"

"Gatesh. My name is Gatesh."

The woman reached out to him and said, "Nice to meet you, Gatesh. My name is Rose."

CHAPTER 21

ESCAPE

†††

Once Mika'el and his family were out the door and headed for the tunnels, Engel disappeared.

Mika'el couldn't leave his friend Gatesh to die in God's punishment on Tophet, so he took a detour to pick up Gatesh on their way to the tunnels. Arriving at the time lab, he found Gatesh was gone. A note revealed to Mika'el that Gatesh had again gone to the time tunnels. Mika'el knew he would never see Gatesh again.

Take care, my friend.

Mika'el and his family continued on to the caverns. When they arrived and went inside, they went to the spot Mika'el remembered the map being on the cave wall. He blew out the flame of his lantern and waited. Nothing happened.

"Wait, I don't understand."

"What is wrong?"

"This isn't right. There is no map on the wall. It is gone."

"Well, what does that mean?"

"It means that I don't know what to do now. I thought we could use the time tunnels to get out of here, but now, there aren't any time tunnels. It looks like each tunnel can only have one activation at a time, and since Gatesh is in there, we are out of luck."

Jacob spoke up. "Engel told us to go to the tunnels, so there must be a reason — a way out."

Shannon added, "He wouldn't send us here just to die. He is on our side. So there has to be another way."

"The kids are right, Mika'el. Angels don't lie."

"Ok, let's keep going. We will see where the tunnel leads. The good news is this tunnel shouldn't morph, since Gatesh is using it."

They made their way down the tunnel, not knowing where it led. The only light was that emanating from the flame of Mika'el's lantern.

"What direction do you think we are going?" Jacob asked.

"I would guess we are traveling south, toward the shore," Mika'el said.

"Hopefully we will come out by the water. Maybe we can find a boat."

When Jacob said that, Mika'el realized just how desperate their situation was getting. Not only did they have to make it out of the cave and to the shore, they had to get across the sea. Mika'el felt tempted to despair.

How am I going to keep my family safe?

Then he remembered everything that had happened over the last month — all the miraculous things; from meeting the stranger, to the wolves, to the dreams, to the angel saving Shannon from being taken for sacrifice. Now was not the time to doubt — one hurdle at a time.

"I think I see light up ahead," Sandrah said.

A hundred yards later, the narrow tunnel opened up into an enormous cavern. As they entered the cavern, they could see a pool of molten lava boiling in its center. It made the entire cavern glow a crimson red.

"Stay close. We don't know what is in here."

"Look, the tunnel continues on the other side." Shannon kept walking across the cavern.

"Dad, what — is — that?" Jacob asked. Mikal stopped to look at where Jacob was pointing.

Across the cavern, behind the lava pool, something was hiding in the shadows. Mika'el looked closer. "Those look like — eyes."

Chapter 22

The Ritual

†††

Soros stood atop the pyramid, next to the temple altar, with the six children to be offered in the Ritual of Consumption and Conciliation. He was not happy that the daughter of the time lab scientist was not among them, but there was still time to track her down for next month's ritual.

The people of Tophet had all turned out to see the children walk into the fire. The drums were pounding, the flames were ablaze, and Soros had worked the people's blood lust into a frenzy. Everyone expected one or more of the children to return from the flames as the two twin girls had the month before.

Soros wondered where his priestesses had gone. He had instructed them to be at his side for the ceremony, and they had not shown up. The Temple Guard could not find any trace of them. They had simply disappeared. This annoyed Soros, but he could not dwell on it — there were sacrifices to be made.

The sun had set and the full moon had risen, shining its pale light upon the volcano behind and high above the altar. Ashtar was hungry for its sacrifice, and it was not advisable to keep Ashtar waiting.

All six of the robed children standing at the altar were between ten and twelve, and Soros had coached them well on how to appear willing and even excited to give themselves over to the flame — whether or not they truly were. Soros had assured the children that serving the people of Tophet in the ritual would make their parents very proud, and he had promised them they would return as priests and priestesses, just like the twins had the month before. Their parents had joyfully accepted a payment of jewels in exchange for their lives.

Everyone was excited about the upcoming ceremony, except perhaps the children, once they started feeling the heat of the flames before them. All six stepped backwards, away from the fire, as their skin baked within the crimson robes. The crowd, from their vantage point far below the altar, could not see the spear tips held behind the children to keep them from fleeing. When the children backed into the tips of the spears, they instantly found themselves caught between certain death and — certain death. At Soros' direction, the temple guards pushed the children back towards the flames with the tips of their spears. While the sound from the beating of the ceremonial drums covered the children's screams for mercy, Soros held his ghoulish smile for all to see; giving the crowd below the impression that all was well.

It didn't really matter what Soros did atop the pyramid; the crowd was in a demonic rage below. Driven to madness by demons, the people of Tophet wanted sacrifice!

The drums beat, the children fell forward into the fire, and the crowd roared their approval! Soros held his hands high into the night sky as the flames exploded, fueled by the tender kindling the children provided. This had been the time in previous rituals when Molech would make his appearance. All the people of Tophet, including their high priest, now awaited Molech's arrival and approval of their sacrifices. After all, what would a Ritual of Consumption and Conciliation be without conciliation?

Soros and the people of Tophet searched the skies above them for their god, but their god did not appear. As the full moon loomed in the dark sky above, an eerie stillness settled upon the altar; the flames reverted to their pre-sacrificial state.

Motionless and silent, the crowd awaited the rest of their evening's entertainment. Perhaps one or more of the children would emerge from the fire.

Soros was anxious. First, the priestesses had not showed up for the ceremony, and now Molech, too, was absent. Soros slowly lowered his arms as his eyes hunted the flames for any sign of his god.

Then came the rumble, very subtle at first; a barely perceivable, deep sound emanating from — somewhere. The people looked around, still smiling and waiting for the end of the show, but now a bit more wary; they didn't yet understand this scene of the performance.

A moment later, the rumble became louder — then louder again! Soros and the people locked in on the rumbling's origin and the faces in the crowd rapidly switched from morbid pleasure to absolute terror. All eyes focused on Ashtar, as the top of its dome exploded, shattering the silence! In its hellish fury, Ashtar instantaneously blasted a million tons of ash and molten rock skyward in all directions.

For a surreal moment, the people of Tophet remained frozen in time, their minds incapable or unwilling to interpret what their eyes were seeing. That moment quickly vanished as the magma vent underneath the temple pyramid erupted up through the temple's center, sending the top third of the temple tumbling down the pyramid and crushing much of the gathering below. The fiery magma, pouring from the top of the fractured pyramid in all directions, overtook the rest of the people as they fled. Soros and the people of Tophet suddenly found themselves burning in hell with their god.

Chapter 23

The Red Dragon

†††

Sandrah stopped beside Mika'el. "They do look like eyes."

Mika'el noticed that Shannon had gotten well ahead of them. He would soon realize that was a big problem.

Before Mika'el could tell Shannon to wait for them, she had passed the midpoint of the cavern. That is when the set of eyes in the shadows moved into the crimson light emanating from the molten lava pool, revealing a creature much more sinister than they could have dreamed. Crawling out of the crouched position it had been in to conceal its massive reptilian presence, the red dragon emerged. This dragon was much larger than the black dragon that the people of Tophet associated with Molech, and even uglier. It looked like it had been around for an eon. Its head, distinguishable as that of a dragon, appeared badly disfigured, as if someone had crushed it.

As the red dragon stepped out of the shadows, Shannon turned to see the monster and realized that by moving too far ahead of the rest of her family, she had allowed the creature to separate them from her. She cried out, "Daddy!"

"It's ok, little girl. I won't hurt you."

"Far wall! Now!" Mika'el barked out the order to his daughter without even thinking.

Shannon turned and ran in the direction she had been moving, attempting to put more distance between herself and the enormous dragon.

"No matter, little girl, you can run, but you can't hide."

Shannon reached the wall of the cavern. She turned and faced the dragon.

Even though I walk through the darkest valley, I will fear no evil. You are with me.

"I am not afraid of you!"

The dragon started moving towards Shannon. "Oh, you will be!"

Mika'el tried to distract the menacing creature. "Over here, you ugly beast!"

"Oh. That's not very nice, is it?" the beast snarled.

Mika'el moved forward toward the dragon with his lantern; he motioned with his free hand for Sandrah and Jacob to hug the wall and try to get to Shannon.

"Oh no, you plan on using a lantern as a weapon against me? What will a dragon do to protect itself from — FIRE?" As the red dragon said the word fire, it blasted the lava pool with a blistering stream of fire from its mouth, vaporizing the ash floating on the surface.

Mika'el fell backwards onto the cavern's rocky floor, dropping his lantern. The lantern smashed into pieces, the burning oil spreading across the ground in front of him.

"Time for another plan, little man."

Mika'el was out of ideas, and the demons of fear, inadequacy, and doubt attacked him.

After everything God has done to get us to this point, has he abandoned us now? Is he not great enough to handle this? Is it too much for him?

The dragon bowed its head down to the man, its nostrils but a few feet from Mika'el's face. "Weak, scared, little man. Who are you to stand against a dragon? My kind is far superior to your kind. You are alone now and defenseless. Prepare to watch your family die. Then I will have you as a snack."

Mika'el recoiled in fear. Tears ran down his face as he thought of his family. He looked to see where they were, but could not find them in the darkness.

God have mercy on me? Please help me? Please, Father, be with me? Do not leave me alone.

Memories flashed through Mika'el's mind and his thoughts landed on a group hug he had with his family a few nights earlier. He remembered something Shannon had said as she looked up into his eyes. She had said, "We are not alone."

Of all the memories for me to think of right now. Just a coincidence? I don't believe in coincidences. Everything happens for a reason!

Mika'el raised his head and stared at the beast. When he did, another memory returned. It was from a prayer he had prayed to God the night of Shannon's walk to the stream.

Please protect your people, Oh God, for without you, we are defenseless. However, with you, no weapon formed against us will prosper. No weapon.

Mika'el stood up to face the dragon head on.

"Oh, the little man sees himself a knight, does he?"

"I am not afraid of you."

"Oh, but you should be. I am the one who owns you and your family. I am the one who will be with you and your family for every moment from now until forever runs out. Oh, and let me tell you, it will be most unpleasant. What are you going to do now, little man?"

Mika'el looked over and saw his family against the back wall, next to the entrance to another tunnel. He gave Sandrah an almost unperceivable nod. Then he did the only thing any man in his position could do and have any hope. He got down on his knees.

"Good. Beg me. You will beg a lot where you are going. You might as well get some practice."

Then Mika'el closed his eyes and bowed his head.

I am not alone.

Mika'el prayed.

When Sandrah and Jacob saw Mika'el drop to his knees, they began to cry. "No, God, please no!"

Shannon saw something else. She saw her father folding his hands in front of him. He was not giving up. He was fighting his best battle!

Sandrah said, "Shannon, Jacob, come on. Your father wants us to make our getaway down this tunnel." Jacob followed, but Shannon didn't. "Shannon!"

Shannon ignored their pleas, looked at her Father, and then got down on her knees. She bowed her head and began praying.

"You can begin begging me any time now!" The red dragon blew smoke from his nostrils into Mika'el's face, but Mika'el didn't open his eyes.

Sandrah looked at Shannon, and then at Mika'el, and she understood. She looked back at Jacob and said, "Pray." Sandrah and Jacob dropped to their knees, bowed their heads, and began praying.

"I can understand you not wanting to watch your family die." The dragon was getting very riled up. His whole body convulsed, his wings slammed into the cave floor and he roared, "Stop your muttering and open your eyes!" Debris flew out in all directions as the dragon's wings slammed into the rocks of the cavern floor.

Without warning, an intense gold light swallowed up the crimson glow of the enclosure, filling every crack and hollow of the cavern. A gentle breeze blew from behind the great red dragon as if something had seized space and forced the air in that space to flow away from it.

"I seem to remember you have had your share of trouble with Michaels."

The red dragon spun around, his mighty tail sailing over Mika'el's head. Facing him was a mighty angel with golden wings, holding a golden sword in front of him with both hands.

The mighty angel added, "No fair picking on someone without wings."

"Engel! This has nothing to do with you. Go back to playing your harp in the clouds."

"I think I'll stick around for a little while. I have some friends in this group — yourself excluded, of course."

Mika'el realized God had answered his prayers, giving him the opportunity to escape. He quickly got to his feet and ran toward his family.

As Mika'el ran across the floor of the cavern, the dragon turned its head and hurled a stream of fire toward him. Engel instantly dematerialized and re-materialized between the flame and Mika'el, holding up his sword and redirecting the fire stream off into a cavern wall.

Everyone praised God for sending Engel and ran into the tunnel. They didn't know where the tunnel led, but they recognized God had provided it for their escape and that was good enough for them!

The red dragon was furious! "You cannot defeat me, Engel!" The dragon fired another blistering attack at Engel as it swept its powerful tail around to swat him. Engel deflected the flames with his sword as he dove over the dragon's tail and returned to a standing position.

"I'm not here to defeat you. We both know how this story ends. It is just a matter of time."

The dragon made several efforts to land blows on Engel, but the mighty angel was too agile and easily evaded each one of them.

"Yes, time. We will see if time rolls out the way you think it will. You may someday find that I have remade the creation in my image!"

"Still trying to rule? How has that worked out for you?"

The red dragon unleashed everything he had at Engel, but Engel held off its attack.

"Well, looks like my work here is done." Engel stepped back out of time and was gone.

The red dragon then realized Mika'el and his family had escaped and let out an ear-piercing roar that echoed down the tunnel.

"It can't get down here, right?" Shannon asked as she heard the dragon and turned around, looking back down the tunnel.

"Not unless it can shrink!" Jacob thought for a moment and looked up at his father. "Dragons can't shrink, can they?"

"I don't think so, but I wouldn't have thought they could talk either, so we better keep moving."

As they moved down the tunnel, it got darker and darker. They no longer had their lantern and the light from behind them — once bright gold, then crimson — was fading. Soon, the light was so dim that every step forward became treacherous.

Suddenly, as they stood in the pitch black, there was a mighty rumbling and the tunnel shook like it was going to collapse down on them. They could hear large rocks falling behind them in the now distant cavern.

"What is that?" Sandrah asked.

"My guess is that Ashtar just erupted. Whatever it is, it doesn't sound good, and I don't think there are any options for us other than to keep moving forward."

The tunnel continued to shake, and everyone's anxiety grew. "How do we keep moving when we can't see anything?"

Mikaël remembered the other tunnels and the glowing stones that were embedded in the walls. No one could see them until someone touched the first colored stone. "Everyone, feel around the walls. See if you can find a stone embedded in the tunnel's wall."

Everyone started feeling the walls in the dark, looking for something that might resemble an embedded stone.

Shannon asked, "How will we know if we've found one? The rock all feels like stone."

"You'll know. Trust me, you'll know."

Chapter 24

Captive

†††

As the molten lava flowed from the vents surrounding Ashtar, it filled the time tunnels and sealed Gatesh's position in the time-space continuum.

Satan had seen where and when Gatesh had gone, and he carefully planned to be waiting for him there in time.

†††

Gatesh or George Zarnakski, as he then called himself, had much to learn regarding the advanced technologies of the time, but having a very analytical mind and a new friend to help him, he caught on quickly. Having secured certified documentation of his family's scientific lineage (from a rather questionable source), and convinced Rose of his immigrant status, George began to fit in.

George had tried several times to find the gateway back to his own time, but soon discovered that it was impossible. There was no way to know if he was just unable to locate the portal entry point or if the portal had simply closed. If he was being honest with himself, he wasn't sure he even wanted to find it. His new time interested him much more than his old one, and the closer he got to Rose, the less he wanted to consider ever leaving her.

George and Rose fell in love, and before long, they made it official. Neither of them had any family in the area, so they had a small wedding before a justice of the peace in Kan; just a few friends attended. George's best man was Thal Blokus, his new boss at Biogen, the technology company that had hired George to work on a new project of theirs. They had said that with George's credentials and family pedigree, he would be the perfect match for the job of project manager. Rose's new best friend and maid of honor was Mirle Blokus, who lived in the pod next to her when she met George. Mirle was Thal's sister and had helped to get George his interview at Biogen. Coincidentally, Rose had met Mirle the same day she had met George.

Funny how things work out sometimes — like it was all destined to be!

It wasn't long before the happy couple were expecting their first child, and shortly after, Hunter was born. Six years later, Joseph was born. Tragically, there were complications during little Joe's delivery. George would never forget the moment the doctor told him they had lost Rose.

For years, George had contemplated telling Rose the truth of the time tunnels and where he was from; or, more accurately stated, when he was from. Someday, when they were both old, he planned to tell her. Unfortunately, that day would never come.

George was never the same after Rose's death. He couldn't help but think that if he could get his project to succeed at Biogen, then maybe there would be hope of reconstructing the time tunnels. He knew the time tunnels existed, or at least the technology — he had seen it with his own eyes. Reconstructing the tunnels might enable him to go back in time and save Rose.

George obsessed over his Biogen project and encouraged his sons as they grew older to do the same. He couldn't really tell them why, but he needed them to excel in the sciences and help him bring the project to completion.

Time held George captive while he worked to develop a future capability that he had witnessed in his past, so that he could one day go back in time and save the one he loved.

Part 5: The Deliverance

Chapter 25

Stones

†††

"I can't find anything!" Shannon was getting frustrated.

"Keep looking everyone. There has to be one here!" Mika'el was getting desperate. It was the only solution he could think of. He kept inching his way farther and farther down the tunnel, running his hands over the wall in the dark, hoping he would find just one embedded stone.

"Wait, is this?" Jacob thought he felt something. "It feels cooler than the surrounding rock. It is glowing."

Everyone looked where Jacob was touching the wall, because they could see the faint blue glow. Mika'el was sure it had to be one of the special stones. "Push on it, Jacob."

Jacob pushed on the stone, and it lit up. Within a second, dozens of the embedded stones lit up down the tunnel ahead of them. They were all at unique positions on the tunnel walls, some high and some low. The stone Jacob pushed on fell out in his hand. He held it. It softened and then ran out of his hand like molasses. Once it hit the cave floor, it hardened again into a stone.

"Shannon, did you see that?"

"I did. What in the world?"

That is when the conditions changed once again. Sandrah noticed it first. "It's getting kind of warm, isn't it?"

"Yes, it is." Mika'el said as he turned around to see the orange glow coming from behind them. "It's the lava flow coming down the tunnel! We have to move! Let's go!"

Mika'el led the way as they ran down the tunnel, following the blue stones. They turned a corner in the tunnel and faced the worst-case scenario — the tunnel just ended with a wall of rock.

"What now?" Jacob yelled.

Shannon looked around. "Look, there are more stones. Maybe the other stones can help."

"The lava is still coming. We have to hurry!" Mika'el started trying to push and pry stones loose from the cave walls.

Shannon grabbed a red stone, and it came loose from the wall. As she held it in her hand, her hand turned red; then her wrist and then her forearm. "Hey, look at this!"

Everyone looked at Shannon and saw what was happening. Sandrah asked, "Does it hurt?"

"No. Doesn't feel any different."

"You better put it back, Shannon. We don't know what it is doing to you," Jacob said.

"Sure, but it is doing something. We need a way out of this mess, and maybe this is it."

Mika'el didn't like it. The red was reaching Shannon's shoulder. "Honey, just put it back for a second so we can think about it."

Shannon went to put the stone back into its place in the cave wall when something impossible happened — her hand kept moving right into the rock.

"What?" She moved her entire arm into the cave wall. Everything that was red passed right through the rock. "Look!"

Everyone looked on in shocked amazement! Mika'el looked behind them and saw the molten lava was advancing quickly, and it was getting hot! He knew there was not much time left.

"Time to throw caution to the wind! We are out of time! Everyone, grab a red stone, hold it tight, and pray we have enough time for this to work."

They all grabbed red rocks, and slowly but surely, Mika'el, Sandrah, Shannon, and Jacob all turned red.

"Ok. I wish we had more time to test this properly, but we don't. Hold on to that stone and follow me!" Mika'el hoped and prayed there was more tunnel on the other side of the wall or this was going to be a very short and unsuccessful experiment.

Mika'el stepped into the rock wall and emerged on the other side. Sandrah and Shannon followed closely behind him, but Jacob didn't emerge on the other side.

Sandrah cried out, "Where is Jacob?"

Shannon said, "Something must have happened. I'm going back for him!"

"No one is going back! He will make it. Let's just give him a few seconds."

Jacob was still on the other side of the wall. He had been eyeing an orange stone. After the others had stepped through the rock wall, Jacob tried to grab the orange stone. He couldn't hold it because his hand passed right through it. So he had to set the red rock back in its place in the wall, let the red in his hand fade until he could use it again, and then grab the orange stone. The plan worked, but it took valuable time. After putting the orange stone in his pocket, he grabbed the red stone again. His hand turned red, and he stepped through the wall to the great joy of his family. "Wow! Ok. Well, that worked!" He said.

They were all amazed at what they were experiencing, and that the plan had worked, but there wasn't really time for a victory lap yet. They weren't even sure where they were going.

Mika'el said, "Let's put the stones down here. I don't think we are supposed to leave the tunnels with the stones."

Sandrah said, "Honey, shouldn't we keep them until we get out of the tunnel — in case there is another blockage?"

"That is a good point. Ok, let's hold on to the stones for a little longer."

They saw that there was some light in the distance, and hoping it was the end of the tunnel, they started moving forward as swiftly as possible. The closer they got, the faster they could move. Soon they were running. When they emerged from the tunnel, they were standing on the shore looking out at the Dark Sea.

They turned around and could see Ashtar for the first time since the eruption. The upper third of her cone was gone. An immense cloud of smoke and ash encircled what once had been the summit of the great mountain and rose high into the sky. Lava streams ran down from the crater and from vents all around the volcano.

They could see what had once been the city of Tophet at the foot of the mountain. A cloud of fire and ash covered it, with lava streams running through and around her.

Sandrah was in tears. "Oh, no! All those poor people. All those children, burning alive! For what? For Molech and a lie!"

Mika'el turned around and looked at the sea and the task at hand. They had arrived at part two of the problem — how to get across the Dark Sea.

Jacob looked at his dad and asked, "Now what?" Mika'el looked back at him. "You know, my boss once gave me some valuable advice. He said that I should bring him solutions, not problems."

Jacob looked out at the sea. "My Dad once gave me some valuable advice. He said, when you don't know what to do, just do something, because doing nothing — gets you nowhere." With that, Jacob waded out into the Dark Sea.

Sandrah went to take Mika'el's hand, and her hand passed through his.

"Ok everyone, time to ditch the red stones."

They threw the stones back into the cave, and when they landed on the cave floor, they melted into the rock and disappeared. In moments, their bodies returned to normal color and function.

Mika'el yelled to Jacob, "Red stone, Jacob!"

"Already left it in the tunnel, Dad."

Sandrah took Mika'el's hand. "What should we do, Mika'el?"

Mika'el pointed at the lava stream coming down the mountain and headed straight for them. "That lava stream is moving fast and will get here within the hour. When it does, it will destroy everything in its path to the sea. That's us. We won't survive. We can't stay here and we can't outrun it in any direction along the shoreline."

"Then what can we do?"

"There is really only one thing we can try. Jacob is doing it."

"Just go into the water?"

"No, that lava will bring the water to a boil when it gets here. We need to get out as far as we can and hope however far we get is far enough."

"We can't swim across a sea."

"I know, but it is all we can do right now. One thing at a time, right? We will do our best and let God do the rest. That is all we can do."

"True. We are in his hands, no matter what. Look at what he has done so far!"

Mika'el, Sandrah, and Shannon followed Jacob into the warm waters of the Dark Sea.

CHAPTER 26

Fins

†††

"We have to swim faster!" Mika'el was working hard to keep Shannon afloat.

"I'm so tired." Shannon struggled to keep swimming. "Can't we float for just a minute?"

Mika'el looked to the shore to see the lava flow coming over the last hill before the shore. It was flattening, burning, and melting everything in its path. Soon it would hit the water.

"We are running out of time."

"The lava stream hasn't even hit the water yet." Jacob supported Shannon's idea of taking a break.

Then the magma hit the water, and the sizzling caused by the hot lava flow forcefully evaporating the water instantly caught everyone's attention. When they looked, they saw the steam from the interaction rising as the two thousand degree magma vaporized the sea. In addition, toxic gases rapidly spread out from the point of interaction.

"Let's go, it's begun! I don't think we want those gases to catch us. Something tells me they are not healthy! Swim!"

Everyone swam away from the shore as fast as they could, but the gases advanced faster. It was an exercise in futility, and Mika'el knew it.

Please Father, help us.

Shannon and Jacob had given everything they had and simply could not go on. They floated in the water, trying to catch their breath. Mika'el and Sandrah swam back to them and held them above the water. As the gases advanced, they all accepted that this was the end of the journey. They just couldn't go on. Short of a miracle, they would soon suffocate as the noxious gases burned both their skin and lungs.

Mika'el and Sandrah prayed with every breath, calling out to the heavens for help. "Please Lord, save us!"

Suddenly, Sandrah hit her wall. "I — can't —" She went under.

"No!" Mika'el screamed, reaching for her as she disappeared under the waves.

"Mom!" Shannon and Jacob both screamed.

Mika'el tried to go after Sandrah, but as soon as he did, both Shannon and Jacob struggled to stay afloat. It was Sandrah or the children; he couldn't save both. It was an impossible choice to make. Watching her descend into the darkness broke his heart, but he knew Sandrah would never choose her own life over that of her children. Mika'el cried as he prayed, "Lord, have mercy."

Sandrah reached for the surface and Mika'el's hand as she sunk deeper and deeper into the depths of the Dark Sea — his hand disappeared, and then the light faded into obscurity.

Mika'el held the children and helped them weather the waves, but the poisonous cloud continued its advance towards them.

As all hope seemed to fade, they appeared.

"Dad, what are those? Are those shark fins?"

Mika'el couldn't believe what was happening. Another impossible choice — die with your skin and lungs on fire or be torn apart by ravenous sharks. "Oh, no. No! Get ready to kick them with everything you have left as you see the fins approach. Fight children, fight!"

Several fins headed right for them at high speed.

"Kick, kick everyone!"

As the lead fin closed to within thirty yards, part of its body showed above the water. Something wasn't right. The water was flowing over the top of the creature and its fin, but something else was there, holding on to the fin.

"That's Mom!" Shannon screamed. "That's Mom!"

Mika'el and Jacob squinted in unbelief, thinking Shannon was seeing things midst her grief and panic. However, as the fin got closer, they realized Shannon was right. Something was pulling Sandrah through the water towards them.

How can this be happening?

Then Sandrah's head rose out of the water. "Grab hold! They're dolphins! Engel sent them!"

There was no time for anyone to think about what Sandrah was saying. The only option for survival was the unbelievable, and the unbelievable was approaching at high speed.

Mika'el looked at the cloud of death approaching from one direction and rescue from the other. "Grab a fin, kids. Do it, now!"

Sandrah went by them and the trailing dolphins slowed for but a moment — just enough time for everyone to grab a fin. Then the mighty tails of the dolphins burst with energy and propelled them out to sea, away from their certain deaths.

Chapter 27

Doppelgängers

†††

Thalia and Mirare watched the couples split up in haste. The fishermen went to load up on heavy supplies of meat while their wives went to the bakery. The sisters smiled at each other as they followed the women into the bakery. They studied the women — their relationship and mannerisms. They listened carefully to their speech and dialect. When the women left, they purchased the same supplies in the same amounts.

When they saw the women went to get vegetables from a nearby vendor, they quickly purchased some clothing and returned to the place they had heard the husbands tell their wives to meet up after gathering the provisions.

Though they had done their best, the doppelgänger's clothing differed slightly from that of the fishermen's wives, but when the men arrived early to the rendezvous, they didn't even notice. They did, however, notice their wives flirting a bit more than then they had been before.

"I know we are in a hurry to leave before Ashtar's anger reaches us, but we didn't know how long our journey would be. We took a little time to clean up for you," one wife said as she gave her man a big hug and kiss. The greeting shocked the man, but he was clearly happy about it. He pulled his wife in close and gave her another big kiss. Her friend reciprocated with her husband, showing him some recently absent affection, and he reacted with similar surprise and joy. Then they all scurried away towards their boat like happy newlyweds. Even fleeing the anger of a volcanic eruption, the elixir of affection can manipulate a man's focus immensely.

"We better push off as soon as possible," Sophia said to her husband.

"Yes, that ash cloud is approaching quickly!" Mason replied.

"I can't believe the merchants are still selling at the dock."

"I talked to the butcher when we were picking up the salted meat. He said everyone was leaving soon, but since they had no time to pack up their stores and would have to leave everything behind, they were trying to sell some of their merchandise to provide some subsistence for their families."

"It is terrible what is happening! But at least we have each other."

"Let's push off and get out of here. We will focus more on us when we get out of port and to a safe distance." He smiled.

"That sounds good, honey." She smiled back.

They kissed again, and together with the other couple on board, they sailed out of port, headed for Omentia.

†††

Their arms full of the supplies they had gathered for their journey, the wives waited for their husbands at the rendezvous point. They were among the fortunate ones who had a boat with which to escape the coming disaster. After they had waited a while, they headed towards the pier where they had moored their boat.

As they approached the dock, they saw their boat was no longer there. They searched all around for their husbands, but they too were nowhere to be found.

Standing on the wharf, looking out over the water, they saw the markings of their boat far in the distance, heading out to sea. They could faintly see four people sitting on the boat, two obviously women. They wept, wondering what their husbands were doing.

Who are the other women on the boat? How could they have left us here to die?

The youngest and smaller of the two held her hands across her belly, against her unborn baby.

How could he?

She fell to her knees, screaming his name as the first of the volcanic ash fell from the sky over the port. The other woman got down on her knees and tried to console the soon to be mom. They then realized that the baby, due to be born in a week, would never see the light of day. None of the left behind would survive what was coming, and the unspeakable had already begun.

†††

Having reached what they considered a safe distance from the shore and the eruption, the fisherman relaxed with their wives on deck with some lunch.

"Just look at that eruption! The cloud of ash is coming down on the harbor." Sawyer said, pointing back at the pier in the distance.

Mason replied, "Those poor people. I can see they are forming up on the pier, trying to get as far away from the incoming lava flow as possible. It is arriving much faster than they thought it would. We got out just in time." He held his young pregnant wife's hand.

Sophia squeezed Mason's hand. "I knew you wouldn't let anything happen to me or our baby. Thank you, honey."

"Oh, my!" Ellie said as she looked back toward the harbor. The lava flow was smashing through the village, crushing everything in its path. A moment later, it reached the pier and lit it and everyone on it a blaze. They didn't suffer long as the magma swallowed them up and buried them in the sea.

"That could have been us," Sophia said, her voice breaking in empathy for the people perishing.

The horror of what they were watching transfixed the men.

Sophia glanced over at Ellie and smiled. Ellie smiled back — through the tears, of course.

†††

A week later, the couples arrived in Mecha. The wives went ashore as the men unloaded the cargo. They were to meet at the Captain Hook Bed and Breakfast later in the afternoon. Mason and Sawyer never saw their wives again.

How could they just leave us? Why would they do that? Did something happen to them?

They would never know the answers.

Chapter 28

Family

†††

The dolphins pulled Sandrah, Mika'el, Shannon and Jacob far out to sea. They watched in horror as the volcano completely decimated the lands to the north. They wondered if anyone would ever live there again.

Mike thought to himself.

All this time we thought Ashtar was under the control of Molech — that paying homage to the demon held back Ashtar from destroying us. In reality, the volcano not erupting was the Lord having mercy and showing grace to us. But when the people sacrificed their own children to the demon, the sands of the hourglass of the Lord's wrath ran out, and the Lord destroyed the city. Soros and the rest of Molech's followers may believe that evil controlled the volcano, but we know the truth.

The dolphins circled in the waters.

"I think they want us to let go," Sandrah said.

"What here? In the middle of nowhere?" Jacob asked, sounding annoyed.

Mika'el let go, and the rest of the family did as well. The dolphins took turns leaping out of the water and saying their goodbyes, and then the pod of dolphins raced off to the south.

"They could have taken us with them." Jacob said as he watched them zip away.

The seas were calm, but there was quite an active weather system building to the northeast — the eruption of Ashtar was making its own weather, and the weather looked as nasty as the volcano's eruption had been. It was another big ugly, and it was heading their way.

"Ok, here we are." Mika'el said. "Now what?"

Shannon was exhausted. "After all that, we are going to drown. There is only so much floating I can do."

Sandrah just shook her head in disbelief. "Seriously people? Come on!"

"How did you and dolphins link up, anyway?" Mika'el asked. "We were totally losing it when you went under."

"Oh, you were losing it? Ok."

"I mean, of course, we weren't losing it like you were losing it but —"

"Well, about the time I was going to meet the one true God, a bright light approached from the depths. As it got closer, I could see it was Engel, and following him was a pod of dolphins. When he got close, he asked me if I was afraid. I told him, yeah, a little. We were talking like we are now."

"Under the water? You were talking under the water?" Shannon asked.

"I guess. It's the way I remember it, at least."

"Wow!"

"So, he tells me not to be afraid, because the Master is always watching out for me and my family. He says he has work for us to do."

"Work? What kind of work?" Mika'el asked.

"I don't know. I guess we will find out. But, some of the good news is that — well — we will find out. So stop all the complaining and worrying about every minor challenge and start focusing on solutions."

"Minor challenges? Really, Mom?" Jacob said with a smile.

"Good points, honey." Mika'el said. "Ok, so, here we are. Now what?"

"Look for boats, maybe? There is a reason we are here. Like Jacob said before, the dolphins could have taken us with them, but they didn't. I think it is time we see with our spiritual eyes."

They all scanned the horizon for boats. They saw nothing but blue water and blue sky. Then, Shannon thought she saw a glint of light to the southwest. Everyone trained their eyes to the waters in that direction, and eventually, they saw a fishing boat reflecting the sun's rays. Their arms felt so heavy that they couldn't even wave their hands to get the crew's attention.

"How are they going to see us?" Shannon asked.

As the boat got closer, everyone could tell that whoever was aboard had not yet seen them.

"They aren't changing course. What can we do to get their attention?" Sandrah asked.

"I don't know, they are going to go right by?" Mika'el replied.

Just as it seemed like the vessel was going to pass them by, something unusual happened. With all the jostling around that Jacob was doing, the orange stone he had in his pocket floated out and onto the surface of the sea in front of them. It bobbed there on the waves like a piece of wood.

"What's up with that?" Shannon asked her father. Everyone focused on the orange stone floating on the waves. "Is that a stone from the tunnel? How is a stone floating?"

Before Mika'el could chastise Jacob for not leaving the stone in the tunnels, the stone dissolved right before their eyes. As it did, it covered the waters in glowing orange algae. It didn't just glow a little, but was so bright that Mika'el and his family had to keep their eyes closed.

"What's happening? I can't see!" Shannon shouted.

"It's ok. It will be ok." Mika'el tried to comfort everyone, though he couldn't open his eyes enough to know what was happening himself.

After about a minute, the orange algae-like substance converged again in front of them and solidified back into an orange stone floating there on the water. Jacob went to grab it, and as he did, it sank out of his grasp to the depths of the sea.

"What was that all about?" Jacob asked.

"Well, for starters, it was about you not listening to me." Mika'el replied.

"I'm sorry about that."

"Guys, look!" Sandrah yelled. "The boat is turning in our direction!"

Despite their exhaustion, everyone in their excitement found the energy to stay afloat long enough for the vessel to arrive at their location. When it did, a couple of sailors helped everyone aboard.

"Hello. My name is Henry. This is my fishing boat and we are happy to have you aboard. We are at your service."

"Thank you, sir. My name is Mika'el. This is my wife Sandrah, my son Jacob, and my daughter, Shannon. We are sure thankful you came along!"

Henry directed a couple of members of his crew to get water, food, and blankets for their guests. He directed Mika'el and his family to a place where they could sit down and rest.

"How did you get way out in the center of the Dark Sea?"

"Well, that is an amazing story, to be sure. How did you see us out here? It looked like you were going to go right by."

"Well, to be honest, we were. We didn't see you at all. My grandson, Lee here, he saw a glowing orange light on the water. We didn't believe him, but he insisted I bring the boat over to check it out. He told me he had a dream last night where an angel of all things told him this would happen. I am not one to ignore angels, you see."

Mika'el looked at Sandrah and then grinned at Jacob. "Looks like the Lord had plans for your stone after-all."

Mika'el and Sandrah looked at Shannon, who was looking at Lee. Lee was looking back at Shannon.

"Lee. Thank you for saving us," Mika'el said.

Lee realized he was staring. Embarrassed, he broke his gaze off from Shannon, and looking at Mika'el, said, "Oh, yes, sir. But I didn't do any saving. I just looked for what the angel told me to look for and when I saw it, I told Pops."

"Well, it is a good thing that you did, or we would have all been goners."

"With all due respect, sir, I doubt that. I think God would have just sent someone else to save you."

After what they had witnessed that day, Mika'el agreed with Lee. But it was Lee's use of the word God that caught both his and Sandrah's attention. Mika'el looked at Lee and then, out of respect to Henry, and asked, "Which God is it you serve?"

"The one true God and him alone. I think we have that in common, don't we?"

Mika'el was a little slow on the uptake. "It is true, but why would you think that? We have just met."

Henry made a small motion of his hand and pointed to Shannon's medallion that was then visibly hanging around her neck. He did the same toward Lee, who wore the same medallion. "Looks like we are of the same family."

"Seems we are." Mika'el said with a broad smile. "Seems we are. And that actually explains a lot!"

"It does, doesn't it?" Henry walked over to Mika'el and gave him a big hug. "Welcome again to my vessel, brother."

"Thank you, brother."

"Do you know where you'll be heading from here?"

Mika'el looked back toward Tophet. "Well, our home is gone. We will look for a new place to live. Do you have any suggestions?"

"I sure do, Mika'el. I sure do."

Henry and Mika'el looked at Shannon and Lee, who were once again having a staring competition; then they looked back at each other. They both grinned knowingly.

"Let's get you all settled," Henry said.

As everyone went to their respective tasks, Jacob walked by Shannon and whispered, "You're welcome."

Once everyone had eaten and changed into dry clothing, they sat on the deck of Henry's fishing boat and marveled at what they saw. The sun was setting, and high over their heads they could see multicolored lights falling in bands as the debris from the mountain volcano fell onto the lands to the west.

"I wonder if any of the special stones are falling with that debris," Mika'el asked Sandrah.

"I think it's a safe bet that some of those stones are indeed making their way to a new home."

Shannon and Lee sat together, off to the side of the deck by themselves, gazing up into the amazing sky above them. It was an evening like none other — one made for falling in love.

Chapter 29

The Accident

†††

It was a cold and rainy night. The lightning flashed, and the thunder rolled as the car traveled down the highway high above the cliffs of the Dark Sea. George and his long-time assistant, Tatiana, were on their way to a secret lab to get an early start on The Project. Tatiana's car had broken down, and she had asked George to give her a ride to the lab.

"So, do you think we are close, George?" Tatiana asked.

"I do. We would have been farther along if Biogen hadn't banned me from the lab for trying different approaches to solving the problem — the problem they gave me to solve. They called the approach unconventional. Um, yeah! When what is conventional doesn't work, you try something else. That, then, becomes unconventional! But, I think we can make it work in this lab. Yes, I think we are close."

It was dark, and the drive was long. They were above the sheer cliffs on the northwest edge of Delvia. The road was slick and curvy, and the drop to the Dark Sea was a good thousand feet.

"Thank you again for letting me work with you, Gatesh." The lightning flashed and there was a loud crack of thunder.

George swerved slightly as the lightning, as well as Tatiana's words, caught him off guard. *Am I hearing things? Who did she just call me?*

George shook it off, thinking the stressful drive had just caused him to hear Tatiana — wrong.

"You are very welcome, Tatiana. You have been a great asset to The Project. Without you, I don't think I would have made it this far."

"You have no idea, Gatesh. Fate destined us to be together long ago."

George griped the wheel more tightly. The rain was really coming down and the windshield wipers were having a hard time keeping up.

Did she call me Gatesh, again?

This time, George knew something wasn't right, but he avoided it out of — fear.

The lightning flashed and the low rumble of thunder vibrated the vehicle as they slipped back and forth on the slick road. Sheets of rain pounded against the windshield as the wind howled outside of the vehicle.

"Let me tell you a story, George."

That's better. She is calling me George. I must have been hearing things.

"Sure, Tatiana. That will make this drive a little easier."

Tatiana smiled.

I don't think so, George. This story is going to hurt. It is going to hurt — a lot.

"When I was a young girl, I had a crush on this guy. He was older and wasn't really interested in me. He may have thought I was too young for him. I told him that we were meant to be together, but he just laughed it off."

George was nervous. He didn't know where this was going. "Well, Tatiana, I think that is a very common thing. We all have crushes on people as we are growing up."

"This was different. I just knew that we would spend our lives together!"

The lightning flashed, and the thunder cracked! The lightning was getting very close.

Where is this going? She sounds a little unhinged.

"It's ok, Tatiana. You are a grown woman now. Any man would be lucky to have you."

Tatiana smiled, though it was too dark to see her face. "Yes, I am older now. And, yes, they would be lucky to have me."

Flash! Crack!

George swerved again. He felt like the presence in the car had changed. It was him and Tatiana five minutes ago — a scientist and his assistant. He was the dominant personality in the vehicle. But suddenly, there was a different force in the car with them, a distinctly different energy.

"I don't think you know me, George."

"Of course I know you, Tatiana. We have worked together for many years."

"Yes, we have. Longer than you know."

Flash! Crack!

George did not respond.

This is freaking me out! Maybe it's the storm affecting her.

George took a quick glance over at Tatiana. The lightning flashed, and for just a moment, he saw an image of her. As the car went dark again, the image seared into his mind's eye. It wasn't Tatiana sitting next to him. It was someone else; someone familiar, but the image was not familiar enough to remember who.

I'm really getting freaked out now! Someone is sitting next to me, and I don't know who they are. Am I having a mental breakdown or something?

"You still don't recognize me?"

George took another look. The lightning flashed, and George was looking at a young girl, maybe twelve or thirteen.

Thunder boomed! "Whoa!" He swerved again, barely getting the car back on the road.

The girl grinned devilishly. "It has been a long time, but c'mon, Gatesh."

Gatesh gripped the steering wheel so tightly his knuckles turned white.

Gatesh again! What is happening? Who is that? A long time? She's only a young girl — how long could it have been?

The girl was small, but her presence felt powerful; Gatesh felt vulnerable.

"I bet if Travork was here, you would remember me."

Her words hit like a ton of bricks.

Tarah? How can that be? I must be dreaming! Unless — unless the tunnels?

"Tarah? I know you!"

"Yes, Tarah, but you still don't really know me."

"Did you use the tunnels?"

"No. It took me a lot longer to get here than it took you."

"How is that possible? It's been thousands of years!"

"Twenty questions. This is fun. Hey, time traveler, you figure it out."

It took a little time, but Gatesh remembered his previous life, before he left Tophet. Tarah had come out of the fire. They said her skin had regenerated. The thoughts of that made Gatesh's skin start to crawl.

"What are you doing here?"

"I'm here to deliver a message."

"What? A message? From who?"

"From my master."

"Your master? Who is your master?"

I don't think I want to know the answer to this question.

"You might think he is Molech, but he is so much bigger than Molech."

Flash! Crack! Boom!

Gatesh swerved. "Molech? What? C'mon. All that was superstitious nonsense!"

"Did you hear about my sister and me returning from the fires?"

"I did."

"Explain that with your science, would you?"

"I wasn't there. It was probably some sort of mass hysteria. You probably didn't even enter the fire."

"What about me being here now? Can you explain that?"

"I am probably just imagining all this. Maybe the thunderstorm is affecting my memories."

"I know things, Gatesh. Would you like to know the things I know?"

"This is probably all in my mind, so whatever you say, you know, I probably already know."

"Ok. Let's just see. Here we go. First, you will not be the one to finish The Project. True, your contributions were invaluable for getting The Project started, but you really don't have what it takes to use its capabilities to their true potential. You see, you think too small."

"Really? Ok, so who is supposed to finish it? Are you working for one of Biogen's competitors? Is that it?"

Flash! Crack! Bang!

"There you go. You think too small. I told you who I serve already. Weren't you listening?"

"Ok. You know, I don't really believe in all that hocus pocus stuff."

Flash! Crack! Bang!

Tarah laughed out-loud and loudly. It was a wicked laugh — an inhuman laugh. "Sorry, that was hilarious. Good one!"

"No really. I believe in science, natural laws, and the logical explanation of things."

"Oh, I see. Ok. So explain to me, scientist, about the time tunnels. Or maybe how you didn't know it was me for all of those years?"

"Wait. So, you are not just appearing here through Tatiana for the first time? So, all this time, you have been my lab assistant and not Tatiana?"

"That is not the half of it, Gatesh."

"What does that mean?"

"You have two beautiful sons."

"Hey, you leave them out of it!"

"I'm afraid it is a little too late for that."

Flash! Crack! Bang!

"If you do anything to hurt my sons!"

"Hurt them? No. I would never hurt them. They are too valuable."

"What do you want with my sons?"

"They will finish The Project. My master demands it."

"I will finish my project! You can tell your master to go to hell!"

Lightning flashed across the sky and the thunder cracked almost instantly! Thalia's sinister laugh echoed within the car. "That, right there, is the funniest thing you have said all night!"

"I am serious! Leave my sons out of it! I swore to their mother I would let nothing happen to them!"

"That is sweet. About that, do you remember my sister, Mirah?"

"Yes. I guess so. What does she have to do with any of this?"

"She really enjoyed playing doctor when your boys were born."

"What are you talking about? She wasn't there!"

"We were both there, Mirah and me."

"She was playing doctor. I had a unique, but different part."

"Mirah was Rose's doctor?"

"Not just Rose's doctor. There were other women giving birth that day in the hospital. Mirah particularly enjoyed telling the other women that their children had died. She has a peculiar sense of humor."

"Why would she tell other women their children had died? You are not making any sense! What does this have to do with Rose?"

Gatesh was all over the road.

"Keep your eyes on the road Gatesh, it is not yet time. I'm not finished with my story."

"I think we have finished! We are almost at the lab, and when we get there, I never want to see you again. You're crazy!"

"Let me answer your question, Gatesh. I think it will all make sense to you in a moment. You see, I cannot have babies. The fire incident on the pyramid had that effect on my body. But we needed to have children for my master's plan, so we needed those other women's babies. Mirah did a great job picking them out for us, don't you think?"

"Us? What are you—?"

Gatesh looked over at Thalia. What he saw brought a flood of various emotions, from shock to love, from terror to confusion, and finally, understanding and intense sadness. It was completely overwhelming! Sitting next to him, where a young Thalia sat a moment before, was

Rose. She was smiling sweetly at him and resting her arms on her belly, where she looked to be very pregnant.

"Honey, I told you a long time ago that we were meant to be together, and so it was. Thanks for the memories, Gatesh, but unfortunately, you have accomplished everything my master required of you. You are no longer useful to us."

Gatesh could not look away. For so long, he had dreamed of someday seeing his beautiful Rose again. For so many years, he had sacrificed everything for The Project, in hopes of someday being able to go back in time and save his beautiful wife, Rose. Even though his mind told him that the monster he was looking at had pretended to be his loving wife, Rose, for all those years, he still could not look away. The truth in his mind did not matter to his heart. The only thing that mattered to his heart were the years of feelings that were stored there. He could not deny those feelings. Those yearnings to see her again took priority over everything, even his life.

Flash! Crack! Bang! The lightning flashed directly in front of the vehicle, and the thunder instantly roared. They had arrived at Gatesh's final destination.

Gatesh did not see the turn in the road. He did not feel the car going through the guardrail and over the cliff. He did, however, see the true charred appearance of the creature that, a moment before, had been his Rose — the creature he had slept next to for seven years of his life.

The horror of the realization was more than any man could take, but he did not have to carry the burden of it for long. As Gatesh's car hit the rocks in the surf below, and his car exploded into a million pieces, hellish phantoms from a different dimension emerged to tear his soul from his body and carry it to their master.

His last thought was of his old friend and what his friend had tried to tell him.

Mika'el, you were right.

The fiery figure of a female body rose from the wreckage. It smoldered as the ocean water evaporated from its skin. As it walked, its blazing red skin cooled and repaired until it was once again beautiful.

I will miss him, but we will be together again someday — after I have finished my work here.

A voice echoed through the void. “Welcome Gatesh to my home. I believe you already know its name.”

Chapter 30

A New Home

†††

"Wow, it is beautiful!" Sandrah stood with her family, Henry, and Lee on the deck of the boat, looking out over the rolling hills and fruit trees of the coastal town of Mecha.

"It is a wonderful place to live. Most of the people here follow the one true God. We live, work, and rest in his will. Bekka will love showing you around, Sandrah."

"That is amazing. We couldn't have imagined a better place to find to make our new home. Our God has been so good to us. I can't wait to meet Bekka and your children!"

Shannon and Jacob smiled from ear to ear. They couldn't wait to explore their new home.

"I'll show you around once we dock," Lee said. He looked at Jacob and said, "There is a large group of kids our age. I can't wait to introduce you."

"Awesome! Thank you!" Jacob replied.

"Do you think there are any openings for scientists in the town?" Mika'el asked Henry.

"Absolutely! We have a large community of scientists and inventors working hard to improve the everyday lives of our people. You will fit right in, and you will all stay with us until you get your own place."

"We don't want to impose, Henry." Mika'el said.

"I wouldn't have it any other way."

"We left everything behind in Tophet. I have no way to pay you."

"We think about things a little differently here. We believe that everything we have is from God, and we simply manage it for him. God doesn't bless us for us to hoard his blessings for ourselves. We are to use his blessings for the good of his kingdom. There really is no paying back Mika'el. There is only helping brothers and sisters when they are in need. Today, your family is in need. Tomorrow, it may be mine."

"Thank you, brother. That is a wonderful way to live."

"It is, isn't it?"

"How did you get such a large community of believers in the one true God? As far as we know, we were the only family of believers in Tophet."

"His name was Kissami."

"You sent him to us?"

"No, Mika'el. He came to us about a year ago. He met with groups of us and shared the truth. Not everyone believed, but large numbers of folks did, and the truth spread far and wide like a firestorm. It has changed Mecha and changed our lives."

"We know all about the changed lives part."

"You have quite the story. I can't wait to hear it again when you tell Bekka and the kids. And about the changed lives part, don't worry, we will take care of you. I think you will enjoy being here more than you did Tophet."

"Already do, brother! Already do."

Within the week, Mika'el and family had their own cabin, land, and furnishings. Their ten-acre parcel was next to Henry's two hundred acres. They had a horse, two cows, twenty chickens, a barn cat and dog. Life had completely changed — and life was good.

"Good morning." Sandrah smiled as she gave Mika'el a kiss on the cheek. The sunlight had just broken over the waters to the west and lit their bedroom.

"Ahhh. Good morning." Mika'el opened his eyes and smiled. "And what a beautiful morning it is."

Sandrah snuggled close and Mika'el put his arm around her. They both faced the window, watching the sunrise over the Dark Sea.

"Mika'el, can you even believe how much our lives have changed in such a short time?"

"It is not really believable, honey. Sometimes, when I wake up in the middle of the night, I think for just a moment that maybe we died in those tunnels, and we are in heaven."

"And the children already have close friends — so many — many more than they had in Tophet."

"And the cabin and land, the livestock, my job at the Science Center — the Lord has blessed us beyond belief. So, no, I can hardly believe it."

They closed their eyes, cuddle close, and basked in the warm golden morning rays.

The red dragon spoke to his chief lieutenants in the void. They think they have gone beyond my reach — that they are safe. Take the girl! Take her where her family will never find her. Do not kill her, but make her suffer much for her beliefs; turn her to me!

Shannon rose bright and early. She walked down to the barn to feed the chickens, gather the eggs, and let their horse, Starlight, out to graze. It was such a beautiful morning. How blessed they were in this new land!

She opened the door to the barn.

"Hello Shannon."

"Mirah? Mirah!" She ran to hug her dearest friend.

The men were waiting in the shadows and surprised her from behind. No one heard her scream for help as they bound her and dragged her away — somewhere her family would never find her.

†††

Mika'el sat alone on the front porch of the cabin, praying. It had been three days since Shannon had disappeared. There were obvious signs in the barn of a struggle. Someone had taken her, and they wanted to send an obvious message that it was so.

Lee rode up on his stallion, dismounted, and somberly walked up to the porch and sat down next to Mika'el.

"Any news?"

"No, sir."

"Where will you look?"

"Everywhere. I will bring her home to you — if it is the last thing I do."

The Promise

Part 6: Darkness

Chapter 31

Taken

†††

Her soft voice whispered into the darkness as she wept in the damp, cold cell — all alone. "I'm not alone."

She could hear others whimpering in the dark.

"Hello. Who's there?"

The crying stopped. "Hello?"

"Hello. What is your name?"

"My name is Lydia. What is your name?"

She thought for a moment, and nothing came to mind — about anything. "My name is — Trista, for I am sorrow. Where are you from, Lydia?"

"I'm from Mecha. Where are you from?"

She thought again, nothing; so she just faked it. "Me too. Do you know where we are?"

"No. I have been in the dark for days. I haven't eaten. Only water. There are rats."

"We will be ok, Lydia. I promise."

Rats. Great. I hate rats.

"How can you be so sure?" Another female voice asked from the darkness on the other side of Trista's cage.

"Hello? Who is there?"

"Another fellow traveler. My name is Lucinda. I've been here for more than a few days. They don't give you food until the third day to make you beg for it. Part of the psychological operations part of our trip, I guess."

"Psychological operations? What does that mean?"

"It's just a fancy way of saying they are playing with our minds."

"I wouldn't know about any of that, since I just turned thirteen."

"I'm fifteen. My dad grew up in Heath. They learned all kinds of things there. He taught me a lot."

"Do you know why they took us?"

"I overheard them talking a few days ago. Not sure what they meant, but they said we were a good batch and would make excellent fighters if Brutus didn't get us. Then they laughed."

"Brutus? Fighters?"

"We are slaves, Trista. I'm slave number one, Lydia is slave number two, and you are slave number three."

"Don't forget me." Another voice from the darkness joined in the conversation.

"Who is that?"

"That is slave number four, Maxine. She came in with you."

"Hi Maxine."

"Hi Trista."

"Do you have any more information on what is going on here?"

"From what Lucinda said, it sounds like they are slavers."

"Slavers?"

"Slave traders. They take people and sell them for a profit."

"What would they want us for?"

"Well, Trista, based on the one thing we all have in common, I would say not to work in the salt mines. Young girls are not very heavy lifters."

"Oh, no. Do you mean?"

"Oh, no, is right. That is what I mean."

Lydia started crying again. "No. No."

Lucinda added her opinion. "I'd like to see them try! Anyone touches me, and I will crack their skull open!"

"I'm with you, Lucinda!" Trista said. "They touch me without my permission and they will pull back a stump!"

Lucinda laughed. "Trista, you can call me Cindie. You've got some spunk. I'll give you that."

Trista smiled in the darkness. It helped a little to have friends, but the not remembering everything bothered her.

Lydia continued to cry.

Maxine had what she needed.

†††

The slave ship hugged the coast of Omentia, headed for the auction. Two days later, the ship arrived.

There were two buyers that day. The first was a hospitality provider, and she snatched up Lydia, who went away crying. "Please don't take me! Please?" Her pleas fell on deaf ears.

Next up was Cindie, and the second buyer claimed her. Cindie struggled against her chains as her captors led her away.

Finally, it was Trista's turn. Both buyers wanted her and bid accordingly. Trista recognized the voice of the second buyer. It was Maxine. She wore some sort of battle armor and obviously carried with her the authority to speak for someone the first buyer feared. All it took was a look from Maxine, and the first buyer backed down. Trista joined Cindie in a wagon cage, and they departed.

Maxine rode her stallion alongside the wagon. She looked to be maybe twenty years old. Leather boots adorned her feet, while protective leather bands encased most of her legs, arms, and neck. She had a knife at her waist, and she had a sword and a bow strapped to her horse.

Trista and Cindie looked at each other in wonder.

"Where are you taking us?" Cindie demanded of Maxine.

"We're taking you to assess your abilities and decide whether to keep you."

Trista asked, “What if you decide not to keep us? Do we go to the other buyer?”

Maxine looked at Trista and laughed. “Oh, they won’t want you after we are done with you. You see, every rose has its thorn. You may soon long for the thorns of the rose that lost the bid for you, because you will find the thorns of our rose are very painful. This is an all-or-nothing kind of test. Pass-fail, if you will. Pass you stay with us. Fail — we bury you.”

Chapter 32

Heartbreak

†††

Lee prayed on the shore of his grandfather's ranch on the Dark Sea as he did every morning.

"Almighty God. I come before you once again, as I have for ninety straight days. Winter is almost upon us, and the shipping lanes to the south will close until spring. I have looked everywhere I know to look for a clue of what direction I should go."

"My promise to Mika'el is that I will tirelessly search for his daughter and ensure her safe return to him and Sandrah. I maintain my pledge to do so, but please show me where to look?"

Lee looked out over the sea and watched the sun rise. The colors of orange and red filled the sky. Lee remembered the night they had watched the debris of the volcano fall on the lands to the west and talked about visiting there someday, together. That now seemed like forever ago.

How will that ever happen now?

Henry saw Lee down by their pier and joined him. He sat down on the pier behind Lee, using Lee's shoulder as support as he sat.

"How are you doing, Lee?"

"Not so well, PawPaw."

"It's hard, I know. But you must not give up hope. The one true God will show you a way."

"That is so easy to say, PawPaw, but when? I feel like I am running out of time. There is no telling what is happening to her. I have to help her!"

"Listen Lee. We don't know why this happened, but we know God has allowed it to — for a reason that only he may know. As hard as it is to accept, that is really your only choice right now."

"So I am supposed to just sit back and accept this? Just move on with my life? Forget her?"

"Look at me Lee. Look at me."

Lee looked at his grandpa.

"Just take a deep breath. I didn't say you should stop searching for her, but what you need to do is trust God has a reason for all of this and that he will tell you what to do in his time, not yours."

"It is so hard, PawPaw. I feel like I lost a part of me. I feel like she is in trouble and waiting for me to find her."

"Both are probably true, Lee, but God has a plan here, even if we can't see it right now. I can't promise you that everything will work out the way you want it to, but I can promise you it will work out the way God wants it to; that it will be the best for both of you. God has this, and someday you will look back and see that clearly he was in control for the whole time. Try to see that day in your mind and hold on to that hope. Until then, keep doing what your heart tells you to do, being certain that every step is one step closer to being with her again."

"For how long? How long will it take?"

"Lee, it may take a very long time."

Tears ran down Lee's face as he heard the words, but as they did, Lee's resolve strengthened from that of a sprint to that of a dedicated marathon.

Someday we will be together again. I can see that day. It will be a long time from now — but she is worth waiting for — and I will wait.

Henry slowly walked back up the cobblestone path from the pier to the house, leaving Lee alone to finish his prayers.

Dear Father in heaven, show Lee where to turn. It will be a long path ahead for him, but please show him which direction to walk.

Chapter 33

Show Him

†††

Kissami sat in the cool of the evening, high on a mountaintop, watching the sunset. He had traveled often, spreading the good news of the God of love. He often wondered why God had chosen him to do this work, but he felt very thankful for the mission of spreading the light in a world of shadows.

As Kissami sat in awe and wonder, marveling at the colors on display before him, the picture changed. It was a gradual transformation of the space before him, as if the colors of the scene were bleeding in all directions. In the center of his perception, a shape slowly formed and then crystallized. Its radiance started as a subtle shade of gold and grew in intensity until he could barely keep his eyes open, squinting to endure the brilliance of it. It was as if the setting sun had suddenly risen again to blaze into his eyes.

Kissami wasn't startled by the arrival of the living being, for they had met many times before. The living being levitated in front of Kissami, hovering in space over the edge of the mountain. Its body emanated endless colors of light, running like streams in every direction as it spread its shimmering golden wings wide in a spectacular display.

"Kissami, I hope I didn't alarm you."

"It is always wonderful to see you, Engel, but I don't think I will ever get used to your arrival."

"We do not choose how we will appear. Everyone and everything perceives us differently, dependent on their spirit and the moment within time. It speaks well of your spirit that I appear in a way that is pleasing. You can trust me when I say that the demons of hell would view me in a far different light."

"I am sure they would, and I would never want to see you in that way."

"I am certain you won't, old friend. You have so much more you will experience when you get to the eternal home the Master has prepared for you. My appearance is a very poor example of the splendor you will witness in that place."

"I can't wait! And yet I am very thankful to do the Master's work here. I hope I can serve him more before I am called home."

"Speaking of that, one of the Master's children needs direction. The Master has sent me to you. You are to assist him in finding his way."

"Do you mean the tunnels?"

"Yes. The evil ones have taken his love away from him. Show him the path to Parlantis, where he will once again find his heart."

"This must be a very important heart."

"It is. You met her in Tophet. You spoke to her family by the stream. She wore the medallion."

"Oh my. That poor girl."

"She will endure much, but her faith is strong."

"Where do I find this lad?"

"His name is Lee, and he is Henry's grandson. They live in Mecha."

"Henry, yes, I know the family."

"The family is a pillar of truth in that place."

"Engel, that tunnel will get Lee to Parlantis well ahead of his stolen heart."

"Indeed. Make sure he knows this."

"Do I go with him?"

"No. He must make this journey alone. Show him the way and return here."

"Very well. It will be as you have instructed."

"It was good to visit with you again, Kissami."

"Amazing as always to see you, Engel."

Chapter 34

A Way

†††

Lee was making his rounds on the ranch when he noticed a man sitting under an oak tree. He was tossing stones into one of the three streams that ran down behind their home into the Dark Sea. Lee had never seen the man before and went to see what the stranger was doing there and if he needed any help.

"Hello, sir, can I help you?"

"Hello Lee. You have really grown since I saw you last."

Lee dismounted and walked over to greet Kissami. "I am sorry, sir. Do I know you?"

"You sure do Lee. I am an old friend of your grandfather's. My name is Kissami."

As Kissami introduced himself, he pulled his medallion out from under his tunic for Lee to see that it was like the one that Lee wore under his tunic.

"Kissami! Yes, I have heard a ton about you! It is thanks to you we know the one true God!"

"Well, thank you Lee, but it is more accurately thanks to him. I just go where I am told, when I am told, and tell people what I know. He does the convincing."

"Hop on my horse, and we will go see my grandfather."

"Actually, Lee, I am here to see you."

"See me?"

"Yes. Why don't we sit down for a couple minutes and talk?"

Kissami led Lee over to some rocks beneath the oak tree, and they sat by the gentle stream.

"You look pretty serious, Kissami. Is this going to be bad news?"

"It isn't bad news, but it is a serious subject."

"Ok. I'm ready. Fire away."

"I hear you have been looking for a certain girl."

"Yes! Do you know where she is?"

"I don't, Lee."

"Oh. Ok."

"But I know where she will be."

Lee rose to his feet. "That is great! We can get some men together and intercept those who took her and get her back!"

"Son, I am afraid it is a little more complicated than that. Please, sit back down for a moment. This is the sit down and talk part."

Lee sat back down. "I am not sure I understand."

"Well, you better get used to that part. You see, it's this next part that is going to be a little hard to accept."

"Ok. I'm all ears."

"I know where she will be, but I don't know the when."

"That is ok. We can go there and wait. When she gets there, we will be ready."

"You still don't understand. You see, it could be a very long time. It could be years — or longer."

"Ok. Now you are losing me. Where is this place?"

"It is Parlantis."

"Parlantis? I have heard of it. Isn't it far to the south of Omentia? I mean, far?"

"Yes, it is. Very far."

"Well, how do you know she will be there?"

"Did she tell you the story of how her family escaped Tophet?"

"Yes, of course. It was pretty amazing!"

"Did she mention an angel named Engel?"

"Yes. If it wasn't for Engel, they wouldn't have made it out. He was critical to their survival several times. Incidentally, he was the one in my dreams; the one who told me to look for the orange light on the water. That is how we found her and her family in the ocean."

"Good. Well, Engel told me to show you how to go where she will someday be."

"Angels don't lie. If Engel said she will be there, then she will be there. The question then is, how do I get there?"

"That part I can help with. I know of a tunnel and a door that will take you to Parlantis. This tunnel will get you there faster than any other way. The problem is that I don't know when it will be when you get there."

"Faster than ship?"

"Much faster."

"Well, that is great! What is the downside?"

"The downside is that when you step through the door, everyone outside the tunnel will age much faster than you do. The girl will age faster, your grandparents will age faster — everyone. Your love will be older than you when she gets to Parlantis, and there is no way to know how long from now that will be or how much older she will be."

"I don't care. I have to see her again."

"Now, Lee, I want you to consider this carefully and discuss it with your grandparents."

"I am old enough to make this decision. I don't need their permission."

"It is not about permission, Lee. Have you considered that your grandparents may not be alive if or when you return from Parlantis?"

The words hit Lee hard. He hadn't considered it. Lee became very serious as he thought of the possibility.

"I could be gone that long?"

"Almost certainly."

"Oh. Then yes. I better talk to them about it."

"Leave nothing left unsaid, Lee. It could be goodbye."

"Right. Good advice. Thank you, Kissami."

"Ok then, Lee. If you decide you want to go, meet me here at nine in the morning."

"I will be here. Thank you, Kissami."

Lee somberly walked to his horse, mounted, and rode to the ranch.

†††

Lee sat on the front porch of their home with his Grandma Bekka and Grandpa Henry.

"I just thought you should know my plans. I have to go find her, but my heart is breaking. It might mean that I will never see you two again."

"Oh, honey," Bekka put her hand on Lee's hand. "Follow your heart. If it is God's will, we will see you again. If not, we will see you there — forever."

"Bekka is right, Lee. I would have done the same thing to find your grandma — a hundred times over."

"I know, but it is still hard."

"Your grandfather and I will pray for you every day. And we will look forward to the day you both return home together. We will be sitting right here on this porch when you ride up. Why, I can see you two riding up to the house right now!"

"We might sit in rocking chairs, though." Henry laughed. "And don't show up after eight in the evening, because we may be in bed already."

Every one enjoyed a good chuckle with their tears. They agreed to hug and go to bed like it was just another evening.

†††

Once Bekka had gone to sleep, Henry rose and walked outside onto the porch. He looked up at the stars and remembered the evening on the boat when they had rescued Mika'el and his family. He thought of Mika'el's little girl.

If that was my daughter, I would do anything to find her. How can I not tell Mika'el if I know of a way for him to rescue her? What kind of friend would I be?

Henry went to the barn, saddled his horse, and rode to Mika'el's ranch.

†††

Everyone was sleeping when Henry knocked quietly on Mika'el's door. Henry knew Mika'el was the lightest sleeper in their family.

Mika'el answered the door. "Henry, is everything ok?"

"Yes, Yes. No emergency. Can we talk?"

"Absolutely. Come in, please."

"Actually, could we sit out here on the porch?"

"Oh. Ok. Let me get a sweater and a couple of mugs of ale. I'll be right back."

A moment later, the men sat on the porch watching the moon rise and drinking their ale.

"I know you didn't come over to watch the moonrise with me, Henry. You do know I am married, right?"

The men shared a chuckle and a sip of ale that lightened the moment a bit.

"I had to come see you, Mika'el, because I learned something tonight that I couldn't keep from you. It just wouldn't be right to do so. That is the reason for the late visit."

"Ok. Is it bad news?"

"No. Not bad news. Could be great news, I guess."

"Is it about my daughter?"

"It is."

"What? Why all the cloak and dagger?"

"Well, let me explain. I think you will have intimate knowledge of the complexity of this situation."

"Engel has told Kissami to show Lee a tunnel that will bring him to Parlantis."

"What? Why Parlantis?"

"Engel says she will be there — sometime."

"Sometime?"

"There is no telling when. Kissami told Lee it could be many years. I don't have to tell you what that means."

Mika'el thought for a moment. "Wow."

"I know. Right?"

"We are talking about my little girl, whether she is thirteen or thirty."

"I'm a father. I understand. That is why I couldn't keep it from you."

"Thank you, Henry. I appreciate you telling me."

"There is more."

"Ok."

"They are leaving for the tunnel tomorrow morning."

"Tomorrow morning!"

"I know. Not much time."

"Well, one doesn't normally bring much with them through the portal, so I guess we don't have to pack much."

"Another big change for your family."

"Yeah. We were really loving it here. Your family has been so good to us."

"Well, you make that very easy, Mika'el. All of you do."

"Henry, do you think you could hold the cabin for us for just a little while? In case it doesn't take that long. You never know."

"For sure, Mika'el."

"Thank you."

"Can I ask you a favor in return, Mika'el?"

"Anything, Henry."

"If possible, and I don't know how these things work, but could you try not to let Lee see you follow him through the portal? I feel like I am betraying his trust a little. The message from Kissami was for Lee, and because of that, I'm still not sure I should have told you."

"I understand, Henry. We will do our best."

"We?"

"Well, I am pretty sure everyone will want to go. It's a family thing."

Henry got up, they gave each other a hug and said goodbye.

"God speed, Mika'el."

"God bless you and your family, Henry, until we see you again."

†††

Henry waited until morning to tell Sandrah and Jacob. He knew they would have no reservations about starting a new life if it meant that the family might be whole once again. They all agreed that keeping the family together was the most important thing; family was everything!

Chapter 35

Caged

†††

Trista woke up, and her head instantly started throbbing as if someone had hit her with a rock. "Oh, wow, what happened?"

Cindie was sitting against the bars on the other side of the cage. "They drugged us."

"Drugged us? Why did they do that?"

"They moved us."

Trista looked around. It was dark and damp. "Why don't they ever keep us in the sunshine?"

"More Psyops. They think they can keep us off balance by drugging us and keeping us in the dark."

"It's working pretty well for those of us on this side of the cage."

"I'm kind-of surprised they put us together in here. Normally, isolation is another tool they would use against us."

"Guess they screwed up."

"We'll see. I'm sure they have done this many times before. There has to be a reason."

Suddenly, men with torches entered the underground room. The light flooded the enclosure, elevating the pounding in Trista's and Cindie's heads tenfold. Squinting to handle the intense change in light, they could see the figure of a woman in combat armor walk into the enclosure and stand next to their cage.

"Hello ladies."

Trista could tell from her voice that it was Maxine.

"Not in a cage this time?"

"I was never in a cage, Cindie. You just assumed I was a prisoner like the rest of you. I had to listen in on your conversation and see which of you had what it took to be fighters."

"Fighters? That is why we are here?" Trista asked.

"Most certainly, Trista."

"I'm not a fighter. I've never been in a fight in all my life."

"Well, I hope that changes quickly. I get paid to make good judgement calls. If you don't fight, the Syth will be very upset with me. We paid the slavers good money for you."

"You should prepare for her to be upset then."

"Ah, Trista, you've got spunk. Something tells me you will rise to the occasion."

"Do we get to fight you?" Cindie asked. "Sign me up for that one."

"Nice. Love you too, Cindie. Hey, we have a treat for you tonight — food. Eat up and get some rest, because you'll need your strength tomorrow."

"Tomorrow?" Trista asked. "We are fighting tomorrow?"

"Sure are. Can't wait. It will be fun." With that, Maxine left, and servants brought in trays of food for Cindie and Trista.

"I feel like they are fattening us up for the slaughter," Cindie said as they ravaged the food.

"At this moment, I don't care!"

"Wake up ladies!"

Multiple guards in metal and leather combat gear entered the underground enclosure, running their swords against the bars of the cages as they yelled for the prisoners to wake up. The noise and light from the guards' torches jolted the girls from their dreams into their grim, new reality.

Within a minute, the girls were standing under the bright light of the sun in the middle of a sandy outdoor field that resembled a makeshift arena. About twenty other girls were sitting on rock formations around the circular arena, and all of them wore some sort of combat uniform. Standing together in what appeared to be the positions of highest honor were Maxine and the Syth, the leader of the organization.

Maxine did the introductions. "Warriors, welcome our new recruits to the Dragon's Lair."

The girls around the ring clapped while heckling the four new recruits.

"You all know this, but I'll review for the sake of the newbies. Periodically, we add two new members to the Hydra to ensure we maintain our organizational strength. As you can see, we have four new recruits — that is two too many."

The warriors around the arena cheered.

"So, how do we solve this problem?"

The warriors chanted, "Fight! Fight! Fight! Fight!"

The Syth raised her hand and there was silence. Then the Syth addressed the new recruits.

"Ladies. You may have noticed that we don't see the title of lady in a positive light. Ladies are not warriors. We view ladies as women who are slaves to a master. The girls who were not as fortunate as you in the auction are learning as we speak what being a slave is like. We are giving each of you the opportunity to become a warrior. True, if you fail the test, you will lose your life, but being a slave is a life that is worse than dying. Either way, your old life died the day you left your homes, and a new life begins here today. You will either join the ranks of the warrior class, or the gods will free you from this life and you will live in Valhalla. Max will explain the rules of the duels."

"Ladies. The girl who was in your cage with you will be your partner. You will each pick one offensive and one defensive weapon. Then you will join me in the center of the ring."

Trista spoke directly to the Syth. "I didn't sign up for this and I won't take part in it!"

The guard in charge of Trista immediately struck her across the face with his hand, causing her to fall to the ground. The arena erupted in laughter and jeers.

Trista turned her face toward the Syth in anger. She got up off the ground and looked directly at the Syth. "Warrior men who beat on young girls? This I should respect?"

Trista's guard struck her more forcefully, and she went to the ground even harder. Cindie bent over to help Trista, and her guard gave Cindie a kick across her face, knocking her to the ground on her back.

Maxine whispered to the Syth, "I told you they had spunk." The Syth replied, "This is going to be good if they aren't dead before they meet their opponents."

The ring erupted. "Stand up. Stand up. Stand up!"

The Syth raised her hand, and there was silence. Everyone watched to see if the two girls would get back up, especially their would-be, much more seasoned opponents.

Both Trista and Cindie shook off the blows and slowly stood before the Hydra.

Trista looked at the Syth with contempt. "I can do this all day!"

The guard pulled back his arm, made a fist, and prepared to deliver a knock-out punch, but the Syth was fascinated. "Halt!"

The arena was in shock. This had never happened before.

The Syth stood and addressed Trista directly. "Young lady, child, just who do you think you are addressing? Don't you know I could have you killed right now? Have some respect for my authority."

Trista wiped the blood from her lip; spit blood and a tooth into the sand; and looked up at the Syth once again. She raised her hands, palms up, asking if she could reply.

The Syth smiled, happy that Trista was showing the ability to control her emotions. The Syth recognized this as a warrior trait. "Yes, you may respond to my question."

"You threaten me with death, but is that not your plan for the day's activities? Indeed, you claim to have the authority over life and death, but we both know that authority rests solely with the one true God."

The ring erupted in more jeers and heckling.

Maxine stepped forward to direct the guards to strike Trista down. The guards, seeing where this was going, placed their hands on their swords to prepare for the order. Cindie looked at Trista like she was crazy.

The Syth smiled, put out her hand, and grabbed Maxine's arm. "Tell me, little girl. What makes a young, weak, little girl like you think you can speak to me that way? You are all alone here, and no one can save you."

Trista was afraid. Anxiety swept over her body as she heard the words. But just as quickly as the anxiety came upon her, it suddenly fled as a small gentle voice reminded her of an event from her forgotten past.

Trista smiled in return, more blood oozing from her torn lip. "The last time the words, little girl, were used to address me, they came from the mouth of a dragon much larger than you are, with teeth much sharper than the swords you threaten me with now. The dragon who threatened me then could not touch me any more than you can now — if my God does not allow it."

Trista scanned the arena. "You say that I am all alone, but those surrounding you now are much greater than those who are with you."

Then Trista looked directly into the Syth's eyes. "I am not alone."

Chills went through the Syth's body as the warriors of the Hydra sat stunned and silent.

"Dragons don't speak, little girl. We will see if this god you speak of can save you."

The Syth looked at Maxine and nodded. Maxine announced the start of the next stage of the event. "Choose your weapons."

The girls that Trista and Cindie were to fight quickly moved to get first choice of their armaments.

Cindie moved towards the weapons area but stopped when she saw Trista did not move and whispered to her. “Trista, we have to defend ourselves. Please?”

Maxine addressed Trista directly. “If you die, your partner dies. Just winning the fight is not enough. If you don’t kill your opponents, the Hydra must kill you. The Hydra has to know that its members can kill to defend its own. If you cannot defend the girl next to you, then you are of no good to us.”

Trista walked to the weapons cache. One of her opponents picked a sword and a shield. The other picked a mace and a shield. Cindie chose a shield and a sword. Trista chose a shield and a helmet. There was quite the stir around the ring, as everyone, including Cindie, couldn’t believe Trista didn’t take an offensive weapon.

“What are you doing? Get a sword. I can’t do this by myself.”

“No weapon formed against me shall prosper. We are not alone, Cindie.”

The four would-be warriors joined Maxine in the center of the ring.

“No rules. Fight to the death.”

Everyone could see it would not be a fair fight. The two girls that Trista and Cindie opposed, Locke and Kyie, were both taken from the mountains of northern Omentia and were a few years older. Cindie had about two years and twenty pounds more than Trista, but Locke and Kyie each had a couple of years and twenty pounds on Cindie. In addition, the mountain girls looked like they were quite familiar with the sword and the mace.

“Ready ladies? Begin.”

Max stepped out of the ring and the mountain girls immediately attacked, slashing and swinging their weapons at Cindie and Trista, who defended with their shields. The Hydra warriors yelled and cheered. There was little question who would join their ranks.

“This won’t take long,” Max said to the Syth.

“We will see what the dragon-slayer has up her sleeve.”

Max laughed. “She doesn’t have any sleeves.”

Cindie landed a couple of swings of her sword on Locke's shield, giving some appearance of offense, but Trista was purely defensive, taking the brunt of Kyie's mace against her shield over and over. It didn't appear Trista could hold off Kyie's attacks for much longer.

Please help me, oh God? Show them you are the only true God!

Cindie and Locke were exchanging sword blows against each other's shields. Stepping backwards, Cindie tripped. She fell on her back and lost her shield. Her opponent charged her, confident in the victory to come.

Trista saw Cindie's predicament, and taking advantage of Locke's distraction, set an intercept course. Kyie pursued Trista, swinging her mace in attack.

"Well, this is it." Max said to the Syth.

"Maybe. Maybe."

Cindie raised her sword to make some defense against Locke, who was almost upon her. But Trista was closing rapidly and planned on hitting Locke at full speed to throw her off her advantage. Just as Trista dove to hit Locke low, Kyie swung her mace, missing Trista. The spiked ball, however, continue its trajectory and hit Locke squarely in the side of her head, taking off half of her face instantly. Locke's head exploding, her lifeless body fell to the sand. Kyie stumbled over Trista, who had hit the ground on her dive, and fell towards Cindie. Cindie still held her sword up defensively, and Kyie fell into it. The sword nearly split Kyie in two, the halves largely falling in the sand on either side of Cindie. Kyie's eyes darted about for a few seconds as the pieces of her body convulsed, and she tried to make sense of her new perspective.

The warriors of the Hydra all stood as the last act of the battle took place. As the dragon-slayer and her teammate stood to face them, the Dragon's Lair was silent.

Max was speechless. A slight smile broke across the Syth's face as if to say she knew all along what might happen.

The Syth stood. "Let's welcome the new members of the Hydra."

The shocked warriors around the ring clapped in obligated reverence.

The Syth raised her hand and there was silence. "I look forward to hearing more about this god of yours."

Then the Syth looked at Max. "Max, you will train Trista personally."

"But —"

"And be personally responsible for her safety. Do you understand?"

"Yes, Ma'am." Max nodded once, demonstrating her loyalty and obedience.

"Hydra warriors. I expect each of you to render our new members the respect you would give to any of the other members of our order. There is no room for dissent in our ranks. Save it for the enemy. Questions?"

Silence.

"Good. I know there are no deaf among you, so I expect I was clear. Now, greet your sisters."

It was surreal. Trista and Cindie stood, barely, in the sandy ring, being welcomed by the very people that had held them captive and ridiculed them just moments before. Max was the last to congratulate them on their most surprising victory.

Trista asked Max, "Does this mean we are free?"

"Once you become a sister to the Hydra, there is only one way to leave."

Chapter 36

The Journey

†††

Lee met Kissami just after sunrise, and Kissami brought him to the hidden entrance to the underground tunnel system that existed beneath the city of Mecha.

"How long has this been here?"

"I'm sorry Lee. I am really not at liberty to talk about the tunnels other than to point you in the right direction."

"Ok. Got it. And thank you again for this. Any point in the right direction is truly a godsend."

"Well, again, it truly is a gift from God, because if he hadn't sent Engel to tell me to do this, I wouldn't be doing it. You should give him all the credit and thanks."

Kissami led Lee to the map on the tunnel wall. They shut off their lanterns and waited. The stones on the map lit up, and Kissami touched the violet topaz stone. Topaz stones all along the tunnel lit up, showing Lee the way.

"Follow the stones and they will bring you to an archway. Step through the archway and you will be in Parlantis."

"Just like that?"

"Just like that."

"This is amazing!"

"God bless you Lee. I hope you find your heart."

"Thank you Kissami. God bless you too."

Lee headed down the tunnel and a moment later, the tunnel swallowed him up. Kissami turned around to leave and was face-to-face with Mika'el, Sandrah, and Jacob.

"Oh, my goodness!" Kissami jumped backwards.

Mika'el stepped forward. "I am so sorry, Kissami! We didn't mean to startle you."

"Ok. Just let me reset here for a moment." Kissami caught his breath.

"Again, we are really sorry."

"No harm done. One has to push that blood through the system really fast once in a while to stay young. What are you doing here?"

"Well, we heard a rumor that Lee was stepping through the portal to find our daughter, and we had to come. Sorry we had to be so secretive about it, but we didn't think you would bring us with if we asked you."

"Well, you are right there. My instructions said to bring one person to the portal, and I fulfilled that task."

"Please understand that we must try to save our daughter. Whatever it takes."

Kissami thought about it for a moment. "You didn't see what color stone I activated, did you?"

"Well, I could lie and say I didn't."

"Hmmm. Well, I'll leave you to it then."

"You're not gonna try to stop us?"

"Would I be able to?"

"No."

"Then what would be the sense of trying? Besides, I wasn't told to keep anyone from doing anything, just to bring Lee to the tunnel and show him the way."

"Thank you Kissami."

"For what?"

"Hey, can we use the tunnel if someone is still in it?"

"Not until they go through the portal on the other side. And the time on the other side will be different for you when you get there."

"By how much?"

"Could be a day, could be years. I must warn you. It could be longer, much longer."

"Years?"

"Yes. Even many years. It's fluid. That's about all I can say. I just want you to know what you are getting yourselves into. God bless you all and keep you safe." With that, Kissami turned and strolled out of the tunnel.

"Ok. Everyone shut off your lanterns."

When all the lanterns were off, the lights of the map came up again.

"I guess Lee is out the other side of the portal. That didn't take long."

Mika'el touched the violet topaz stone and the tunnel lights came on, showing them the way. They followed the lights, and the tunnel closed behind them.

†††

He couldn't believe what he was seeing. A moment earlier, he had stood in the dark tunnel looking at the portal. He had taken a couple of steps forward and everything had changed.

Red flowers covered the rolling hills, shining brightly before him as far as the eye could see. It was morning, and the sun had just risen, casting its rays across the horizon and illuminating the towering clouds in vibrant colors of red and orange.

Lee thought he heard thunder. Turning to see where the sound was coming from, he saw hundreds of horses crossing the hills to his left and heading for his position. Just before they reached him, they altered their course, which was good, since he had nowhere to take cover. He stood in silent awe as the countless number of horses passed by him. A white stallion ran directly towards Lee and came to an abrupt stop right in front of him. It reared up on its hind legs, kicked its front legs in the air, and let out a loud neigh. Then it dropped its front legs to the ground, kneeling in front of him.

He didn't have to contemplate what to do for long, because he needed a ride, and this seemed to be an obvious invitation. He jumped on the stallion, it rose, and quickly joined the rest of the herd.

†††

Mika'el, Sandrah, and Jacob stepped through the portal. Mika'el figured they were maybe thirty minutes behind Lee.

Hopefully, Lee has moved on from the portal. I don't want him thinking we don't trust him to find our daughter on his own.

When they emerged on the other side of the portal, they found themselves in the middle of something they had never even imagined before. Buildings towered high into the sky all around them, strangely dressed people were everywhere, and machines passed by rolling on wagon wheels.

"Where are we?" she asked.

"More like when are we?" he replied.

They knew they belonged together, but couldn't remember who they were.

The third, younger one asked, "Dad?"

"Yes, son."

"What's my name?"

He thought for a moment. "I'm sorry. I don't know."

Chapter 37

Tannin

†††

One more foothold!

The man hung two thousand feet above the floor of the mountain valley of eastern Parlantis. He has spent twelve-plus hours climbing the face of the mountain that towered over the crimson fields of spice flowers covering the valley below, and he was exhausted.

Just one more foothold.

He swung across the precipice, reaching with one hand to grab hold of the ledge above. If he could not grab the ledge, there was little chance he would get another opportunity to lift himself to the shelf above, in which case things were going to go south quickly. By south, he meant down. As he swung, every muscle in his body screamed, but the adrenaline forced them all to give every bit of effort, as it was absolutely critical he succeed in this maneuver. Reaching the ledge with the very tip if his fingers, he latched onto it and with an immediate second effort, released his other hand and pulled it over to join the first. With the last bit of energy he had remaining, he lifted his body and secured the edge of his foot in a small rock wall indentation. He slowly crawled onto the rock ledge, unable to move.

It slowly opened its eyes. Resting within the rock cave high above the valley, it could feel the vibrations in the rocks outside of its den. It was not used to being disturbed, as few creatures could reach, let alone purposefully approach, the entrance to its domain. Most creatures had an instinct about such things and thus avoided disturbing the creatures within the mountain. If a creature did make the mistake, it never made it twice.

Ah. I can't believe I made it. I underestimated just how hard that was going to be. Thank you, God, for helping me.

The man's name was Tannar. He enjoyed the challenge of climbing the mountain faces — it made him feel alive. While most of his friends had figured out what they wanted to become, Tannar was still wrestling with what exactly he would do with his life. He had shown he could be anything he wanted to be and accomplish great things in any field, but what field exactly he would pursue remained elusive, and he was still searching. His father wanted him to pursue a leadership role, but he was still looking for a sign of what God wanted him to do.

Tannar rolled over to face the cliff. When he did, he could clearly see the cave entrance; the ledge had concealed the opening from below.

"Whoa, what do we have here?"

His muscles slowly regaining energy, and Tannar struggled to get up. He walked over to the cave entrance. He could see a few feet into the cave, but beyond that, the shadows concealed everything within.

It took a long time to get here and a lot of effort. Might as well see what's inside.

Tannar slowly entered the cave, letting his eyes adjust as he stepped inside. Once inside, he still couldn't see much.

The creature did not move, but its eyes tracked the two-leg as it entered. Its kind was very familiar with the man-kind.

They fear what they do not understand, and they kill what they fear.

Tannar felt something was watching him and he instantly regretted entering the cave. He could smell something was present in the cave and could also hear what he thought was the beat of a heart, though it wasn't like any heartbeat he had heard before.

The creature's long reptilian tail slowly retracted from its extended position down the adjacent cavern tunnel. It tensed its claws, ready for the fatal strike upon the man should he offer any threat to the lair.

Tannar soon realized that he could go no further because of the lack of light entering the cave.

Bummer, now what?

He turned to leave the cave, but stopped.

How much easier it would be to find out where this cave leads than to climb my way either up or down outside the cave's entrance. It is getting late in the day. Perhaps I will spend the night here in the shelter that is provided. In the morning, when the sun rises in the west, it will illuminate the inside of this cave, and I can decide if there is any value in seeing where it leads. If I decide to not investigate the cave further, I will have many daylight hours remaining for a climb down.

Tannar went back out to the ledge and sat down with his legs dangling over the edge, enjoying the view. He had brought water and rations in a small backpack, and he pulled them out of the pack and had dinner while he watched the night arrive.

The beast within the cave gave the two-leg little more thought.

When Tannar had watched the sunset and the stars come out to sparkle brightly in the sky, he moved inside the cave to stay warm. He couldn't go far because of the lack of light. He settled just inside the cave's entrance, curled up as best he could, and fell asleep.

Tannar had the strangest dreams. He dreamed he was flying through the night skies high above the hills. He loved the flying dreams — he had them so rarely.

†††

As the sun slowly lit the western sky, Tannar awoke. He faced the inside of the cave, and though still half asleep, he could faintly make out the contours of the walls within. His imagination ran wild as he saw all the abstract possibilities of what the shapes might be as the light from the entrance changed in direction and degree.

As the sunlight slowly panned across the far wall, Tannar could see far more expansive of an enclosure than he had first imagined. He then imagined images he had never contemplated before — images of long reptilian tails, giant lizard bodies, enormous wings, and powerful claws all mingled together within the cavern. His peaceful waking calm changed to one of restless anxiety. He sat up and rubbed the cobwebs from his eyes, only to find the images became clearer.

At first, his mind could not accept what his eyes were reporting. His imaginations were not imaginations at all. Before him within the cave was a countless number of creatures; all their bodies lying intertwined. It was impossible for Tannar to make out how many of the creatures there were within the cave, for their number extended deeper into the cavern and beyond his view.

Tannar slowly stood, evaluating his situation and various courses of action. As he did, a pair of eyes opened in the middle of the brood before him. The eyes were like those of a snake. They blazed a golden-red hue, reflecting the sun that was shining in through the cave entrance.

Instantly, dozens of eyes opened. A moment later, the forms of the creatures separated, unwrapping themselves and becoming independent entities. The creatures stood on four sturdy legs with long sharp claws upon their feet. They had powerful wings tucked close to their bodies and were covered in layers of jagged scales. Their heads resembled those of the snake-kind, with long ears and large nostrils.

The winged reptiles all glared at Tannar, and he knew he was in trouble. There really weren't any good escape options. The choices were to move down farther into the tunnels filled with the winged serpents or do a freefall out the cave entrance, neither of which was very appealing.

Tannar slowly stepped backwards toward the entrance, attempting to show he meant the creatures no harm.

Two of the creatures slowly approached Tannar from both sides of the cavern.

I don't think that worked.

The largest beast in the middle of the cavern continued to study Tannar. It had watched him throughout the night, ever since he had arrived.

As Tannar backed away from the creatures and toward the ledge, he stepped on his pack and lost his balance. He stumbled backwards and fell. As he did, the medallion he wore slipped out from the neck of his tunic. The golden rays of sunlight entering the cavern glinted off of the medallion for but a second — but a second was enough.

Tannar continued stumbling backwards, his momentum taking him out of the cave and over the edge of the ledge. In a streak of lightning, the creature in the center of the enclosure burst forward and latched on to Tannar's leg, holding it in its jaws and keeping him from falling to his death. It dragged him back to the center of the cave, where Tannar found himself surrounded by the winged monsters. Tannar screamed the whole time, thinking he was about to be devoured, until the creature released his leg.

What's happening? Why am I still alive?

The creatures separated and a smaller one made its way forward, stopping a few feet in front of Tannar.

"Hello. My name is Snuffy."

"What is happening? How can you speak my language?"

"I don't think I am."

"What does that mean?"

"I think it is the medallion you wear around your neck. It processes and converts air vibrations into understandable sound. I understand you too, and I don't think you can speak the language of my kind, can you?"

"No. As a matter of fact, I cannot. Still, how is this possible?"

"The ancients of this land used such a device to communicate with my kind. It isn't just a decoration. With the one we serve, all things are possible."

"You mean your kind knows about the one true God?"

"The one true God? Of course. All creatures do."

"I don't know what to say. Thank the big one of your kind for saving me, and not eating me."

"Ha! We don't eat your kind. We eat the red flower here in the fall and the El Tigran lion in the winter."

Tannar stood. "My name is Tannar."

"It is good to meet you, Tannar. My father asks that you keep our presence a secret between the medallion bearers and us. The ones who do not serve our God would hunt us, and it would prove to be a most unfortunate mistake for them. We wish to spare them that mistake."

"Of course. Oh, and what shall I call your kind?"

"There is no name for us. There are others like us in the world, but they do not serve the master we serve, therefore they should not bear the name we bear."

"I will call you, tannin."

"Tannin." Snuffy looked to his father, Valdo, for approval and then back at Tannar. "My father approves."

"Do you always speak for your kind? For the tannin?"

"No. My father just thought you might need someone smaller to speak to you — so you would stop screaming."

Tannar thought about that for a moment and was noticeably embarrassed. But after another moment, he started laughing. "Yes, that was probably an excellent idea."

"Well. Would you like a ride to the bottom of the mountain?"

"I'm sorry, what?"

"I can give you a ride down to the valley below."

"You mean, on your back? Yes, that would be — amazing!"

Snuffy made his way out onto the ledge. "All aboard!"

"I can't believe I am doing this?"

"Now, don't let go."

"Don't worry!"

"Here we go."

Snuffy dove for the valley, and once he got enough airspeed, he leveled out. Tannar could not help but scream. Snuffy could not help but smile — inside, since dragons have a hard time smiling on the outside.

The two spent a significantly longer time flying than it took to get Tannar to the valley below, and they formed a friendship.

Once Snuffy dropped Tannar off in the valley and said his goodbyes, Tannar could not believe what had just happened. It was the most amazing thing he had ever experienced, and he soon found himself missing his new friend. It would be awhile, but they would meet again.

PART 7: Opportunity

Chapter 38

Arrival

†††

Flash!

"Do the travelers realize how much time has changed for all of them? That the farther they travel within the tunnels, the more time they skip compared to those on the outside of the tunnels? That even the travelers within the tunnels skip different amounts of time compared to those who traveled before them?"

Flash!

"No. Nor will they. They will lose their memory of most things as they cross the dimensional boundaries; but not all things. The Spirit transcends all, and their faith will remain. Indeed, the bond of love between them is strong. God is love, and time will not erase love."

Flash! Flash!

†††

The soldiers knocked on the door, looking at each other apprehensively.

"Enter."

They opened the door and escorted the prisoner in, standing him up in front of the Colonel's desk. Colonel "Grumpy" Sanders, the Commander of Parlantis' famed infantry, sat with his back to the door.

He slowly rotated his chair to face his soldiers and their prisoner. He sat for a moment, assessing the prisoner.

"How old are you?"

"I'm not sure."

"Well, you're a little young to be a spy, don't you think?"

"A spy? I'm not a spy."

"Perhaps a horse-thief then?"

"I'm not a horse-thief."

"My men caught you stealing horses."

"Your men took me prisoner while I was riding a horse."

"Hmm. Where are you from?"

He thought. *Nothing.* "I — don't remember."

"You don't remember. What is your name?"

He tried to remember, but nothing came to mind. "I'm not sure."

The guards both yanked on him, letting him know the Colonel expected answers to his questions.

He thought about his options. He could keep telling the truth and sound dishonest, or he could just give his best lie and hope it convinced these men he was telling the truth.

"My name is Christian."

"Christian. Ok. How did you get here, Christian?"

"Ships. Lots of ships and lots of time."

"Hmm. Ships, you say. Did you work on these ships?"

Christian knew he was sinking, but kept digging the hole. "Not at first. I was a stowaway. My mother died and my stepfather beat me, so I ran away and hid on a ship. Once it set sail, I learned my way around."

"I see. So, you're a fast learner, are you?"

"Yes, sir."

"My men tell me they first spotted you riding point of two-hundred wild stallions — bareback on top of the lead stallion. How did you learn to ride like that?"

"I learned as a child. My Grandpa taught me."

"And how did you come to find yourself leading hundreds of wild stallions across my countryside? Where were you taking them?"

Great. Another tough question.

"If you are insinuating —"

"Son, I wasn't insinuating anything. If I want to say something, I will say it to your face. You walked into that one all by your lonesome. Now I will ask you again. Where were you taking those horses?"

"Nowhere, sir. It is they that were taking me."

"Really? And where were they taking you?"

"Here, sir."

"Hmm. Well, I don't know what they do wherever it is you came from, but since we don't shoot children around these parts, I am tempted to throw you in the stockade until you are eighteen and then shoot you for being a spy."

The guards smiled.

"But Sir —"

"Wait. I wasn't done. When I want you to talk, I will tell you to talk."

"Yes, sir."

"On the other hand — whether it be that a wild herd of Parlantian stallions brought you here to me, as you maintain, or you mounted the over stallion of that herd to take the herd to a band of horse-thieves — either way you are of great value to Parlantis."

The guards frowned.

Colonel Sanders looked at each of his guards. "And in these parts, all in my charge, accept what I judge to be the right way forward — as absolute. They follow my orders or find themselves in the brig."

The guards wiped their disappointed expressions off their faces and stood at attention.

"Now, as I was saying. Since you are still underage, you will stay with my family until you are sixteen. However, you will work in the Parlantian Guard. You will teach my cavalry how to ride like you ride, and we, in-turn, will teach you how to be a cavalry soldier. You will report directly to me. Once you are sixteen, you will have the choice of joining the Parlantian Guard or spending two years in the stockade, followed by execution."

"That sounds — fair, sir."

"Good. That's that then."

Colonel Sanders addressed his soldiers. "You two, get him everything he needs to do his job, and do it with smiles."

"Yes, sir!"

"Christian, my wife, Christen, will make sure you get the rest of what you need."

"Thank you, sir."

"Dinner is at six. Your new best friends here will show you how to get to my house. Don't be late. Christen is the tough one in our house."

"Yes, Colonel."

The men left Colonel Sander's office and closed the door.

†††

Everyone around the table stood as Christen took her seat. Colonel Sanders sat at the head of the table, but the place of honor was to his right.

Christen acknowledged the gesture. "Thank you everyone. That was very nice."

As Christen picked up her fork, Colonel Sanders, their daughter Maria, and Christian began as well.

"Christian, we love that you have decided to join us for a while. Maria will be happy to have someone else in the house her age. Ever since she came to live with us last year, she has been wanting someone to hang out with."

Maria smiled at Christian across the table.

"So, Christian, isn't it amazing how similar our names are? What are the odds?"

"Yes, Ma'am. It is amazing."

"Tell us about where you grew up — your childhood."

"Well, Ma'am, I honestly remember very little. I think maybe I hit my head or something. I am sure my childhood was much like childhood is here."

"What do you remember?"

Christian glanced at the Colonel. Colonel Sanders gave him a look as if to say, "See, I told you she was tougher than I was."

"Ok. Well, we filled our days with work and school, and our nights with family and love."

"What would your family do in the evening?"

Christian tried hard to remember. Only blurred bits and pieces came to his mind — very disjointed and unclear. "We would eat dinner together, just like this. Then we would do homework and join before bed to read the Word, pray, and give thanks to the one true God."

"The one true God?" Christen looked at Grumpy and then back at Christian. "In Parlantis, we worship many gods. We have many temples dedicated to them. Which one do you call the one true God?"

Christian's memory of this topic was surprisingly very clear to him. "None of them, from what I figure, based on your question. If you worshipped the one true God, there would certainly be no other temples for false gods."

"Yes. I guess that makes sense."

Grumpy and Christen looked curious and interested. Maria was no longer smiling.

Grumpy asked, "How would I know your one true God? Is he the god of war, the god of food, or the god of gold? What is his image? A lion? A dragon?"

"None of those, sir. He is the God above all authority, sharing his throne with none other. He is a righteous judge; a God of justice, but also of love. He does not take on a form as from the imagination of a man, but is spirit. He made everything that exists, is everywhere, knows everything, and can do anything."

"Well, that about covers everything, doesn't it? Tell me, Christian, why would it matter if I worshipped your god versus any of the other gods that we have built temples to in Parlantis? What difference does it make?"

"The difference? The difference is in truth. If not for worshipping the creator of all things, the one who loves you, the one who sustains you, the one who can help you, and the one who will decide your eternity after you leave this place — what would you waste your breath and time in worship for, if only to praise a piece of brass or gold? Would that not be the epitome of foolishness?"

Maria spoke up. "Isn't foolishness praising a god who took your mother away and gave you an abusive father? A god who abandoned you to stowing away on ships only to be caught here and forced into servitude? Is that a loving god, as you say?"

"Maria, we will have none of that! Apologize to Christian!"

"It is ok, Ma'am. I understand her confusion."

"Confusion?" Maria asked. "What is the confusion?"

"Well, the most basic confusion is that in your concept of a god, god exists to serve us. That he did this to me and failed to do that for me, so I should be angry with him for his failures in serving me. That is backwards, for we exist to serve him. He is God, not any of us. Granted, we all want to be served. It is in our nature, and many of us spend our lives looking for others to serve us instead of serving them."

"We exist to serve? You make yourself a slave to this god of yours? Speaking of foolishness!"

"Oh, most certainly, I do, and for several reasons."

Christian looked at Colonel Sanders, who had been listening intently to the discussion.

"Colonel Sanders, would you think it foolishness for me to submit to you in your house?"

"No, Christian, it would be most wise, as I have the authority to take your head." Grumpy laughed, looking at Christen. When Christen did not even crack a smile, Grumpy became very serious and looked back at Christian. "It would be most wise to respect those with authority within this house."

"And, sir, would it be wise or foolish for you to serve the queen of Parlantis, doing as she directs?"

"It would be wise, Christian. Wise, indeed."

"So how much more wise is it to recognize the King above all kings, the maker and ruler of this world and the next? As a matter of fact, how unwise to worship or recognize any other."

Maria spoke up again. "So, it is out of fear that you worship your god, just like a soldier would serve his commander? Or like you would serve Grumpy? For the commander holds authority over life and death."

"True. I serve the one true God out of reverence, awe, and respect — for how can one not do so given the awesomeness of God? But it is not out of fear that I would die for him. What gain is there to die out of fear of one over that of another? Either way, one dies."

"What then, if not out of fear of your awesome God? What compels you to serve him and even die for him?"

"It is out of love for him that I would die for him. He truly holds my heart with his love."

"We already went over that. He has not loved you. Look at your life!"

"That is where you are wrong, Maria. He shows me in all things how he loves me. It is not his doing that these troubles have befallen me, but those of the evil one, the great dragon that revolted against him and leads man into rebellion. The dragon has led all of us into sin via our thoughts, our words, and our actions. We see it every day all around us. Because of this sin against the one true God, we all deserve for God to separate us eternally from himself."

"Well, that doesn't sound very loving, does it?"

"Nope. It doesn't."

"There you go, Christian. You said it."

"You are right Maria, it doesn't sound very loving, but it sounds just, does it not?"

Grumpy acknowledged, "It sounds just."

Christian continued. "But God has not stopped there. He has promised in his Word that he will send a savior that will bear all the punishment for us, pay for all our sins, and thus redeem us to himself — perfectly meeting his demand for justice while showing his boundless love."

Christen asked, "Why have we not heard of this God before? Had I known of him, I would not have spent so much time in useless sacrifice to gods that man has made; gods that do not exist."

Christian paused, and then he looked at Christen straight in the eyes. "You have heard of him now."

A tear ran down Christen's cheek. "Yes, I have."

Maria smirked, and Grumpy was deep in thought.

"So, Maria, I thank God for everything that has happened in my life. Everything that has brought me to this place, at this time, with all of you. Had it not happened, you would not know the truth. But now that you know the truth, what will you do with it?"

Chapter 39

Apprentice

†††

"Hold your sword up higher!"

"Max, this is where I hold it to pull you in. I make you think you have the advantage, that I am giving you an opening. Then you go for the high slice attack, miss, and end up on the ground."

"Trista, of course I have the advantage. I've been doing this long before you arrived, and I am the best here. You are giving me an opening."

"Go for it."

Max made her best move and missed. Her momentum took her to the ground, where Trista repositioned with the tip of her sword at Max's throat.

"You — were — the best here."

"Maybe I am just getting old."

Trista extended her arm to Max, offering to help her up. "Maybe you have just trained me too well over the last year and a half."

Max took Trista's arm and pulled herself up. "That's possible." Max smiled. "I suppose we will find out soon. The Syth has you scheduled to fight next week."

"What?"

"Yeah, no worries though, just animals."

"That's good. What animals are we talking about?"

"Oh, just the usual. Lions, tigers, and bears."

"Say again? No warm-ups with like coyotes?"

"Ha! No. Be happy. It could be worse."

"It could be worse? How so?"

"Elephants."

"Elephants?"

"Yep."

†††

The warriors sat below the spectators on stone seats in the arena outside of Krieg, Omentia, awaiting the assortment of competition between warriors and beasts. There was to be much bloodshed and much death; usually the creatures died, though the warriors always sustained some mementos of the encounters, and more than occasionally, fatal ones.

The more death and injury sustained by the warriors during the competitions, the more entertained the crowd; and the more entertained the crowd, the greater the likelihood the patrons would return in the future to make the managers of the competitions richer.

To fire up the crowd, the managers instructed the Syth to send in Trista. The Syth did not want to sacrifice Trista before she ever became the warrior the Syth thought she could become, but the managers held all the power, and the Syth could do nothing but comply. Number one to fight was an especially bad position as all the wild animals were still available, and thus, the managers could throw an endless stream of carnivores at the warrior in the ring.

Max delivered the news to Trista. "Trista, you're up."

"I'm up? Already?"

"Seems the managers want blood to fire up the crowd, and they think you, being a rookie, will provide it."

Trista was concerned. "Ok."

"Hey, you are not alone, right?"

Max was the last person Trista ever thought would give her encouragement, but having worked together for eighteen months, Max had heard her confess her faith countless times. Perhaps the Spirit was working on Max's heart, or maybe she was just being callous. Either way, it had a positive effect.

"You are right, Max, I am not alone. Thanks for reminding me."

"Plus, you keep saying heaven is an awesome place, so how sad can you be to go there?"

"Ok, Max, that will be about enough encouragement for now. Thanks."

Max helped Trista get her battle armor on and pick out her weapons. "It is normally a little easier to pick out the weapons to bring, based on the creatures that are left. This time, not so much. There is a spectrum of possibilities from the most likely to the most dangerous — which way do you want to go?"

"Well, we all know I am not getting through this without God's intervention, so I'm going with speed, maneuverability, and the blade."

Trista picked up a short sword, two daggers, and a sling.

"Seriously, a sling? What are you going to do with that?"

"Well, there should be lots of rocks out there. That means endless ammunition. And I can use the ammunition on all my opponents at a great distance from their teeth and claws."

"If you have the time."

"Goes without saying, Max. But they have various obstacles out there that I can use to my advantage, right?"

"I guess."

"Well, I'm as ready as I am ever going to be."

Max walked to the door to inform the guards that the first competitor was ready. She turned to wish Trista good luck and stopped when she saw her on her knees with her head bowed. Her lips were moving.

She's praying to her one true God. Please, God of creation, be with this girl.

It surprised Max to hear the voice in her head pray to Trista's God, but she didn't rescind the prayer. When she saw Trista had finished, she said, "Good luck, Trista."

"Luck has nothing to do with it. Luck doesn't even exist. God's will be done!"

"God's will? That's it?"

"I mean it when I say it. I just need to accept it when I see it."

"Ok, so whatever happens will be good then, right?"

"That is right, Max, now you get it! See you in a few, or hopefully, I will see you later."

Max thought she knew what Trista meant, but wasn't sure.

The doors opened and Max watched the petite fifteen-year-old girl walk by her and into the arena.

Maybe there is something to this one true God thing after all. Never have I seen such courage in the face of certain death.

†††

The crowd roared its approval as Trista entered the arena. Eager for action, the spectators had been waiting for the show to start. The crowd quickly quieted, however, when it saw how young and petite this warrior was and realized that no one was joining her in the fight. Even being as brazen an audience as they were, they understood that the event managers were simply sacrificing this small girl for their bloodlust.

The announcer addressed the crowd. "Welcome to the games! Now entering the arena is Trista, the dragon-slayer."

The crowd erupted in laughter, assuming Trista's appearance was now simply a clown show to begin the event.

"Though you cannot see her companions, the dragon slayer is not alone. She says she serves the one true God, and that his servants protect her."

The crowd roared with ridicule and mockery, for no one in this audience would serve the same god as Trista. Indeed, the legion of demons hovering over the thousand in attendance yelped their amusement, though a few wiser demons grew suddenly apprehensive at hearing the announcer's words.

"Let us see how she fares against the lion!"

A door opened at the opposite end of the arena and a giant lion entered, running at full speed toward Trista. Trista instantly sprinted for the obstacles in the center of the arena. The spectators screamed in fear for Trista, as it was unlikely she would make it before the lion tore her to pieces.

I can do this. Just a little farther!

Just prior to the lion intercepting Trista, she threw herself into a narrow tunnel carved from the trunk of a redwood in the very center of the arena obstacles. The lion could squeeze through it in pursuit, but at a much slower pace. Trista emerged on the other side and drove her sword into the sand about two feet beyond the exit of the tunnel.

"What is she doing giving up her sword?" the Syth asked Max as they watched their young dragon-slayer.

"No idea."

The roar of the crowd hushed as Trista crawled up the side of the redwood tunnel, pulled her two knives, and crouched down above the exit. As the lion emerged from the tunnel, it stopped momentarily as it maneuvered around Trista's sword.

Trista leaped off the tunnel obstacle and onto the back of the lion. As she did, she swung both of her arms as forcefully as possible and drove her knives into both sides of the lion's neck. The lion jumped into the air and ran around in panic as it spewed blood in every direction. Trista rode the lion like a bull, holding both knives as would-be reigns.

The crowd stood dumbfounded at the girl's ingenuity. They watched in amazement as the lion quickly lost energy and collapsed onto the ground. Trista leaped off the lion as it faltered. She retrieved her sword and approached the lion as it breathed its last. Standing over the lion, she raised her sword and swung, effectively chopping off its head. She drove her sword into the ground, took a knee, and bowed her head.

Thank you, Father in heaven, for delivering me from the lion. All praise and glory be to you!

The spectators were stunned and stood in silence, unable to decide what to make of what had just happened. Having just made fun of the girl and her god, the managers of the games could not allow the girl to survive the competition, so they released the wooly mammoth. To fuel its aggression, the managers of the games had subjected the male mammoth to hours of torture. It was angry.

Spotting Trista at the center of the arena and smelling the lion at her location, it charged. Controlled by their spiritual tormentors, the crowd suddenly cheered the mammoth, siding with the managers against Trista in a surge of blood lust.

"Oh, oh. I don't know how she gets out of this one," The Syth said to Max.

Max didn't say a word. She just stared at Trista.

Run Trista. Run.

Trista stood and faced the giant mammoth.

I am not alone.

She looked down on the ground in front of her. Immediately in front of the lion's head was one spherical stone. There were no other stones within sight, just the one. She bent down and picked it up.

The crowd roared as the mammoth closed in on Trista's position. Twenty more seconds and this competition would be in the books.

Trista removed the sling from the rope belt around her tunic, placed the stone within the fabric, and swung it above her head.

The crowd erupted in laughter at the obviously futile gesture from the girl facing off against a mammoth!

Because they mocked the name of my God! Please, Oh Lord, let your name be praised! And if not praised, feared!

Trista released the stone toward the mammoth. It penetrated the right eye of the giant and sent it into a panic! It swerved past Trista and ran full speed into the stone wall surrounding the arena. As it hit, several of the spectators jumped and others fell from the wall into the arena. The mammoth fell over onto its side, stunned.

Again, the crowd stood in shock and silence as they watched Trista walk over to the mammoth, climb up its leg, walk along its back to its head, and drive her sword down into its good eye — into its cranial cavity and then its brain. It convulsed and died.

Trista stood atop the colossal creature, raised her hands into the air and praised the one true God!

"Let all know that you, Oh Lord, are the only true God!"

The managers could not allow this to stand. They released three El Tigran tigers and a pack of wolves. The crowd howled their delight as the carnivores entered the arena, wanting this young girl who had insulted their gods to be torn to pieces.

The wolf pack detected Trista first, darted across the arena, and, climbing the mammoth, surrounded her. One tiger charged the group of spectators that had fallen from the wall moments earlier, mauling them mercilessly and adding to the injuries they had sustained from their fall. The other two tigers approached the mammoth.

Trista removed her sword from the mammoth's eye and held it high above her head. She was now surrounded by a pack of wolves and two El Tigran tigers.

I am not alone.

†††

A golden angel hovered over Trista. Its glorious rays of light shining in all directions. The crowd of scoffers could not see the angel. Trista could not see the angel either, but she didn't need to — she already knew it was there. The wolves, however, could see the angel, and they froze in their tracks.

As if commanded by some unspoken word, the wolves turned and faced the two tigers. The tigers then froze in their tracks.

†††

The Syth and Max stood with a thousand others in the stands of the arena. They could not believe what they were seeing.

Max looked at the Syth and asked, "Who is this girl?"

"She has told us countless times she is nobody, just a believer in the one true God. The real question is, who is this one true God she speaks of?"

Without warning, storm clouds rolled over the arena, unleashing bolts of lightning and thundering their anger. The crowd became fearful and ran from their seats to the exits as the winds howled from all directions.

Trista maintained her position, and the wolves stood their ground. The tigers noticed the crowds running and their instincts took over. Defenseless prey is much less a threat to survival than armed resistance. The tigers launched from the mammoth into the stands in pursuit of the easy prey, mauling countless unarmed spectators fleeing the storm. Once free of the arena, the tigers escaped into the countryside. The wolves then followed the alpha male along the same track to freedom as the tigers had taken.

As Syth and Max ran out into the arena, they looked up to see Trista standing atop the mammoth. The arena was empty, and the storm thundered above. The sky flashed, and the thunder rolled as lightning shot in all directions.

"This is something I never thought I would see," said the Syth. "Not in a million years. How did this young girl do this? It is impossible!"

"We have witnessed something here today much bigger than a young girl surviving a competition," Max replied. "We have witnessed the power of the one true God."

They looked at each other in awe. Then they looked up at Trista again. She was on her knees with her head bowed. Without thought, they both fell to their knees and bowed their heads — though they did not know what to say to such an awesome God.

Chapter 40

Cavalry

†††

Christian taught the Parlantian Guard cavalry recruits how to ride, and over the next two years, the Parlantian cavalry increased their speed and riding ability tremendously. In return, Colonel Sanders made sure Christian received weapons training from his best officers.

By the time Christian turned sixteen, he was ready to commit to joining the Parlantian Guard. He didn't think execution was still on the table, but didn't want to ask Grumpy Sanders for fear of reminding him of the original ultimatum.

Colonel Sanders and Christen made sure Christian had the best education Parlantis offered, and Christian joined the Parlantian Cavalry as a lieutenant.

Christian and Maria became best friends even though Maria had much different ideas about their relationship. Though it was not an easy thing to resist Maria's charms, Christian couldn't help but feel there was another — though he couldn't recall who that person might be.

†††

Christian was soon leading his first patrol as a Squad Commander. He had ten men under his command, and they were riding border patrol to the southwest of Pferd. Command had received reports of unusual activity on the outskirts of the city and had sent Christian's squad to find out what, if anything, was going on.

Christian's second in command was First Sergeant Red Clark. Red was a crusty old cavalry man that Colonel Sanders had directed to teach Christian how to be a good leader. There was no question where Red had earned his nickname, as he still had a full head of red hair.

The squad rode for half a day to the mountain area where the locals had reported seeing groups of men that no one recognized. It was a hot day, and the horses were tired and thirsty from their ride, so the squad went to a treed area in the center of a valley to give them some water. Christian and Red rode ahead for a bit and then also stopped at the river for a rest.

"How long have you been with the guard, Red?"

"Oh, ever since I was about ten," Red said. "Guess that means about sixty years."

Christian looked at Red, trying to figure out if he was pulling his leg? Red looked like he could have been seventy, but Christian thought maybe that leathery skin might just be from decades riding out in the hot Parlantian sun.

Red held his serious look as long as he could and then let out a friendly laugh. "No, son, I'm old, but not that old!"

Christian laughed along with Red as the horses drank some of the cool spring water, weaving its way casually down the valley.

"Red, what would you say is the most important characteristic of a good leader? For men in this profession of arms."

"You are asking me?"

"Yes, Red, I am. You've been doing this for a long time, and I'd be an idiot to not learn everything you can teach me."

"You are the first person ever to ask me that question."

"You're kidding."

"No. I'm afraid not. Most just like to just shout the orders and learn through their mistakes."

"Well, I value your opinion on all things related to the profession of arms."

"I appreciate that, Lieutenant. I really do. Well, let's see. There's courage, wisdom, discipline, mental strength, judgement, ability —"

Christian held up his hand, signaling Red that he thought he heard something. Red immediately stopped speaking and listened. Then Red heard it too.

Christian and Red both crouched low behind the bushes, looking across the stream. As they watched, approximately fifteen men were escorting eight prisoners through the trees — the prisoners were the rest of Christian's squad.

Christian couldn't believe it! Somehow, intruders had got the jump on all of his squad except for him and Red and were leading them somewhere, maybe back to their camp.

"Take your horse and go get reinforcements."

"Excuse me, Lieutenant?"

"We need more firepower. One of us has to go, and since I am the guy in charge, I choose you."

"Those are my guys. I'm not leaving them. You go, Lieutenant."

"Red, those are my guys now, my family. I go when they go."

"I guess we are both staying then. What's the plan?" Red expected a "follow and look for an opportunity" response.

"The plan? What do you do when someone threatens your family?"

"Copy that Lieutenant. That is what I was hoping you would say."

"Let's go."

†††

Christian and Red low-crawled up to the rocks just above the campsite where the enemy rebels were holding their squad mates. It was dark, an hour past sunset. All their squad mates were bound and on their knees in a line, eight of them. They were all roughly Christian's age, in their late teens or early twenties. Christian saw them as brothers; Red saw them as sons. Each one of them bore the signs of a vicious beating, some more severe than others.

Their minds raced, trying to figure out a tactic to free the soldiers from their captors. They could see seven of the rebels relaxing by the fire as one walked up and down the line of prisoners; interrogating them and hitting them with a club when they refused to answer. It was getting pretty brutal.

"Options?"

"Well, Lieutenant, there are two of us and at least eight of them, probably more around their perimeter — maybe even behind us now. Granted, we have the element of surprise, but they probably know our units typically have ten men and they only caught eight, so they are probably expecting us."

"And the good news?"

"That was the good news."

"Oh. It didn't sound like good news."

"I never said there was good news."

"Right."

They listened to the interrogation while trying to decide a course of action.

"Hey soldier-boy, I'm asking you a question!"

The rebel wound up and hit the young man in the face with the club, knocking him backwards and unconscious.

"Well, I guess you won't be answering questions until morning."

Christian began to move when the rebel hit the young soldier, but Red held him still.

"We have to think. Need a plan. Too many of them to just rush in."

Christian knew Red was right, but those men were his responsibility. He couldn't let this go on any longer.

"Here is the best option I can think of, Lieutenant. You go over yonder in the rocks and create a distraction. That will draw some men away. Then I will go in under the cover of darkness and do what needs to be done."

“That sounds like the only course of action, Red, except one slight change. You create the distraction, and I will go do what needs to be done.”

“Apologies for pointing this out, Lieutenant, but I am pretty sure you have never done the kind of doing that needs to be done right now, and any hesitation down there will get you and those men killed.”

“You might be right, Red. I don’t know what will happen down there. What I know is that it will be me that does the doing. Now get on your way. We are running out of time. Make that distraction good and loud to pull as many of these guys out as possible.”

Red never hated rank more than he did at that moment.

This kid is going to get himself killed. Can’t help but respect him for his decision, though.

Red put his hand on Christian’s shoulder for but a moment, and then he slipped back into the darkness to execute his orders.

Christian slowly and quietly made his way down to the trees behind the campfire, where the interrogation continued.

“Who is your commanding officer, and where is he?”

Christian was standing in the shadows right behind the interrogator, his sword drawn.

The interrogator stood in front of the youngest soldier in Christian’s squad, Private Liam Smith. Liam had just completed his training. Christian had met Liam’s mom and dad. They were so proud of young Liam.

Liam looked up into the interrogator’s eyes, and it seemed to Christian like Liam was looking past the interrogator and straight at him. He could see the regret on Liam’s face; regret he would probably never see his parents again, never have a wife, and never have a family. But Christian did not see fear in the young private’s eyes. Liam simply said, “My commanding officer? Who is he?”

“What are you deaf or just stupid? Yes, your commanding officer. Who is he? Where is he?”

"He is your worst nightmare, and he is where you least expect him to be."

The interrogator laughed, and all his buddies around the fire laughed with him.

"Remember that sentence well, because it is the last thing that your mouth will ever say."

Time stood still for Christian. He had never killed a man before, and he didn't want to. He regretted the decisions that had brought him to this moment, but he was here now, and there was no turning back. Whatever decisions he made in the next few seconds would live with him for eternity. On the one hand, ending a man's time of grace, time to get to know the one true God, was a decision that would affect that man for all eternity. God hated murder and held every man responsible for the blood of another. But Christian did not want to kill this man — he wanted to save another. He didn't know how else to do it. The dilemma was tearing him apart.

Christian raised his sword, waiting for his mind and spirit to resolve the conflict; dreading the moment that Red would create the distraction; hoping it came in time to save Liam and yet, hoping it would never come.

The rebel interrogator raised a different club, one with spikes on it, high into the air, preparing to unleash a hellish blow on the defenseless Liam. "Where is your God now? Since he isn't showing up to help you, I will send you to see him."

At that moment, Christian remembered something his Grandpa Henry had taught him many years earlier. God doesn't always show up directly to help us. Sometimes, God uses masks in this world to help us — indirectly. The doctor is one of God's masks for healing. God uses the farmer as one of his masks to feed us. The soldier is one of God's masks for defending the defenseless.

Christian remembered something else. He remembered Liam's mom hugging Liam and saying, "I love you, son. Do not be afraid. The one true God will always be with you. Trust him. He will protect you and defend you."

It was the moment of decision. In a second, the interrogator would kill Liam.

"Where is his God?" The voice came from the shadows behind the interrogator.

The interrogator, who had been looking towards the campfire, turned. As his eyes slowly adjusted to the lack of light, he strained to see into the darkness — to identify the voice.

The voice spoke again. "Today, God wears a mask."

The interrogator's eyes adjusted just in time to see the razor-sharp blade swinging from the shadows — just the blade. It passed in front of him from left to right and sunk into the club he was holding high in his right hand, where it stopped.

It is said that a man's eyes continue to send signals to his brain for five seconds once losing blood pressure. The first second the interrogator made out Christian's face, staring at him from the shadows. In the second, he saw his life flash before his eyes. During the third second, he observed the world around him descending into chaos, like a turbulent fall, down a steep hill. As his head came to rest on the ground in front of Liam, he saw the young private close his eyes and a tear of relief roll down his face. In the interrogator's last moment of life, he saw demons descending on him to drag him to Hell.

At that moment, Red began making a commotion on the other side of the rebel camp. Several of the rebels sitting around the fire instantly bolted in that direction. Three snapped their heads toward Christian, and seeing him, picked up their weapons and rushed in his direction.

There was just enough time to cut Liam free before the first rebel made it to the line of prisoners. Christian jumped in front of Liam to intercept the rebel's blade, while Liam rolled behind the man next to him and used the knife from the interrogator's belt to free the man.

As the two freed soldiers dispatched the third rebel and subsequently untied the remaining soldiers from the squad, Christian fought two rebels at once. Not yet being as experienced as the rebel fighters, Christian sustained several sword wounds. By the time the freed members of his squad made it to him to assist, Christian had sustained a life-threatening stab wound to the abdomen. With the help of his men, he finished taking out the last rebel.

After establishing a future rendezvous point, Christian directed two of the wounded soldiers to take the unconscious soldier to safety. He instructed the remaining five men to cover the evacuation of the wounded and set up a perimeter around the rendezvous point. Over the objection of his men, Christian took off alone to help Red.

When he arrived at the rocks where Red had created the distraction, he found three dead rebels and Red actively fighting two more. Christian jumped in alongside Red and together they eliminated the remains of the rebel force.

"What are you doing here, Lieutenant? What about the rest of the squad? We have to free them!"

"It's done. They are all going to make it."

"Well done, Lieutenant, well done!" Red slapped Christian on the back.

"Christian smiled and then collapsed."

†††

Christian opened his eyes to see Christen, Colonel Sanders, Maria, and eight other men gathered around the room. He was flat on his back on a bed. When he tried to get up, he quickly found that it was not going to happen, at least not anytime soon.

"There he is." Grumpy said thunderously as he walked over to the bed. "Just relax, soldier. That's an order."

"Where am I, Colonel?"

"Well, you're in a hospital in Pferd. Your squad got you here just in time. It was touch and go for a while."

Christian looked around the room to see a bunch of smiles.

"We are so glad you are going to be ok, Christian," Maria said as she took Christian's hand.

Christian's eyes rolled back into his head for a moment. "I feel kind of weird."

Christen grabbed Christian's other hand. "That's the morphine, Christian. It will wear off. But I don't think you want it wearing off too soon."

Just then, Corporal Liam Smith entered the room with his mom and dad.

Christian noticed Liam's rank immediately. "Whoa, Corporal Smith. Nice." Christian looked at Colonel Sanders. "How long have I been unconscious?"

"Just a couple of days, Christian. If you look around the room, you'll notice a lot of promotions."

Red walked across the room and stood next to Christian's bed.

"Red, good to see you!" Realizing his error in front of the Colonel, Christian rephrased, "I mean, Sergeant Clark."

Colonel Sanders chimed in. "Red is fine, Christian. He earned it."

Christian smiled and then grimaced as he shook Red's hand. Once he shook Red's hand, Christian reached for his right cheek.

Red said, "Don't worry about that, Christian. Chicks dig scars."

Maria added, "Yes, they do."

Red said, "Your wounds will all heal, Colonel. You just have to take it easy for a couple of weeks."

Christian frowned. "Colonel?"

Red motioned towards Christian's chest with his eyes and a head nod.

Christian looked down at his chest. There was a colonel's eagle, and another medal pinned to his shirt. "I don't understand."

Colonel Sanders said, "I know you haven't had one yet, but that would be called a promotion, and a rather hefty one at that."

A tear filled Christian's right eye.

"Oh, and that other colorful piece of fabric on a pin next to your rank, Colonel, is the Medal of Valor. It is for choosing to risk your life to save those under your charge. Your men, all of them, insisted you receive it. Who was I to argue?"

"But Colonel, Red should have —"

"Red should have received the medal? Oh, he did. Seems we have lots of medals to go around this battalion."

"I'm sorry, sir, you mean squad."

"Don't correct me, Christian. I mean battalion, a few soldiers of which are here today."

"You mean —?"

"That's what I mean. The queen promoted me to brigade and asked if I had any recommendations of who should take my battalion. I could only think of one fast learner who could step up; someone I could trust. Congratulations! She accepted my recommendation. Oh, and you can call me General Sanders."

†††

After everyone shuffled through, thanking Christian for saving their lives and congratulating him on his promotion, only Red remained in the room with Christian.

"We never finished our conversation."

Christian looked at Red, puzzled. "Our conversation?"

"Before all the action, we were discussing what a good leader looks like."

"That's right. I remember now."

"Well, the most important characteristic of a good leader is that he loves the men under his command. He understands they are not just numbers to be used for power projection and winning battles, but also that they are somebody's sons and that they mean everything to their families. A good leader will be in the front lines of the conflict and willing to sacrifice his life for his men if required."

Christian started to tear up.

"That is the characteristic I witnessed out there, and I am proud to be under your command, Colonel."

Before Christian could reply, Red left the room.

Chapter 41

Survival

†††

It had been two years since the incident in the arena. The Hydra was no longer welcomed in the northern areas of Omentia, because of what had happened. So the Hydra traveled to the southern and eastern regions of Omentia.

Max had continued training Trista as she grew bigger and stronger. No longer did Trista have to depend on her intellect alone to be victorious against her opponents, though doing so remained her first choice.

Trista had shared much of her faith with Max, and Max had professed her faith in the one true God. Though her faith was new, it was strong from having already seen several amazing acts of God in person.

The Syth, however, was resistant to the Spirit, despite having seen the mighty acts of the one true God. As such, the Syth insisted Trista stay with the Hydra and threatened harm to Trista's friends should Trista decide to slip away.

So Trista stayed with the Hydra and had no alternative but to fight others just like herself. Though she had sustained considerable injury from the battles, Trista had been victorious twenty-seven times. At just under seventeen years of age, the Syth considered Trista the most formidable of the Hydra warriors, and her would-be opponents feared her for both her intellect and for her fighting expertise.

Trista's battle for survival had been especially brutal. She had tried her hardest to avoid being responsible for anyone's death, but as time passed, her opponents became more and more challenging. Before long, Trista's fight became the last and main event of each competition, with challengers coming from far and wide to take a shot at Trista, the Dragon Slayer.

Trista became a battle-hardened warrior.

†††

"If my parents saw me now, they wouldn't even know it was me."

"C'mon Trista. Your family never forgets you or stops loving you."

"Max, I'm telling you, they wouldn't understand."

"What — that traffickers kidnapped you, sold you, threatened your life? That the Syth forced you to fight to survive?"

"No. That I am a killer!"

"You are not a killer! You have gone to great lengths to avoid killing and you've simply done what you've had to in order to survive!"

"But all those people!" Trista put her head in her hands and cried.

Max hugged Trista and tried to console her. "Didn't the angel tell you that God had important plans for your family?"

"Yes."

"Well, if you don't survive, then how can he use you?"

Trista thought about it for a moment. "I guess."

"Now c'mon. Get up. It's time I taught you how to ride."

"I know how to ride."

"No, I mean really ride!"

Max brought Trista to the stables.

"C'mon. Let's go look at the horses."

"Max, I've seen horses."

"Not like these, Trista. Not like these."

They turned the corner of the barn.

"Wow!" Trista said.

"Did I tell you or what?"

They walked up to the training corral where a few of the stallions were being trained.

"They are incredible!"

"Pick one."

"What?"

"Pick one."

"Pick one for what?"

"Pick one to be your horse, of course."

"You mean?"

"Yep. That's what I mean."

"How? I mean, why?"

"Well, I wish I could say it was all for a good reason, but the Syth signed us up for some competitions on horseback. But the good news is, it will be your horse, even when we aren't competing."

Trista thought about it for a moment and looked at Max. "I guess we have to take our wins where we can get them."

"Isn't that the truth?"

The black stallion walked up to Trista like he knew her.

"That is really odd," Max said.

"What? What is odd?"

"Well, that horse has been aggressive and unpredictable. They were considering releasing it back into the wild."

"Ok. I'll take the black one, and I will name him Fury. Like me, he wants to be released back into the wild. Like me, his captivity has made him aggressive and unpredictable. Someday, I will be free and I will release him. Until that day, we will lean on each other and we will survive together."

Trista hugged Fury's head, and the trainers looked on in bewilderment.

"That is the first time we have seen that horse calm — the first time anyone has even touched him!"

Chapter 42

Where are we?

†††

"Excuse me sir, may I ask you where we are?"

The man looked at Shawn like he was crazy.

"You don't know where you are?"

"No sir, we don't know where we are."

"You are in Kan, Kandish. The country of Trinian."

The man joined the crowd again; like a fish that had momentarily departed the school and then scurried back into formation.

The amount of people rushing past them, the blinking lights, the strange carriages, and buildings towering to the surrounding clouds overwhelmed Shawn and Diane.

Christopher couldn't stop looking at the passing women, all wearing skimpy tunics and adorned with shiny objects.

"Christopher, close your mouth," Diane scolded. "You're going to catch flies."

Diane stopped a passing woman about her same age. "Excuse me, ma'am, could you help us, please?"

The woman gave her a look, snorted smugly, and continued on her way.

They looked at each other in frustration and helplessness. Shawn pointed out a tall building to the right, and they maneuvered their way across the flow of people to the corner of the building, where they sat down at a small table.

Diane said, “What are we going to do? We don’t know anyone here. We don’t know how to get around. Everything is different!”

Shawn tried to calm her down. “It’s going to be alright, honey. Someone will help us.”

As he was speaking, a woman approached their table. “Excuse me. I couldn’t help but hear you talking. My name is Dawn.”

“Hi Dawn. My name is Diane. This is my husband Shawn and my son, Christopher.”

“It is very nice to meet all of you. Are you new to Kandish?”

Everyone exchanged smiles, and Diane took the lead in talking to the woman.

“Yes, we just arrived. Our plans changed at the last moment, and we found ourselves here, in a brand new land. We are at a bit of a loss as to your customs as well as how to find a place to stay or a place to work.”

“I understand. It has been hard for many of the refugees coming here. The wars have caused so much misery. As the owner of this restaurant, it would be my honor if you would let me serve you a warm meal. I could join you, and we could get to know each other better. I have a lot of connections in the city, and maybe I could help you find a place to stay until you can get things sorted out.”

“That would be most kind of you Dawn. We could repay you as soon as we can find work and —”

“I’ll not hear any of that kind of talk. Just take some deep breaths and be at peace. I’ll be back with some biscuits, meat, and potatoes in a few minutes. Then we can talk more.”

“Thank you so much, Dawn. You are an angel sent straight from the one true God!”

Dawn froze. “What did you say?”

Diane was confused. It was like a bucket of cold water fell on Dawn’s head.

“I said you are an —”

“Don’t say it. Shh.”

Dawn sat down and put her hand on Diane's hand. "I'm sorry if I startled you. Please forgive me. Be very careful what you say. They are listening. I will explain later when we can talk freely. I will be right back with some food. You will stay with us tonight. We have a place with lots of room above the diner."

Dawn squeezed Diane's hand and then hurried off into the corner coffee shop to get their dinner.

"What was that all about?" Christopher asked his Mom?

"I don't know Christopher. I guess we will find out in a few minutes."

Shawn suddenly noticed that a man sitting a few tables away from them was watching them a little too closely. "I think we should be very careful about what we say out in the open."

Christopher asked, "Can we talk about our names? I've been thinking—"

"Let's just stick with the names we chose, ok?"

†††

Shawn, Diane and Christopher sat around a table in Dawn's home above the coffee shop later that evening.

Dawn came around the corner with another younger man. "Everyone, this is my son, Josh."

Shawn stood and shook Josh's forearm. Josh took Shawn's hand. "This is how we shake here, Shawn."

"I'm sorry, Josh. I guess we have a lot to learn."

"No problem, Shawn. My Mom told me your story, and quite a story it is!"

"We didn't think anyone would believe us, because it feels like someone has erased our previous lives. Our memories are so scarce that we can't even recall our names; we just picked these names out of the blue.

"But you remember the one true God?"

"Oh yes. Each of us. Absolutely!"

"But you don't remember how?"

Shawn, Diane and Christopher all shook their heads from side to side. "No. We don't."

"Well, my mom is an excellent judge of character, and we trust you."

Diane asked, "What is the issue? Why is trust required when it comes to the one true God?"

Dawn answered. "Well, things have been changing here in Trinian. The One Church is cracking down on talk of the one true God. It teaches all religions are a pathway to god — no matter what they teach. Today, here, not offending anyone is more important than truth."

"Well, that is crazy," Shawn said.

Josh replied, "You are preaching to the choir, my brother. I have friends who work with the government, and they have been flat out told they have to support wholeheartedly the inclusion of every religious concept, sexual orientation, and ridiculous notion that comes about in the name of personal truth. Not just coexist with it, but support it. It is like belief can be in both a thing and its opposite at the same time. Those that professed science last year now profess purely anti-scientific and illogical ideas this year."

"Like saying one and one makes three. Believe it all you want, but try to build something with that mathematical model and you will soon see the folly of your acceptance of it. It gives a new definition to irrational numbers." Shawn chuckled to himself at his joke.

"What do you do, Shawn? It sounds like maybe you might be a scientist."

"Wow, Josh, I hadn't even thought about it. I don't remember what I did for a living, but I know numbers and equations and such. Perhaps I am a scientist."

"I have a friend who works at a company called Biogen. It just started up. Would you like me to see if maybe they can use a guy like you?"

"That would be great, Josh. Obviously, I need a job. Maybe I could work as an intern for a bit and see where I can fit in?"

Dawn asked, "And Diane, where do you see yourself working?"

"Well, I'm not sure. Maybe helping in a school? I love children of all ages. I think I would have something to offer." Having the thought, Diane turned and looked at Christopher. "And speaking of schools, we need to get this young man into a school."

"That is easy. We know the perfect school, don't we Josh?"

"Sure do, Mom. I will talk to Steve and Jill about getting Christopher in right away."

Shawn asked, "Well, are you sure it is a good fit, given our — beliefs?"

"Oh yes, and the after-hour programs will definitely impress you."

Diane grabbed Dawn's hand. "Thank you for everything you are doing for us. I just can't believe it. I don't know what we would have done without your help."

"You are our brothers and sister. God brought you to us for a reason, and I am so glad he did."

Part 8: Preparation

Chapter 43

The Queen

†††

Queen Tharice sat at her window in the palace overlooking the city. Historically speaking, it was not typical of so young a queen to rule the kingdom; but hers was not the typical story.

It had only been a year since her husband, King Edward, had tragically fallen ill with an evil specter. For many weeks, the medicine men of the kingdom had tried to heal him of the menacing spirit, but none had been successful. One stormy night, the trying ended when the king threw himself from the castle wall. The next morning, Queen Tharice became the ruler of Parlantis.

The sun was setting over the mountains that surrounded the city of Pferd, and the full moon was just rising in the west. It was nearly time.

Before making her way through the secret chamber door that led to the stone staircase behind the wall, the queen donned her outer garment. She lit a torch and then descended the staircase thirteen stories to another chamber deep beneath the castle. Built before the castle itself, the ancient chamber was located five stories below the castle walls and two stories below the bottom of the moat that surrounded the castle.

Entering the ancient chamber, she used her torch to light an oil moat that ran the perimeter of the enclosure. Starting beside her, the flames rapidly spread, forming a ring of fire around the room.

In the center of the chamber, there was an unnaturally black hole, surrounded by a massive stone walkway fifty feet wide. The flames growing around the chamber lit the stone walls to reveal the many chained skeletons that hung there, remnants from ages long past.

Queen Tharice approached the hole and dropped the torch into the chasm. She watched its flame light up the rock walls of the abyss as it descended into the depths of darkness, until eventually, the darkness swallowed up all the remaining rays of light.

Tharice stood at the edge of the abyss, waiting. It wasn't long before the scratching sounds coming from within the pit announced the imminent arrival of the hellish creatures climbing up the walls of the chasm. First, their long spindly fingers appeared at the edge of the abyss, followed by their bloodied and smooth heads without faces. The only features on their heads were an oversized mouth with rows of razor-sharp teeth.

Six of the creatures emerged from the pit. They had pale skin, six arms, and resembled spiders more than any other creature that walked the face of the planet. Daarak, the oldest and largest of the six, stood in front of Tharice while the others crawled upon the skeletons hanging in the chamber, gnawing on the old bones as a dog would savor the remnants of a deer kill.

"You summoned us?"

"I summoned six of you, not one!"

The heads of the others snapped toward their queen, and they scrambled over to the edge of the pit to join the largest standing before Tharice.

"Remember who you serve!"

The mouths of the aaranae chattered with their teeth clamoring together as they raised their heads high into the air and their bulbus white-skinned bodies convulsed as if they were having a seizure.

"Bring a message to Trajan. Tell him it's time to begin the second phase of our plan."

"Yes, my Queen."

Daarak and the others turned and scurried down the walls of the pit until they disappeared into the depths below.

Chapter 44

Aaranae

†††

The aaranae delivered the message to Trajan and returned to their lair, deep underground in the catacombs beneath Parlantis.

Daarak traveled through the many tunnels and chambers where the spider kind lived. Daarak and his mate, Loathe, were the alphas of the gladiator order of aaranae. After three hundred years, there were many orders or tribes of aaranae to include the gladiators, recluses, goliaths, and huntsman.

Daarak and Loathe were the first of the aaranae kind. They had once been of the human kind. As two-legs, their hearts had been cold. They had lived a life of plenty and pleasure, swindling others and leaving their victims destitute.

The couple, Derik and Loita, had lived a life of decadence and harm to all those they came into contact with in their lives. Unfortunately for them, they came into contact with and swindled an old woman named Wendrine. Wendrine was not pleased, and unbeknownst to the couple, Wendrine was a witch and a servant of the crimson dragon.

Wendrine cursed Derik and Loita, transforming them into a new species of creature, the aaranae. She cursed Daarak and Loathe to live underground with the creatures that hid there from the sun. Their lot was to feed on the rotting corpses of the dead to survive.

Unable to live and hunt for food above ground, lest they be hunted down and killed, the aaranae kind tunneled entirely underground to the freshly buried bodies within the cemeteries of Parlantis. They pulled the decaying bodies from their graves to their underground lairs and devoured them.

When couples of aaranae shared the corpse of a two-leg, doomed to hell, the female of the couple would become pregnant. After a three-week gestation period, a baby aaranae would be live born. The baby aaranae would hold the consciousness of the unbelieving soul fed upon by its parents until its death.

Daily, baby aaranae were born. They immediately let out terrifying screams as their eight eyes first opened to see their new parents, and their consciousnesses realized their new lives within the arachnid family. The numbers of the aaranae grew into the thousands as there was no shortage of lost souls in Parlantis.

Daarak crawled into his dark burrow to find Loathe there, giving birth to another aaranae with a lost soul. A moment later came the high-pitched shriek, reminding all that as horrifying their current predicament, a worse one awaited them upon death. So they clung to their pitiful existence, fearing the day they would meet the dark lord they served.

CHAPTER 45

DISCOVERY

†††

Christian had largely recovered from his wounds, but to ensure he had completely healed, Colonel Sanders insisted he take a few more weeks off before returning to duty. Christian used the time to explore the more remote mountainous areas surrounding Pferd. The more he could learn of the area, the better he could perform his duties defending it.

One day, while out riding, Christian saw a man ahead of him go into an area of the mountains he hadn't yet explored. Wishing to meet the man and maybe visit with him for a while, Christian followed him into a winding dry stream bed, surrounded by steep cliffs and copious caves.

After a few minutes, Christian found the man's horse tied to a tree outside of a cave entrance.

I wonder what this guy is up to. I don't want to intrude on his activities, but this seems a little strange. What if this is rebel activity?

After wrestling with the decision for a minute, Christian decided it was his duty to investigate. He tied his horse up next to the stranger's horse and headed into the cave.

The cave entrance was narrow and the tunnel beyond dimly lit. Christian stopped once inside, unable to see the way ahead. After a moment, Christian's eyes adjusted to the low light, and he continued on deeper into the cave.

The air in the cave was humid, unlike the dry air outside, and the temperature must have been thirty degrees warmer.

Wow, I have experienced nothing like this before. Something strange is going on here. Why would it be so much warmer inside this cave? You would think it would be cooler out of the scorching sun. That has been my experience.

As Christian moved forward, the cave divided into two separate tunnels, one branching off to the left and one to the right.

Great. Now what? There really isn't any way to know which way to go, so it doesn't pay to stand here and try to decide. Today, we're going to the right.

Without delay, Christian made his way to the right, down the tunnel. He walked slowly, as he was unsure of what he might find ahead. The tunnel became more and more narrow, until soon he could only move forward by turning sideways and squeezing through a crack in the rock.

This doesn't really seem much like a passageway at this point.

Still, Christian pressed on as he could see there was a faint crimson glow beyond the crack in the tunnel rock. Emerging on the other side of the crack, Christian saw the unbelievable. The tunnel opened up into an enormous cavern. Everywhere Christian looked — the ground, the ledges, and the walls — were all covered with giant eggs. A faint crimson light emanated from within the eggs. The light moved or pulsated, as if to mimic the movement of the unhatched creature within. Together, the light from the eggs lit up the entire cavern.

Christian could not believe his eyes! He slowly walked to the closest egg. He stood before it, marveling at its size. Slowly, ever so slowly, he reached out his hand and touched the top of the egg that must have stood waist high. When his hand contacted the outer shell of the egg, whatever it was within moved and the crimson light within the egg moved up to contact his hand.

"Hi!"

Christian did not hear the greeting with his ears, but he just heard it in his head.

What in the world?

He felt the creature repeat his words. "*What in the world?*"

As he heard the words in his head, the medallion that he wore around his neck heated. It didn't burn, but he was aware of the increase in the temperature.

"Are you speaking to me from inside of this egg?"

"I'm speaking to you, but what is an egg?"

"Ok, sorry. I'm getting a little too far ahead of you."

"*What does that mean?*"

Ok, this is getting off point. How can I understand what is talking to me from inside of this egg?

At that moment, Christian felt a breeze above his head. As he looked up, a giant creature dropped from above. It landed on the ground behind him. Enormous wings collapsed around him and massive claws latched onto Christian's abdomen. He had less than a second to live.

The reptilian jaws drew near to Christian's head as the nursery protector's threat elimination protocol required the intruder's decapitation.

Christian squeezed his eyes shut, waiting for the pain. "Father, help me?" Christian's medallion glowed as he spoke the words.

A moment before Christian met his maker, the mighty dragon froze.

"What did you say?"

Christian opened his eyes and searched for the person who asked the question. He only saw the dragon. "Where are you? Help me! Don't leave!"

"I'm right here."

Christian could not believe his eyes or his ears. "You. You are speaking."

"Yes, I am. So are you."

"Yes, I know, but dragons don't speak."

"Oh, well, I guess it wasn't me then."

As the dragon said that, Tannar entered the egg nursery from the tunnel. "Stop! Release him!"

The dragon released Christian and stepped back away from him.

Tannar ran up to Christian, who stood staring at the dragon. Once he got close, Tannar's medallion also glowed.

"Are you ok? Did he hurt you?"

"No, I think I am ok."

Tannar noticed Christian's medallion glowing and threw his arms around Christian. "Brother!"

"Brother?"

"Do you believe in the one true God?"

"Yes. Of course."

"Then we are brothers!"

"What about the dragon?"

"What about him?"

"Well, aren't you afraid of him?"

"Afraid of Aryon? No, he's a teddy bear!"

"The dragon has a name?"

"Of course he has a name." Tannar looked up at the immense dragon standing next to them. "Aryon, introduce yourself."

"I would, but our visitor says that dragons can't speak."

Tannar looked back at Christian. He held his hands out in front of himself, palms up, and shook his head side-to-side. "Dragons."

"What is your name?"

"Christian. Yours?"

"Tannar. Come with me and let's talk." Tannar gestured toward the tunnel.

Christian walked slowly away from the dragon with Tannar, still unsure if anything that was happening was real.

Aryon flapped his enormous wings and flew back to his perch high above the eggs, keeping careful watch over his charge.

Tannar led Christian down the long tunnel to another chamber. This chamber wasn't nearly as large as the egg nursery.

"This is quite a system of caves," Christian said.

"Indeed. Over the centuries, the tannin have constructed quite the elaborate maze of tunnels and chambers within the mountains of Parlantis."

"The tannin? That is an amazing coincidence, Tannar."

Tannar stopped, smiled, and looked back at Christian. "Yes, I may have had something to do with that."

"Dragons wouldn't do?"

"Actually, no. They said all dragons are not alike, and they didn't want to be associated with the — bad — dragons. These dragons serve the one true God. The others serve the dark master."

"The others?"

"Yeah. Apparently, there are others living in other lands that are a different breed, if you will."

"Great. Just what we need, right?"

"I know. I had the same reaction as you did when I met them for the first time. Once Snuffy explained some things to me, I could relax a little around them."

"Snuffy?"

"Snuffy is the son of their leader, Landris."

Tannar sat down with Christian on a large rock next to a stream that ran through the mountain chamber. A hole high above the chamber let in ample sunshine to light up the many crystals embedded within the chamber's walls; which, in turn, reflected the sunlight around the chamber in a glorious and surreal fashion.

"This chamber is amazing!" Christian said.

"It is, and there are many more like it — absolute marvels!"

"Speaking of marvels, what is up with our medallions? I thought they were just fancy necklaces that maybe spoke to our historic tribe or people."

"Yeah, me too, until Snuffy told me that our ancestors designed this tech to allow us to speak to the dragons of the land. Apparently, neither our ancestors nor the dragons knew they were on the same side; that of serving the one true God. This led to conflict whenever the two sides encountered each other. Once they could communicate, the misunderstanding was resolved."

"But how could our ancestors have tech that we still don't have?"

"I know, right? Apparently, we aren't as smart as we think we are."

"Makes you wonder where they acquired that tech or what else they had."

"It does."

As they were speaking, Snuffy made an impressive entrance. First there was nothing but a shadow passing over the ground in front of them, which made Tannar and Christian look up towards the hole in the cave's ceiling. Gliding from high above, the Prince of the Tannin descended in a spiraling fashion, flared at the last moment, and landed in front of them.

"Speaking of the devil, here's Snuffy."

"Hey Tannar, I don't think I like that classification."

"Sorry, Snuffy, just a figure of speech."

"It's ok. I get it. We have some tannin that say that you two-legs taste like chicken. It is always good for a good cluckle-chuckle."

"Point taken Snuffy. Whether a figure of speech or a joke, we should be careful not to insult our friends."

"You two-legs are pretty smart, after all."

"Sometimes, Snuffy, sometimes."

Snuffy looked at Christian. "So, Christian, what do you do in Parlantis?"

Christian froze, not knowing what to say.

Oh, oh. Telling him I'm a Parlantian Cavalry Commander will not go off well. At the same time, lying to a new friend would eventually prove problematic.

I will not lie to you. I'm a Commander in the Parlantian Cavalry.

As expected, that went over like a bag of rocks. Christian could see it on Tannar's face, as well as on Snuffy's — though reading a dragon's face was questionable at best.

"So, were you in the caves in an official capacity?"

"No. I just saw Tannar, and I thought I would see what he was doing. We have had a growing drug smuggling problem. The smugglers are coming in from El Tigre. I wanted to make sure he wasn't involved with that operation."

"I see. What are your intentions regarding disclosing the tannin's presence in these mountains?"

"Well, I haven't thought that through yet."

"We really hope you will consider not revealing our presence. In the past, fear on both sides has led to bloodshed. We wish to avoid that."

"That makes sense. But at the same time, I have a duty to my commander and my soldiers."

There was a moment of tension in the air.

Honesty is the best policy unless your guests can tear you to pieces.

"The Master's will be done." Snuffy nodded, flapped his wings, and exited the chamber from high above.

"Those aren't the words I ever expected to hear from a dragon."

"That makes two of us," Tannar said.

Tannar and Christian sat in silence, mesmerized by the dancing reflections all around them on the chamber walls.

"Do you think they'll let me leave, Tannar?"

"Oh, sure." After a few seconds passed, he added, "Pretty sure. Well, fifty-fifty."

Chapter 46

Rise

†††

Christian had mostly recovered from his wounds at the hands of the rebels. It had taken several weeks of bedrest and close attention by Christen and Maria following a nasty infection.

Recently promoted, General Grumpy Sanders had kept Christian filled in on the higher-level aspects of his new battalion's operations. Red assisted with several visits discussing personnel and the more mundane administrative details. Both were highly invested in Christian being up to speed when the day came for him to take command of his battalion.

That day came sooner than Christian expected it to. He was to be the youngest battalion commander in Parlantian history, and there was quite the promotion ceremony required. Christen, Maria, and Red took care of assigning the duties and planning the details. Everyone would be there, to include Queen Tharice.

"Are you ready?" Christen asked Christian as he walked out of his room.

"No, I don't think so."

"Oh, sure you are!" Grumpy thundered. "You'll fall right into the position when you see the thousand men at your command sitting upon their steeds in their dress uniforms on the parade field and the queen waiting for your words of wisdom."

"Thanks, General, I think I am going to be sick."

"Well, do it on the way. Queen Tharice will not take kindly to us being late."

"I'll be waiting to ride back with you after the ceremony, Christian," Maria said as she walked up and gave Christian an unsolicited kiss on the cheek.

Christen smiled and left with Maria. Grumpy raised his eyebrows and winked as he slapped Christian on the back and walked him out to their saddled horses.

"Sir, I want you to know that I —"

"Oh, I know, Christian. The girl has a mind of her own. All I can offer for advice is to look out! Throughout the time I've known her, she has consistently gotten what she wants."

"General, as you know, I have a lot going on right now. I don't think I have anything left over for that kind of business right now."

The two mounted their steeds.

"I get it, son. Trust me, I do. I'm just not sure it makes any difference. By the way, how are your shoulders?"

"My shoulders, sir? They feel fine."

"Good, because they will carry a lot more weight in a few hours."

†††

The Parlantian Color Guard had just placed the Parlantian flag and the Parlantian Guard flag in position. A thousand mounted cavalry faced the stage and saluted with sabers held high as the Parlantian Anthem was played. All stood, soldiers saluted, and Queen Tharice led all the people of Parlantis in attendance in placing their hands above their hearts.

Following the presentation of the colors and the anthem, Brigade Commander General Grumpy Sanders took the stage.

"Queen Tharice, fellow Parlantian Cavalry Commanders, soldiers, ladies and gentlemen; it is a hot day, and I am going to keep this short. The queen, my wife, and this battalion have all heard my opinion about our defense many times, and you don't need to hear it again today. I will, however, speak for a few minutes about this battalion and its new commander.

"There are several battalions in my soon to be brigade, but in my humble opinion, the 90th Battalion is the most important for one reason and one reason only; it protects central Parlantis, the pathway to Pferd, and the Capitol itself. It cannot fail, ever. Nor has it!

"In our long and storied history, the 90th Battalion, Parlantian Guard, has never failed to rout any would-be invaders. If you gaze upon the 90th Battalion's standard, you will see the many banners hanging with distinction. They represent the many victories on the Golden Fields and throughout Parlantis. Our enemies know they cannot defeat us. No one has and no one ever will. Always watching, always ready, the 90th Dicemen will protect our Parlantian Paradise and our loved ones at all costs; to the last man.

"Now for the elephant in the room. Some of you have reservations as to the age of your new commander. I assure you, he is ready for this command. There is no one I have more faith or confidence in to carryout the duties of the 90th Battalion Commander.

"So, without further delay, it is with great pride that I have led the Dicemen, and it is with great confidence that I introduce to you my adopted son, your new commander, Colonel Christian Sanders."

Christian rose from his chair and walked to the podium, shaking forearms with General Sanders as they passed each other.

"Your majesty, General Sanders, commanders, soldiers, ladies and gentlemen.

"I stand before you today in great humility. Never did I dream this day would happen, let alone this quickly. I am tremendously honored.

"Thank you, Queen Tharice, and General Sanders, for your confidence in me. I would also like to thank the one true God for all he has done for me; for his protection, his providence, and his love."

Everyone was largely in shock when they heard Christian's words for different reasons. General and Mrs. Sanders were concerned about how Christian's words would be taken. The soldiers and civilians in attendance were shocked because they had largely never heard of the one true God and felt threatened by Christian's mention of him. But none was more shocked than Queen Tharice. She seethed with anger, struggling to control her rage.

"To you, Queen Tharice, I pledge I will defend Parlantis, your city, your palace, and your throne with my life.

"To my commander, General Sanders, I pledge to you my loyalty, my service, and my sword.

"To the people of Parlantis, I pledge my gratefulness and love.

"Finally, to the soldiers of the 90th Dicemen, I pledge to you that I will lead from the front, never ask you to do something I won't do, and never risk your lives unless it is absolutely necessary.

"The men of the 90th will defend our land with our lives. We will never surrender and we will never retreat!"

General Sanders and Colonel Sanders met at the center of the stage. General Sanders handed Colonel Sanders the 90th colors, and at that point, Christian was the commander of one thousand men.

†††

Following the Change of Command, the family and top brass took part in a formal reception at the Parlantian Guard Officer's club.

"So Christian, how do those eagles feel on your shoulders?"

"They feel heavy, General Sanders, very heavy."

"I told you they would. That weight is responsibility to Parlantis and responsibility to the men you lead."

"How do you handle it?"

"Well, it is really pretty simple. If the stress you are feeling is you worrying about your own performance, you are spending a lot of energy on worrying about you instead of using that energy to serve your country and perform your duties. Are you looking inward or outward? At some point, you need to let — you — go. You need to trust you were chosen to commmmand for a reason and spend your energy executing that charge. You may fail sometimes; that comes with trying. Don't stress it. Just get up, brush it off, and press forward."

"That is good advice, sir."

"Well, you know, I have a vested interest in my adopted son doing well; the last name and all."

"I won't let you down, sir."

"Son, Christen and I are very proud of you, and we love you. You could never let us down. Just keep doing what you know is right in your heart."

"Like thanking the one true God in my speech?"

"That roiled some feathers to include the queen's, but whatever. You have to be you, and I am thrilled you gave credit where credit is due."

"Well, that almost sounds like you are a believer."

"Funny you should mention that, Christian. I was meaning to show you this. Ten years ago, when my grandfather passed away, I found it while going through his chest. It wasn't until last night that I remembered I had saved it, thinking it was an interesting medal. I woke up from a strange dream. I couldn't remember the dream, but I felt I needed to go through grandpa's chest and war medals. That is when I saw it."

General Sanders reached into his pocket and pulled out a medallion. He held it cupped in his hand for Christian to see.

"What? Your grandfather has an identical medallion? Maybe we are family."

"Maybe so."

"This is mind-blowing! I mean, what are the odds of this happening?"

"I don't know, Christian. I don't know of anyone else having a medallion like this."

"There are probably more in Parlantis." *I feel so guilty for not telling him about Tannar. But if I do, I have to tell him how we met, and that means the tannin. Then I need to tell him what the medallion is really for and that his grandfather was a believer in the one true God. That is outstanding news, but I don't know if he is ready for that yet.*

"What do you mean?"

"Well, again, what are the odds of you having the only one in Parlantis?"

"True. My grandfather might have got it during his travels abroad."

"I guess that is possible."

"Anyway, I wanted you to see it. I'm not sure about showing Christen."

"Why?"

"She jumps to the conclusion of everything. I enjoy doing more research before deciding on things. I don't like being rushed. Don't get me wrong; if I have to make a quick decision on something I can and will, but I like to have sixty percent of the information — not twenty — before reaching a conclusion."

"How will you do more research on this?"

"I don't know yet. I may just have to go with my gut."

"What does your gut tell you?"

General Sanders stared at the medallion for a moment, while he moved around the cigar he had in his mouth with his lips.

"My gut tells me there is more to this medallion than meets the eye. It's not just jewelry; it has a purpose. Wouldn't you agree, Christian?" Grumpy Sanders stared at Christian, waiting for his answer. "Well?"

"Well, I —"

"I'm just kidding with you. There is no way for us to know the answer to that question. Right? I just wanted to see if you were just going to be a yes man, or if you thought before giving your opinion. You passed. Ok, enough of this. Let's go have some shots of Jeremia Weed! This is a celebration!"

"Jeremia Weed? What is Jeremia Weed?"

"I'm sorry, son. What did you just say? Let's go. We have to rectify this situation."

Grumpy Sanders threw his arm around Christian as he stuffed a cigar into Christian's mouth and led him back to the celebration.

Maria was the first to intercept them, grabbing Christian's hand and leading him to her table to introduce him to all her friends. Between Maria and the introduction to Jeremia Weed, Christian had his hands full.

Part 9: Another Time

Chapter 47

New Life

†††

Steve and Jill ran the Foundation Elementary School in Kandish. It had been over ten years since Dawn had introduced Shawn and Diane to Steve and Jill; it had been a Godsend.

Diane had bonded instantly with Jill, and Jill had been excited to have Christopher for a new student in their eighth-grade class at the school. Additionally, Diane was the perfect fit to replace the elementary school counselor and sixth-grade teacher the school had recently lost. The timing had been perfect. Shawn and Diane also found Foundation Worship Center to be their new church home.

On a sunny Monday morning, the teachers were making their way into the school building to start their day.

"Good morning Jill."

"Good morning Diane. You are here early."

"Oh, you know, early bird gets the worm, and all that."

"That is true. Oh, Diane, I know you are getting ready for class, but can I talk to you about something for just a minute?"

"Of course, Jill. What's up?"

"We have some incredible news. We just adopted a little girl."

"What? That's great! What is her name?"

"Her name is Grace, and she'll be starting school here today in the second grade."

"Oh, what a beautiful name! I can't wait to meet her!"

"She is so precious, and so amazing! You will see. We are just blown away by how she shares her heart. She speaks like an adult but with a child-like faith. So smart and so aware."

"I'm sensing you have some concerns?"

"Well, she came from a very unpleasant situation. You can read about that in her file. I was hoping you could you schedule a time to sit down with her and talk. Just see if everything is ok? She puts on a pretty tough front, but I know she is really hurting inside."

"Oh, I would love to Jill. I will make it a priority to figure out a good time that works best for you and Grace. I really can't wait to meet her."

"Thank you, Diane."

"You bet, Jill."

"Oh, and you also have a new student. I almost forgot. His name is Ethan. His Father, David, is bringing him in this morning. Ethan's family just arrived in town and wanted to get Ethan into school right away. Steve and I met with Ethan and his parents on Saturday. Great people! Sorry for the short notice."

"Wow. That is wonderful! The more the merrier! Well, I better get to work."

"Happy Monday!"

†††

Josh had wasted no time in scheduling Shawn for an official interview with the Biogen hiring manager. Though Shawn lacked some of the computer skills that Biogen desired for the new position, he scored high marks on the aptitude and imagination portions of his interview; which was just what Biogen was looking for in new employees working in their artificial limb department. Shawn had quickly excelled in his duties and moved up in the department.

It was just past sunrise, and Shawn sat at his desk in his office at Biogen, working on his computer. He was always the first one into the building and the last one out. There was so much to learn, and it was exciting work.

To Shawn's surprise, his boss, Lieutenant Colonel Austin, was suddenly standing at his desk. "Shawn, can I see you for a moment?"

"Yes, sir."

Shawn followed Lieutenant Colonel Austin down the hall and into his office. Lieutenant Colonel Austin was the Artificial Limb Department Chief at Biogen. They went into Austin's office and closed the door.

"Good morning Shawn. Please, have a seat."

"Thank you, sir."

This can't be good.

"I have been looking at your work for us here over the past few months."

Oh no. I knew it.

"And I have to say —"

Here we go.

"I'm very impressed."

Oh, good.

"When you were first placed here by human resources, I had my doubts about how you were going to contribute to our research. Honestly, it seemed like you had never seen a computer before."

Truer words were never spoken.

"Then, in a matter of days, the lights came on and you have been on fire!"

Oh, good.

"Which is why this next part hurts me so much."

Oh no.

"I have to let you go."

I knew it. Now what am I going to do?

Shawn's gaze dropped to the table between them. "I understand, sir."

"I don't think you do, Shawn."

Shawn looked up and saw his boss smiling. "I'm promoting you."

"Sir?"

"We are starting advanced trials of our latest artificial limb technology on human volunteers, and I would like you to lead the effort."

This is too good to be true!

"Sir, I would be honored!"

"That's great Shawn! It is a highly classified program. Are you ok with leaving your work at the office? You can't speak about anything you are working on; not even to your wife."

"Yes sir. I can handle that."

"Good. Then we will read you into the program this morning. The program is called Nexus Rex."

Chapter 48

Grace and Ethan

†††

Ethan and Grace were both new to the school, and as such, they had to figure out where they fit into the social structure.

Children will be children no matter what school they go to, and Foundation was no exception. In the classroom, under the watchful eyes of their teachers, all the students followed the rules of respect and inclusion. However, once recess was announced and all the children went out to play, a new set of rules went into effect. The new students had to earn their place.

Grace sat alone on the merry-go-round, when the clique of girls wandered by. They were all older by a couple of grades, but that didn't matter; it just made the ridicule easier for them.

"She doesn't have a mother. That's what I heard," said one girl. All the other girls laughed. Then they all joined in a chant. "She doesn't have a mommy. She doesn't have a mommy."

The playground bully and his entourage swiftly converged on the event, joining in the ridicule of the defenseless little girl.

Ethan was sitting across the playground under a shade tree and reading a book. He heard the commotion and looked to see what was going on.

That's the other new kid. Why are they all yelling at her? She's just a little girl.

Ethan ran over to the merry-go-round and stood by Grace.

"Why are you all yelling at her? What's wrong with you?"

The playground bully, seeing his opportunity to solidify his position as the kid in charge, stepped forward. "What is it to you, weirdo?" His entourage of four laughed.

Ethan looked at Grace and reached out to take her hand. "Come on, Grace, let's go."

"I didn't say you could leave," the bully shouted.

Ethan turned back to the boy. He was an eighth grader and obviously larger than any of the other students on the playground. His size advantage had given him the confidence to assume no one would stand up to him. This had proven true for sometime with everyone else at the school. However, Ethan was an unknown quantity; a variable in the bully equation.

Ethan's father had taught him that fighting was bad. But Ethan also knew that what the children were doing to Grace was also bad. It came down to the worse of two evils.

Do I fight or do I let this continue and maybe even get worse?

Ethan felt a gentle tug on his shirtsleeve and looked down to see Grace looking up at him. She whispered, "It's ok. I'm not afraid."

Ethan smiled. "I'm not either."

Grace smiled back. "Fear not. Be strong. God is nigh."

"Hey, wimpy boy! I'm talking to you!"

Ethan looked back at the bully. He gently set his bible down on the merry-go-round next to Grace. The martial arts bookmarker he was using hung out from the page he was reading.

Ethan captured everyone's attention as he set his bible down. All eyes then watched him as he turned around to face the bully; all eyes except the bully's. His eyes were still looking at Ethan's book marker.

Ethan ignored the bully and rolled up his left sleeve.

"Hey punk. You some sort of tough guy?"

Ethan rolled up his right sleeve.

"You want to fight, punk? Let's do this! I'll knock you out right here!"

Ethan's father had taught him that most bullies were cowards inside, which is why they presented themselves the way they did. He taught Ethan that cowards die a thousand times and that heroes die just once.

I will not die every time I come out to this playground, fearing this guy. Though I'll be on the receiving end of some blows today, I'll get my fair share of hits in too. I don't think he wants that. We're going to find out right now.

Ethan slowly took off his glasses and handed them to Grace. Then, for the first time, he looked the bully in the eyes.

"Ok, four eyes. You want some of this? You got it!"

The bully's buddies egged him on. "You go, Richie! Take this punk out! Put him down, Richie!"

Ethan just looked at Richie. They locked eyes. Richie glanced down at the book marker and then back at Ethan.

Ethan could see Richie was thinking. He surmised Richie had just figured out that he had a lot more to lose than to be gained by this encounter. If the new kid knew martial arts, and he lost this fight, his status would forever change. On top of that, it would probably hurt a lot.

Ethan remembered what a friend of his had told him. True freedom is being ready to accept the consequences of your actions. Ethan was prepared to face whatever would come from defending this little girl; whether that meant enduring a beating, being suspended from school on his first day, or facing his father's disappointment. Ethan was free.

Richie was not willing to face the consequences of a loss. He had created a social status for himself and was bound by it. He was afraid of losing it. Richie was not free.

"C'mon boys, this loser isn't worth getting dirty over. Let's leave the two losers to be together."

One of Richie's friends clearly did not get the message and said, "C'mon Richie, I want to see this kid bleed!"

Richie gave the boy a look that said he had better fall in-line or else. The boy bowed his head in submission and followed the group away from the merry-go-round. The girls that had initially teased Grace sensed that something had changed in the playground dynamic and also left the scene.

Grace handed Ethan's glasses back to him. "Thank you."

"Oh, it was nothing."

Grace smiled. "It wasn't nothing."

"My dad taught me that all it takes for evil to prosper is for good men to stand by and do nothing. I want to be a good man someday. I figured this would be a good place to start."

"You are already a good man. You just have to get bigger."

"Ethan looked at Grace. A moment later, they both started laughing."

"Why weren't you afraid, Grace?"

"I guess for the same reason you weren't afraid, Ethan."

"What do you mean, Grace? The martial arts book marker? Oh, that is just something I picked up from the library."

"Martial arts? I don't know what that is. I meant the bible."

Ethan smiled and nodded. "Yes, Grace, I guess that is ultimately why I wasn't afraid."

"The bible tells us we never have to be afraid. The one true God is always with us. We are never alone."

"You are right, Grace. It is true."

Ethan and Grace heard the school bell and knew it was time to return to class.

"Will you be my friend, Ethan? Even if I am only a second grader?"

"Of course, Grace. I can't think of anyone else that I would rather be friends with."

As they walked back into the school, they noticed Ethan's teacher in the window of her classroom. Mrs. Diane was watching them. She had a big smile on her face.

"How long do you think she has been watching?" Grace asked.

"That is a good question," Ethan said. "Maybe the whole time."

Chapter 49

Christopher Crisp

†††

Christopher finished his education and moved towards a career in law enforcement. Having completed his training, Christopher became a sheriff's deputy in their small town. He attended the Foundation Worship Chapel with Shawn and Diane and made many close friends.

One Sunday morning, Christopher sat down next to a beautiful young woman in a light blue dress. Her name was Angella or Angel, as her close friends called her.

Christopher was instantly love-struck! Following the church service, Christopher introduced himself and invited Angel to go out to lunch with him and a group of friends. Angel accepted, and love quickly bloomed.

Angel had a close friend that also attended FWC. Her name was Mary Lou. Mary Lou's husband, Randy, had recently died in the war with El Tigre; their son, just twelve years old, had lost his father. When Mary Lou met Christopher and got to know him, she asked Christopher if he might spend some time with her son. Her son was spending a lot of time in the forest by himself, and she was worried about him. Mary Lou wanted her son to have a powerful father figure in his life.

Christopher gladly agreed to spend time with Mary Lou's son. They explored mountain trails together, camped, hunted, and practiced shooting with different weapons. Deputy Crisp made sure the boy stayed on a righteous path.

As Christopher and Angel grew closer and fell in love, Christopher struggled with how to tell Angel about his past; a past he didn't even know himself. The mandatory background check for a sheriff's deputy required his history. Christopher had claimed immigrant status, and that he was too young to remember where he had been born. If the country of Trinian hadn't relaxed their immigration standards, he wouldn't have even been able to get his job.

One sunny day, as Angel and Christopher were walking a path in the park, Christopher approached the subject of his past. The birds were singing and ducks were relaxing in the lake as the couple strolled down the path that led sleepily through the towering trees and mountain flowers.

"Angel, I'd like to speak to you about something."

"Sure, honey. What is it?"

"Well, we haven't talked a lot about my past — about my childhood."

"That's ok, Chris, I know the man you are now. That is most important to me."

"I know, dear, and I appreciate that. But something happened when I was young, and I think you should know about it."

They sat down on a bench in the shade of a large oak tree. Angel listened intently.

"Ok. So when I was young, Shawn, Diane and I found ourselves here in Trinian. We didn't remember who we were, where we came from, or really what our relationship was to each other."

Angel took on a much more serious expression. "Are you serious?"

"I am very serious. We knew we loved each other. We felt we were a family, but we couldn't be sure."

"None of you can remember anything before that day?"

"No. Nothing. We know we love the one true God. We know we love each other. But not much of anything else."

"Wow. That is strange, isn't it? I mean, what could cause that kind of thing to happen?"

"I know. Trust me, we have talked about it many times. We all felt like we were missing someone. Like we were looking for someone. But that is it. Nothing else."

"Well, wherever you came from, we are better off for having you here. Me especially." Angel pulled Christopher in close and gave him a gentle hug."

"Thank you Angel. I bring it up, because I don't know if we will ever remember. If we do someday remember, we may feel we have something we must do. We may feel like we must go home."

"I understand."

"If that happened, how would you feel about it? I mean, If I had to go home, how would you feel about—?"

"About going with you?"

"Yes."

Angel looked into Christopher's eyes. Your God is already my God. And I know I love you. If that were to happen, then your home would be my home."

A tear ran down Christopher's cheek. "Thank you, honey. You don't know what that means to me."

They leaned into each other and kissed tenderly.

Part 10: Darkness

Chapter 50

Pull Back

†††

Queen Tharice summoned General Grumpy Sanders to the palace to discuss the defense of Parlantis.

General Sanders entered the throne room and waited just inside the majestic doors for the queen, who was sitting on her throne, to acknowledge him and signal for him to enter.

Queen Tharice motioned for General Sanders to approach. He approached the throne and bowed.

"General Sanders, come and sit by me." She pointed to the chair next to her.

"Yes, my queen."

This is weird. Who ever sits on the throne with the queen?

General Sanders walked to the chair and sat down.

"That was an interesting change of command, don't you think?"

"How so, your majesty?"

"Your 90th Battalion replacement. His faith in an unknown God that he says is in the one true God."

"He has a fervent faith."

Where is this going?

"I found it offensive, personally. Had I known of his belief in a non Parlantian God, I would have not approved his promotion."

"I wasn't aware there was a requirement to believe in a particular God?"

"Do you believe in his God?"

Grumpy knew it was a trap. If he said yes, his command would be in jeopardy. Denying his God is what he would do if he said no; if he believed in Christian's one true God. Truth was, he didn't know what he believed. He didn't feel like he had an answer to the queen's question.

"Well, do you?"

"Your majesty, I'm not sure."

"I see." *Good, doubt. I can work with that.*

"You are a married man, aren't you?"

"Yes ma'am. 21 years."

"So then, comfortable."

The queen opened a small jewelry box that lay on a table beside her throne chair. It had a purple stone in the center, with some ancient writing carved into the metal around the stone. She put it on the little finger on her right hand.

Instantly, General Sanders felt a little dizzy.

"As you know, I recently lost my husband, and I need a new husband to fulfill my needs. Plus, Parlantis needs a new king."

Grumpy Sanders became very sleepy. He rubbed his eyes to wake himself up. He looked at the queen. She was different. She wore a long crimson dress with a slit in it, showing her long, toned legs. The queen took on a much more alluring appearance. Her long blonde hair flowed over her ample breasts. The dress fit tightly over her body, clinging to her curves in a most appetizing way. General Sanders couldn't help but hang on her every word, every word coming out of her ruby red lips.

"Why don't you come over here, general?"

General Sanders could hardly think, but the thoughts still flowed through his words said by his spirit.

God of Christian, the one true god, please help me? I do not want to break my covenant with my wife, nor with you; now that I have learned who you are. Please save me?

Instantly, the vision of the queen blurred. Soon, her form returned to that which he knew. She was still attractive, but now he could resist her charms.

Queen Tharice could see General Sanders' resistance, and she knew that only one who was filled with the spirit of the one true God could resist her magic.

"You disappoint me, general."

General Sanders was slowly becoming lucid again.

"I want you to pull back our forces along the Pferd corridor, leading to the dark sea."

General Sanders knew what that would mean.

"But your majesty, doing so would leave the capital vulnerable to attack from the sea if the Golden Fields fell."

"I know what it means, general. I'm not an idiot."

"No, ma'am, I didn't mean to—"

"We need to weed out those rebels–the ones who have been sneaking about the countryside."

"Let's give them a clear prize and see if they take the bait."

"But your highness, I—"

"General Sanders, I gave you an order. If you can't follow my directives, I can find a new general."

"Yes, ma'am."

"Guards!"

Four Parlantis palace guards entered the chamber.

"Escort the general off the palace grounds!"

The four soldiers helped General Sanders down from the throne and out of the chamber. General Sanders wasn't sure what had happened. He could barely walk.

One thing was for sure: he had changed. He now knew the answer to the Queen's question.

Yes, I do believe in Christian's one true God.

Chapter 51

Trustworthy

†††

General Sanders called an emergency meeting with Christian, his number one.

"The queen ordered me to pull back from the Pferd corridor."

"What?"

"I know, but it was a direct order. Either I agreed to it, or I would be relieved of my command."

"Wow. What in the world is going on?"

"I know. I need you to patrol the center of the Pferd corridor for me. This will be extremely risky for you. If there is anything going on there, I won't be able to help you. But I need someone I can trust to be my eyes if something is going on there."

"Yes, sir. I will do it myself."

"There's something else. I met with the queen today and something strange happened."

"What do you mean, strange?"

"She changed right before my eyes, and it affected me. If it hadn't been for—"

"If it hadn't been for what?"

"For God helping me."

There was silence.

"My God? The one true God?"

"Is there another? Yes. I asked him for help and he saved me."

Christian smiled, and Grumpy smiled back.

"Welcome, my brother."

Grumpy pulled out his medallion, but this time, it was under his shirt.

"For the first time in my life, I—"

"I know."

Christian thought long and hard about what he was about to say.

"There's something I have to tell you, General."

"Ok, what?"

"Dragons."

"What?"

"Dragons."

"Ok. What about them? They don't exist. They are myths. Legend."

"There are dragons in the mountains."

"Say again. What?"

"But that's not the big thing."

"Dragons in the mountains is not the big thing?"

"This medallion, our medallions," Christian held up his medallion, "they communicate with dragons."

"The medallions communicate with dragons? Son, suddenly you're worrying me."

"No really. I know it sounds crazy."

Christian told Grumpy about his cave encounter. Grumpy was speechless; well, almost.

"Ok, I'll take your word for it."

"I don't think we should let this news get out. The dragons are on our side. They always have been."

Silence.

"Ok, if it hadn't been for what happened with the queen today, I would have said no way. But something is up."

"Thank you, general. I think the tannin could help us someday, if we ever need them."

Chapter 52

Stones Return

†††

The queen retreated to her basement chamber, one level above the pit. Two dozen stones levitated above the platform that overlooked the pit below. Each of the stones was a different color or shade and each held unique powers.

Queen Tharice grabbed the black stone and walked over to a rocky pit where several cobras hissed at her and stood ready to strike as she approached them. As soon as she closed her hand around the black stone, the cobras relaxed. Queen Tharice reached into the pit. She grabbed a cobra with her free hand, held it to her face, and gave it a kiss. It was as calm as a kitten. She placed it back into the enclosure with its kind.

She returned the black stone to its hovering position, and the cobras went crazy once again. Several cobras were so riled that they leaped from the pit and streamed her way.

She quickly grabbed the red stone. As the cobras reached her position and struck, their fangs passed directly through the queen as if her legs were that of a ghost. Tharice smiled as she left the area and proceeded back to her throne room.

I'll have the servants go down and clean up.

Chapter 53

El Tigre

†††

El Tigre was a vast continent of jungle and desert, mountain and valley in the southern part of the world. It was an ungoverned place, composed of various tribes, each dealing in their own crop of agriculture, drugs, prostitution, and special favors. There was no norm of morality or civilized behavior.

The life expectancy of young men averaged somewhere in the mid twenties. The old men ran the show, while the young men took the risks, fought the battles, and suffered the payback from rival gangs for any miscalculations.

The life expectancy of young women was about the same. I won't describe to you why.

Overall, fathers died early, children served the tribal power-brokers, and mothers mourned their dead family members. The scenery was beautiful, but it was an ugly place.

Ulhorn emerged from a mountain cave entrance that was still securely hidden behind many bushes. It was about five miles from the small village he was planning to visit.

Ulhorn had visited the village for centuries in their time, seeing their families and the faith of many grow tremendously. The last time he had visited there, there were well over one hundred believers in the one true God living in the small village. That was most of the population.

He traveled his normal route over the mountain ridge and to the overlook where he normally stopped to look down upon the village and see the hustle and bustle of the many families in the fishing village preparing for the day. He couldn't wait to see his friends. They were just children the last time he visited, but now would be adults; perhaps with children of their own.

What Ulhorn saw shook him to his core. The thriving village he left, but a short time ago, was no more. There was no movement whatsoever. The same cabins that had existed there the last time he visited were nothing now but rubble, burned to the ground.

Who would do such a thing? What would be the purpose?

There was no way for Ulhorn to calculate how long it had been since his last visit, and certainly no way to know how long since the fishing village had been destroyed.

Oh Lord, have mercy on them, for you showed them the truth and the way. I know this prayer is late, but please have mercy on their souls and bring them to be with you.

Ulhorn knew there was no cause for mourning. He knew those he loved were now in heaven with the one true God.

Soon, I too will be there with them.

As he was praying, a small band of rebels emerged from the forest below and entered the village. They did not appear to be surprised by anything they saw there.

They made their way to what used to be the village center, drop their packs, and sat down. To the last man, they pulled some contents of their packs out, smoked it, and reclined.

Ulhorn watched the men quickly become affected. They all became like dead men on the ground.

What is happening?

Suddenly, there was the sound of approaching horses. Several men rode into the village from the same direction the others had emerged from the forest. A man on a black stallion led them. The men on horseback rode to the position of the others lying on the ground and tried to wake them. None of the men responded. They just moaned as if in a deep sleep.

The man on the black stallion wore all black clothing with silver buckles. He had a red sash around his waist and a long, thin sword with a pearl handle. He also wore a black turban and a black mask.

The commander of the horsemen stopped above the men that lay unconscious upon the ground. "I told them to move it, not use it! They are no good to me if they are using the merchandise. Gather up their packs and kill them. Divide up their belongings amongst yourselves."

The riders followed their commander's orders. The unconscious men never knew what happened.

Ulhorn was in shock. He had seen brutality before, but the callous disregard for life exhibited by these men was pure evil. The men who had been killed had souls, and deserved much more than to be butchered like animals.

Once the deed was done, the men rode off after their commander toward the sea.

Ulhorn made his way down to the fishing village and to the dead and dying. Most of the men were dead when he reached them. However, two, we're coming out of their dreamy state; the immense pain turning their peaceful dreams into a nightmare.

"Ulhorn, is that you?"

Ulhorn kneeled down to hear the man's words.

"Ulhorn, it's me, Benjamin."

Ulhorn recognized the face of the man. He hadn't seen him for many years — ever since he was a boy.

"Benjamin. It is you!"

"It has been so very long, and so much has happened."

"What happened to you, Benjamin? What happened to this place?"

"They came many years ago and destroyed everything. They took us away. I cannot describe the horror of it. Those they did not kill became their slaves."

"Oh, you poor lad. Your parents? Your family?"

"All gone. They turned us into addicts to control us — so we always have to return and we can never get away. I am so happy to be leaving this place. I will be free again, and I will see my family again. Thank you, Ulhorn, for teaching us the truth of the one true God. I can't wait to see him with these eyes — my Redeemer lives!"

And with a smile upon his face, Benjamin left for a much better place.

Ulhorn bowed his head, prayed, and wept.

Ulhorn spent the day digging graves and burying all the men that had died that day, including his friend Benjamin. Exhausted, he returned to the caves and to his time.

Chapter 54

Trajan

†††

Trajan led the men on horseback to the ship waiting at the port for the product.

The mind-dust had had been mixed with middle-mist red from eastern Parlantis and was headed back to Parlantis to meet the growing demand from the city dwellers for the drug. Slowly but surely mind-dust was turning the fighting age men of Parlantis' population into zombies. Soon the warriors of El Tigre would sweep across weakened Parlantis and subjugate it like they had El Tigre.

Trajan had left Heath when the rival family had forcefully taken back the throne from his family. Most of his family had been executed for the insurrection that they had once conducted. Trajan was the lucky to escape, but not really; he had special qualities that none of the rest of his family possessed.

Trajan had learned to survive in the rugged and lawless lands of El Tigre. He had to be merciless in order to survive, but he was already merciless when he arrived in El Tigre. Ten years later, he knew exactly what he wanted and how to get it. First, he would take Parlantis, and then, once his power was consolidated in the south, Trajan would return to Heath and have his revenge. He would reclaim his family's kingdom and hold it forever.

†††

Trajan watched the full moon rise through the mountain fortress window. It was almost midnight as the clouds passed by the full moon in a foreboding and mystical way.

Trajan could see the enormous raven approach. He had received a message the week before that the raven would carry something he needed.

The raven entered the window and landed upon the perch prepared for it. A small pouch was attached to its left leg. Trajan removed the small pouch and opened it. Inside was a small black stone. Trajan smiled.

Perfect.

Trajan attached his return message to the raven's leg. It read, "Dearest Tharice, thank you for the gift. I will put it to good use. Condolences on the loss of your husband. Soon, all the impediments to us being together will be gone, and I will join you on the throne in Parlantis."

The raven launched through the window for its return flight to the palace in Parlantis.

Trajan secured the ebony stone in a locked chest to keep it secure until the next day's test.

†††

Early the next morning, Trajan removed the small stone from the locked chest and went out to the courtyard, where the mama bear and her cubs were caged. Trajan gripped the stone in his clasped fist. He concentrated on the mama bear and ordered it to kill its cubs. Going against every instinct the mama bear had to protect her cubs, she immediately attacked them and ripped them to shreds.

Ok, I guess that's proof enough that this works. Our enemies will not understand what hit them. I will turn nature itself against them, and they shall be destroyed.

Chapter 55

Lions, Tigers, and Bears

†††

Mankind was the glorious apex of the creation, but mankind was not the apex predator. That distinction belonged to the lion kind. Working together in a pride, the lions dominated the landscape of El Tigre.

The lion kind did not look for conflict with mankind. They avoided it at all costs. Any interaction between mankind and the lion kind always ended with losses on both sides.

The lion pride had devoured an enormous meal earlier in the morning and we're relaxing besides the water hole. Instinctively, it was with great surprise that the pride sensed mankind approaching.

A single man approached. He did not conceal himself or disguise his movement. The pride snapped to attention and converged on the man. Preparing for the attack, the alpha male lion gradually gained speed as he closed on the invader. The rest of the pride stood by and watched in deference to their leader.

Just before the alpha lion had reached the point of no return in his assault, the man, all dressed in black, removed the black stone from his pouch. Squeezing the stone tightly within his fist, he commanded the attacking lion to stop.

The lion screeched to a halt, the dirt beneath its feet rising into the air and scattering in the wind. It did so with the look of shock on its face, not knowing why it had broken off its attack. The rest of the lion pride had the same look, instinctively wanting to attack, but they knew they could not defy their alpha.

Having the lion attack was one thing, but having it understand the language was another. Trajan had bet his life on the experiment and still it amazed him it had worked.

Trajan took the experiment to the next level. He had stopped the lions from attacking him, but could he make the lions attack another creature?

Would they attack their alpha? They no longer have a need for him. They have a new alpha now.

Trajan ordered the pride to kill their alpha male. Without hesitation, they surrounded him. He put up a fierce battle but could not handle defending against all the pride at once. Within moments, he succumbed to their attack, and they tore him to pieces.

Trajan commanded the pride to follow him. He turned his back to them and walked back toward his horse and the men that awaited him there. The men on horseback could not believe what they were seeing as they watched Trajan walking ahead of a pride of the lion kind, approaching thirty lions. His men once followed him out of fear, but now they did so out of reverence, seeing him as a god.

The word went out throughout El Tigre that all sightings of lions, tigers and bears were reported through channels to Trajan. Enclosures were erected to contain the vast number of alpha predators that were gathered. Trajan's army would use these creatures to their advantage when they attacked Parlantis.

Trajan was having dinner with one of his commanders, Morticus. Trajan and Morticus had been friends for many years. They were on their second bottle of wine.

Morticus asked Trajan, "Commander, how are you able to control the animals?"

"Do you really wanna know?"

"Yes, I do."

Trajan pulled out the black stone and laid it on the table before them. "It's with this stone."

"Come on, that's impossible."

"Well, let's do an experiment?"

"I'm game."

Trajan picked up the black stone and squeezed it tightly in his right hand.

"Drop your pants."

"Excuse me?"

"Drop your pants."

"I'm not gonna drop my pants."

"I guess it doesn't work on people."

"That's too bad. It could have been useful."

They both had a good laugh.

Trajan suddenly became very serious. He realized he had told his friend the secret of his greatest weapon. Morticus probably didn't believe the stone had power and being drunk, Morticus probably wouldn't remember the conversation; but if he ever did casually tell the story, it could mean disaster. Everyone thought he, Trajan, held the power over the animals. If anyone thought it might be a stone, he might have a hard time keeping control of it.

Trajan waited until Morticus passed out, and then he suffocated him. There were faster ways, but this way would be less contentious. The old man's heart just gave out. Morticus had drunk himself to death. Not a bad way to go. Time for a new commander.

Chapter 56

All the World

†††

All The world.

There was only one thing that was important to them, only one mission; spread the truth of the one true God throughout the known world. It was for this reason that they existed. It was this purpose that gave their life meaning.

After all they had been through, they knew that this work and the value of it were infinitely greater than all the hardship, loss, and loneliness they had endured.

Nomen, Veteris, Donstup, Kissami, Krohn, Mertz, and Ulhorn had walked through the fire and come out the other side. For they were not alone in the fire, there was another.

Those who knew their names thought of them as angels; but they were not angels. They were simply helpers who appeared at the right time to make a difference; a difference that was determined by his-story.

For how will they know if no one tells them? And who will tell them if no one is sent? These were the messengers of his Word. These were the witnesses to the one true God.

For what is the value of an empty jar of clay? If it contains nothing, then its existence had no purpose. If its contents taste bitter and cause sickness and pain, it would have been better for it to have never existed. The jar should be broken and cast out.

What is the jar of clay worth if it contains contents of infinite worth? How beautiful and precious is the site of that jar!

And so it was at the sound of the names of these witnesses; they were beautiful and brought joy. For theirs was the commission to share the love, peace, joy, and salvation of the one true God; to share it with all the world.

Nomen, Veteris, Donstup, Kissami, Krohn, Mertz, and Ulhorn; beautiful jars of clay.

Part II: The Players

Chapter 57

A Mission

†††

The Syth summoned Kristana to her chambers. "I have a mission for you."

"I'm done with the missions." Kristana replied. "I want out."

"I don't think so. You belong to me.

"Nobody owns me. Do you have any doubts that I could just leave and no one here could stop me?"

"That's true, but what about the girls you'd leave behind? Need I remind you what will happen to them if you just disappear?"

"I think I'm getting a little tired of that threat. Your keeping me here indefinitely is a death sentence. Eventually, someone is going to be bigger, stronger, or faster than I am."

"I thought your God protects you? It shouldn't matter if someone is bigger, stronger, or faster than you. Actually, they've all been bigger, stronger, and faster than you, and you're still here. I'm getting a little tired of that complaint."

"What you say is true, however, we are not to tempt the Lord our God. I have done well for you. It is time for you to release me."

"I decide when it is time to release you. That's the end of this discussion."

It was not the end of the discussion, but Kristana knew this was not the time; the Syth was not in the mood.

"The reason I called you here today is to accomplish a mission that is critical to the Hydra. An old friend has requested that we escort a shipment of a flower from eastern Parlantis through the mountains and to the western coast for pickup. You and ten other hydra warriors will leave tonight to meet them."

"What is so special about these flowers that you need ten warriors to escort a shipment?"

"That's none of our business."

"So our business now is to escort flower salesmen?"

"Look, all you need to do is follow your orders. If anybody tries to stop this shipment from getting to the coast, you are to use whatever force is necessary to ensure mission success."

"Whatever force is necessary? We are to kill to protect flowers?"

"Yes. And if these flowers don't get to the coast, you know what will happen, or do you need me to remind you?"

Kristana knew what the Syth was capable of, and she feared for her friends, who were staying behind. "No, I got it."

"Good. Then go prepare. I've put you in charge, so don't let me down."

†††

Because of his new position, Christian no longer needed to go out on patrol. He had people to do that for him. Still, he preferred to keep his finger on the pulse of Parlantis' defense, so he found himself once again leading a patrol along the western coast of Parlantis. He was his own boss, so no one told him he couldn't.

"It's beautiful here this time of year; all the flowers blooming in the sunshine with the ocean as a backdrop."

Red responded, "Yes sir, it surely is."

"You're gonna continue to call me sir, aren't you?"

Red smiled. "It's what we do here, Colonel."

It was a casual ride for most of the day, and they observed nothing out of the ordinary; until suddenly, they did.

"Hey Red, do you see what I see?" Christian pointed to the south-west of their position.

"Yes Sir, I surely do. That looks suspicious, doesn't it?"

"Let's go check it out; quietly."

†††

Kristana and the Hydra escorted the five cartel members and their two wagons of middle-mist red flowers toward the coast and the boat that awaited them there.

The cartel had laboriously dug a tunnel over the course of a year; from the cliffs overlooking the Dark Sea, down five hundred feet to the ocean below. It was quite the undertaking, but worth it to the cartel if they could acquire the flowers.

"How much farther?" Kristana asked?

"About a mile or so," the cartel boss, Slip, replied.

"What's so special about this flower?"

"I'm really not at liberty to tell you."

"Well, maybe I'm not at liberty to get you to where you're going."

Slip thought about it for a moment. Realizing Kristana didn't look like the kind of woman he wanted to mess with, he gave up the requested information — kind of.

"Well, it seems the flower has certain characteristics."

"What characteristics?"

"Certain properties that allow other things to be magnified in intensity, if you know what I mean?"

"I don't know what you mean. That's why I'm asking. And if I don't have to stop asking pretty soon, there may only be four cartel members making it to the boat."

"All right, all right. The flower makes our drug more powerful; more addictive."

"Drug? What drug? What are you talking about?"

"You must be new to Parlantis. This place couldn't survive without our drug. The demand is through the roof. We can barely meet the requirement now, and the demand is growing every day."

Drugs? I can't be involved in the drug trade. It's wrong. It imprisons people until it kills them. I know exactly what that's like. How can I imprison people, hoping to set myself free?

"That's it? No more questions? Good, my boss would probably kill me if he found out I told you anything."

I feel sick. How did I get myself into this situation? And how do I get myself out? If I don't get this drug supplement to its ferry, what will happen to Cindie and the other girls?

"Masks! Riders approaching from the rear! Parlantian Guard!"

Kristana turned to see the hydra warrior posted at the rear of their formation riding towards them at high speed, followed by ten Parlantian Cavalry.

"Slip, continue on with your men. We'll hold them off!"

Kristana turned towards her warriors. "Defensive line! Now!"

The hydra warrior from the rear swiftly rode through Kristana's defensive line and continued on to join his comrades around the wagons.

Christian and his men rode to within one hundred feet of the hydra warriors and stopped when Christian raised his arm to signal a halt.

Christian alone rode slowly toward the Hydra. Taking his cue, Kristana met him halfway between the formations.

Christian greeted Kristana. "Hello. Lovely day for a ride."

"It is a beautiful day, isn't it?"

"What's with the mask? I can't see your face."

"Protecting ourselves from the sun. What's with the beard? I can't see your face."

"What are you all up to out here?"

"It's like you said, just taking a ride."

"Must get hot in all that armor, wearing a mask."

"No. Not really."

"And the wagon?"

"Oh, just some fellow travelers we happened upon. We talked for a few minutes. Now they are on their way."

"I see." *This gal is loads of fun.* "Well, we've had a problem with drug smugglers as of late. You haven't seen any around, have you?"

"Nope. Hate the stuff."

"Ok, good. You have a nice day. We are just going to ride up and check on your new friends; see if they need anything. If you all wouldn't mind moving to the side."

"We kind of like it where we are."

"I see. What if I said to move aside on the authority of the Queen of Parlantis? What would you say?"

"I would say that we are new to Parlantis — just passing through — and not subject to your queen."

"In the law's name, I must demand you move aside."

"In the name of freedom, I must not comply."

Everyone was getting anxious. Hands were slowly gripping swords, and both sides were summing up their potential opponents.

Kristana thought. *This is getting dangerously close to that "whatever it takes moment."* Right before things got nasty, Kristana said, "How about this? Instead of everything getting uncomfortable, why don't we have a little duel?"

Christian thought about it for a moment. He looked at Red; Red subtly shook his head no.

"Sounds like a lot of fun. Let's do it."

Both Christian and Kristana rode back to their respective lines.

Christian looked at Red. "Ok. Give it to me."

"What are you doing, Colonel?"

"I'm just taking a minor break. That's all. You guys can dismount and have some lunch."

"What about your injuries? You're only half recovered!"

"Oh, I'm fine! Besides, it isn't like I'm fighting a battle-hardened warrior. It's just a girl, and she looks cute."

"What's the upside to having a dual?"

"The upside is we make some new friends."

Red took another look at the armor the "girl's" entourage was wearing. *Just a girl, he says.*

"How do you know she's cute? You can't even see her face?"

"Well, she sounds cute."

"Look, Colonel, don't underestimate her. There's more to a cactus than just the flower. She suggested the duel. There are only two reasons I can think of why she would do that. The first is she has summed you up and thinks she can take you."

"Red. C'mon. Really?"

"The second is–"

Christian interrupted him. "She thinks I'm cute."

Red frowned. "I don't know how that could be."

Christian laughed as he left his horse with Red, dismounted, gathered his sword, and turned back toward the ladies.

Kristana did likewise, and they met each other in the middle.

Christian said, "No one brings a knife to a sword fight."

"I never said it was gonna be a sword fight."

"So a knife fight then — up close and personal. I like that idea."

Christian looked back at Red and give him a small smile.

Christian replaced his sword with his knife. "Ok, anything else I'm missing?"

"I think that's it, other than maybe some skill deficit."

"Oh, nice one." *I think in another life, I could have been buddies with this one.*

A voice from the Hydra's side yelled, "Begin!"

Red subtlety shook his head. *That is not a good sign. Seems they are all too familiar with this process.*

Kristana lowered her stance. "Shall we?"

"Surely," Christian replied.

The two paced slowly in a circle, eyes locked.

Christian's smile slowly faded as he observed the moves that Kristana was making as she expertly varied her stance, alternated her knife hand,

and maneuvered her body in such a way that all of Christian's would be attack moves were negated before he even started them. *Seems like maybe she's done this before.*

"Are you sure you want to do this?" Tristana asked.

"Oh yeah. I'm just a little unsure of what exactly we are doing."

"We're dueling."

"Well, yeah, but what are the terms? We are using knives, so are we fighting to the death here or what?"

"Of course. To the death. What else?"

Christian stopped and stood upright. "Really?"

Kristana paused, letting Christian think about it for a moment.

"No, of course not! I don't even know you. Why would I want to kill you?"

"Well, I'm not sure."

"No. No. No. Hey, I have an idea. Let's toss the knives and just go hand-to-hand. We will keep it friendly."

"That sounds great. I would never hurt you on purpose, but I can't trust my reflexes. You know?"

"I know. Trust me, I know."

Red shook his head from a distance. *The young lad stepped in it, and he still has no idea.*

"Being a gentleman, I have to ask—"

"Oh, you're a gentleman?"

"Well, of course."

"Ok."

"So, you being a girl and all, should I hit you in this dual?"

"For sure! I'm not making any special dispensation for you being a man."

All the girls on the Hydra side chuckled at that.

"Ha, ok." *I'm getting a little annoyed now.*

"Are you ready?"

"No rules then, right?"

"No rules."

As Kristana said the words, she faked a punch to Christian. He expertly dodged it, but he wasn't ready for the front snap kick that followed. His head snapped back. Christian took a step back and shook it off, but he didn't see the roundhouse kick that quickly followed, snapping his head to the left.

Christian blindly threw a punch with his right hand in an attempt to use offense as defense. It went well over Kristana's right shoulder. Kristana took advantage of Christian's open right ribcage and threw a succession of punches into his right side, not knowing of his recent injury. Christian walked right into them.

Christian took a knee, wincing in pain. Red grimaced. The hydra warriors cheered. The guardsmen moaned. And Kristana smiled. Then she stopped smiling.

Something isn't right. That shouldn't have hurt him so badly.

"Ok. So that's the way it's going to be?"

"I'm sorry. I thought we agreed—"

"No. We're good." Christian painfully stood and shook it off. "Again then?"

Kristana lowered into her fighting stance. Christian did the same.

This time, Christian made the first move. Lunging forward and throwing a punch with his right hand, he baited Kristana.

Kristana took the bait. Spinning in a roundhouse, jumping kick, Kristana spun in a circle expecting to land a blow on Christian as he overextended. But Christian did not overextend. Once Kristana had begun her spin, Christian pulled his punch. As Kristana's leg came around, Christian grabbed it with both hands. Kristana, still being airborne, had no control.

Kristana was completely off balance; Christian twisted her leg and threw her to the ground. He immediately fell on her with his hands controlling both of her arms.

Kristana writhed in pain underneath Christian, having had all the air knocked out of her lungs. When she could once again breathe, Christian had her pinned.

Christian and Kristana were face-to-face, staring into each other's eyes. Just then, something happened. The world stopped turning.

"Good thing I don't have a knife, or it might be all over for you."

"Is that what your instincts are telling you to do right now?"

Hurting her was the farthest thing from Christian's mind. He could barely think at all.

"I think it's time for the mask to come off."

Kristana didn't object.

Christian gently pulled down her mask. She wasn't cute. She was drop-dead gorgeous.

"Now I know why you are wearing a mask."

"Why?" she whispered.

"Because the flowers would lose their beauty."

That is when she saw it; the medallion hanging from Christian's neck. She stared at it in surprise.

Christian noticed Kristana's gaze drop. He looked down and saw his medallion.

Kristana slowly reached up and pulled her medallion out from under her tunic. They were identical.

A sudden flood of awareness overcame them as they realized they were family. More than that, they didn't know.

Christian raised his medallion up next to Kristana's. They stared at the medallions in disbelief.

"Coincidence, we meet like this?" Christian asked.

Both of their eyes focused on their hands holding the medallions and the identical leather bands there.

"I don't think so. There is no such thing as a coincidence."

"I think we are on the same team."

"I think you're right."

"I feel like I know you, but—"

"But you can't recall from where?"

"Do I take your breath away, like you do me?"

"Yes. You're very heavy!"

Christian immediately stood and pulled Kristana to her feet.

"Are you ok?" Christian asked.

"Oh, sure, I'm fine. You? You looked like you had a previous injury."

"Oh, that? Yeah, I can barely feel it. It's fine."

"Cause that is why I let you drop me like you did; I felt sorry for you."

"Oh, really? That's what happened? Ok."

"Hate to interrupt, Colonel, but just a reminder — the wagon."

"Right, the wagon!"

Kristani grabbed Christian's arm. "You can't! They are holding my friends captive, and I was told they would kill them if I didn't get that wagon to the coast."

"You did your part. The wagon is at the coast. You aren't responsible for it after that."

Christian returned to his horse. He winced as he pulled himself up and into the saddle.

"That would be the other part of the cactus, sir," Red said with a smile.

"True. But the needles are worth the life-sustaining waters within."

Red rolled his eyes.

Kristana mounted her steed and directed the hydra warriors to stand down.

Together, they all rode to catch up with the wagon, but it was too late. As they stood high upon the cliffs overlooking the sea, they could see that the boat, far below, was loaded with its precious cargo and was departing.

"Torch, do you think you can make that shot?"

The young private replied, "Yes Colonel, might take two attempts from this distance, but I have elevation on my side."

"All right then, light 'em up!"

Torch dismounted, grabbed his bow, and with the help of a fellow guardsman, he lit an arrow on fire. Quickly making his corrections for wind and elevation, he let the arrow fly. Everyone watched as the arrow rose and then descended to find its mark. It was a direct hit!

It didn't take long before the boat went up in flames.

"Well done Torch!"

"Thank you, sir!"

Christian turned to Kristana. "Let's go figure out how to rescue your friends."

†††

Flash!

The tunnels have stolen their memories.

Flash! Flash!

But the feelings remain. Love crosses all dimensions.

Chapter 58

Rescue

†††

It seemed like a lifetime ago. Growing up in Heath, they had enjoyed the best of everything. They were royalty, after all. A future king or queen depending on how it all worked out, but they were too young to worry about that. They had their whole lives ahead of them and not a care in the world.

Sure, there were some rumors of troubles with rebels claiming to be rightful heirs of the throne, but their father, Nod, had stayed ahead of any viable challenge that surfaced in the kingdom.

One day that all ended, suddenly, without warning. While they were out riding, the castle came under attack. A traitor working with the rebels opened the castle gate. Their guardian, Mordock, whisked them away from the fray and safely transported them to the coast, where they fled to Omentia. Mordock did not survive the trip. He died of a mysterious illness on the way.

They were all alone in a strange land. They changed their names to disguise their identities. Cindy became Syth, and Tray became Trajan.

Fortunately for them, a mysterious woman named Thalia took them in. She brought them to monthly bonfires in the forest, where they met other unfortunate souls like themselves. They became family and soon their family found purpose.

As they grew older, that purpose took on shape, and that shape became a plan. Ten years later, that plan was nearing completion. The

Syth's brother, Trajan, was building an army in El Tigre; the Syth had arrived in Parlantis with her contingent of warriors known as the Hydra; and finally, Thalia had become queen of Parlantis and would soon usher in a new era of royalty there with their help. Once power was consolidated in Parlantis, an army would return to Heath and take back what was stolen from them.

†††

Kristana returned with her contingent to the hydra encampment. As they rode in few of the hydra warriors were visible. The Syth was waiting for her.

"How did it go?"

"Mission accomplished."

"Did you run into any trouble?"

"Nope. Where is everyone?"

"They're guarding the prisoners. Did you run into any Parlantian Guard on the way?"

"I told you, we didn't have any trouble. You can let the girls go now."

"That's not what I heard. I heard you stopped with the Parlantian Guard for a significant amount of time."

"That had nothing to do with the mission. There wasn't a problem. The product was loaded on the boat, and it set sail for its destination."

"But it didn't get very far, did it?"

"That had nothing to do with me. I got the product to the boat as instructed."

"Why did you stop and talk to the guard for so long?"

"I was buying time for the wagon to get to the boat, and it worked!"

"But the boat didn't get very far, did it?"

"Again, that had nothing to do with me. I can't be held responsible for that."

"Come inside."

Kristana followed the Syth into her bunker. When she got inside, she saw one of the hydra warriors was holding a knife to Cindie's throat.

"Hey, let her go! I did what you asked. I kept my end of the deal!"

"That's not the way I see it. You knew the mission was to get the product on the boat and safely away. You failed, and for that, there must be consequences!"

"Now tell me who you were talking to in the Parlantian Guard. Tell me or you will force my hand!"

"It was nobody. Just some guy in charge of a small patrol."

The Syth looked at her new second-in-command.

"Guard, execute the other girls! Start with Max."

"Yes, ma'am!"

"No!" Kristana yelled. "No, I did what you told me to!"

Christiana went to stop the guard from leaving.

"Let her go, or else you force my hand!"

Kristana stopped. She could see tears running down Cindie's face.

"It will be ok, Cindie. Don't fear. Have faith. God is nigh."

The Syth scoffed, "Your God can't get you out of this problem?"

Just then, Christian walked in the door, dressed like a normal working man.

"You should really have a guard at the door."

"Who are you?" The Syth asked as she reached for her sword.

"Me? Oh, I'm nobody. I was just passing by and I heard yelling. Then I heard something about a problem. I kind of see myself as a problem solver and thought I'd drop in and see what I could do." He smiled. "So, is there anything I can do?"

"What's going on here? Guards!"

"Oh, I'm afraid the guards have left. I didn't see anybody else out there when I came in. Now that I think about it, there were a bunch of warrior-looking types, but they were riding away as quickly as possible. Something about the Parlantian Guard. And there's a bunch of other gals walking around celebrating being free. It's a party out there."

The Syth was furious! "Enough of this. Kill the girl."

"Ok, now wait. Let's not do anything rash. Let's just talk about it for a bit."

"I'm done talking. It's time for action. Kill the girl!"

Christian was still standing in the bunker's doorway. All it took was a flick of his finger and Torch released the arrow. It traveled approximately seventy-five yards before entering the window of the Syth's bunker. It traveled another ten feet before it entered the guard's head and severed any communication with his hand holding the knife. He dropped to the ground like he had never existed, his knife clanging on the rock floor.

"Sorry about that. That was a little rude, but you forced my hand. Actually, it wasn't my hand. It was my archer's hand. He's very good, as you can see. If I were you, I'd be very careful about your next move."

The Syth looked at Kristana. "You know the code. No surrender, no retreat."

"Is that why so many stand with you right now? Where are the faithful Hydra members?"

"Cut off one head and the rest will grow more powerful."

The Syth's eyes noticed the medallion hanging from Kristana's neck. She looked at Christian and saw he, too, had a medallion. "I should have known."

"Should have known what?"

"I should have seen who you are!" The Syth grabbed her sword and lunged forward toward Christian. She didn't make it halfway there before two more arrows came through the window, both direct hits. She fell to Christian's feet.

As she breathed her last, Christian said, "He's that good."

Note to self — give Torch a raise.

Kristana and Cindy were hugging before the Syth hit the floor.

When they were done, Cindy looked at Christian, gave him the once over, and said, "Ou La La, where did you pick this guy up?"

Kristana said, "Oh, he's just a guy I know."

"Anymore like that where you found him?"

"Maybe."

I don't think so. I think he's one-of-a-kind.

"Ladies please, I'm right here."

Chapter 59

Jealousy

†††

Christian and his men rode into the city of Pferd with Kristana and her warriors to ensure everyone received them as guests and not as a threat.

"After we get your warriors settled, you should have dinner with my family."

"Slow down there, soldier boy, meeting the family? That's a little fast, don't you think?"

"Ha, ha. My father is in command of the Parlantian Guard. If you and your friends want to join the Parlantian Guard, there is no better person to ask. If he agrees to it, it's done."

"So I'm asking for his blessing, but not for us?"

"Not yet." Christian smiled and winked. "I'll let you know when it's time."

†††

Christian told Kristana how to find General Sanders' residence. He was waiting outside for her that evening when she rode up on horseback.

He had seen nothing like it before. Kristana rode in wearing the most beautiful red dress. It was sleeveless, her shoulders were bare, and she wore a gold necklace with the medallion. When she dismounted and approached him, she completely captivated him. He stood speechless.

"What's wrong? Am I late?"

"Um, no. Um."

She is the perfect mix of gorgeous and wild. And the medallion. Perfect.

"Hey! Soldier boy. Snap out of it!"

"I'm sorry, Kristana. You're just, beautiful."

Kristana smiled. "Well, thank you, Colonel Sanders. You're rather dashing yourself."

Christian gave her his arm and escorted her into their home. Before they went any further, Kristana stopped him.

"Hey, I've never been in this situation before. Will you try to help me through it?"

"You'll be fine. Just be yourself."

"Ok."

They rounded the corner of the doorway and entered the den where everyone was having a drink and visiting before dinner.

General Sanders walked up and met them as they entered. Christian introduced Kristana.

"Dad, this is Kristana. Kristana, General Sanders."

Grumpy extended his hand. "So, this is the young lady that knocked my son on his rear end."

Kristana gently shook Grumpy's hand. "Oh, I think maybe he just fell."

"Well, now I can see why that just might be true."

Christen joined them. "Hi Kristana. I'm Christian's mom. Let me rescue you from these two." She took Kristana's hand from Grumpy and led her away. Everyone smiled as she did.

"Well, son, now you have your hands full."

"Don't I know it?"

"Let's have a drink."

Grumpy led Christian over to the bar. "Whiskey?"

"Yes, please. Two fingers."

"Don't blame you. I'll join you."

"Dad. Did you notice the medallion?"

"Notice. Ah, yea."

"She's one of us."

Grumpy gave Christian his drink and held up his glass. "To one of us."

Christian touched his whiskey glass to his father's glass. "To one of us."

"So, she wants to join the guard?"

"Yes, general, she and her fellow warriors."

"How do you see that working?"

"Well, at first I was thinking of embedding them with our soldiers. But then I got to thinking that as a group, they are probably a lot more inconspicuous than we are, and in small groups, they might more effectively uncover illicit operations being conducted in the Pferd corridor."

"Makes sense. Are you sure they're really up to the task?"

"Trust me, father, I know we joked that I had taken a fall for her, but it was touch and go. If she hadn't underestimated me the third time —"

"Whoa, whoa, whoa. Come back, say again? Did you say the third time?"

"Ah, yeah. Didn't I tell you that?"

"No. You did not."

"Well, it's true. She has some skills."

"I look forward to seeing them sometime. Perhaps the men might profit from some additional training sessions?"

"That's a great idea. I'll ask Kristana if she wouldn't mind."

"Mention that her general requested it."

"Her general? Does that mean?"

Grumpy lifted his glass. "That's what it means."

"Thank you, General."

"You're welcome, Son."

†††

Christian was visiting with Kristana — Grumpy with Christen — when Maria entered the room. Christen saw her first. "Oh, oh."

"Oh, oh? What's, Oh oh?" Grumpy turned to see Maria. "Oh, oh."

Maria was decked out. She looked like she was dressed to go to the Parlantis Officer's Ball; black, low cut, short skirt dress and jewelry to boot.

"General, this could get ugly if not managed properly."

"I love it when you call me, general."

"Not now, honey. Focus. Let's get in there."

"Right. On it."

Everyone converged on an unsuspecting Christian who had his back turned to the developing storm.

"Maria entered like a hurricane. "Hi, I'm Maria." She made eye contact with Kristana as she gently brushed up against Christian and let Kristana know, as only women can, exactly where she stood without saying a thing. *He's mine. Back off.*

"Hi. I'm Kristana."

Kristana smiled back at Maria and then raised her eyebrows ever so slightly as she looked at Christian.

Christian suddenly had the look like he had walked into quicksand. He looked at Maria, then Kristana, and then Maria again.

Fortunately, at that moment, the cavalry arrived. To Christian's delight, Christen and Grumpy jumped in.

"Who is ready for some dinner?"

Christian responded immediately. "Excellent idea, Mom. I'm starving!"

Christen led Kristana toward the dining room.

Grumpy took Maria by the arm. "C'mon, honey, let's go get you some ice water."

Grumpy gave Christian a look as if to say, "You are in neck deep. Good luck!"

Christian just stood there staring at a war picture on the wall of two armies, duking it out.

Oh, man. Here we go.

†††

Everyone dished up their plates and Grumpy asked, "May I say a prayer of thanks?"

Maria looked at her dad like he had just lost his mind.

When Christen said, "Yes, dear, thank you," and bowed her head, Maria looked at her mom like she had just lost her mind. *Who are they and what happened to my parents?*

"Thank you to the one true God for this food and this company around the table. Please bless us and help us serve only you. Amen."

Everyone except Maria repeated, "Amen."

After a moment, Christen said, "So Kristana, tell us about yourself."

"Honestly, I wouldn't know where to begin."

"How about the beginning? Where are you from? Do you have any family?"

Kristana was silent, wondering how to answer. "I'm sorry. I've never talked about this before."

"Oh dear, I'm sorry. I didn't mean to be nosey. There's no need to talk about it."

"No, it's ok. I probably need to get this out. It has been so long since I've allowed myself to think about it."

Maria sensed vulnerability, and she liked it.

"I don't remember who or where my family is. When I was a child, I was taken. My first memories are of waking up in a cage. Since that day, the only family that I've had are the other girls."

"Oh Kristana, I'm so sorry for asking. I didn't know."

Maria was seething inside at the empathy around the table for Kristana. She saw the way Christian was looking at her with the puppy dog eyes. She couldn't resist.

"A cage? What, were you some sort of sex slave?"

"Maria! Enough!" Grumpy exclaimed, getting everyone's attention.

Christen put her hand on Grumpy's and he settled down.

Christian said, "Please, Kristana, continue. If you want to."

Kristana looked at Christian and then at Maria. “No, we weren’t sex slaves, but we were slaves. They taught us to fight and to kill. If we didn’t, they said they would kill us.”

Christen reached across the table and put her hand on Kristana’s. “Honey, I am so sorry.”

Maria looked at Kristana. “You don’t look like much of a killer to me.”

Kristana fired back, “You would be surprised.”

Grumpy jumped in again. “Ladies. Please. Enough.”

Christian asked, “How long?”

Kristana looked into his eyes.

“How long were you in that situation?”

“Best guess, about five years.”

Christian, Christen, and Grumpy all exchanged glances.

Kristana asked, “What?”

Christian looked at Kristana. “I showed up here five years ago with no memory of who I was or where I came from.”

“What? Are you serious?”

Grumpy answered that question. “It’s true. All he knew was that he was looking for someone. That he had made a promised he would bring someone home.”

A tear formed in Kristana’s eyes. “Excuse me, may I use your powder room?”

Christen said, “Of course, dear. It is right down the hall on the left.”

Kristana excused herself and went down the hall.

Christian gave Maria the look and excused himself.

Maria said, “What?”

Grumpy said, “Maria, it might be best if you retire for the night.”

“But–”

“Goodnight.”

“Goodnight.” Maria reluctantly went to her room.

Grumpy looked at Christian. “I think you should take it from here.”

Christen added, “Please ask Kristana to stay with us for as long as she wants. The guest bedroom is hers.”

"Thanks Mom. Appreciate that."

Kristana gathered herself and returned to the dining room. Christian was waiting for her.

"Where did everyone go?"

"Oh, they just thought a little relaxing time would be good for everyone. Let's go out on the deck."

They walked out onto the deck at the back of the house where they could watch the orange and red sky as the sun set over the mountains in the east.

"It's so beautiful."

"I know. Whenever I have the chance, I come out here and watch the sunset."

"I'm sorry Christian, I haven't really done anything like this before. I did not intend to ruin dinner. What happened is making me feel sick."

"No, no, no. You did nothing wrong. Sometimes it's just difficult to sort through life. Sometimes personalities and agendas and emotions don't help with that. Don't beat yourself up. It's ok to feel. Being vulnerable is perfectly fine. It's ok to let other people in. That's what family is."

Kristana started to tear up. Christian slowly moved in close. "Come here."

Kristana moved in the rest of the distance between them. Slowly, gently, their lips met, and they kissed.

"We want you to stay with us as long as you like."

"Maria won't have a problem with that?"

"She will, but I think you can take her if it comes to that."

They both smiled.

"Mom wants you to stay. So does Grumpy."

"And you?"

"Yes. I do too."

They stared into each other's eyes.

"Well, I guess I'll stay then."

"Good."

Another gentle kiss.

“I’ll show you to your room.”

Kristana followed Christian inside and to the spare bedroom.

“Thank you for coming over tonight and staying with us. You’re important to me.”

“Thank you and your family for being so warm to me. Even Maria. She just knows what she wants and feels threatened. I can’t blame her for that.”

“I’ve never given Maria a reason to expect we were a thing. That has always been a one-sided deal. Truly.”

“The heart sees what it sees.”

“Yes Kristana. It does.”

“Goodnight Christian.”

“Goodnight Kristana.”

†††

Bright and early the next morning, Christian was taking a shower. He was singing, because it was spring; the sun was out, and he was in love.

Maria knocked on his door and entered. She was only wearing a bathrobe. Upon hearing him in the shower, she looked around. She had done it secretly many times before, so it wasn’t a big deal; at least not to her.

Maria enjoyed looking at Christian’s things. She picked up the leather band and looked at it closely. *What an odd little ring.* She had asked Christian about it before, but he never had an answer for why he wore it.

While she was looking at the ring, there was a knock at the door and Tristana walked in. Maria slid the ring on her finger.

“I’m sorry. I was coming to see Christian.”

“He’s in the shower.”

“Tristana noticed the leather ring was on Maria’s finger.”

Maria smiled. “I told you, he’s mine.”

“Tristana turned around and left.”

Just then, the door to the bathroom opened.

Oh no, he's done.

Maria quickly put the ring behind her back.

Christian walked out of the bathroom with just a towel on. "Maria, what's up?"

"I was just coming to tell you breakfast was ready."

"Ok, thanks. I'll be right down."

Maria dropped the ring behind her back onto the table where she had found it and left the room.

I win.

Christian got dressed and went down for breakfast.

"Good morning, Mom."

"Good morning, Christian."

"Have you seen Kristana yet?"

"Yeah, actually, she stormed out of here about five minutes ago. She seemed very upset. I thought maybe you guys had words."

"No. I hadn't even seen her yet. I wonder what that was all about?"

Chapter 60

Chambers

†††

The beast summoned her.

The queen had heard from her sister that the girl had been liberated from the control of the Syth and was now in Pferd. This was a problem and somewhat of a delicate situation for several reasons.

Her general in charge of security of the country, General Sanders, had taken a liking to the girl and this would make it more difficult for the girl to have, shall we say, an accident?

Additionally, the Syth had been killed in the girl's liberation by the Parlantian Guard, and once Trajan heard the news, he would surely rush in and get his revenge. His reaction would thus need to be controlled to not unravel the plan that they had all so carefully set in motion.

There were many moving parts over multiple continents that needed to come together in just the right order and at just the right moment for the operation to be successful.

The queen descended to her underground chamber for her meeting with the dragon. As she descended, the flames from the pit rose high into the cavern, setting the air and everything around it on fire. The queen's garments incinerated instantly and her body glowed a crimson red.

The beast rose to the second, third, then fourth level of the voluminous cavern. It soared as it threw flames in every direction throughout the enclosure. Everything was ablaze!

Tharice froze. She knew now was not a time for her to speak, for the beast was angry.

"Why does she still live? We must cut off her offspring! Kill her!"

The fiery red figure amidst the flames acknowledged the beast's orders. "Yes, Master."

"I have secured control over El Tigre through Trajan. Prepare the way for him in Parlantis. When we control all, we will march on Heath."

"Yes, Master."

"And who is this Christian? Where did he come from? Isn't he the one responsible for the death of the Syth?"

The voice thundered through the cavern. Tharice did not know how to answer that question. The beast had the power to bring her back to life again or to bring her to the pit for eternity. How could she admit what the beast already knew — that she allowed this Christian to be in the position he was in — the position to execute the Syth?

The fiery figure squirmed. "Master, how was I to know?"

"How were you to know who he was? How were you to know what he would do? Did you know he believed in the one true God?"

"I had just found out."

"Yes, you knew."

Though she was already on fire, the intensity of the fire suddenly increased, and she felt intense pain, like the pain she had first felt when she walked into the fire of the altar upon the pyramid.

"Master, I'm sorry."

"Yes, you are sorry, because you knew what he believed and who protected him; and you did nothing about it!"

The fiery figure fell to its knees, writhing in excruciating pain. "Master, no!"

"I will teach you what service to me means."

The figure fell to the ground and curled up into a fetal position as it screamed in torment.

"I should bring you to the pit right now. I should show you what it means to disappoint me."

"Master, have mercy!"

"I'm afraid you have me confused with another master. Mercy is not in my repertoire, and mercy is no longer possible in your future. You are mine now, and I will do with you as I please. Consider this a preview of coming attractions."

"I'm sorry, master!"

"You are sorry, but I don't care. All I know is that you have failed me. I will make you sorrier!"

"Please make it stop?"

"I will make it stop for now, only because I need you to serve me! But you must do what I tell you to do and not fail me again!"

"I will, Master. I will."

"Know that I can make this worse and know that I will."

The dragon took away the pain from its servant, and slowly the fiery figure rose to stand before the great, crimson dragon.

"Are you ready to serve?"

"Yes, Master."

"Kill the girl!"

Part 12: Somewhere in Time

Chapter 61

Seeds

†††

Diane accepted a position to teach at the college in Aanot. She had loved her teaching job at the Foundation Elementary School and would cherish those memories forever. Moving to the college was an opportunity to follow the students she had at the lower school and continue to nurture and encourage them in a higher phase of their education.

Diane taught both Ethan and Grace Ethics as they passed through the college as freshman. Three years later, Ethan went off to join the Trinian Guard as an intel officer, and Grace, following a brief sabbatical serving overseas at a mission in Patagonia, returned to Aanot College as a professor.

Jason, the young man that Christopher had mentored in the summers after Jason's father had died in the war, ended up returning after his service in the Trinian Guard and became a history professor at Aanot College. He and Grace became close friends.

Diane loved men in uniform and so she took a special liking to Professor Jason Ramhart. She thought of him as another son. They ran into each other in the hall one morning at the college.

"Good morning, Professor Ramhart."

"Good morning, Diane. Do you have any intel for me today?"

"I do." She spoke in a hushed voice. "Only one bandit spotted. Richard Crandall has been sneaking in and watching your classes. I think he is up to no good. You better keep your body armor on."

"Thanks for checking my six, Diane."

"You got it." She returned to reality. "Do you ever miss being in the guard?"

"Sure do. The comradery, the action, and the close friendships. I miss it a lot!"

"Well, we're glad you're here with us teaching."

"Now, just a boring old college professor."

"You're not old and certainly not boring."

"Well, thanks, Diane. I appreciate that. Sometimes when you have a normal, quiet life, you wonder if you really did all that crazy stuff back in the day."

"I would ask you to tell me about all the things you did, but I'm sure you would just say—"

"I could tell you, but I'd have to kill you."

"Nice."

They both laughed.

"What's up?" Grace asked as she joined them.

"Just reliving our military days."

"Oh, Diane, I didn't know you were in the guard."

"I wasn't."

"Ok. I'm a little confused."

"We were just joking around."

"Ah. Gotchya."

"Hey Grace. Can I walk you to class?"

"Thanks Jason. I was hoping you would."

"Later Diane," Jason said as he and Grace went to teach their respective classes.

"See you guys later." Diane went into the college office to get to work.

None of them saw Professor Randall and a young brunette student following the professors.

†††

Across town, Shawn had a meeting with his new boss at Biogen. Shawn knocked on the door.

"Come in. A man stood up from his desk and walked to the door to meet Shawn. Hi, my name is Joe. You must be Shawn."

"Yes, sir. I'm very glad to meet you."

"Likewise Sean. I've heard nothing but good about you."

"Thank you, sir."

"I try to meet all the new hires before they start work to give them the ten thousand foot picture of what we're doing here. You'll be inundated with the day-to-day workings of the lab, but I want you to truly understand why we are doing what we're doing here, and all the good being accomplished through our work."

"I appreciate that, Joe."

"We'll be working side-by-side in the lab, and you may find that often I'm working very late some nights. That does not mean I expect you to stay. I'm just a little obsessed with some of this work and sometimes I work through the night to reach my goals."

"Got it, Joe."

"Now, why are we doing what we're doing? Contrary to what some may believe, we are not building super-soldiers. What we are trying to do is make our soldiers super once again, after they return from war with injuries and amputations. Of course you know this from your work on the Nexus Rex Project."

"That's a very honorable mission, Joe, which is the main reason that I wanted to further my previous work with the Nexus Rex project with your project."

"Excellent! We'll be working on an AI to help optimize the movement of the artificial limbs."

"AI?"

"Oh, sorry, artificial intelligence."

"What exactly is that, Joe?"

"Well, we are not sure yet, Shawn."

"I see."

Shawn noticed a picture on Joe's desk.

"That's my brother and I with our dad, George."

"He looks familiar to me for some reason. Maybe I saw him around the building."

"No, I am sorry to say you didn't. He died in a car crash some time back. I lost my mom, Rose, when I was born."

"I am very sorry, Joe."

"Thank you, Shawn. Yeah, it was tough, but it happens to all of us eventually, right?"

"True."

"Anyway, my father was passionate about creating an AI. He thought it could change the world for the better. I guess he passed that passion down to me."

"Passion is good, sir. It's how we get stuff done."

"On target, Shawn!"

"I heard I could also work on another project of special interest to me — common learning?"

"Yes. Thanks for bringing that up. Lt. Colonel Austin mentioned it to me. Cleared hot, Shawn. We are happy you have so many interests and areas of expertise."

"Oh, that's great! Thank you, sir!"

"Don't thank me for that one, Shawn. Thank Lt. Colonel Austin. He was so impressed with your ideas about common learning that he convinced me to let him work with you on that project. It can get more funding if we have a military sponsor. So, you will get to continue to work with the Colonel in that capacity."

"That is great! He's a great guy!"

"Yes, he is. And his wife is a real sweetie, too."

Chapter 62

Colonel Austin

†††

It was Friday evening and everyone went out to the Officer's Club for a drink or two. Lieutenant Colonel Steve Austin was no exception. It was a long week, and he was tired.

A couple of drinks later, Steve was feeling better. Music, alcohol, and a very attractive young woman sitting down next to him had a significant impact on Steve's attitude.

"Hi. My name is Rachel."

"Hi Rachel. My name is Steve."

"Hi Steve. Buy me a drink?"

"Sure. What the heck."

I probably shouldn't, but it's just a drink.

Two drinks later. "C'mon Steve, let's get you out of here."

"Ok."

Two other guys at the bar helped Rachel walk Steve out to an SUV waiting outside the club.

"This isn't my car."

"Steve, you can't drive. I'll get you home."

"Thank you Rachel. That is so sweet."

Ten minutes later, Steve felt like he was dreaming. He had obviously been drugged.

"Where am I? What's happening? This is not my house."

Five more minutes and things were happening in a bed. Steve was confused, dizzy, disoriented.

"What is happening?"

Sounds. A woman. Rachel? What is happening? No, stop.

Steve woke up in his front yard without his clothes. It was still dark. He stumbled into his home and collapsed in the spare bedroom. Fortunately, Helen hadn't heard him come in, and he was up and showered before she woke up the next morning.

By Monday morning, Steve had anonymously regained his clothes, wallet, keys, and other belongings. The event wasn't forgotten, but it wasn't as raw as it had been — at least until he received the videotape.

Steve watched in horror. He couldn't remember any of what he was watching.

Is this a deep fake? How can this be real?

Then Steve realized it must be true.

How did this happen? Why?

A very short and simple note accompanied the tape.

Standby for instructions. We own you now.

The next morning, Lieutenant Colonel Austin was promoted to Colonel Austin and reassigned to the New Horizon Space Station.

Chapter 63

Wedding Bells

†††

Christopher was in love. Angel was in love. Christopher popped the question, and Angel said, "Yes!"

Christopher wanted to make an impression on his entrance to the wedding venue. Josh was an avid parachutist. Having jumped over eight hundred and fifty-seven times, he talked Christopher into jumping with him into the wedding.

Angel did not know that this was going to happen. She had almost finished preparing to walk out for the ceremony when she was summoned to the entrance of the Foundation Worship Chapel and told to look up into the sky. She saw the two men jump from an airplane that flew overhead, but she did not know who they were.

What am I watching? Where is Christopher?

Somewhat annoyed, she observed the parachutists exiting their freefall and descending under their canopies to the wedding venue. She never considered for a moment that it could be Christopher and Josh. She thought maybe it was some kind of entertainment that Christopher had arranged, and she planned on having a moment with him about it. It was not really appropriate for a wedding.

When the jumpers made stand-up landings, disconnected their parachutes, and walked over to Angel, she simply didn't know what to expect. Then they raised their visors, and she was flabbergasted!

Angel threw her arms around Christopher and hugged him. Then, for a moment, when she realized the danger that he had put himself in, as well as the risk to the memory of their once in a lifetime ceremony; she wanted to slap him. However, she realized it had been important to Christopher to do this, and since he didn't get hurt, it was water under the bridge.

Angel made a decision that her wedding day was not the day for Christopher and her to have their first fight. Surely, there would be countless other times in their marriage when they would disagree on what to do or how to do things. They would have to recognize that they were different and gradually come to an agreement on how they would address their differences. All that could wait. She was just glad Christopher's testosterone-laced adventure had turned out well.

Christopher took off his jumpsuit to reveal a tuxedo underneath. He and Angel traveled back to the Foundation Worship Center, where hundreds of people were waiting for them.

It was quite the elaborate wedding. Pastor Steve led the service. His wife, Jill, was Angel's maid of honor. Dawn's son, Josh, was Christopher's best man. Everyone from Foundation came to see the happy couple say their vows, and there was an enormous potluck following the service.

The reception in the park was crazy! Music, dancing, singing, air guitar and a plethora of desserts entertained and satisfied the attendees. It was a loving and celebratory time, as joyful as any in memory.

At the end of the evening, Christopher and Diane walked hand-in-hand over a small bridge extending over a babbling brook in the park. It was a moment for the couple to be alone and reflect on the wonders of the day they had just shared.

They stood in silence on the small footbridge, looking down at the water that passed below them, reflecting their images in the moonlight.

Angel asked, "What are you thinking about, honey?"

"Oh, about all the memories from this wonderful day."

They turned to face each other and held each other close.

"What was your favorite part of the day?"

Christopher smiled. "The moment I saw you in your wedding dress, walking down the aisle towards me, knowing that it was the beginning of our life together as husband and wife."

Christopher asked, "How about you? What was your favorite moment?"

Angel thought back over all the day's events. "Honestly, I think it was watching you play air guitar."

They both cracked up uncontrollably. When the laughter subsided, Christopher said, "Ok. That was pretty funny. But I'm gonna give you a mulligan here; one more shot to redeem yourself."

Angel looked up into Christopher's eyes, and a tear ran down her cheek. "It's when you said you would never leave me. When you said you would always love me. When you promised me — we would grow old together."

A tear ran down Christopher's cheek. "I meant every word."

"I know you did. And I meant every word too. I will never leave you, and I will never forsake you. Where you go, I will go. Where you are, that's where I want to be. I hope you remember what I looked like walking down the aisle towards you, because you'll have to look at me when I'm old."

"You will be just as beautiful to me in a hundred years."

They kissed gently in the moonlight; the first night of a very long future together.

Chapter 64

Middle-Mist Red

†††

The most beautiful flower, called middle-mist red, covered the eastern third of Parlantis from the beginning of spring to the end of summer.

The El Tigre drug cartels had figured out that middle-mist red augmented the potency of their drugs by freeing up the restriction of blood vessels in the brain.

But unbeknownst to the drug cartels or the government of Parlantis, there was another consumer of middle mist red. The tannin of Parlantis, living in the mountain caves mostly undetected, regularly left the caves in the pitch black of moonless nights to consume the beautiful flower. The dragon naturally discovered that middle-mist red promoted blood flow and freed the restriction of blood in their brains; allowing them to more adequately access the fire-breathing abilities that their enemies so feared.

So the flower was in outrageous demand. Locals of the provinces of east Parlantis were often amazed when they stumbled upon the bare fields, emptied of plant life, that just the day before were covered in the red flower. What could do such a thing in just one evening? No one knew the answer.

The theft of the natural resource by a competitor country, if El Tigre was truly a country, would not have been such a security danger had it not been for the fact that the theft would soon create a more potent drug that was wreaking havoc on the urban inhabitants of Parlantis. The drug augmenting compound found in the flower was literally turning large swaths of Parlantis' population into zombies and affecting both the safety and economy of the country. Something had to be done to stem the tide of both the theft of middle-mist red from the countryside of Parlantis and the import of the destructive drugs into the country.

The counter argument, voiced by the pro-libertarian section of the country, argued that though reprehensible, the drug cartels were simply supplying the people of Parlantis with what they wanted. They argued that regardless of the increase in crime, decrease in public safety, decrease in economic productivity, and dismal outlook for the future of the country; that the government should not restrict the flow of drugs within Parlantis.

It seemed like it was a losing battle. The death spiral had already begun and the numbers of people demanding more product was growing by the day. The proponents of the freedom to use drugs did not know where their drug use would end up and they didn't care. Once they got a dose of whatever El Tigre cartels were selling, boosted by middle-mist red compounds, all they cared about was getting more. Getting more drugs took priority over their jobs, their well-being and their families.

But it got worse. El Tigre began lacing their product with poison. Why would a drug producer poison the consumers of their product? A more nefarious agenda was in play. The cartels were not just supplying their consumers with what they wanted; they were killing them.

Middle-mist red was not just entertainment. Middle-mist red was an existential threat to Parlantis.

General Sanders had informed the queen of what was going on several times, but she hadn't seemed concerned. Something was wrong.

Part 13: The Plan

Chapter 65

Amends

†††

It was five in the morning on a Saturday when the knock came at the door.

Seriously? Don't they know this is the only day of the week I get to heal?

Kristana did all she could to crawl to the door of her small apartment in the city. She put on her robe and stood at the door. Doing a quick check that everything was in order, she took a deep breath and opened the door.

"Rise and shine."

"Maria, what are you doing here?"

"I brought you some breakfast."

"No, I mean, what are you really doing here?"

"I wanted to apologize. I want us to be friends. Nothing happened between me and Christian. I was just looking at the band while he was taking a shower."

"I see. Thanks for telling me that."

"Oh, and Christian wanted me to tell you he found out something amazing about the medallions. He said to meet him at Tannin Mountain Cave at ten this morning."

"Where is that?"

"Oh, you are new here. I forgot. I can show you where the cave is, if you like. There are tons of caves. I would just tell you how to get there, but it's really hard to describe."

"Ok. Give me a minute to get dressed."

Chapter 66

Targeted

†††

Maria waited while Kristana saddled up her horse, and then they rode into the mountains south of Pferd.

After about an hour, they reached a remote cave entrance, and they tied their horses to a tree.

Kristana grabbed her short sword from the side of her saddlebag.

"You think you'll need that?"

"It's better to have it and not need it, than need it and not have it. I don't go anywhere without it."

"To each their own."

"That's right."

"Where is Christian's horse?"

"He must not be here yet."

They lit their lanterns.

"Shouldn't we wait here for him?"

"There's more than one entrance. He probably entered on the other side of the ridge. My bad. Anyway, the place he described is just inside. C'mon."

Maria disappeared inside the cave entrance.

I don't like this.

"Ok. Wait up!" Tristana enter the cave entrance and followed Maria into the tunnels, following Maria's light the best she could. "Wait up!"

Maria made a couple of turns. Kristana missed one of them, and Maria's light disappeared.

"Hey!"

Kristana moved forward, working through several forks in the tunnels. Kristana heard Maria call out ahead. Echoes of Maria's voice rang out from multiple tunnels. Kristana took one, then the other. Then there was no sound at all.

I knew this was a bad idea! Ok. Now what?

Kristana turned around and realized she didn't know the way back. She was trying so hard to catch Maria that she didn't keep track of her turns!

Stupid me!

Then she heard it — the chattering.

What is that?

Kristana turned around and saw the most horrific thing she had ever seen. It had six hairy legs and resembled a spider; but on its bulbous torso sat a flattened head and the smooth, bloody face of a person with just a mouth. Its mouth was very wide with many teeth. The mouth was opening and closing repeatedly; the upper and lower teeth were hitting each other rapidly, making the chattering noise.

I've seen spiders and I've seen people, but spider people? No. I don't think so. You might just be smiling, but something about your body language tells me you are not friendly.

Kristana drew her sword and turned to retreat down the tunnel to her right. Then she heard the same chattering ahead of her and froze.

Another one of you guys? Did I crash a monster party?

Kristana turned in a slow circle. The creatures surrounded her. A couple of these things were even hanging from the ceiling of the cave tunnel.

So, I want to be friends. Christian wants to meet you. I'll show you the way. Sure, Maria!

The creatures closed in on Kristana.

One true God, please have mercy on me? Please show me the way out of this, or give me the strength to fight?

Kristana noticed there was one tunnel the spider-people were avoiding. She darted down that tunnel as fast as she could with the arachnid-like creatures right behind her.

It sounded like a herd of cattle was chasing her. Each of the creatures' legs pounded against the cave floor as they ran and the echoes of the combined impact were thunderous!

The tunnel opened into an enormous cavern ahead. Kristana sprinted across the cavern and climbed up a steep rock. She barely had enough room to stand at the top. She thought, by doing so, maybe she could force a fight against just one creature at a time. That hope quickly faded as the creatures easily climbed up all sides of the rock simultaneously.

This is not looking good.

Kristana didn't know where the thoughts — the feelings — came from; but suddenly the words formed: *Fear not; have faith; God is nigh.*

That is when everything changed. Enter the ancient enemy of the aaranae — the giant huntsman spider. The giant spider emerged from the dark shadows of the cavern in a full charge toward its primeval enemy.

The heads of the aaranae snapped as one toward the huntsman, and they screamed. Suddenly, the aaranae, whose directive from the queen was to kill Kristana, had a different priority; survive.

As a unit, they redirected their attack on the greatest threat to their kind, the huntsman. The huntsman and the aaranae collided in the center of the cavern. The aaranae covering the huntsman took chunks out of it as it tore them apart one by one.

As the clash of titans raged, Kristana took full advantage of their distraction. She slid down the rock and ran full-speed to the nearest exit.

Kristana made it into a new tunnel, but the original problem still existed — how to get out of the caves.

She felt light-headed. Her heart was still racing.

It won't be long before those creatures come after me again. I have to find a way to get out of here! My God, please help me?

From nowhere, she had the memory. She was sitting beside a peaceful stream and talking with a friend. It was a very unusual friend. He was dressed entirely in white and spoke with calmness and gentleness.

The Lord is my shepherd, I shall not be in want. He makes me lie down in green pastures. He leads me beside the still waters. He restores my soul. He leads me in the paths of righteousness for his name's sake. Though I walk through the valley of the shadow of death, I will fear no evil, for you are with me. You prepare a table before me in the presence of my enemies. You anoint my head with oil. My cup runs over. Surely, goodness and mercy will follow me all the days of my life, and I will dwell in the House of the Lord forever.

Her heart rate slowed, and she regained her composure. Suddenly, she saw the light. Faintly at first, then brighter, and then brighter again. The light lit up the tunnel in front of her. She was reticent to move forward, because she didn't know what the light was leading her into.

What choice do I have?

Within a few minutes, the light led Kristana to an opening. She shielded her eyes from the ever-increasing brightness. Then she crawled through a hole in the tunnel wall and stood in the sunshine.

It took a few minutes for Kristana's eyes to adjust to the light. Once they did, she couldn't believe what she saw.

From her position at the top of the ridge, she watched Maria approach a stranger, but that wasn't the strange part. The stranger stood amidst a pride of lions.

"I was wondering when you would get here," Maria said.

"I had to gather up some friends to come with me."

"I see that. May I approach you or will your kitties get upset?"

"Approach."

As Maria approached the stranger, all the lions rose from their reclined positions to a heightened state of alert.

Maria stopped.

"It is Ok. My kitties won't hurt you."

Maria suddenly regretted using the term kitties. She moved in closer to the stranger until she stood before him.

He asked, "Is everything prepared?"

"It is. There are very few that suspect anything out of the ordinary. I left one of the suspicious ones in the caves behind me with our friends, the aaranae."

"Oh. That should be fun!"

Kristana could hear every word clearly as the sound rose from the canyon below in the crisp, early morning air.

"Yeah. She won't be giving us any trouble."

Kristana was fuming.

No trouble? You haven't seen trouble yet, Maria!

Kristana understood Maria's jealousy over Christian, but this was a betrayal of the worst kind! Not betrayal of her; they weren't even friends, but betrayal of her family and her country!

The stranger asked, "What about the Pferd corridor?"

"They are pulling out. Should be clear within the week."

"Perfect! The plan is coming together nicely. The Master will be pleased."

I have to get this information to Christian!

Kristana turned and headed quietly back down the ridge. She had to get back to her horse before Maria, or she would certainly lose her ride. And she had to do it quietly, so those lions didn't here. Fortunately, she was downwind from them or she would already have been in big trouble. She would have a hard time fighting a pride of lions alone; but then she wasn't alone.

Kristana could see the horses below her in the valley.

Oh good, they are still there.

She sprinted down the rugged terrain, sliding down many a stony hillside. By the time she reached the horses, she was covered in cuts, scratches, and bruises. It didn't matter; she was used to beating her body into submission.

She mounted her horse.

But what about Maria's horse? What would Maria do?

Kristana grabbed the reins of Maria's horse. C'mon honey, you're coming with us.

Kristana rode as quickly as she could to get the word to Christian and General Sanders. General Sanders and Christen would be shattered when they found out about Maria.

Chapter 67

Holiday

†††

The queen stood on the palace balcony high above the courtyard where everyone who was anyone had assembled for her special announcement.

"By my hand, I hereby declare, this week will be an official holiday, set aside to honor our armed forces; a freedom holiday! To the maximum extent possible, the men and women of the Parlantian Guard will stand down, reconstitute, and spend time with their families. There will be no exceptions other than a small peace-keeping contingent."

General Sanders was in shock. The queen had given him no warning of her decision.

What is she thinking? This will leave our border completely open and our entire country vulnerable to attack! A small contingent for peace-keeping?

Christian came through the door and into General Sander's office. "I came as quickly as I could."

"Have you heard?"

"About the holiday? Yes, sir."

"I tried to persuade the queen that it was insane to leave the country completely undefended, but it was to no avail. It was one thing to evacuate the Pferd corridor, but it is another thing completely to sit down the entire military, except, of course, for the small peacekeeping contingent."

"May I assume that I have command of the peacekeeping contingent?"

"Yes, you may."

"Excellent. The queen didn't say how small the small peacekeeping contingent had to be, did she?"

"Son, I like the way you think."

"Then I'll be ready with, say, five hundred men in the hills just outside the Pferd corridor, awaiting any disorderly conduct that needs peacekeeping."

Grumpy smiled. "That's perfect. Of course, if the worst-case scenario unfolds, that won't be enough. You might still be vastly outnumbered."

"That would be excellent! Just the way I like it!"

"You might not think it's so excellent if the entire Army of El Tigre is staring you in the face."

"Oh, come on. Are you kidding? That would be incredible."

"Well, if that's what you want, you might just get it. Ok, have Red handpick the best five hundred men. Tell him to have them ready to ride in the morning."

"Yes, sir."

"Any idea where Kristana is?"

"No, I haven't seen her since the day before yesterday."

"Something happen?"

"Not that I know of. Things were superb the night of the party."

"Really? How good is superb?"

"Can't kiss and tell."

"So, there was a kiss?"

"Ok, we're getting a little off subject. Anyway, yesterday morning I came out of the shower, and Maria was standing there in my room — wait. Something must have happened between Kristana and Maria."

"That'll do it. I told you that you had your hands full with Maria. If she sensed Kristana was a threat to her relationship with you, then she would have acted on it."

"But there is no relationship between me and Maria."

"That all depends."

"Depends on what?"

"Depends on whether Maria thinks there's a relationship. By the way, Maria is nowhere to be found this morning either. Coincidence?"

"I think not."

"At that moment, Kristana came through the door."

Christian said, "Kristana? Where have you been? I've been looking everywhere for you?"

Kristana walked right by Christian and directed her comments to General Sanders.

"General Sanders, I just came from the mountains to the southeast of Pferd. Maria led me into a trap with some crazy human spider creatures there."

"Some what?"

"Anyway, sir, with all due respect, that's not what's important. What is important is that after I got out of the caves, I overheard Maria talking to a stranger in the canyon just inside the Pferd corridor. They were discussing a plan that was about to happen. It involved an invasion happening this week."

"That makes sense because the queen has just put the entire Parlantian armed forces on vacation for a week to celebrate Armed Forces Day."

"What? That will allow an enemy to advance all the way to Pferd!"

Christian interjected, "Unless we stop them."

Kristana finally turned and addressed Christian. "Stop them with what?"

"The general said that the queen is allowing us to have a small peace-keeping force available. If we take that force, along with your warriors, into the Pferd corridor, we can hold back an invading force long enough for General Sanders to join us with the rest of the Parlantian Cavalry."

Kristana paused. "There's something else."

"Go ahead Kristana," the general said.

"There was an entire pride of maybe thirty lions at the command of the stranger who was talking to Maria."

"Excuse me?"

"I know it sounds crazy, but it seemed like he could tell the lions what to do."

"That's not good. We're going to need some help."

"Christian looked at General Sanders. They nodded together."

Kristana asked, "What?"

Christian said, "I think I know a guy."

"A guy?"

"A guy with some friends that might help us cover much more territory from the air."

"From the air?"

"Dragons."

"Dragons?"

"Well, tannin, to be more precise; but yes, dragons."

Christian addressed General Sanders. "General, if it is alright with you, I'll fill Kristana in regarding the dragons. Then I'll see if I can get in contact with Tannar."

"That sounds good, Christian. Let me know if you have any success, please."

†††

Christian took Kristana to the study and filled her in on the dragon story.

"So these medallions allow us to talk to dragons?"

"That's right. Apparently, our ancestors not only could do that, but had a reason to."

"That is amazing!"

Christian looked into Kristana's eyes.

"So are we ok?"

"Yes, we're ok. I left the other morning, because I saw Maria in your room while you were in the shower, and I thought that, well, you know."

"No! Never!"

Kristana pulled Christian in close and kissed him. The talking ended.

Part 14: Complicated

Chapter 68

The Cross

†††

The day that Shawn, Diane and Christopher arrived in Parlantis, Dawn gave them a place to stay. It was life-changing. But when Dawn brought them with her to the Foundation Worship Center, it was life-saving.

The sermon they listened to on their first Sunday at Foundation Worship Center was from Job 19:25-27: "I know that my redeemer lives, and that in the end he will stand on the earth. And after my skin has been destroyed, yet in my flesh I will see God; I myself will see him with my own eyes—I, and not another. How my heart yearns within me!"

They had heard this passage and many more like it from Henry when they arrived in Omentia. Henry had taken the time to teach them who the one true God was. They believed, but their faith was immature.

But Pastor Steve expanded his sermon to verses they had never heard before; versus that even Henry had never heard before. One of such verses was John 3:16: "For God so loved the world that he gave his one and only Son, that whoever believes in him shall not perish but have eternal life."

This verse shocked them. They looked at each other with such joy. They couldn't believe what they were hearing. Everything changed in an instant! They had heard the promise, but not the promise fulfilled! They could hardly sit still in their chairs until the end of the sermon.

Once the sermon was over, everyone in the Foundation Worship Center was focused on the newcomers. Their joy was contagious! It opened everyone's eyes to what they had taken for granted. Their Savior had come! The promise had been fulfilled! They were so happy they were in tears and had to hug everyone they saw.

Pastor Steve gave each of them a bible, and they devoured the contents. Bible classes, bible studies, bible readings, bible devotions, bible memorization and prayer; they were on fire with the Spirit, and couldn't get enough of the Word.

Chapter 69

Security

†††

Before Christopher served as a sheriff's deputy, he worked security for an established politician named Scott Swalwell. The paycheck was good; but there was a lot of travel involved and frequently, Chamela, a personal romantic aid to Swalwell, would flirt with him. Fortunately, Christopher had a policy to never be alone with a woman he didn't trust, even in the elevator. He always found a way to not draw Chamela's security detail. He did the best he could to keep his distance from her.

Other things that bothered Christopher about Swalwell were the mysteries that surrounded him. Supposedly, he had risen to prominence from apparent obscurity, his supporters met by moonlight around bonfires in the forest, and they unofficially called his movement "the Order." It was all very opaque and disconcerting.

Almost immediately, Christopher saw the security job with Swalwell wasn't right for him. He noticed more and more things that just didn't seem on the up and up; things that troubled his spirit. Something was very wrong, but he couldn't put his finger on it.

When Christopher heard shocking information about a scroll that foretold of Swalwell's rise to power and a dark apprentice that would follow, Christopher decided being a sheriff's deputy was good enough for him.

One day, in the course of his duties, Christopher met a man named Kiethan who shared a secret with him. He talked about being a truth-keeper and the history of truth-keepers all the way back to Heath and the Veteri. Kiethan told Christopher, "Those who resisted the Veteri then are still around today, and they are rising again."

He made a pitch to Christopher to join them. According to him, the truth-keepers also required security personnel and would highly value and well use his skills. Christopher liked what he heard and joined them.

Christopher kept his job as sheriff's deputy. It provided an excellent cover.

Chapter 70

The Diamond and the Cross

†††

Years earlier, Kiethan had been working for Joanne for a few months when she called him to discuss a matter of utmost importance.

Knock, knock.

"Come in."

"Hello Joanne."

"Hi Kiethan. Thanks for coming to see me."

"Oh, it's my pleasure, ma'am."

"Have a seat. I'd like to discuss something with you."

Kiethan sat down at the table across from Joanne. Joanne pulled out a diamond and set it on the dark wooden table between them, along with a cross on a necklace.

Kiethan looked down at the diamond. "Whoa, that's beautiful."

"Isn't it though? Let me tell you something about this diamond. Have you ever heard of Truin's timepiece?"

"No ma'am, I haven't."

"Well, here's the condensed version. Truin was the founder of Trinian. His seven sons had a timepiece made for him for his birthday. Each son had a stone from their province inset in the timepiece's face. There was one stone inset into the twelve o'clock position of the timepiece."

"Let me guess, a diamond."

"Correct. This diamond."

"This diamond?"

"This diamond."

"Wow."

"All the rest of the stones have been lost over the centuries. This is the last stone."

"Ok."

"What I would like to do is have the diamond set into this cross."

"Ok."

"I can't overstate how important this is. At no time can you let this stone out of your sight, not even for a moment. Do you understand?"

"Yes ma'am. I've got it. You can count on me."

Kiethan carefully placed the diamond and the cross necklace into a pouch. He went to see Adrian, the jeweler, who was already expecting him.

†††

"Good day, sir."

"Good day to you, young man. How may I be of service?"

"Joanne said you'd be expecting me?"

"Oh yes. You must be Kiethan."

"That's me."

Kiethan walked over to the table where Adrian was sitting. He opened the pouch and withdrew the diamond first and laid it on the table.

"Oh, that's exquisite!" Adrian said, "Where did you ever find such a diamond?"

"I'm sorry, sir, I'm really not at liberty to say."

"Kiethan then pulled out the necklace for the cross."

"We would like the diamond to be placed at the center of this cross."

"That'll be no problem, no problem at all."

"We need to make sure that the diamond doesn't fall out of the necklace."

"Oh, don't worry. I'll make sure it doesn't. When would you like to pick it up?"

"I'm Afraid I'm going to have to stay until it is complete."

"I understand."

†††

Three hours later Adrian was finished, and the cross with a diamond in the center was beautiful.

"Thank you so much Adrian. This is fantastic. I'm sure Joanne is gonna love this."

"I'm so happy you like it. Joanne has already wired me the payment, so you are free to take it to her."

"Once again, Adrian, thank you so much."

†††

Kiethan handed the pouch to Joanne. Joanne opened the pouch and remove the necklace. As she lifted it out of the pouch, the cross dangled from the necklace, and the diamond reflected the sunlight coming in through the large bay window. A multitude of colors from the refracted light covered the walls all around them.

"This is spectacular. It is exactly what I wanted."

"I'm so glad."

"Kiethan, promise me that if anything ever happens to me, you will get this necklace to my daughter, Charlene. You must protect this neckless at all costs. My daughter is next in line to be a truth-keeper and it is critical that she has the Truin Stone."

"Yes, ma'am."

"Promise me."

"I promise."

†††

It was a frigid winter morning just before sunrise. Kiethan was driving Joanne through the fog to a highly secretive meeting deep within the Tobarian forest. As they crossed the bridge over the Tobarian River, a single shot rang out in the distance. A fraction of a second later, the front right tire of their vehicle disintegrated, and Kiethan lost control. The car crashed through the right side-rail of the bridge and catapulted off into the river. It instantly sank into the murky depths of the Tobarian.

The cab of the vehicle quickly filled with water. Kiethan could free himself, but Joanne was pinned between her seat and the crushed right side of the car.

Kiethan continued to pull and cut at Joanne's seatbelt as the water in the car rose higher and higher. Almost all the light was gone, and he struggled to see what he was doing.

"Take it!"

"There is still time! I am getting you out of here!"

They both struggled to keep their heads above water as the river poured in through the smashed windshield.

Joanne held the necklace out above the water. "Take it!"

"There is still time!"

"Take it! You promised me!"

The water covered both of their heads and filled the car as it sank ever deeper into the depths of the river. The light was almost gone, but Kiethan saw a faint glint of light and reached out for the cross.

He couldn't see anything, but felt the hand holding the cross relax and release it as he pulled it toward him. Then he held Joanne's hand until he felt her grip ease, and he knew she was gone.

Kiethan knew he was almost out of time. The car continued to sink, and deprived of oxygen, his body panicked.

Goodbye Joanne. I have to go. I am so sorry. Someday, we will meet again. Don't worry, I will keep my promise and get this to Charlene.

Kiethan made it out of the car and to the surface of the river. As he took a deep breath of air, he saw the searchlights scanning the river.

They must be here to help.

Right before he called out to them, they opened fire with automatic weapons, barraging the river surface at random, attempting to kill anything that might have survived the crash into the frigid waters below.

Nope. Not here to help.

Kiethan took another quick breath and dove under the surface, swimming for shore. He had to get there before he froze; he could already feel consciousness slipping away.

Just before the searchlights started scanning the shoreline, he made it out of the river and took cover among the trees.

I guess it wasn't an accidental tire blowout. It was a targeted assassination.

†††

Charlene was alone in the small apartment when Kiethan arrived to give her the tragic news that her mother was gone. She knew instantly her mother was gone when Kiethan gently handed her the cross necklace; there was no way her mom would have parted with it as long as she still breathed.

†††

Joanne's death on his watch haunted Kiethan. He knew he had done everything possible to save her, and he knew her death wasn't his fault. But he still found it nearly impossible to sleep.

One night he could sleep, he had a dream. A voice spoke to him through a bright golden light.

"Kiethan. Be at peace. It is how it needed to be. You have done well."

He couldn't make out who was speaking to him. The voice sounded familiar, but he couldn't place it.

He awoke. A sense of calm and peace settled upon him, and he fell back to sleep. He never had problems sleeping again.

†††

For several years, Hunter and Charlene were committed to studying God's word and serving in the church. Then, suddenly, Hunter stopped attending church with Charlene.

Hunter started hanging out after work with a new set of friends. Not long after, Charlene and their children went missing from Foundation all-together. Pastor Steve and Charlene's many friends tried to find her, but it was like she had just disappeared.

When Kiethan saw Hunter was running for office, he confronted him. Hunter told Kiethan that he and Charlene were divorced and that Charlene had taken the kids and left. He did not know where.

Chapter 71

Reconnaissance

†††

Tannar return to the caves at the request of Christian. The Tannin security was so good that he didn't really have to look for Snuffy. He just waited at the entrance of the cavern system, and Snuffy showed up a short time later.

The two friends were happy to see each other.

"Hey Snuffy, how are you doing?"

"Great Tannar, how are you?"

"Doing alright, doing alright."

"What brings you around today, Tanner? Do you want to go on a flight?"

"Are you kidding? I would love to go on a flight. But there's something I have to talk to you about first."

"Sure, shoot."

"We've got ourselves a bit of a problem. The Queen of Parlantis has told the Parlantian Guard to stand down for a week as a rest and celebration of our armed force's warriors. Normally this would be a good thing, but we have reports that show that El Tigre may be preparing to attack."

"That sounds like a problem."

"Now I know that the tannin want to keep a low profile. Your kind has survived without conflict for hundreds of years by staying hidden in the caves and the caverns of Parlantis."

"That is true."

"You have told me that there was a time, in a place far away to the north, when you lived in harmony with the medallion holders."

"Yes, those were time thousands of moons ago, before the War of Annihilation."

"I come to you today as a medallion holder. I come to you today to ask for your help once again. We have a defensive force that we think can hold off any invading army long enough for the main Parlantian Defense Force to arrive and assist us. However, we don't know where the enemy will attack. The territory is just too vast for us to cover. We need a reconnaissance capability that only you can provide."

"That is a pretty tough sell. I don't think my father and our kind will want to come out of seclusion and safety to expose ourselves to your kind again."

"Snuffy, my friend, what I'm proposing is for you and me to go on some night flights. Under the cover of darkness, just like when you go out and feast on the middle-mist red; you and I can patrol the night skies over western Parlantis. We can see where the enemy is advancing and direct our defensive force to delay their advance long enough for our larger force to converge on them. This should be of no-risk to you or your kind."

"That sounds fair. It doesn't seem to me like there would be very much risk in that plan. I would think my father would go along with that."

"I hope so, because we really need your help. And I hate to say this, but it's kind of an emergency. The attack could come at anytime."

"I'll bring him the proposal and be right back."

Tannar sat down on the edge of a rock ledge. A very large maroon tannin approached him from behind. It stopped about ten feet behind Tannar. It was there to protect the tannin and Tannar until Snuffy returned.

Snuffy returned about ten minutes later with good news.

"My father agrees it is in the best interest of both our-kind and your-kind to maintain the status quo, so we must repel any El Tigre attack."

"Thank you, Snuffy! Thank your father for us!"

"No need, Tannar. This helps us all."

"So, when can we start?"

"I guess as soon as the sun sets."

†††

The sun had just set, and both Tannar and Snuffy were eager to launch. Tannar got on Snuffy's back and off they went.

"Woohoo!" Tannar could not keep from showing his excitement.

"Get it out of your system," Snuffy roared, "you can't make that much noise over the enemy when you find them. This is a covert flight, right?"

"Right. Right. Absolutely. I'm trying."

Part 15: Battle

Chapter 72

Attack

†††

Christian and Snuffy had flown the western coast of Parlantis all night. After ten hours, Christian thought of himself as experienced.

A low fog deck had blown in from the West and obscured the coastline for the past few hours. They hoped it would dissipate as soon as the sun rose.

"Can't we stay a little longer, Snuffy? I know the sun is coming up, but if we stay high enough, no one will see us."

"My father gave me strict instructions to be in the caves when the sun rose. If I don't listen to him, I may jeopardize our entire kind."

"I understand, and you have to do what you have to do, but I'm asking you as a friend to do this for me. It is absolutely critical that we know if and where the enemy is coming ashore."

"Well, my father didn't definitively say which caves to be in at sunrise. So, that gives us a few more minutes."

"That's my buddy!"

†††

Christian had most of his force of five hundred cavalry and infantry concealed in the trees and ready to move on a moment's notice. He took one hundred men and actively patrolled his area of responsibility. He didn't want the defenses to look too soft, but wanted to force the enemy to show their hand.

Kristana and her warriors held halfway between Christian and the principal fighting force under Red's command.

Red awaited the signal to converge on the enemy. A single flaming arrow into the air would tell him which direction to go.

Christian saw them first; lions. They emerged from the trees on the coastline in a full charge toward Christian and his men. There must have been hundreds of them.

Fortunately, Parlantian horses could outrun the lions, even though the lions had the element of surprise. Had the lions waited just a little longer, their sprint speed could have caught many of the guardsmen.

Directing the lions to attack while the guard patrol was still out of range was the first major error of the enemy's plan. Having a brilliant plan is always a prerequisite to launching any attack. However, the execution of that plan is as critical to victory.

No plan survives first contact with the enemy, for the enemy always has a say; but committing an unforced error is not the best way to begin a competition. And that's what warfare is — a competition with deadly consequences.

Tannar and Snuffy, having seen the lions emerge from the tree line, focused their attention on that area of shoreline; that of the Golden Fields.

When they saw the sun break over the western horizon, and the fog dissipate, their worst fears were realized. Hundred of ships were unloading thousands of troops; cavalry, infantry, and archers.

"That's an overwhelming force. The Parlantis Guard cannot hold them off for long."

Snuffy asked, "Do you want me to bring you home to the eastern tribes?"

"No. bring me to your father. We need to talk."

†††

Tannar stood and addressed the leaders of the eastern tribes.

"Fellow descendants of Nomen, warriors of the medallion, and keepers of the truth. I come before you today with urgency.

"Parlantis is under attack. As I speak to you, a massive invasion force disembarks upon the western shore from the Dark Sea. Traitors in the Parlantian government are abetting the destruction of our lands.

"It was not long ago that I came before you, the leaders of the eastern tribes, with the revelation of the medallion. Our ancient ancestors were entrusted with the ability to speak to and work with the dragon-kind. They did so in defense of their land and their people. This sacred honor and burden has now fallen on us.

"The defensive forces of western Parlantis are overwhelmed and will soon fall. Then the enemy will set its sights on the eastern tribes.

"I come before you today not as your prince, but as your brother. I ask you to join me in the defense of our land, our children, and our people. We must not falter and we must not delay.

"Just as our fathers fought the ancient enemy of our people so many years ago in the lands far to the north, so we must do so today. None of us would choose this battle, but the one true God has laid it before us.

"I do not know why this challenge falls upon us now. The ways of the one true God are far above our ways, and his thinking far above our thinking.

"I know he has promised to always be with us, and that he is with us now. Knowing that he is with us, do we shrink from this challenge or do we embrace it? Do we run from the enemies of the one true god or do we engage them?

"I have just come from speaking to the leader of the tannin. He has promised the dragon-kind will rise once again with us to stand against evil. He awaits our decision.

"I will now ask the leaders of the seven tribes. What say you?

"Sheryl?"

"We stand!"

"Tina?"

"We stand!"

"Holly?"

"We stand!"

"Kaiti?"

"We stand!"

"Kayla?"

"We stand!"

"Brock!"

"We stand!"

"And Hayden?"

"We stand!"

"The seven tribes have spoken. We are at war!"

Chapter 73

Combat

†††

Christian and his men retreated towards the trees as quickly as possible, but the lions kept coming. Christian ordered three archers to stop and fire the alarm, so Red knew to deploy the main force.

The archers obeyed. One archer drew an arrow and lit it on fire, while the other two archers defended him. Three lions attacked. The arrows of the defenders brought two of the lions down, but one lion leaped and hit the archer with the flaming arrow just as he was about to release it into the sky. The archer released the arrow as the lion took him off his horse, but the flaming arrow did not reach its intended target; instead, it lodged itself in a fellow archer's chest. The archer screamed in horror as flame consumed his body, and he and his horse rode off into the countryside, ablaze. The remaining archer tried to light an arrow and send the signal, but additional lions took him and his horse down.

As Christian and his men retreated to the tree line, the rest of Christian's forces emerged from the trees and headed towards them. Just before they met, Christian ordered the retreating men to reverse and join the emerging forces; they charged as one towards the pursuing lions. At that point, the lions never had a chance and were defeated quickly.

Christian and the Parlantis Guard continued on to the trees where the lions had emerged. Once Christian had signaled Red of the location of the enemy invasion, he divided his cavalry and begin disruptive operations to impede the enemy in organizing their forces.

Kristana and her fellow warriors joined Christian in the fight, eliminating El Tigre's scouts as they attempted to advance ahead of their principal fighting force to get intelligence on any Parlantian defenses that might remain.

By nightfall, Red arrived with the Parlantian main fighting force, and Christian took charge of it once again. Early the next morning, Christian led an assault on the El Tigrans. It was a bold move since the Parlantians were massively outnumbered, but the El Tigrans were taken by surprise and lost many men.

†††

"What's wrong? You seem nervous."

General Sanders was very uncomfortable. The queen had called him to the palace once again, and he was sitting with her alone in the throne room.

"Oh no, your majesty. There's nothing wrong. I'm fine."

I think she knows.

"Really? Because it seems like you're waiting for something."

"No. Pretty much everyone is off duty under your proclamation that this week is a celebration. I guess I'm just not used to relaxing."

"Why don't you come over here next to me and relax?"

General Sanders felt dizzy. *Not again.*

Just as General Sanders stood, there was a knock on the throne room door.

"Enter."

A Guard entered the room and rushed over to the queen.

"Your majesty. There is an urgent message."

"And?"

"It was brought by — special messenger."

"I see. General, if you will excuse me?"

"Of course, my queen."

Queen Tharice followed the guard out of the room and proceeded to her private chambers. There, the raven awaited her arrival.

"What is it?"

It spoke. "The attack has begun. Why are we meeting resistance?"

"Resistance? What resistance? There isn't any resistance, there isn't any guard on duty. There is only a small police force."

"Do not contradict me."

As the raven spoke, a powerful wind entered through the window, and everything in the room flew against the walls and stayed there.

"Are you questioning me?"

"No, my lord, of course not."

"Fix this!"

"Yes, my lord."

The raven flapped its wings, lifted off its perch, and exited through the window. Everything plastered to the walls fell with a loud crash.

Resistance.

Queen Tharice stormed from the room.

Someone is going to pay.

General Sanders didn't know what hit him. One moment he was relaxing and waiting for the queen to return. The next moment, he was pinned against the stone wall, three feet above the rock floor. He couldn't move a muscle.

Queen Tharice entered the room.

"Did you think I wouldn't find out? Did you think I was stupid? Now you will pay for your insubordination!"

General Sanders struggled to speak. "My queen, I do not understand."

"You do not understand a lot of things, but I will teach you to understand!"

The invisible phantom that held General Sanders against the rock wall tightened its grip, sending General Sanders into immense pain. He screamed in agony and then from the shock of the sound of his own voice — he had never heard himself scream before.

†††

Evie was the best rider on the fastest horse in the cavalry, and it was critical she carried the word of the attack to Parlantis' main defense force as quickly as possible — the survival of all Parlantis depended upon it.

No one knew how long the peacekeeping force assembled would last against the entire El Tigran invasion, but everyone knew it wouldn't be long.

Then from no where three riders were converging on Evie — El Tigran scouts!

†††

Christian and Kristana had engaged the El Tigrans from both the south and the east, respectively, but they continued to disembark from their ships onto the Golden Fields. The Parlantians fought valiantly and took three to five El Tigrans for every Parlantian that fell, but that wouldn't be good enough. Wave after wave of El Tigrans continued to come ashore, and the Parlantian forces were quickly being depleted. The situation was looking grim.

Christian met Kristana on the field of battle.

"We can't hold much longer, Christian!"

"We have to hold them off until General Sanders brings the main force! There is simply no alternative!"

Their eyes met and said the same thing.

There isn't much time, and there is so much more I have left to say.

Christian reached over and grabbed Kristana's hand. The two simple rings they wore contacted each other as their eyes met.

"I'm not sure we will be together again, Kristana."

"We will, Christian. I know we will. Although I am unsure of the details, I have a firm belief that we are supposed to be together."

"I believe that too."

For a moment, it seemed as if the battle raging around them had faded into the background, but then that moment ended. The battle closed in around them, and the fury of combat engulfed them once again.

Chapter 74

Heavenly Host

†††

The heavenly realm glowed in unimaginable color as the living beings deployed from the throne of light in route to engage the demons of darkness.

Flash! A streak of silver. "The dark spirits once again inhabit the creatures of the earthly realm."

Flash! A streak of majestic gold. "The ancient enemy of the faithful attacks. The medallion holders are once again at war."

Flash! Every color imaginable and unimaginable. Thousands of living beings arrived in a single streak of light.

The Chief Living Being spoke to the multitude. "These are the messengers of the Faithful and True, and they will deliver a message to darkness this day! Give the enemy no sanctuary!"

A silver flash! "He has found the girl, and they are targeted."

"Protect them. The Master has a plan. They are important to His-story."

†††

In the same space and time, there was darkness. It stunk with the rancid stench of death. Those that lived within the cloud of hate and destruction lived in fear of their master and transferred their anxiety to the physical forms they persecuted in the corporeal realm.

Portentous, Obaminous, and Scire glided over the legion of lesser demons as they settled over the wild creatures and members of the El Tigran attack force. All the bodily forms instantly reacted to the demon infestation as their empty spiritual vessels conformed to the evil presence that now made its home within their physical shell.

The soldiers of the El Tigran army, having given all control of their actions to the mind altering-drugs in their systems and the soul-destroying darkness in their hearts; joined their savage allies of lion, tiger, and bear in not knowing or caring to know the difference between right and wrong.

This was the wave of man and creature that swept against the Parlantian shore and crashed into the guard defenders. It had no conscious thought, no perception of pain, and no remorse. Its purpose was to destroy, and its master had complete control over it.

The lesser demons revealed over their new found hosts. Being spiritual creatures, they spent most of their existence influencing the spirits of mortals in the physical realm with temptation and deception. The opportunity to actually inhabit a physical form and control its actions was a relatively rare and especially pleasing opportunity.

The evil entity move ashore in a fluid motion; more resembling that of a vapor; as its diabolical consciousness contemplated its sinister intent. *Maim, kill, and destroy; but most importantly, find her.*

Chapter 75

Heavy losses

†††

Christian and ten of his men charged the enemy formation. Their stallions raced towards the forward line as the invaders prepared to meet them with long spears.

As Christian's stallion launched over the enemy defenders, the El Tigran archers fired a barrage of enemy arrows from close range. One arrow hit Christian square in the chest and knocked him from his stallion. He landed hard on the ground.

Christian thought he was a dead man. He laid on the ground face up, and could see the arrow lodged in his chest. Christian reached up and snapped the arrow in half. At that moment, he realized that had it not been for his medallion hanging from his neck, the arrow would have penetrated his chest just above the heart. Instead, it had simply penetrated his tunic and fell away, leaving Christian unharmed.

As Christian struggled to recover, a tiger appeared from nowhere. The ferocious tiger charged Christian, and in that moment, Christian knew, yet again, that he would not survive.

Almighty God, please have mercy on my soul.

Christian scrambled across the ground to reach his short sword.

Just as the tiger launched and was about to take Christian's head, a large man with blonde hair stepped in front of Christian with a long spear. It was too late for the tiger to stop its charge, and the spear lethally impaled the charging beast through the neck. The tiger was dead, but it didn't know it yet. It flailed upon the ground for a few seconds with blood hemorrhaging from its neck.

Time seemed to stand still. The stranger turned his head toward Christian and said, "Be strong, have faith, God is nigh." As soon as the man finished speaking, he disappeared once again into the melee.

Who was that man and where did he come from at just the right moment to save my life?

There was no time to contemplate an answer to the question. Christian rose quickly and reengaged the enemy. Though he and his men fought valiantly, Christian's eyes told him it was a losing battle.

Still, Christian had learned not to trust his physical eyes, but his spiritual ones. So he fought on!

†††

Trajan watched the battle from a safe position high upon a ridge to the rear of the brutal combat. He had confidence that his troops would win the battle; after all, his men outnumbered the Parlantians, four to one.

Trajan was so focused on the battle that he did not see the sudden opening of the portal behind him. What was discernible suddenly became a doorway of the undiscernible.

Through the gateway walked a man whose name was Nomen. Nomen approached Trajan and stood beside him.

"Your father was like a brother to us. Your family was our family."

Trajan did not react. He knew the voice well.

Nomen continued. "Then one day, having been tempted by Satan himself, your father, Nod, turned on us. Out of jealousy for his brother, Veteris, he betrayed those that loved him. He broke the moral code and used the tunnels to take you, your mother, and your sister into the future. Choosing the path of our enemies, he opposed the guardians of the truth. Now, in this time, he continues to cause mayhem and destruction through his son."

Trajan turned and faced Nomen. "Your clan believed fairy tales. Your clan wished to use these myths to control the people. My father did what he did; I do what I do; to free the world of your superstitions, and share with all the knowledge of the mystics and the hidden powers of the natural world."

"There is more than you know, Trajan! There is another place — another time. Your father knew of it."

"Save it, Nomen! Just more superstitious nonsense!"

"Your sorcery cannot win. Your alliance with demons cannot give you victory. The one true God created all, and he rules over all—both here and throughout time."

"And yet, here we are."

"End this madness, Trajan!"

"It is not madness. We will bring order to the world."

"The one true God has given order to the world. He has set the celestial bodies in their place. He gives life to all creatures. All exist to give him glory."

"Your one true God is a God of chaos. Individuals with freedom destroy order. Only through control can the weak-minded be productive in a society. We will give this order and productivity to the world."

"Trajan, the demons you serve have no interest in order. They only wish to enslave and destroy. You are being deceived. Stop this madness!"

"My master will never stop. There will be many more like my father and me. We will never stop until we control all and provide order to all. Wave after wave of soldiers will follow me until the end of time, and we will be successful. The master of this world will take control of the world and remake it in his image!"

"Trajan, I will ask you one more time to turn from the darkness and follow the light. Turn from hate and follow love. Worship the creator, not the created."

"Be gone, old man, with your superstitions. Go back to your time. You do not belong here. You're not even alive anymore. I am talking to a ghost."

†††

Daarak and Loathe weighed their options. They had spent many years feeding on the dead and growing the number of the aaranae kind. There wasn't really a future in this course of action.

They knew if they continued to serve their dark master, they would never be clear of the shackles of slavery, sorrow, and pain.

However, opportunity was on the horizon. They carefully contemplated the possibility that if they fought on the side of the one true God, perhaps they would be shown mercy. Maybe they would not be lost for eternity.

They decided they would fight against the queen and the evil forces invading the country. They owed no loyalty to the queen or her kind. It was her kind that had cursed them in the beginning, and it was her kind that had enslaved them ever since.

As alpha aaranae, their council held much weight, and so, they could convince the rest of the aaranae that this option held the most promise for their kind.

When the El Tigre attack began in earnest, the aaranae were prepared to make a difference.

One advantage of living underground was that the aaranae did not need to breathe very often. Therefore, they could not only tunnel through the ground for long periods of time, but they could also stay submerged underwater for extended periods.

When the El Tigran invaders came ashore, they wondered about the dark squishy sand they walked upon under the last couple feet of water leading up to the beaches of Parlantis.

What is this strange sand we walk upon? It shifts beneath our feet. It is almost as if it is alive.

The invaders soon found out that it was alive. Thousands of the aaranae lie in wait for their uninvited guests, and as the enemy marshaled its forces upon the beaches of Parlantis, the aaranae moved as one.

The second echelon of the El Tigran attack force was about to leave the beach and ingress into Parlantis. As hundreds of troops disembarked the El Tigran ships and made their way up the beach, the aaranae latched on to them, both from beneath the water and from beneath the sand. The invaders screamed in absolute terror as an entire corps of soldiers was pulled beneath the water and the sand, and there was nothing any of them could do about it. As the aaranae feasted, the waters transformed into a crimson hue.

Filled with horror, the next wave of troops about to go to shore watched in disbelief as their comrades vanished from existence, never to be seen again. They didn't want to follow in their brother's footsteps.

Unfortunately for the aaranae, this display of affection for the one true God came a lifetime too late. Their time of grace had passed, and any attempt at this point to show their loyalty or love for the creator was worthless. They would eventually join in the eternal condemnation of those unbelieving souls whose lives they had just ended.

†††

Christian and the men of the Parlantian Cavalry fought valiantly, but their numbers were not enough to keep up with the wave after wave of invaders.

Christian had sent a rider to inform General Sanders that the invasion had begun, but reinforcements still had not arrived. He wondered if they ever would.

Christian and Kristana soon found themselves alone and surrounded. There were still pockets of cavalry engaged in skirmishes with the enemy, but Christian and Kristana were basically all that was left. They stood back-to-back on a knoll, surrounded by El Tigran warriors.

"Ok. Well, I thought it was a good plan."

"Thanks Kristana. Unfortunately, it doesn't look like it is going to work out."

"It's not over yet, soldier boy! Buck up!"

"Oh no. Don't misunderstand me. We've got this! They don't know who they're messing with!"

"That's better!"

"I think it is time to call in reinforcements, though."

"I thought you already did that. Didn't you send a rider to tell General Sanders to send reinforcements?"

"Those aren't the reinforcements I'm talking about."

"Oh, I see. Yes. I agree."

Christian and Kristana planted their sword's tip down in the sand. Then they each got down on their knees, bowed their heads, and prayed.

Chapter 76

Intercession

†††

Kristana prayed out loud. "The Lord is my shepherd. I shall not be in want. He makes me to lie down in green pastures. He leads me beside the still waters. He restores my soul. He leads me in the path of righteousness for his name's sake. Yeah, though I walk through the valley of the shadow of death, I will fear no evil; for thou art with me. Your rod and your staff, they comfort me. You prepare a table before me in the presence of my enemies. You anoint my head with oil; my cup runs over. Surely, goodness and mercy will follow me all the days of my life, and I will dwell in the house of the Lord forever."

She remembered the words but couldn't place from where. As she said the words, the ground surrounding them glowed.

Christian prayed. "Almighty God, maker of the heavens and the earth. To you we give all glory and honor and praise — for you alone are the one true God."

"Father in heaven, once again we call upon you to save us. We exist to give you glory, and our lives are in your hands. Please use us to honor you whether we live or whether we die. We know that whatever you choose will be for our ultimate good. Our faith and our trust are in you, the rock of our salvation. We are at peace. Your will be done."

As Christian prayed, a dome of golden dust glittered in an arc around the mound on which they kneeled.

Kristana and Christian slowly stood and marveled at the strange sight. They looked out at the surrounding hills. They could clearly see hundreds of El Tigran soldiers searching frantically for them, and yet the El Tigrans could not see them.

"Why can't they see us?" Christian asked.

"It's like this dome of light is masking us from their view."

Christian cradled Kristana's hands in his own. They both looked down at the leather bands on their fingers.

"I don't know where these came from, but I think they mean something."

Kristana looked lovingly into Christian's eyes. "I think they do too."

"No matter what happens to us now, Kristana, I'm glad I could be here with you."

Time stood still and their lips met in a soft kiss. As they opened their eyes once again, they witnessed a miracle.

"Do you see what I see, Kristana?"

"It's amazing! They're everywhere."

"What are they?"

"I think they're angels of the one true God."

"What does it mean?"

"It means we are not alone, and we have nothing to fear."

As they looked at each other again, something else changed. They remembered a boat, an amazing sunset, and the pledge they had made to each other many years earlier.

Chapter 77

The Sky

†††

The 3rd Corps of the El Tigran assault force approached the shore of Parlantis and prepared to disembark. Trajan had directed the 3rd Corps to land on a different beach to avoid whatever had happened earlier to the 2nd Corps. Still, anyone who had seen the earlier bloodbath was very apprehensive.

It was an hour before sunrise, and the El Tigran ships approached by moonlight. All their attention was on the shore and any threat that might arise from there.

Admiral Teagan was responsible to Trajan for getting the assault force safely to Parlantis. He stood at the helm of the command ship, pondering what had happened to the 2nd Corps.

I've seen nothing like it. It's like the earth just opened up and swallowed them. My responsibility was getting them to the shore. After they disembark my ships, I have no control over what happens.

Admiral Teagan wasn't sure that Trajan would see it that way. Trajan was unpredictable; he directed his anger toward anyone in the vicinity. But that was a future problem. For now, Admiral Teagan had to get the 3rd Corps safely to shore.

Teagan relaxed for a moment and allowed himself to appreciate the beauty of the full moon, low over Parlantis, casting its beams of pale blue light off of the wave-tops. What a glorious sight it was to behold; so peaceful and serene.

I wish my Genevieve could be here to see this.

He pictured how she would look in this light. Her long hair flowing in the breeze like the waves tossed here and there upon the sea.

Oh, how I miss you, my darling.

Out of the corner of his eye, Admiral Teagan noticed a momentary aberration interrupt the tranquility of the moment.

What was that?

The glint of the moonlight had highlighted something. But what?

Without warning, one ship in the troop convoy erupted in flames. All eyes shifted their focus to the fiery beacon of death, announcing to all the position of the El Tigran attack force. The screams of hundreds of men burning to death in the night terrified every El Tigran soldier to the bone.

What could have caused that ship to go up in flames so quickly?

Teagan snapped his attention back to the moon.

What did I see right before that ship went up in flames? Are the two related?

Suddenly, a second ship in the fleet erupted in flames. Instantly, the possibility of an accident disappeared. Something was attacking them in the darkness and for the first time in his life, it petrified Admiral Teagan.

Then he saw them highlighted by the full moon over Parlantis — dozens of them approaching the fleet.

"Archers at the ready!" The command echoed through the fleet, but it was too late.

Another glint of light caught General Teagan's attention. It was straight off the bow and approaching at incredible speed.

Oh no.

The whispering death descended to just a few feet off of the surface of the sea. The descent had given it so much airspeed that it now glided directly and effortlessly toward its target.

It was an effortless approach. The waters of the sea rose high into the air in the wake of its swept wings. It locked its eyes upon the lead ship and the man standing at the bow. Valdo's eyes burned with fury.

How dare these foreigners think they can attack our land and subjugate the creatures here to their evil endeavors. Let our enemies forever know that as long as the tannin dwell in Parlantis, she shall remain free.

A barrage of arrows flew by as Valdo released his payload upon the ship. The man at the helm burst into flames shortly before the rest of his men and his ship did the same.

Dozens of tannin struck their targets simultaneously. The ships of the invasion fleet erupted into flames and sunk into the depths of the dark sea. The El Tigran fleet and its men were no more.

†††

Christian and Kristana sat beneath the glowing orb that engulfed them. The moon was low upon the horizon to the east, and a bright orange flame suddenly burned beyond the trees to the west.

"What do you think is happening on the coast, Christian?"

"I know what I hope is happening, Tristana, but I can't be sure."

"I share your hope, but I hesitate to even say it out loud."

They closed their eyes and prayed that it be so.

Christian opened his eyes and looked out upon the many bonfires that burned in the valley below the knoll.

"Why don't they attack us? Surely, they can see us below the glowing orb that surrounds us."

"I think it's precisely because of the glowing orb they don't attack us."

"They don't understand it anymore than we do, and because of that, they are cautious, maybe even fearful."

"Of course. That makes sense."

Christian and Tristana rested within the protection of the golden orb, looking up at the stars.

"How long are we going to stay here?" Tristana asked. "I'm getting pretty hungry."

They both laughed.

"I don't know. I guess until the enemy moves on or help shows up."

"Help? We don't need any help. I think we can take 'em."

"Let's get some rest and we can take 'em in the morning."

They both drifted off into a deep sleep. Suddenly, they awoke to the sound of a whoosh and jumped up to their feet.

"What was that?" Kristana asked.

"I don't know."

Whoosh! Whoosh!

Two enormous shadows flew low over their heads, momentarily silhouetted by the moon. A second later, the tents of the enemy encampment burst into flames, the inferno lighting up the early morning sky.

Kristana stared in awe at the nearly instantaneous destruction of the invaders taking place in the valley. "Whoa! What is happening?"

"I think I might know what is going on here." Christian had no sooner said the words, and a tannin landed on the knoll where they were standing. As if on cue, the golden orb glowing around Christian and Kristana dissipated.

Kristana instantly prepared to fight the dragon. Before Christian could tell Kristana to stand down, Tannar peeked around the giant neck of the tannin he was riding and said, "Anyone around here want a ride?"

"Wow, are we glad to see you!" Christian screamed.

Tristana maintained her fighting stance, unsure of what was happening.

"Hop on, Tristana!"

"Say again?"

Christian jumped on the dragon and repeated his plea to Tristana.

"We have to go. Hop on!"

"That's a dragon!"

"Actually, it's a tannin. Let's go!"

Kristana didn't care for dragons. She wasn't sure why — not that anyone really needs a reason.

Tannar peeked around the dragon's neck again and smiled. "We're the good guys. Promise."

Tristana looked at Tannar, looked at Christian, and then looked at the dragon. “Fine. But it is against my better judgement!”

She climbed onto the tannin’s back; the dragon flapped its mighty wings, and away they went.

Chapter 78

Love

†††

The El Tigran assassins could not catch Evie. There was a reason she had been entrusted with the urgent message; she was the fastest rider in Parlantis.

First Evie went to Parlantis Command Headquarters to deliver the message to General Sanders, but the headquarters were closed because of the week-long stand-down of the guard.

How stupid!

So Evie went directly to General Sander's residence to find him.

Evie arrived at the residence, dismounted, and frantically pounded on the front door. The door opened.

"I need to speak to General Sanders immediately!"

"Slow down now. How can I help you?"

"I told you I need to speak to General Sanders right now! It is absolutely urgent!"

"General Sanders is not available at the moment."

"I need to give him a message immediately. It is of absolute importance!"

"I'm his daughter, Maria. Give me the message, and I'll give it to him as soon as he's available."

"I'm sorry. I can't do that."

"Alright then, come on in, and you can wait for him. It shouldn't be too long."

Evie followed Maria to the den.

"You can have a seat anywhere you would like. Can I get you something to drink? You look exhausted."

"I think I'll stand. I've done about as much sitting as I want to do anytime soon. Water, please?"

"Coming right up."

Evie walked to the large window that overlooked the rolling hills behind the residence.

Where is he? What is taking so long? There's only one thing I could think of that could have him occupied at this moment.

Maria snuck up behind Evie as she was looking out the window. Maria held a small marble statue in her hand.

Evie slowly relaxed as she watched the gentle breeze blowing through the trees at the back of the residence. Her long ride caught up with her, and her heart rate slowed. Even though she was standing, drowsiness invaded her consciousness; her eyes started to close.

Evie wondered if she was dreaming as she noticed an image in the window's reflection; an image that was approaching her from behind. Evie felt so peaceful. Her mind told her to not believe her eyes, and to just enjoy the moment of rest — a moment that she deserved so much. It wasn't until the image raised the club-like item in its hand that Evie's sense of survival trumped the voice of deception.

Christen entered the room. "Maria, what are you doing?"

It surprised Maria momentarily, and she turned her head away from her target.

Evie spun around with lightning speed as her consciousness returned and her trained combat reflexes took over. With a single motion, she grabbed Maria's arm and flipped Maria backwards onto the floor. Maria landed with a thud, knocking all the air out of her lungs.

"What is going on here?" Christen screamed as she rushed into the room.

"Mrs. Sanders, I have an urgent message for General Sanders. It is of the utmost importance — life and death — that I get this to him immediately."

The distraction gave Maria just enough time to kick Evie's right knee with such force as to shatter the bone. Evie fell to the ground next to Maria. Maria picked up her weapon and raised it to strike Evie in the head.

"Maria stop! No!"

Christen had only a moment to decide what to do. She didn't understand what Maria was doing, but Maria was her adopted daughter. She loved Maria and would never choose to hurt her. So Christen did the only thing she could do in this situation, the only thing she had time to do — she kicked Maria in the face.

Desperate times.

Maria flew backwards into the wall behind her, seemingly unconscious.

Christen kneeled down next to Evie. "Are you ok? I'm so sorry. I don't know what got into my daughter."

"I'm fine. I have to speak to General Sanders."

"He's not here. He was called to the palace to speak with the queen."

Evie held her knee as tears rolled down her face. She knew she'd be unable to get the message to General Sanders.

"Get him this message. We are under attack! The invasion has begun! The guard must respond immediately!"

"Oh no! But what about you? What about my daughter?"

Christen looked to see if Maria was ok, but Maria was gone.

"Don't worry about me. Get that message to the general. The fate of the country now depends on you. Go now!"

Christen leaped to her feet and ran out the door.

"Let her in."

The guards allowed Christen to enter the queen's throne room and closed the doors behind her.

"So you must be Mrs. Sanders? It is so nice to meet you, finally."

"Yes. The pleasure is all mine, your majesty. Unfortunately, I must insist on seeing my husband right away. I was told he was here?"

"Bold. What's the rush? Let's visit a bit."

"No. There is no time for that right now. I must get him a message immediately."

"I'm afraid you misunderstand the rules. In my throne room, as it is throughout my kingdom, I give the orders. Not you."

Christen was stunned.

"Come closer to where I can see you."

Christen approached the queen, who was sitting in her judgment seat on the throne.

"Where is my husband?"

"We'll get to that in due time. For now, he is adequately entertained."

"You don't understand. The country is under attack! There is an invasion! We have to tell General Sanders, so he can deploy the guard to defend us."

"I know all about that. I'm the queen."

"But don't you care? Your country will be destroyed!"

"It won't be destroyed. It will just change, and be how it should be."

Suddenly, Christen understood. "You're in on it!"

"In on it? No. Again, I'm the queen. I'm not in on it, I'm behind it."

"I demand to see my husband."

"Again with the demands? I thought we went through that already. But if you insist, walk this way."

The queen led Christen to the chamber behind the throne room, where Grumpy Sanders was pinned against the wall. He writhed in excruciating pain. As soon as Christen saw him, she ran towards him, but was stopped by some invisible force.

"Not so fast," said Queen Tharice. "Let's play a little game first."

Tears ran down Christen's face as she watched her husband suffer.

"You must love him very much."

"I do."

"Do you believe in his god?"

"Not only his God, but the one true God."

Christen and Grumpy made eye contact; pain and tears.

"Deny your God, and I will release him."

Christen thought about Tharice's offer, but her thoughts were interrupted by the painfully spoken, barely audible words Grumpy could get out of his mouth between clenched teeth. "No weapon — formed against me — shall prosper."

Tharice instantly responded by doubling Grumpy's pain. "Quiet! The ladies are talking."

"Now, where were we? Oh, yes. Deny your God, and I will release your husband."

"No!"

"No? You say you love him. Why would you not take away his pain?"

"I cannot deny our God."

"Then you have no love for your husband. You can't even say a few simple words to take away his pain."

"I will not deny our God. He has promised to always be with us, and he will save us! This battle is already won! I know how the story ends!"

Tharice increased Grumpy's pain yet again.

"Foolish girl. Deny him."

"No."

"Deny him."

"No."

"Deny him!"

"No! Get thee away from me, Satan!"

Tharice reacted to the words as if she had just been punched in the chest. She stumbled backwards, noticeably shaken. The crimson light within the room faded as Tharice retreated.

Christen said the words again. "Get thee away from me, Satan!"

Again, Tharice was thrown backwards as if struck by lightning, and the crimson light in the room faded. A golden glow took its place.

A third time, Christen screamed the words. "Get thee away from me, Satan!"

Tharice could take no more and ran from the room.

The force that was holding Christen back from Grumpy dissipated, and Christen ran to him. He was still pinned against the wall and in excruciating pain. Christen did not know what to do.

"Please father, have mercy on us? I love you, and I love him, the man you gave me. Help us?"

Christen wrapped her arms around her husband's head and kissed him. Instantly, the light in the room filled with bright golden rays. The force that held Grumpy against the wall released him and he collapsed into Christen's arms.

Christen helped Grumpy out of the throne room. She did not know how they would get past the guards, but strangely enough, the guards stood like stone statues, not showing that they even saw Christen and Grumpy leave.

Chapter 79

Victory

†††

Valdo helped Christian, Tristana, and Tannar join Red and the remaining guard troops. General Sanders and the reinforcements still hadn't arrived. Even though the 2nd and 3rd Corps of the El Tigran army had been decimated, the 1st Corps was more than enough for the few remaining guard infantry to contend with. The 1st Corps of El Tigran troops still outnumbered the Parlantians one-hundred to one, and it surrounded the survivors. As the sun rose, the few Parlantians stood against the many.

A delegation approached on horseback under a white flag. The horses stopped about a hundred yards from the rocks where the Parlantians had taken cover.

Christian, Kristana, Tannar, Red, and the others watched the delegation approach.

"I wish we hadn't sent the tannin back to the caves." Kristana thought out loud. "They could have made a short order of the rest of these invaders."

"True, but I promised them we would restrict their operations to darkness to minimize their exposure." Tannar offered. "They are trying to remain discrete."

"Well, they certainly made a difference in this battle. We wouldn't have made it this far without them." Christian said. "Now, what do you make of this? Why would they want to talk?"

"They probably feel a little uneasy after losing two-thirds of their fighting force the way they did," Tannar offered.

"Perhaps." Christian said.

"Or maybe it's a trap. Who knows if they honor a white flag?" Kristana offered.

"Only one way to find out." Christian decided. "Tannar and I will ride out and hear what they have to say. Red, you and Kristana stay here in the rocks and ready the archers to reign down hell on them should there be any trickery."

Kristana wasn't happy about staying behind, and once they all split up, she let Christian know it. "Why am I staying behind? I'm probably the best fighter we have."

"You are the best fighter we have, and in case this is a trap, I don't want them to take the best fighter we have off of the field."

"That is a bogus argument, and you know it. I should go with you."

"Look, I've made my decision."

"You don't get to decide what I do. I'm not formally part of the Parlantis Guard. I'm an independent contractor!"

"Can't you just stay here? Why do you have to make this difficult?"

"For the same reason that you're making it difficult!"

"And why exactly is that?"

"Because you're trying to protect me. And I want to protect you. And that's why I'm going with you. Because if something happens to you, it is gonna happen to me too. I've made my decision."

Tristana had finished saying what she needed to say, and she stomped off. Christian just watched her walk away and didn't try to stop her. She had made her own decision, and there was nothing Christian could do about it.

I love her.

†††

Christian, Tannar, and Tristana rode out to meet Trajan, the 1st Corps Commander, and one of their cavalry champions.

"Behold, the defenders of Parlantis!" Trajan announced as the Parlantians approached. The El Tigran delegation laughed aloud.

Christian responded with a smile as he stopped before Trajan. "I think you got a little taste of Parlantian defense last night, didn't you?"

The El Tigrans immediately stopped laughing, their anger exploding across their faces.

Christian asked, "What do you want?"

"I am Trajan. I am here to discuss your surrender."

Christian smiled. "Why would I surrender?"

"You are defeated."

"We are? I think you have lost far more men than we have. Our primary force hasn't even joined us yet. I thought we were coming out to accept your surrender."

"You expect to stop me with your measly force of surviving cavalry fighters?"

"Seems we have been doing alright so far."

"You will all die, slowly. I will make sure of it! My forces will swarm your positions and bury you!"

"You're a pretty scary guy, Trajan, and somewhat pompous. Haven't you learned that he that is with us is greater than they who are with you? Your reinforcements are gone."

Trajan was incensed at Christian's lack of reverence toward him. He pulled out his special black stone and directed the Parlantian horses to buck; throwing the Parlantians from their horses to a hard landing on the rocks. Trajan laughed.

Christian and Tannar helped Tristana up off the ground. "Nice Trajan — classy."

Trajan saw the medallions hanging around all of their necks. "Veteri! I should have known! Now the night-fire makes sense. I will have to deal with those miserable creatures once we take Parlantis."

Tannar replied, "How did dealing with them work out for you last night?"

Trajan moved forward toward Tannar.

Christian, with a flick of his wrist, signaled Red.

By the time that Trajan's horse moved two feet forward, three arrows were in the air. By the time that Trajan's horse had moved five feet forward, the three arrows landed in front of Trajan's horse, stopping it in its tracks.

Trajan exclaimed, "You attacked me under a white flag of truce!"

Christian replied, "If we had attacked you, you would be dead."

"I'll see you on the field of battle, Christian!"

"Count on it, Trajan."

The battle lines were drawn. The two armies stood facing one another. Ten exhausted Parlantian defenders stood against one thousand fresh El Tigran invaders. By all rational consideration, the outcome of the battle had been determined before it had begun. There was no logical way that ten soldiers, no matter how good they were, could defeat a trained army of one thousand; and yet, the Parlantians stood before the invaders, confident of victory.

Their confidence did not stem from hubris or bravado. Rather, it emanated from the leaders of the battle-weary group to every cavalry soldier upon the field of battle.

Christian and Tristana were confident of the outcome of the battle. Even Red was confident, though not as much. Christian and Tristana had spoken to Red about all the amazing things they had seen. They had witnessed to him extensively about the one true God. Indeed, Red himself had seen many amazing things. Still, Red was hesitant to believe with all of his heart; he had doubts.

Red stood beside his comrades, ready to die. He had faced many enemies before, sure that he would not make it until the next morning, but this time was different. Christian had convinced Red that death was a fork in the road leading to two completely different eternal destinations.

One was eternal bliss, and the other was eternal pain. For the first time in his life, he was anxious about which path he might be on.

There is an old saying that offers there are no atheists in foxholes. While enjoying a normal existence of experiences and pleasures, a person is well distracted from considering the greater philosophical truths of life and their eternal ramifications. However, when suddenly faced with the reality that one will soon know the destination of their eternity, terror can grip the soul of even the most battle-hardened warrior.

Red turned and faced Christian. “My friend, may we speak for a moment?”

Christian was a bit taken aback at the timing of the impromptu discussion. However, time itself was in God’s hands, and God often chose the most inopportune times to speak to his children.

“I have doubts.”

“It’s ok, Red, we are all human, and we all have our doubts.”

“I’m not sure about where I am going.”

“My friend. Remember, our God has promised to be with us. Whether we live or whether we die, the one who created us has numbered all our heartbeats. When he calls us home, nothing will keep us from leaving, nor should we want anything to keep us here. He has an amazing place prepared for all those who call upon his name and trust in his salvation. He loves us, and for the sake of the one he promised will someday come to pay for our failures, he forgives us. If you have faith in this promise, you will be saved.”

“I believe all that.”

“Then there is nothing to fear, Red. You will be saved.”

“Thank you, Christian.”

Their attention returned to the mission at hand.

Red prayed a silent prayer to the God who listened and always heard. *I believe, Father. Please forgive my unbelief? If it be your will, please give me one last sign you hear my prayers.*

The El Tigrans formed three battle lines in front of the Parlantians; one directly in front of them and one on each side of them. It was comical to behold, as the Parlantians were so outnumbered that it made the situation seem ridiculous.

Their fearless commander, Trajan, watched the battle from high above on a nearby mountain ledge to ensure his safety. In addition, he had five archers with him for his defense.

Tristana looked at Christian. "So I'm pretty confident we can take the three hundred men directly in front of us, but who's gonna engage the two forces to the sides of us while we do that?"

"Yeah, I've been asking myself that same question."

"Has yourself come up with any suitable answers?"

"Not yet, but I'll let you know as soon as it does."

Trajan signaled the commander of the 1st Corps to advance. A moment later, all three El Tigran formations began moving on the Parlantians.

"Fight's on!" Christian screamed, though it wasn't really necessary, based on their proximity to each other.

Red asked Christian, "Any tactical instructions regarding the battle plan?"

"Yeah. Kill the bad guys as quickly as possible."

"Copy that, sir."

Tristana asked, "Do you think we'll see any unexpected visitors to even out the odds here a bit?"

"You tell me, Tristana. It seems you have had more experience with that than I have."

"Well, I've been praying since sunrise, and the one true God has never let me down yet. I say we step forward in faith by charging the El Tigran commander and his troops in front of us."

"That is a great idea! Charge!"

On Christian's command, the ten-strong Parlantian formation charged the El Tigrans. Trajan and his entire invasion force thundered in laughter as they saw the pitifully outnumbered Parlantians charge the vastly superior military machine in front of them; but they didn't laugh for long.

As the small, ragtag force charged forward in faith, fully expecting their God to go with them, their numbers suddenly multiplied tenfold; adding fifty to their left and fifty to their right.

Numerically, the Parlantians were still massively outnumbered, but suddenly, their numbers assumed a distinct advantage. Those who had joined them from out of nowhere were not your average run-of-the-mill fighters. Charging beside the Parlantians were one hundred golden angels. Equipped with golden armor and flaming swords, these angels had fought demons in the heavenly realm for ions, and to say they were experienced in the art of war would be to understate the obvious. The angel formations lit up the El Tigran formations to the left and right.

The armies merged at full speed and the brutal hand-to-hand fighting ensued. Like a hot knife through butter, the angel formations effortlessly passed through the El Tigrans, sending them mercilessly to their maker.

The middle of the battlefield saw a much more balanced match. Encouraged by the recent additions to their battle-line, the Parlantians fought beyond their abilities, holding their own, though growing more and more weary by the minute.

As the golden angels quickly routed the two side formations of the El Tigrans, they curved inward and converged on the El Tigran center formation, which quickly began to crumble.

Trajan could not believe what was happening. A certain victory was becoming an unmitigated defeat. His heart burned with rage!

"Target the Parlantian commander!"

Without delay, Trajan's archers lifted their bows and fired on Christian. Unaware of the lethal arrows that were inbound, within seconds, Christian would be dead.

The fighting in the center formation was quickly coming to a close. Having completed the tasks assigned by the Master, the angel warriors faded back into the heavenly realm. The Parlantians had all sustained injuries, but everyone had survived. They hugged each other and celebrate their unlikely victory.

As they let their guard down, only one man saw what was descending on them from above, and only one man had any time to do something about it. Red had glanced up toward the mountain ledge where he had seen the El Tigran commander before the battle. He saw the archers release their arrows, and his eyes followed the deadly darts as they descended.

"No!"

There was no time to direct Christian to move, or to push him out of the way. All Red could do was stand in front of death, and like a good soldier, that is what he did.

Christian never knew what was happening until his eyes met Red's in that final moment. Red's eyes were filled with love for his commander and his friend; they beamed a determination to do what needed to be done; and they signaled the knowing pain as each enemy arrow pierced his skin, diving deep into his back and out of his chest.

Christian caught Red as he fell; Red's life ebbing from his body.

Red spoke his last words, sharing one last thought with his friend; the friend who had given him the most precious gift anyone could give another; truth. "I know that my redeemer lives." Red smiled, and then his eyes closed.

No greater love has a man than to give his life for a friend.

Tears filled Christian's eyes. Christian looked up to the mountain ledge to see Trajan laughing. Their eyes met. Christian's sadness turned to anger, and then his anger turned to rage. He leaped on a nearby horse and rode as fast as he could toward the mountain ledge where Trajan stood.

†††

Christian arrived at the place he last saw Trajan a few minutes earlier. Trajan was there, waiting for him. He stood with his sword and shield in hand. Oddly, it appeared his sword hand and sword were connected, as if they were one solid piece of metal. His arm had strange markings on it — like small lights that were flashing together.

Christian dismounted his horse, drew his sword, and walked toward his nemesis.

"It took you long enough."

"I didn't think you'd still be here, Trajan. You are a coward; not leading your men into battle."

"Some say cowardice; some say wisdom. When things don't go well, I live to fight another day. Kind of like today."

"I think that is the definition of a coward."

"Wise coward then. It's settled."

"Well, if you think you're gonna live to fight another day, let me tell you that you're about to be disappointed. You will soon be a dead coward. Now it's settled."

"That's pretty tough talk from a guy that doesn't have his surprise guests here to help him."

"I don't need any guests to help me with what I'm about to do to you."

"Bring it on, bad boy. I've been waiting."

Christian began his charge. There was about twenty meters between him and Trajan. About halfway to his target, Christian realized that his anger and impetuousness had allowed Trajan to bait him into a trap. The ground beneath him gave way, and Christian fell ten feet into a rock pit. He wasn't alone.

After recovering from his hard landing, Christian backed up against the wall facing the three monster bears. They didn't look happy.

Trajan looked down into the pit.

"Surprise! Especially prepared just for you! You see, there was another reason I was up here. Let me introduce you to your new best friends; three giant browns from El Tigre. We El Tigrans know the browns for both their ferocity and their appetite. Don't worry, there won't be remains for anyone to mourn over. They devour everything after tearing it to pieces. Bone appetite everyone! Enjoy the rest of your day."

Christian picked up his sword and fell to his knees, facing the bears. Then he bowed his head and prayed. *Almighty God in heaven, your will be done. If it is your will on this day that these bears should show me into your presence, then so be it. However, if it is your will that I should dispatch these bears with urgency, please give me the strength to do so.*

The pit suddenly filled with a bright golden light. Standing before Christian was a golden angel with a streak of silver across his head.

"I am Engel. Your request has been granted."

Christian was in awe and could barely speak. He bowed on his knees before the angel. When he spoke, he said, "Oh, powerful angel, thank you for what you and your friends did to help us on the field of battle. May I ask you which request was granted?"

Engel responded, "Rise to your feet, warrior; I am not the almighty God, who is the only one worthy of our worship and praise. Your life is to be spared today, for there is much your line will accomplish in History. Your children will accomplish great things in this world and the truth will spread far through their offspring."

Engel looked at the bears on the opposite side of the pit. They clawed and tore at the ground as if chained or some invisible force held them back; which, of course, it did.

"As for your circumstances today, it is unfortunate that these magnificent creatures must be sacrificed. The infection of the evil one is strong, and there is only one way to resolve this situation."

Then Engel's sword glowed. Engel took it in two of his hands and handed it to Christian.

"I'm afraid your sword won't do, but this one will do the trick."

Christian was in awe! An angel of the almighty God had just handed him a flaming sword and directed him to use it. Suddenly, the apprehension of fighting the three giant bears turned to sympathy.

"Are you certain there is nothing else we can do?"

"These creatures have tasted human flesh. They can no longer be allowed to roam this land. Do not enjoy this task I lay before you. Rather, just think of it as something that must be done."

The smile on Christian's face faded and his attitude took on one of empathy and sorrow for the bears he must now kill.

Engel and the golden glow faded from the pit, but the glow of the sword kept it lit brightly. *Why do these creatures not fear the sight of the flaming sword? It must be evil's infection within them. I mourn for what they once were, but I have no sympathy for the evil that they now are. Their time has passed and their life is forfeited. I take no pleasure, but in the fulfillment of righteous anger.*

†††

Thirty minutes later, Christian heard Tristana calling from above.

"Down here. I'm down here!"

A moment later, Tristana was looking down at Christian in the pit.

"Umm, what's going on here? It looks like someone gathered all the parts of hunted creatures for a BBQ and then just scattered them about."

"Yeah, I know. I kind of went beast-mode. It's messy down here, too. Would you mind throwing me the end of a rope if you have one up there on your horse? I'm assuming you brought a horse?"

"Yep, sure did. I'll go get it. Oh, did you take care of that scum, Trajan?"

"No, unfortunately he had this trap prepared for me, and I didn't see it coming until, well, you know. Then I had to contend with three giant bears. Trajan will have to wait for another day."

Tristana was disappointed but happy that Christian was alright. She tied one end of a rope onto her saddle and then threw Christian the other end. When Christian was ready, she pulled him out of the pit with the help of her horse. Tristana stood over the pit, ready to meet him when he emerged.

Christian carefully crawled from the pit, disconnected the rope from his waist, and smiled. He walked toward Tristana with his arms open wide, ready to give her a big bear hug. He was covered in mud and blood.

"Honey, I'm home."

"I don't think so, soldier boy."

"You aren't glad that I'm alright?"

"A bear hug? Really? How corny! I'll save my happiness for another time — thank you very much."

"So that's the way it's gonna be?"

"I hate to tell you, but that's the way it already is. Maybe that works on your hunting parties, but as far as the female psyche goes, blood and hug don't mix. What happened down there?"

"Three enormous bears."

"How did you do all that?"

"I had a little help. I'll tell you about it later."

"Oh, by the way, you'll be happy to hear that one of our scouts just reported seeing an enormous formation of Parlantian cavalry approaching from the east. Looks like the rider finally made it to General Sanders."

"That's great timing, isn't it?"

"Exactly, but we got to see the power of Almighty God and his messengers. It will make for quite the memory to tell our children." Kristana had a sparkle in her eyes.

"Our children?"

"Hypothetically speaking, of course."

Christian smiled. "Of course."

Chapter 80

Dark Instructions

†††

The dragon called them, and they heard their master's call.

Trajan, Tharice and Maria stood frozen before a roaring inferno in the pale moonlight of a full moon as they had all done countless times before; waiting for their dark master.

The flames exploded high into the sky as the crimson beast appeared from within the fire.

"My children. Do you remember when I first joined with each of you?"

"Yes, Master."

"Trajan, we have been together the longest. It was many moons ago that your father, Nod, did my bidding. He served his purpose in establishing my kingdom in Heath. However, his years were not sufficient, and my kingdom there did not last. When you, his son, fled Heath, I was determined for your years to last longer than his did. We joined, and you have lived the equivalent of many lives since then."

"Yes, Master."

"Thalia and Mirah, our time together has more recently begun. Still, you have served me well. When we first joined with each of you in the fires of Tophet, we knew we would be with you until the very end. I am certain there is much more that we have to do together."

"Yes, Master."

The beast reached out with his long, sharp claws and touched the marks it had given to each of its servants. Instantly, their new instructions flowed. Instantly, they each knew what their master wanted them to do.

"In time, after you have accomplished your tasks, we will meet in person again. Until then, remember well what I have told you and do not forget who it is that you serve. Move as stealthily as the leopard, be as cunning as the fox, and strike as deadly as the serpent."

"Yes, Master."

"Now go."

The beast spun swiftly within the flames and then dove back into the fire. Its long, scaly tail followed behind it and disappeared. A moment later, the fire went out.

Trajan, Thalia, and Mirah headed north in the darkness on their long journey to Heath; but there was something they had to accomplish along the way.

Part 16: Recovery

Chapter 81

Coronation

†††

It had been two weeks since the defeat of the El Tigran invasion and its conspirators. Christen and Grumpy were still recovering from the loss of their daughter, Maria. They just did not understand where they had gone wrong and how she could have gone so far off course. There had been no sign of her anywhere in Parlantis since that day.

Still, Christen's and Grumpy's relationship had never been stronger. When the going got rough, Christen had stood toe-to-toe with the Queen of Darkness to save her husband. None of this had been lost on General Sanders. He doubted whether many of his men, men of tremendous bravery, would have done the same. Though his men loved him, they didn't love him like Christen loved him. For Christen, Grumpy shared a one-of-a-kind love, and for that, he would be forever thankful.

Christian and Tristana had arrived early in the morning to spend the day visiting with Christen and Grumpy. At Tristana's suggestion, they sat down to play a board game. The game Tristana had picked typically took a couple of hours. Grumpy wasn't particularly fond of games that lasted that long, but what could he say? Tristana was a new friend and potentially his future daughter-in-law, so he didn't want to offend her.

The game was almost over when Christian asked Grumpy the question.

"Have you heard any news about who the people might choose as their new king?"

"Not yet. Trying to get the council to agree on something so momentous is nearly impossible. Getting a majority of the population to approve is equally difficult. Historically, it has taken years, which can prove quite perilous for the country. During these periods of time, the country is vulnerable to both internal strife and external attack. With any luck, we have just withstood the only onslaught from a foreign enemy that was in the works, but the internal strife can also prove quite catastrophic."

"What types of men have historically proven the best candidates to be king?"

"Well, you want someone relatively young so they can serve for a while, but you don't want him to be so young that he isn't wise enough to lead a country."

Tristana joined the discussion. "It seems someone with military experience would also be a good idea. After all, an understanding of military operations can mean the difference between survival and the destruction of the entire country."

Everyone around the table nodded in agreement.

Christen added, "I think he should be a married man. The king needs to be aware of how his decisions will affect not only the men of the country but also the women and children. We also don't need a king who spends the entire time running around trying to find a queen."

Again, everyone nodded in agreement.

Christian added. "Well, I would think that leadership experience would be an absolute must. I mean, you're picking the guy that's responsible for and to the entire country, after all."

Grumpy looked at Christian and smiled. "If you were to find yourself a bride, you could be a contender."

Everyone laughed at Grumpy's joke.

When everyone stopped laughing, Christian looked at Grumpy and replied, "You already have yourself a bride. That makes you a contender."

“Ha! That’s a good one! I’ll bet you my best horse that doesn’t happen.”

“Alright then! I’ll take that bet!”

“What? You can’t be serious, Christian. Why would you do that?”

“Well, have you looked outside lately?”

Grumpy pushed away from the table and looked out the back window.

“What the—? What is happening out there? There must be thousands of people in our backyard. What is going on? I am going out there and—”

“Your majesty, you might want to change your clothes.”

Grumpy stopped dead in his tracks and turned around. He looked at Christen, and then at Christian. “Are you saying?”

“The people have spoken.”

†††

Grumpy wasn’t looking for the great pomp and circumstance that accompanied the coronation of a king, but the people insisted. Coronation was a big deal, and tradition dictated everyone knew it. It was a celebration more festive than any could remember or imagine. For so long, the country had been in decline, and now there was a birth of new hope. The people of Parlantis not only had a new king and queen, but also faithful witnesses to the one true God. The faith spread like wildfire throughout the land.

The king charged Christian and Tristana with sealing up the border and stopping the illicit flow of drugs that were pouring into Parlantis from El Tigre. They pursued the task with a vengeance.

Having stemmed the flow of mind-altering chemicals into the cities of Parlantis, the cities healed. It was accidentally discovered that middle-mist red, when consumed without other chemicals, had healing effects on the body and actually countered addiction. Having bountiful amounts of the flower available, the medicine quickly healed the drug-addicted population.

Tannar took his rightful place as leader of the eastern tribes. Under his leadership, the tribes enjoyed a golden age of prosperity and peace. They lived together with western Parlantis in a glorious peaceful coexistence.

The tannin retreated once again to the seclusion of the caves, where they had existed undetected for so long. Before long, Snuffy became the leader of the tannin.

Christian and Tristana fell deeper and deeper in love with every passing day. It was like a dam had broken, and they could no longer hold their emotions back. Before long, Christian asked Tristana to stay with him until the end of time. She said, "Yes."

Chapter 82

Going Home

†††

It was a beautiful fall day. Christian and Tristana were out riding through the mountains and enjoying spending time with each other. They had so much to do. Their time together as a couple was just beginning, and there was a wedding to plan.

As they were riding, they noticed a circle of rocks outside the entrance to a cave. They decided they would stop there, relax a bit, and discuss the future.

While they were tying up their horses, they noticed a large man in a black hooded robe sitting outside of the cave entrance. They were startled because they hadn't seen the man sitting there a moment earlier.

Christian approached the man. "Good day, sir."

"That it is, and a good day to both of you."

"Do you mind if I ask how you got here? This is kind of in the middle of nowhere."

"Oh, is it? I didn't realize. My name is Nomen."

"My name is Christian, and this is Tristana."

"Well, it is very nice to meet both of you."

"Where are you from, Nomen?"

"I'm originally from Heath."

"You're a long way from home."

"You have no idea."

Christian and Tristana looked at each other, and without saying a word, communicated their shared concern about the situation.

Tristana then approached the man and asked. “Nomen, what are you doing here?”

“Oh, I assure you, my dear, there is no reason for concern. It is a wonderful day. I have come to take you home.”

Tristana slowly backed away from the man, stopping a respectful distance away.

Nomen stood. “Oh my, I’m afraid I’ve given you the wrong idea. I’m not here to bring just you home, but both of you home.”

Nomen pulled off his hood to reveal a full, jolly face with a bright smile. Instantly, the persona of the man changed dramatically and a sense of ease and well-being came over both Christian and Tristana.

Christian said, “I don’t understand.”

Both Christian and Tristana felt strange; as if their minds were suddenly foggy. Tristana placed her hand on Christian’s shoulder to maintain her balance. Suddenly feeling sleepy, both of them rubbed their eyes, trying to wake up.

“Don’t worry, the feeling will pass in a moment. You will feel much better. You think you are getting sleepy, but in fact, your mind is actually coming out of the fog that it’s been in for a very long time.”

A moment later it was just as Nomen had foretold. They both regained their composure and felt wonderful. They looked at each other in amazement!

“Lee, it’s you! You found me!”

Tristana threw her arms around Christian’s neck and hugged him. Christian hugged her back. Tears filled both of their eyes as the memories of old and new, the distant past and the present, merged; and they remembered everything.

Nomen’s smile widened. *I love this part.*

Christian and Tristana kissed. It was a gentle kiss. It was a kiss like they had not shared before; a kiss that they would remember always.

Christian looked into Tristana's eyes. "I made a promise that I would find you and bring you home — if it was the last thing I ever did."

They kissed again.

"Ahem."

They suddenly remembered that Nomen was standing there beside them.

"And I am here to help you keep that promise. It's time to go home."

Tristana said, "But we have to say goodbye. We can't just leave Christen and Grumpy without saying goodbye — without explaining."

"I'm afraid there could be no explaining that they would understand. And I'm afraid there isn't time."

Christian asked, "What do you mean, there isn't time? We have been gone for years, and there isn't time for us to say goodbye?"

"I'm very sorry for both of you, and I'm also thrilled for both of you. If you want to go home, it must be now."

They looked at each other with tears of both happiness and sadness in their eyes. Tristana gave Christian a slight nod.

Christian looked at Noman. "It's time to go home."

Noman smiled. "Yes, it is."

Christian asked, "By the way, where is Kissami?"

"Another time."

"So there are more than one of you?"

"Oh yes, there most certainly are. This way."

Christian and Tristana followed Nomen into the cave entrance.

Christian comforted Tristana, who was looking anxious. "Don't worry honey, I've done this before, and it's amazing!"

"I can't wait to see my mom and dad. It has been so long!"

They followed Nomen down a long tunnel of glowing emerald lights.

A moment later, they were gone.

Henry and Bekka were sitting on their porch watching the sunset over the Dark Sea as they tried to do every evening. Their golden retriever, Beckett, lay curled up at Henry's feet.

As the sun set on the horizon, a burst of color erupted across the sky and reminded Henry of the sky so many years ago when he picked up the family that had meant so much to him.

Where had they gone for so long?

Beckett raised her head off the wooden porch floor and let out a soft whine.

"What's wrong, girl?"

Henry looked out towards the sea and noticed a pair of silhouettes walking towards them up the grassy hill.

Beckett stood and bolted towards the strangers that approached.

"Beckett, come!"

Beckett didn't listen, but ran up right up to the two strangers who immediately showered her with their love.

Well, I guess they can't be too bad if they love dogs.

Bekka said, "Looks like Beckett gives her approval."

Henry and Bekka slowly rose and stood in front of their rocking chairs.

Henry said, "Seems kind of late for visitors. You would think people would have more common sense."

"Henry, keep your voice down! Don't be rude!"

The couple arrived at the edge of the porch. It was a man and a woman. Both looked to be in their mid twenties.

Henry reached for his spectacles and realized he had left them in the house.

The young woman said, "Sorry to be troubling you so late. We only just arrived."

Bekka said, "That is all right, my dear. How may we help you?"

"We were wondering if you would have room for us for the night. Staying in the barn would be more than adequate. We don't want to cause any trouble, but just want to get out of the cold. It looks like it may rain."

Henry was biting his tongue. *Who do these two think they are? You just don't show up at sundown looking for a place to stay. We don't know them from Adam and Eve.*

Henry gently pulled on Bekka's elbow. Bekka turned to look at him, and he subtly shook his head and whispered, "I don't like it."

As he did, the young man spoke. "PawPaw?"

Chills ran up and down Henry's body. Tears instantly flooded his eyes. He could not believe he had just heard that greeting. For years, he had not heard the word "PawPaw" and had given up hope of ever hearing it again.

Despite all but accepting that it was gone forever, he dared to say the name. "Lee? Thomas Lee?"

Lee jumped onto the porch, wrapped the old man in his arms, and they openly cried tears of joy. Bekka joined them in a group hug and added her love.

After a moment, Henry realized he had left someone out of the hug. Henry looked in the low light at the shadow of a woman standing before them.

"Lee, is this who I think it is?"

The woman slowly approached the group.

"It is Grandpa."

Henry and Bekka opened their arms and welcomed Shannon into the fold, where they laughed and cried together until there was no more light left in the sky.

They gathered around the fireplace inside the house. Out of respect, Shannon held her questions until Lee and his grandparents had reconnected. When she could stand it no longer, she asked the question — the question she was afraid to ask — the question burning a hole in her brain to get out.

"How are my parents?"

Henry and Bekka looked at Shannon like they had seen a ghost. No one answered.

Shannon instantly looked concerned, fearing for the worst. She asked again. "Henry, how are my parents?"

Henry didn't know how to tell her.

Lee asked, "Henry, what is wrong? How are Mika'el and Sandrah?"

Bekka reached over and put her hand on Henry's hand. "Tell them."

Henry squeezed Bekka's hand, looked at Shannon, and shared his secret.

"Lee, Shannon, we haven't seen them since the day you left. Jacob either."

Tears filled Shannon's eyes. "What do you mean you haven't seen them?"

"Lee, the night you told me what you were going to do, I went to see Mika'el."

"You did what?"

"I knew he would never forgive me if I didn't tell him you were going to find Shannon. That there might be a way to find her. So, I went to see him, and I told him."

"Ok, PawPaw, and?"

"Well, he told Sandrah and Jacob. The next morning, they followed you into the tunnel. We haven't seen them since."

Shannon asked, "What does that mean?"

Lee answered her. "It means they also went somewhere, sometime."

"What do you mean, Lee? Where? When?"

"I don't know. I didn't see them in Parlantis. Did you?"

"No. So where are they?"

Both Christian and Lee looked at Henry. Henry just raised his palms and said, "I don't know."

A sadness settled over the four as they cuddled under blankets by the fire and stared at the flames.

Chapter 83

Wedding and Babies

†††

Months passed, and there was still no sign of Mika'el, Sandrah, or Jacob. No one knew when they would return or if they would return.

Shannon and Lee decided they had to go on with their lives. They planned their wedding, and before they knew it, the day had arrived.

It was a beautiful spring morning; the birds were singing in the trees, and everyone who was anyone was in attendance.

Shannon was beautiful in her wedding dress as Henry walked her down the aisle and gave her over to Thomas. Thomas Lee took Shannon's hand and before friends, family, and the one true God; they said their vows to each other. They pledged their lives to each other and in service to God.

Henry gifted the newlyweds with a generous plot of land and the construction of a small but beautiful home.

Not long after the wedding, illness spread throughout the land of Omentia, and with it, tragedy. The sickness spreading through the port town was much worse for older adults. Bekka was the first to fall ill. Within a week, she went to see God. Henry was heartbroken, but found comfort in the sure hope that she was in a much better place. A week later, Henry fell ill. He was rapidly getting sicker, and he called for Thomas to visit him.

Thomas entered the room. "Pawpaw, how are you doing?"

"Come closer Thomas. It's hard to hear you."

Thomas had already been exposed to the illness, so there was no increased risk in him getting closer to his grandpa. Thomas sat down on the edge of his grandpa's bed. "I'm right here, Pawpaw."

"I was lying here thinking about how many years I waited for you to return, and I was feeling sorry for myself that once you returned, this illness swept through and took so much from us. I was telling myself that it just wasn't fair. And I guess I was blaming God."

"Oh no, Pawpaw. Don't say that."

"Yes, it's true. That's what I was doing. So I prayed about it, and God changed my perspective and my attitude. I can see now all the blessings that have been given to us. This illness was going to sweep through our town whether or not you had returned. But the Lord answered our prayers, and we got to see you one more time before we went to our eternal home."

Tears welled up in Thomas's eyes. "I love you, Pawpaw. I'm sorry it took us so long to come home."

"I love you too, Thomas Lee, but don't be sad for us. Bekka and I had a wonderful life, and we were so blessed to see you and Shannon come home and start your lives together."

"I am leaving you everything, Thomas. May God bless you and your family with many children and many happy years together."

"Don't worry, the Lord will bring Mika'el, Sandrah and Jacob home safely. You just have to wait for his timing. It is His-story."

"Yes, Pawpaw."

"Please tell my old friend, Mika'el, that I tried to hold on until his return. It just wasn't the Lord's will. It was time for Bekka and me to leave this place. Please tell him I will see him in our eternal home."

"Yes, Pawpaw."

"Savor every minute with the ones you love, Thomas. When it is time to go, it hurts so much to say goodbye. So very much!"

Thomas buried his head in his grandpa's chest and cried. Henry patted the back of Thomas' head.

"You have been like a son to me, Thomas. Goodbye, son."

Thomas looked up into Henry's eyes. "Goodbye, Pawpaw."

Henry's eyes closed, and he went to be with God.

†††

The years passed and the one true God blessed Thomas and Shannon with their first-born son. They named him Anders. A few more years passed and God blessed them with a daughter. They named their daughter, Anne.

Thomas, Shannon, Anders, and Annie had a quiet little home on a hillside looking down over the sea. Several other dogs and cats, cows and goats, horses and pigs, joined Beckett on the ranch. Three shepherd dogs named Ruth, Brandy, and Thor guarded the homestead and made sure no predators arrived unannounced.

They had a wonderful home, a wonderful family, and a wonderful life. Only one thing was still missing — Shannon longed to see her mom, dad and brother again.

Where are they and when will they return? Please God, bring them home?

One morning, while Shannon was praying and meditating on the twenty-third psalm down by their dock on the Dark Sea, a stranger sat down on a rock close to where she was sitting. It startled her until she saw who it was.

The stranger smiled. "Hello friend."

"Engel? Is that really you?"

"It is."

"It has been a long time."

"Has it? We don't really have a good feeling for time."

"I don't think I have seen you since Tophet."

"That may be true, but just because you didn't see me doesn't mean I wasn't around. I've been watching."

Shannon remembered the golden orb over her and Christian on the hill overlooking the El Tigran army, the golden angels that routed the invading forces, and Christian's story of the angel that gave him the golden sword he used to eviscerate the bears in the pit.

"I guess you have. Thank you."

"When all is said and done, all I have done is my duty."

They sat quietly by the sea, just as they had so many years ago by the gentle stream. Engel's presence gave Shannon peace.

Shannon asked, "It is so comforting having you here, but aren't you busy? Don't you have work to do?"

"What makes you think I'm not working now?"

"Oh. I hadn't thought of that. I guess I just see you fighting with your sword and things like that."

Engel smiled. "Certainly that is part of the job description, but comforting his children is just as important as protecting them. If you think about it, they're kind of the same thing."

Shannon nodded in agreement. "I guess they are."

A few more moments of quiet passed.

"I really miss my parents. It feels like an eternity since I've seen them. I'm worried about them. I'm worried about my brother. Do you know when I'll see them again, or if I'll see them again?"

"I'm sorry. Angels can't see the future. I will tell you, though, that everything works out for good for those that love the one true God. You can rest on the Master's promises."

"I know. And that promise brings me comfort. But it is still so hard not knowing where they are, and if they are alright."

"Have faith, Shannon. God is nigh. All things are done in his timing."

"Thank you Engel. I feel better having visited with you. Sometimes I just start feeling alone, even though I am surrounded by people who love me."

"It was good to visit with you, Shannon. Always remember that you are never alone."

Shannon closed her eyes and meditated once again on the twenty-third psalm. *The Lord is my shepherd, I shall not want —*

When she opened her eyes, Engel was gone.

But not gone.

Chapter 84

Space Station

†††

The medical teams were hurriedly rushing through the various levels of the New Horizon, inoculating everyone.

Shawn and Diane had been assigned to the New Horizon Space Station a year earlier. Shawn was working on advanced mechanics, and Diane was teaching the dependent children of permanent party personnel. The two were enjoying their lunch period with each other when the no-notice immunizations began.

"What is the big deal with getting immunizations today?" Shawn asked. "Normally we just go in when we need them or on our due date."

"I don't know, but they're certainly being serious about it. Why is security here, toting their big guns? What's that all about?"

A large man in a lab coat approached their table. "Is this seat taken?"

"Nope. All yours, bud. Welcome."

"Thanks."

Diane asked Shawn, "Where should we go get our shot?"

"You can't get that shot," the man in the lab coat said. Both Diane and Shawn looked at the man in surprise.

Shawn asked him, "Why can't we get the shot?"

"They aren't being honest about what it is." Shawn and Diane looked at each other and then back at the lab tech.

"You're not one of those conspiracy theory nuts, are you?" Shawn asked.

"You can't get those shots. It'll wreak havoc on the historical genome once you go home."

"I'm sorry, say again?"

"There's no time to explain right now. Follow me."

The lab tech stood and then started walking toward the door. Shawn and Diane looked at each other, not knowing what to do.

The lab tech stopped about twenty feet away from the table and looked back at them. He had a very serious look on his face.

Shawn said, "Whatever." Then he got up, left the table, and followed the lab tech down the corridor. Diane followed suit.

When they got to the end of the corridor, the man stopped and turned around. "It's been a long time."

Shawn Looked at the man. "Wait, do we know you?"

"My name is Kissami. We met a long time ago. You may not remember, but you will in a few moments."

Everything got blurry for Shawn and Diane. Then, suddenly, everything made sense as they remembered their old friend Kissami.

Shawn remembered first. "Kissami. It is so good to see you. We didn't remember how we got here, but now it's all coming back. We entered the tunnels to find Shannon. But when we lost our memory, well, we got a little distracted."

"No worries. I came to bring you home."

"But how? Where would a tunnel be?"

"You'll be surprised. You are going to have to trust me."

"We trust you. Lead the way."

Shawn and Diane followed Kissami to the elevator and down to refuge elimination.

"Um, this looks hazardous."

"I told you it would require you to trust me. It is the fastest way off the ship, and the tunnel is out there." Kissami pointed outside of the space station, in space.

"Ok, but how do we get from here to there?"

"Well, we join the garbage leaving in five minutes from that room. When the outer hatch opens, it will suck us out of the station and into the tunnel."

Diane had to ask, "So will we get into the tunnel before we die?"

"For sure. We have about fifteen seconds."

"What do we do, swim to the tunnel?"

Kissami laughed. "No, the air being released from the station will transport us into the tunnel. You don't have to do a thing. Just enjoy the ride."

"Enjoy the ride. Ok."

They followed Kissami into the trash room. It was largely empty, which was good for a lot of reasons. The trickiest part of the maneuver was to not get impaled on the way out of the hatch.

Fortunately, there wasn't much time to think about what was about to happen. Before they knew it, they were being propelled into the space tunnel. A moment later, they were gone.

†††

Thomas and Shannon were at the local grocery store picking up supplies. Shannon was inside picking up groceries, while Thomas was outside watching Anders and Annie play on the playground. Thomas was also talking to a fellow rancher about his cattle.

No one really noticed the strangely dressed couple arrive. The man entered the store to ask for directions and the woman went to the playground to enjoy watching the children.

Shannon noticed the woman approaching her children on the playground. She ran out of the grocery store and caught up to the woman, who was simply watching the kids play.

"Excuse me. Ma'am, excuse me."

The woman turned around with a pleasant smile. "Yes?"

They locked eyes, and for a moment, time stood still. Neither could make sense of what they were seeing.

Shannon was looking at her mom, who didn't seem to have aged a day since she had last seen her.

Sandrah was looking at her daughter, now a middle-age woman.

"Mom?"

"Shannon?"

"Mom! You're home!"

They rushed to each other and hugged as the tears ran down their cheeks.

Thomas noticed what was happening and ran over to the kids. About the same time, Mika'el exited the grocery store and saw the women hugging. They both joined the women in greetings and hugs.

"Mom, Dad, come and meet your grandchildren! This is Anders and this is Annie."

Sandrah and Mika'el smothered their grandbabies in hugs and kisses.

After a little while, the women took the children for a stroll. Thomas and Mika'el had time to talk.

Thomas looked Mika'el straight in the eyes and said the words he had dreamed of saying to Mika'el for so many years. "I told you I would bring Shannon home if it was the last thing I did."

"Thank you, Thomas. Thank you."

"You guys look like you haven't aged a day. We look the same age as you. How can that be?"

"Well, Thomas, I guess the relative time thing depends on how far one goes distance-wise and time-wise in the tunnels. We went way into the future, so the time in the tunnels made time all but stand still for us, relative to you. So we are effectively the same age now."

"That is amazing!"

"You think that is amazing? We were in space, Thomas! We were aboard a small city way up there!" He pointed into the sky.

"Well, we have a few stories of our own to include an army of golden angels, magnificent dragons, and epic battles. Let's just say you don't want to mess with Shannon. She has skills."

"I'll remember that, Thomas. Let's find the girls and you can show us your home. We have come a long way, and I can use a nap."

"Sounds good, Dad."

Chapter 85

Completion

†††

"Come out with your hands up!"

Christopher gave Angel a look of desperation. He didn't feel desperate for himself, but for her. He never meant to put her in this situation, but here they were.

They had been married for just under a year. Angel knew about Christopher's work with the Alliance, and she knew the risks. She had agreed with Christopher that his undercover work was just. The Order was slowly taking control over all of Trinian, and someone had to stop it. She had told Christopher, "If not us, if not now, then who and when?"

Christopher never wanted Angel to be caught up in this situation.

The Order had surrounded their home and demanded that they come out. This would not end well, and they both knew it.

"Give me the shotgun," she said.

Christopher handed her the shotgun. "I'm sorry, Angel. I never meant—"

"Don't be sorry, be ready! I knew what I was getting myself into. Freedom is not just your fight, honey, it's also my fight. Women are warriors too, you know?"

Christopher smiled.

There are so many reasons I love her, and this is certainly not the least of them.

"Come out with your hands up. Now!"

It wouldn't be long until the flash bangs came in through the window and the storm troopers right behind them.

Christopher and Angel backed into the far corners of the room. Those positions would give them the best crossfire available for the situation.

Christopher picked up his SCAR Heavy and prepared to give his last full measure.

Just then, the closet door opened and a man wearing a black-hooded robe stepped into the room. He had a black patch over one eye.

"It's time to go. Now! Into the closet! No questions!"

Christopher and Angel were at the end of their rope, and they knew it. This was possibly a way out and there was no need for questions. They darted into the closet and the door closed behind them; just as the room they had just left exploded in gunfire.

The man in the hooded robe placed a magenta stone against the wall of the closet. Instantly, a swirling tunnel of lights appeared in front of them.

"Is this ringing any bells, Christopher? You've done this before. Do you remember?"

"Yeah. I think I do, but barely. Who are you?"

"My name is Donstup. It'll all come back to you in a moment. Just hold on and enjoy the ride."

Angel looked at Christopher and asked, "Is this what you were talking about when you said there might come a day when you would have to leave?"

"Yes, honey. This is what I was talking about."

"Do you remember what I told you?"

"You said that my God is your God, and that where I go, you will go."

"That's right. And I just want you to know that this is way cool!"

Christopher held Angel in his arms.

"By the way, it made this trip a lot easier to accept when it was the only alternative to dying!"

"I'll remind you of that when you see there are no microwaves where we are going."

"Wait. What?"

A moment later, they were basking in the warm morning sunlight on a hill overlooking the sea.

"Where are we?" Angel asked.

"We're home, honey. We're home."

†††

Knock—knock—knock.

Christopher and Angel stood at the front door of a small home.

"Are you sure this is the right home?"

"It's the one the storekeeper said."

The door opened. They say that a man's life flashes before his eyes right before he dies. It was kind of like that, though no one was about to die. Mika'el stared at the man that had just knocked on his door. His heart told him instantly who it was. But his mind was still coming to terms with it. He saw the face of his son, and all the memories that his mind had stored with Jacob came rushing back in a flood that overwhelmed his senses. Then the dam broke, and the waters ran freely.

"Jacob? Jacob, my son!"

Everyone enjoying Sunday brunch in the room behind Mika'el leaped to their feet and rushed to the door, screaming the name of Jacob.

A broad smile broke across Jacob's face, and he could not hold back his emotions. Jacob was smothered in hugs from all of his family members as his dad stood watching. Mika'el's heart was full. His son was home. His family was finally complete.

After all the reunions and introductions were finished, they all gathered in a circle holding hands, their hearts bursting with joy. Mika'el prayed a prayer of thanksgiving to the one true God who had brought them all back together again.

A radiant golden glow surrounded the home as heaven showered the family with protection and love.

Chapter 86

Abducted

†††

It was just after midnight. The full moon lit up the terrain just enough to make every tree look creepy and every creature sinister.

The massive brown bear approached the homestead, triggering the shepherd dogs' response as it crossed the ranch's outer boundary. Eager to complete their mission, the three shepherd dogs dashed towards the intruder. The bear sensed their approach and retreated, pulling the dogs farther and farther away from their defensive area of responsibility.

Anders thought he heard something. He rubbed his eyes and woke up just enough to hear the dogs barking in the distance. It sounded like they were getting farther and farther away, until eventually he didn't hear them at all.

Anders rolled out of his bed and went to the outhouse. He was just old enough where his parents allowed him to go outside at night for such purposes.

As he was going back into the house, he thought he saw something on the roof. It scared him, so he hustled back inside and scrambled to his room. As he passed by Annie's room, he heard a strange sound.

He cracked the door open just enough to see if Annie was ok. He couldn't believe what he saw. A large monkey had grabbed Annie and was pulling her out of the window. Annie was struggling and trying to scream, but the monkey had put something in her mouth. Anders burst through the door and into the room, but it was too late. Little Annie was already out of the window, on the ground, and the monkey was dragging her to a waiting wagon.

Anders bolted down the hallway and back outside. He saw the monkey drag Annie into the wagon and the wagon pulling away. All he could think of was catching the wagon. He ran as fast as his little legs would carry him and jumped into the back of the wagon. He covered himself up with a tarp.

When the wagon stopped, he peeked out from under the tarp. A bear was on the side of the dirt road. He watched as the bear turned into a woman and then hopped into the wagon. The monkey that was holding Annie had also turned into a woman.

Anders didn't know what to do, so he did nothing. He just stayed as quiet as he could, hoping it would all be ok.

Before long, the wagon stopped. Anders peeked out again to see what was going on. He couldn't see the man that had been driving the wagon, but the two women were carrying Annie up a ramp and onto a waiting ship.

Andrew got out of the wagon. Suddenly, a man grabbed him from behind. The man stuffed a rag in Ander's mouth and carried him up the ramp onto the ship. Anders struggled as much as he could, but the man was too strong for him.

"Did you really think we didn't see you? Two for the price of one. Now we have both of the little rats."

The man threw Anders in a cage with Annie and locked the door. The two women joined him, and all three stood and stared at the two toddlers.

"We waited a long time for this. They actually thought they had won. It's not over. Their pain has just begun!"

"Trajan, what did the Master say we should do with them?" Thalia asked.

"He said that if we couldn't kill them, we should take their seed. After that, he didn't care what we did with them."

Annie cried, "Mommy!"

"Your mommy can't hear you, little one. And she can't help you either."

The three shepherds returned to the ranch. They had lost the scent of the bear. When they arrived at the house, they went crazy — barking and running around the home.

Thomas and Shannon ran out of their room. Thomas bolted outside to see what the dogs were barking at, and Shannon ran for the children's rooms.

"Easy boys, what's wrong?"

The dogs were inconsolable.

Shannon burst through the door and ran to Thomas' side, tears flowing down her face.

"Thomas, the children are gone!"

To be continued.

The Faithful Stand Forever!
The Promise Time Redeemed.

Epilogue

†††

Royalty. That is what we are.

Do you think of yourself as royalty? You should, but not because of anything you have done. I'm not talking about any hidden rooms or secret handshakes. This isn't a secret club. It's completely out in the open. It's not hidden in darkness, but is in the light for all to see.

We were once poor and lost. But God adopted us through his son, Jesus Christ. We are no longer poor and lost. We have been found and given a crown.

Hopelessness, anxiety, depression, and anger no longer dominate our lives. We are now new creatures. God adopted us into his family and put a crown of salvation upon our heads. We are now sons and daughters of the King of the Universe.

Greater than any crown of jewels upon our head, God blesses us with the gifts of his Holy Spirit. Love, joy, peace, patience, kindness, goodness, self-control, faithfulness, and long-suffering. These blessings are greater than the jewels of any earthly crown. These gems adorn our heads in a kingdom that is not of this world.

So do not doubt and do not fear. In this world, there will be trouble, but our Savior has overcome the world. Those with us are greater than those that are with the enemy, and no weapon formed against us shall prosper. The King of Kings and Lord of Lords is looking out for us, and his mighty angels do his bidding.

See with spiritual eyes. Hear with spiritual ears. As those of this kingdom, this world, approach death with fear and trembling, the sons and daughters of the king of the universe approach death with confidence and peace. We trust in the promises of the Almighty God that cannot be broken. We know he has prepared a place for us in his kingdom, and we already reign with him.

Praise God for his promises, his providence, and his character. He will never leave us or forsake us. We belong to God because he has bought us back from death with an unfathomable price and given us his Holy Spirit as a guarantee of our inheritance in heaven.

Royalty. Sons and daughters of the King. Adopted children of another kingdom that will last forever.

Know who you are! Walk in power, confidence, and peace. Our life of eternal joy has already begun.

"Be thou faithful unto death and I will give you a crown of life." (Revelation 2:10)

The Faithful Stand Forever!
The Promise Time Redeemed.

LIST OF NAMES

Angel: (Angelic): Wife of Christopher.

Aryon: (Enlightened): Large tannin egg protector.

Ashtar: (God of the wind, warrior): The volcano rising above Tophet.

Bekka: (Bound): Wife of Henry, Mother of Lee.

Brock: (Badger): Leader of Eastern Tribe.

Brutus: (Stupid): Leader of sex-slavers.

Christen: (Anointed One): Colonel Grumpy Sander's wife.

Christian: (Shelter, Healer): Grandson of Henry.

Christopher: (Christ Bearer): Son of Shawn and Diane.

Cindie: (The moon personified): Fellow prisoner and friend of Trista's.

Daraak: (Rock): Leader of the aaranae. Mate of Loathe.

Dawn: (Pleasant); Owner of the Bohemian Coffee Shop. Mother of Josh.

Diane: (Divine): Wife of Shawn, Mother of Christopher.

Engel: (Angelic disposition): Living Being.

Gatesh: (Shock of corn): Tophet scientist studying time.

Grumpy Sanders: (Irritable): Colonel in charge of Parlantian Guard.

Hayden: (Fire): Leader of Eastern Tribe.

Henry: (Rules the home): Fishing boat Captain. Lee's father.

Holly: (Clearing by the hollow): Leader of Eastern Tribe.

Jacob: (The Planter): Son of Mika'el and Sandrah. Brother of Shannon.

Josh: (God saves): Co-owner of the Bohemian with his mother Dawn.

Kaiti: (Pure): Leader of Eastern Tribe.

Kayla: (Beloved): Leader of Eastern Tribe.

Kissami: (Bright and compassionate): Veriti. Missionary of the one true God.
Kiethan: (Wind): Truth-keeper who gets cross to Charlene.
Krohn: (Power): Veriti to Heath. Missionary of the one true God.
Landris: (Settles where there is a forest): Leader of the tannin.
Loathe: (Repulsion): Mate of Daarak, the aaranae.
Lowen: (Beloved): Chief trillium sword maker and brew master.
Lucinda/Cindie: (Light): Friend of Trista's.
Lydia: (Noble one, maiden): Friend of Trista's.
Maria: (Seductress): Adopted daughter of Grumpy and Christen Sanders.
Mertz: (Brave): Veriti. Missionary of the one true God.
Maxine: (The greatest): Second in command of the Hydra.
Mia: (Mine): Mother of the twins; Mirah and Tarah. Wife of Travork.
Mirle: (Blackbird): Rose's Maid of Honor. Sister of Thal.
Mika'el: (Who is like God): Believer, Husband of Sandrah, Father of Jacob and Shannon.
Mirah: (Sea of bitterness): Twin sister of Tarah.
Mordoch: (Protector of the sea): Heathian protector of the royal family.
Morticus: (At the point of death): Friend of Trajan.
Nod: (Fugitive): Enemy of the Veritas.
Nomen: (Blessings): Veriti. Missionary of the one true God.
Sandrah: (Defender of man): Believer, Wife of Mika'el, Mother of Jacob and Shannon.
Shawn: (Gift from God): Husband of Diane, Father of Christopher.
Sheryl: (Beloved): Leader of Eastern Tribe.
Slip: (Escape): Drug Cartel member.
Snuffy: (Horned one): Parlantian Dragon.
Soros: (Unknown origin): High Priest of Molech.
Syth: (Anointed): Leader of the Hydra.
Tarah: (Tower): Twin sister of Mirah.
Tatiana: (Fairy queen): George's assistant in the laboratory.

Tannar: (Tanner of hides): First son of Teroth and Therisa.
Tharice: (The Hunter): Queen of Parlantis.
Tina: (River): Leader of Eastern Tribe.
Travork: (Flat): Father of Mirah and Tarah.
Trajan: (Dark Warrior): Leader of El Tigre Cartel.
Tristana/Trista: (Little wise owl): Daughter of Mika'el and Sandrah. Sister of Jacob.
Ulhorn: (Standing Up): Veriti to El Tigre. Missionary of the one true God.

Valdo: (Powerful): Father of Snuffy; Parlantian Dragon.

†††

The Faithful Stand Forever!
The Promise Time Redeemed.

Note: Visit Chroniclesoftrinian.com, and watch for "Time," the next release of "The Foundation Chronicles."

POEMS

The Seed (Kissami's Creed)
As one seed becomes a forest, only He can fill its needs,
I don't control the sun and rain, I just control the seeds.
We pretend to have the power to make things bud and grow,
But as I observe the world around me, there is one thing that I know.
Our hands do not hold the power, yet they are vital in the chain,
Just as the hitches hold the cars to the engine of the train.
I am not here by accident. I am an important part of the whole,
He asks to give what was given me to others who don't know.
I see now not to worry, their faith I cannot feed,
He only asks, I do my part,
He asks — I plant the seed.

Unbelief (Tophet's denial)
Unbelief is in constant struggle, a constant battle with belief.
As such, it is not simply the absence of belief, but an active entity in itself.
Regarding faith, unbelief is the thistle Satan grows to strangle the faith that the Spirit sows.
This seed of unbelief is manifested as man's reason. "If I can't understand it, it cannot be so." Like a man denying his inevitable death, some things are whether or not you believe them.
This grand illusion we live in where all that is visible is the sideshow as the invisible battle rages.
Unbelief is the barrier that binds men and denies men — faith.

Not of Old (Wisdom of the Scribe)
Write only about what you know. All else is but a lie.
One cannot write of sun and moon, not even of the sky.
Write of what you know the best, write of what you feel,
For you to write of anything else is but an attempt to steal.
All we know is what we are, what is in our heart,
It is this and this alone that sets us all apart.
And when we find the other, the one whose dreams we'll share,
It is then and only then we'll find of more we are aware.

Rainbows
I saw a rainbow up in the sky, so many shades of color; beautifully accented by the sun.
I thought, if only I could fly, how fun it would be to soar through it; not to mention how fun.
Alongside it was a thunderstorm, the beauty to adorn with sparks of fire and angered roar.
It brought rain to desert floor; first drizzle, then downpour; thirsty ground hungering more.
As I reflected on the day, on all that I had seen and all that I had done,
I couldn't help but hear the rainbow say, it reflected each scene; feelings and it were one.
The spectrum of our emotions on each page of our story runs together; composing a portrait.

That altogether showered daily with overwhelming turmoil — the harmony endeavoring to spoil — still emerges more priceless than anything which on canvas has been set.

The Shadow (Trinian's Specter)
I have riches, I am loved; greatly blessed by God above.
Yet knowing all of this, I find, how sad I am is on my mind.
Is it chemical? Is it fear? Why is it I shed these tears?
Always wanting and hungering for more, contentment is by desire torn.
It is surely a state of mind. Our emotions play a trick — they steal our thoughts and make them sick.

For not what we know, it is I find, but what we see that is on our mind.
The world doesn't tell us what we have; it plagues us with what we need.
The serpent in this way our path to lead.
For once accepting all those lies, no earthly riches can satisfy.
Beware, my friend, of the shadow we have that follows wherever we go.
Your eyes are fixed on it, you know.

Soon it will interpret all you see and then will determine what will be.
It's a relentless struggle, a constant fight to see through the darkness and find the light.
Where do you fall?
Which side of the line?
Do your eyes face the gloom or sunshine?

As The Sun Sets (Regrets before Battle)
Only so much time to say what we want to say. To give each other of our love and bask in the warm rays. How did we spend yesterday?
If only you knew how important you are to me. If only there was enough time, then truly you would see.
If only I knew better how to set priorities. I sit and wonder where our lives have gone, why so short now what once seemed would last so long.
I was so quick to know how to spend our time. It was so easy to be wrong.
As the sun sets.

Goodbye (Warrior's lament)
They float safely upon the waters, the waters one with the sand, a lonely seagull upon a beacon, the place he chose to land.
Who will remember the unique shades or the portrait that they made?
What is the gain to those I love for the life that I now trade?
The sun in rainbow slowly sets and softly caresses the clouds that twist and turn beneath its gaze in endless colors found.
Goodbye, my love, goodbye. I cannot tell you why. Remind my sons, I love them so, for I go away to die.
I, like the sun, have had my time. I've shared my reds and blues. But colors fade, darkness comes and steals the life they knew.

Too Short — Too Soon (Lover's Regrets)
If emotion it takes to open the heart, then open my heart is now.
Once again, here, missing you, more than I can allow.
It's only been two hours since we said our goodbyes.
The mind repeats, "We'll touch again," but the eyes feel the need to cry.
Missing my best buddies, the best in all the world,
Going forth again, alone — into the night, I'm hurled.
And lurking in murky shadows, dark specters, roam the night.
Separating us from loved ones and stealing us from their light.
Given more time, our love would once again have bloomed,
But our time together was too short,
I had to leave too soon.

Do Angels Cry? (Prophesy)
He was the Light; he was the Word, to his creation he came.
We knew him not, though foretold from old. We expected not the same.
A dark day it was, the darkest of days, the son of man betrayed.
Betrayed by the ones that he loved and who he came to save.
As we beat, the Son of God, and upon his body trod, legions of angels' fists clenched in rage, and so they set the final stage for the destruction of man and end of his age!

But God the Father knew the love of his only Son, and why this plan of love was begun.
He held back the horde from destroying mankind, and the Son saved us all for all of time.
But, as we nailed Him to the cross, did the angels feel the awesome loss?
And though they all knew why the Son of God must die; I have to ask, "Do Angels cry?"

A Toast (The future)
80... 100... 135, Rotate.
Enter the genesis of an altered state.
Altitude increasing; preparing for G's,
Death offers no forgiveness; not at these speeds.
Thunder is storming; static fills the air,
Chaff clouds are rising; dancing of flares.
Four millennia of jousting going before,
Man has ascended to new heights of war.
The bass is pounding; electric guitar is alive,
Looking for honey; departing the hive.
Amraams, sidewinders and a 20 millimeter gun,
Play with this fire and you're gonna get stung.
Hordes of angels in black leather tights,
Await the victors in the O-Club tonight.
The losers join thousands who no longer boast,
Swarming from darkness; night revealing its ghosts.
58,000 pounds of thrust–pulling inverted, and going for bust,
Blowing through the Mach–enemy RHAW screaming and echoing our lock.
One excellent riff and this tribute will end. A flip of the coin decides the fate of foe and friend.
We toast all those warriors who aren't here tonight,
Their spirits remain, though their shapes fade from sight.

The Warrior Knows (The warrior of all times)
The warrior knows pain, down to the bone, the bone that withstands, and stands up for its own.
The warrior knows hope, hope he will return, return to the ones for whom his heart burns.
The warrior knows fear, fear which must be controlled,
Gaining control from experience, experience being bold.
The warrior knows love, love for all men, even men who like him, their loved ones must defend.
The warrior knows heartache, heartache leaving home,
The home he protects, he'll protect (if he must), all alone.

The Light (Prophecy)
What a quiet night; What a peaceful night; one like any other, and none ever before.
In the heavens, a new light; high above burning bright; with love, its radiant beams to earth soar.
Thousands of years for this men have waited; yet they sleep while the moments quietly pass,
The angels now bring, to earth, their heavenly King, in a lonely manger, his glory is masked.
Though man has been blind through the ages, and more ages of blindness, he'll see,
The remnant of God's glorious creation, pausing in bridled anticipation,
This night, in silence, bows down on bended knee
His Word had given life to creation, but man's rebellion had then given birth to death,
Atonement demanded the sacrifice. Only he could pay the price.
Be still; the infant, now takes His first breath.
Oh, so serene, and yet, miraculous night, the most spectacular, and yet hidden from sight,
By night, the Savior comes, and the night will soon succumb; for so long, darkness —

Now, "Let there be Light!"

The Warrior's Farewell (The fallen warrior)
This day in battle a warrior falls; and to the sky, his Maker calls,
As from his body, his spirit flows; he leaves behind, here, all he knows.
Will she know how hard he tried to make it back before he died?
That dying in the mud, he cried, unable in her arms, to say goodbye.
His thoughts then turn from battle cries, as on the field of death, he lies.
To all he leaves on Earth behind, these things, then overwhelm his mind.
Will his sons know of their dad and know about his final stand?
With shield and sword held firm in hand, he died protecting their homeland.
His thoughts are first of his one true love, as he looks down now from high above —
upon the corpse lying in the sand, and the wedding band upon its hand.
Then, as to Heaven, his soul soared, this fallen warrior-to his Lord,
One last wish this man was given, to touch once more his wife yet living.
Does she sense the final blow? Does she know that he must go?
How long upon her heart will weigh the pain and sorrow of this day?
A soft breeze blew in from the plains, and to the home came peaceful rains.
A gentle mist caressed her face, and on her lips left but a trace.
As she gazed, on setting sun, at that moment knowing what was done.
Quietly to her knees, she fell, for she had felt —
His last farewell.

The River of Time (Time)

As a child, I knew her not; as a collection of fun times, I saw yet, no plot.
Now, a man of more years, through the haze, she sometimes appears.
Softly, slowly, her pages turn; and little of her still we learn.
Reflecting all she passes through, her image changes from every view.
She takes her color from the sky; it gives nothing of her away, for it is but a lie.
Though she feeds all the surrounding life, her current causes all our strife.
Though some above and some below and some all around her grow, we pass through cloud, and then through sun, memories of pain and memories of fun.
How much evil lies within? The ripples hide from us her sin.
How much good lies with her? Will good follow when she turns?
I try to plan for where she'll flow, but none can tell where next she'll go.
I cannot hold her, she is not mine, but only a few drops at a time.
She touches all with each new mile and takes us with her for a while.
Some with her move all around, some will fail, and quickly drown
and settle in the murk below, never light again to know.
Sometimes peaceful–sometimes still, all she passes over she fills.
Whether over, under, or around, we tread; she provides us with the common thread.
She maintains the plane we live upon, and she'll be there when
we are gone.
Do not be bitter and angry about this, though time before or
after you miss.
She holds no malice, there is no crime, equity to all,
The River of Time.

This World (The warrior's departure)
I leave the world, my world; the world as I know it.
Though I feel the pain, convention dictates I don't show it.
"Have a good trip, Daddy, and take care. Any Dad who has been in my shoes would agree it isn't fair.
To require a man to leave his home, to leave behind his family and all he's ever known.
Though I've done this before, sure to do this again, each time leaving gets harder, truly harder than it's ever been.
Saying goodbye to their little faces (that echo little hearts), wondering if inside they're breaking (knowing yours is), this is the hardest part.
I leave now, the world, my world; the world as I know it.
Though I feel the pain, convention dictates, I do not show it.

Clouds (Departure)
Clouds are forming.
Tears within.
Waiving goodbye.
Leaving.

The Spell (The Mirare Effect)
Words cannot say, only time will tell,
The full effects of current spells.
What once was real, now is the past,
Yet in memory's web, forever lasts.
As life treads on, much goes unseen,
With distant song and hidden dreams.
When once we've felt never again the same,
For deep inside, we cannot tame —
The passion known, the contact made,
The seed we sowed, and the card we played.
So beware, my friend, and guard the heart,
Once affection we send, we become a part —
Of another's world, and another's life,
Our thoughts we hurl into secret strife.
Like the hidden virus infects the machine,
What attacks the heart will go unseen,
Forever secret and forever hidden —
Hearts away — Hearts away.

Thoughts on Time (Gatesh's Dirge)

As the years quickly pass, many memories. The past — still the present in my mind.
Sometimes it's hard to believe what time's cobwebs will weave today for my conscious to find.
Was that me in those places? Old friends, I can still see their faces.
Where have they all gone? Just like an old song; still there, only now in small traces.
Sometimes at night I awaken, as if by some spirit of the past, softly shaken.
Am I awake or do I dream? Familiar times again stream. In a blink of an eye they are taken.
I close my eyes and I see you, but a glimpse of what was at best.
Though the moment is gone, for your touch I still long, as my heart breaks apart in my chest.
It is true you are gone now forever? Some cruel hoax you still exist in my mind.
Or can there still be time for you and me? My eyes open, you fade — so unkind.
It's but a maze this — time, don't you see? A matrix, memories of you and me.
Have we met before? Will we meet again? Only time will tell what will be.
Is this time real or imagined? Did we create it to structure our day?
False security, I think, like an ice-skating rink that will melt away as we play.
If our time could be kept in a bottle, all the bottles adrift on the sea,
An ocean of time, held neatly in rhyme, sailors of time, you and me.
I leave you with a last observation. Time is simply a measure of what has been.
The present is now dead, as you can see. Its moment already fled, never again to here be.
So do not spend time in the present as the sands in the hourglass quickly run.

Live for the future, or fall victim to the past, 'cause this moment may be your last one.

Illusion (Life)

You've given me eternity, told me not to fear, told me you will provide for us for all our years.

Giving us everything, now and forevermore. You say, "Put your trust in me; no need for stores."

I say I believe you, Lord. My faith, my trust, in you. I believe your promises. I know they're true.

You're all powerful, quite able to defend. With a heart that loves us so, your love to us will send.

So why do I hesitate to give it all to you? To use my time and energy for what you want me to?

Life here is an illusion, soon to quickly end. What we sow for eternity is just around the bend.

Time (Old Man's Lament)
Youth.
Filled with fancy and senseless notions.
When it seems that all we do and say,
Is driven by emotions.
At this time, I could not see,
What time would have in store for me,
And that with all its subtlety,
Time would someday flee.

A busy life, so much to do,
Always on the move, or lest I stall.
I will not slow or fall off the pace,
Oh, I can do it all.
Blind this time, I didn't see,
That time was then besieging me.
And that in assured subtlety —
I stood convinced; it had no hold on me.

Then one day I awoke to find,
That, in reflection, I spotted time.
And though the distraction quickly changed the song,
Ignorance was forever gone.
Though for a moment, I could see,
I chose to think it could not be.
Ignore it, and it will go away,
I'll worry about time another day

Now I stand in the twilight years,
Though many are gone, time brings new fears.
And failing, I plead through heavy tears,
"Time — I need more time!"
All this time, it took to see,

That time was only teasing me.
And that with no more subtlety,
Time — is — gone.

Freedom (Fury Falls)
Entering the skirmish, I hear the battle cry.
And know it is for certain that many men today will die.
But not for want of glory, as it is sure for some.
That I today will fight; it is alone for our freedom.
So tell not of this day with pride, for what this hand has done.
But rather of my dream for peace, this song my heart has sung.

Wishing It Away (The deployed warrior's lament)
The Lord says every day is grace,
A chance to serve Him in this place,
Though I know that this is true,
I see a different aspect too.
I find that when I go away,
To some far distant land, to stay.
It doesn't take long until I'm blue,
Realizing how far I am away from you.
Then I find you're on my mind,
So hard to leave those thoughts behind.
Of wife and kids and our warm home,
So far away, so all alone.
But know it's true, alone I'm not.
Nowhere on earth by God forgot.
He guards my thoughts; he guides my way,
He promised by my side he'll stay.
Now, to do what He has planned,
Directed by his almighty hand.
And though his guidance I obey,
I find the time I wish away —
So I can be home with you.

Out of the Depths (Louis' lament)
Out of the depths, out of the depths I cry to you, Oh Lord. Oh Lord, hear my voice.
Let your ears, let your ears, Oh Lord, be attentive to my cry.
I wait, I wait for the Lord, my soul waits. In his word, I put my hope.
I do not concern myself with this world; you have stilled and quieted my soul.

Keep falsehood and lies far from me. Give me neither riches nor poverty. But give me only my daily bread. So I may not disown you, or dishonor thy name.
The name of my God.

Praise the Lord, praise the name of the Lord our God. Praise him, you who serve the Lord.
Praise the Lord, praise the Lord for he is good, his name will last always.

Keep falsehood and lies far from me. Give me neither riches nor poverty. But give me only my daily bread. So I may not disown you, or dishonor thy name.
The name of my God.

Remember the Trees (Song for the children)
In the cool of the trees, in amongst all the leaves,
There's a buzzing of the bees, and the laughter of monkeys,
In the calm of the day, as they all swing and sway,
There are no worries today, only peace.

As the sun starts to set, and the sky turns to red,
No fears in their heads, as they snuggle into bed,
In the shadows of the night, they know that all is right,
There are no worries tonight, only peace.

They don't worry; they don't stress,
They aren't anxious; they aren't depressed,
They know who's up there, high above the nest,
They do their part; He does the rest.
As we go through our lives, many trials will arise,
Our Lord reigns high above, and our God, He is love,
Let us always remember that He loves us more than ever,
There are no worries then, only peace.
We don't worry; we don't stress,
We aren't anxious; we aren't depressed,
We know who's up there, high above the nest,
We do our part; he does the rest.

Lead You Home (Henry's song)
When I was just a little boy,
Playing with my little-boy toys,
My Father took me on a walk,
He said it was time to have a talk.
Walking slowly with my dad,
He bent down close and took my hand.
And looking just a little sad,
He spoke these words to me:

He said —

Son, you got to know,
I will always love you so,
Don't you put your trust in me,
I won't always be here with you.
Put your trust in the Lord,
Walk, my son, by His word,
And He will lead, He will lead you home.

I always doubted what I'd heard,
When I remember my daddy's words,
'Cause he had always been there for me,
So, I refused to see.
Then suddenly that day was here,
That day that all sons have to fear,
As I kneeled down by his side,
I held his hand and cried

He said —

Son, you know, I have to go,
Son, you know, I love you so,

And you know I can't always be,
I can't always be here with you.
Put your trust, Son, in the Lord,
Walk now son, by His word,
And He will lead, He will lead you home.

Mom and Dad have now gone home,
And on this land below, I still roam,
Blessed with sons now, I can see,
Clearly, what will be.
So, feeling just a little sad,
I found those words I've always had,
I sat my sons down on my knee,
And told them, like my dad told me.

I said —

Sons, you've got to know,
I will always love you so,
Don't you put your trust in me,
I won't always be here with you.
Put your trust in the Lord,
Walk, my son, by His word,
And He will lead —
He will lead you home.

Kind Words, Kind Ways (Wise guidance)

It is so easy to lash out in anger — to pass on some uncaring words.
But to stop and evaluate such actions will reveal that one's vision is blurred.
For what we say to another will ripple to many that day,
And all we convey to each other will surely return to us someday.
Don't expect loved ones to know what you're thinking; don't forget what a smile can do.
Know a hug can keep a spirit from sinking, never pass on saying, "I love you."
So STOP, when you speak to another and think before deciding what to say.
For truly you too will discover that through kind words...
You can build our kind ways.

Freedom (Fighter pilot need)

Entering the fur ball, I hear the battle cry, and know it is for certain that men today will die.
But not for want of glory, as it is sure for some; that I today will fight, it is alone for freedom!
So tell not of this day with pride for what this hand has done.
But rather of my dream for peace, this song my heart has sung.

Time (Guidance on time travel)
Face to face with eternity, time has no meaning. It is death and decay that give time purpose.
Without death and decay, time is irrelevant.
How will time cease to exist? Time will cease to exist when death ceases to exist.
A day to God is as a thousand years, for God is eternal. Death cannot touch God, nor can time.

Like me (Realization)
I fight the wars that keep us free; I fight for our beliefs.
And when it's time for my duty, I fight men just like me.

CHRONICLES OF TRINIAN.COM

BLOG/Devotionals

†††

Tophet

20 April 2024

Pretty interesting story about "Tophet." Still makes the hair on the back of my neck stand up when I tell it.

When writing "Forever" I realized I had a place left on my map that hadn't yet been named. I planned on this "place" being the place where a demon and his followers sacrificed children in the fire (The bad guys, if you will). So, I thought, *Why not take the first letter of each place that had been named, in order of when they were introduced, and see if it gives me something useful?* So, that is what I did.

"T" for Trinian, "O" for Omentia (Trinian in 1st edition, "Stand," 2005, Omentia replaced Dexilia in 1st edition, The Faithful, 2010), "P" for Parlantis, "H" for Heath (both in 1st edition, The Faithful, 2010), and "ET" for El Tigre (1st edition, "Forever," 2024). It spelled Tophet. Sounded kind-of cool. It meant nothing to me and didn't ring any bells.

A couple of days later I Googled "Tophet," and this came up: "In the Hebrew Bible, Tophet or Topheth, (Latin: Topheth) is a location in Jerusalem in the Valley of Hinnom (Gehenna), where worshipers engaged in a ritual involving 'passing a child through the fire,' most likely child sacrifice. Traditionally, the sacrifices have been ascribed to a god named Moloch."

Shocked

I was shocked! Shivers ran down my spine and hairs on the neck stood up! What? What are the odds of the first letters, in order of introduction, over twenty years, spelling out the name of the place where ACTUAL CHILD SACRIFICES took place? Even if I had the name bouncing around in my subconscious, for the first letters of the random names (again, chosen over twenty years) of the other places in the book to spell it out? Weird! Something is going on here!

Having fun through spreading the Word

21 April 2024

Share the truth through the Chronicles of Trinian! Join us on the adventure! The Faithful Stand Forever! #chroniclesoftrinian

"The Chronicles of Trinian" trilogy takes the reader along on epic quests for survival over three separate ages of time; embarking on countless adventures, witnessing untold wonders, encountering fantastic creatures, battling evil enemies, and navigating the arrival of aliens and sentient artificial intelligence. The reader is front and center as the spiritual war between good and evil rages and the powerful forces of hell itself are intent on destroying the faithful in both the physical and spiritual realms. Heroes of faith will emerge amidst deadly conflict as the angels of God and demons of hell battle for the eternal souls of men. The Chronicles of Trinian trilogy focuses on love, family, and faith; and will leave the reader satisfied, edified, and strengthened in their faith. No matter what is to come, God and the spiritual forces of good are in control. The times change, the struggle continues, but the faithful will stand forever!

The Good Shepherd

22 April 2024

Doesn't the Good Shepherd leave the ninety-nine and go after the one sheep that is lost? Yes, he does. There is a heavy dose of this truth in "Forever," but I don't want to give too much away.

I'm patiently waiting for the publisher to send me the typecast for the three books in production. Once I approve of their efforts, it is off to the races. Weekends are the hardest time as I know no work is being done. That is ok though, as everyone needs their rest.

Meanwhile, I'm diligently at work on book four — Tophet, the Foundation! I'm on chapter twenty. Released later this summer attached to STAND (2nd edition), it will add elements that both expand the Trinian universe while tightening the existing trilogy into an even tighter bundle. I'll leave it there for now — you will see.

Two standard deviations of blow your mind

23 April 2024

"Forever" takes the adventures of The Chronicles of Trinian to the first Standard Deviation of blow your mind! Truly! Aliens, sentient AI, covert agents operating for control of Trinian, key revelations from "The Faithful" and "Stand," "Forever" really expands the Trinian universe!

Then, Tophet, two-thirds finished, just takes everything you thought about the trilogy to the second deviation of blow your mind! Seriously, it's like I'm a reporter investigating the story. I get up in the morning and I do not know what is going to happen next. Then, I am blown away!

This afternoon I was typing away and was like, "Wait. What?" I had to sit down. Really! The reveal was so huge!

Nothing boring in T.C.O.T. World! It's an ever-expanding universe!

Great news; Forever has gone to print!

24 April 2024

"Forever" has gone to print! The third book in the Chronicles of Trinian Trilogy should be available within the week for preorder at Amazon, Barnes & Noble, etc!

Hopefully, "The Faithful" will follow suit soon. Should be any day now.

The entire Chronicles of Trinian Trilogy should also follow soon. It has "Stand" included.

So, the motto for this book effort is "Just one soul." If God uses these books to bring just one soul closer to him–if just one eternity is altered–it all will have been more than worth it. Who can put a value on an eternity? Please God, bless this effort and have it accomplish that which you have prepared for it to accomplish.

God bless you all!

More great news!

26 April 2024

"The Faithful" has gone to print! The first book in the Chronicles of Trinian Trilogy should be available soon for preorder at Amazon, Barnes & Noble, etc!

I expect "The Chronicles of Trinian" (all three books in one) to be sent to print today or Monday.

Working hard on "Stand" (w/Tophet). Although "Stand" is included in the full "Chronicles of Trinian" (full three book set), this release of "Stand" will include "Tophet" setting the foundation for the trilogy. Tophet expands the trilogy and includes several shocking tells that reveal previous unknowns. You'll be like, "What!"

Twenty years in the making — here we go! I'm excited! It's going to be fun! Tell your friends and family. Forward the blogs and website on your social media. Spread the Word. If we can reach "Just One Soul — that's the Goal!"

Songs that inspired the Chronicles of Trinian

26 April 2024

Here are some songs that have inspired the victorious stories of the Chronicles of Trinian!

1. You've Already Won (Live)
   by Shane and Shane.
   ☆ "I know how the story ends!"
2. Don't Tread on Me!
   by We the Kingdom.
   ☆ "No Weapon Formed Against Me Shall Prosper!"
3. Threads
   by Geoff Moore and the Distance.
   ☆ "And there's a hand that sows the threads together–around one strand of saving scarlet thread. Come and take your place among the threads."
4. Running Home
   by Cochran & Co.
   "He called my name, and he stole my shame. Out of the dark and into his arms. I'm running home!"

All the Chronicles of Trinian are being printed right now!

26 April 2024

"The Chronicles of Trinian Trilogy" has gone to print! All books should be available soon for preorder at Amazon, Barnes & Noble, etc!

The no later than ship date, which gives the big boys time to get their online act together, works out to be NLT 6 June, D-Day! Isn't it funny how things work out?

Working hard on "Stand" (w/Tophet). Although "Stand" is included in the full "Chronicles of Trinian" (a full, three book set), this release of "Stand" will include "Tophet" setting the foundation for the trilogy. Tophet expands the trilogy and includes several shocking tells that reveal previous unknowns. You'll be like, "What?"

Twenty years in the making. Here we go! I'm excited! It's going to be fun! Tell your friends and family. Forward the blogs and website on your social media. Spread the Word! If we can reach "Just One Soul — that's the Goal!" The value of one infinity simply cannot be measured!

The waiting is the hardest part

27 April 2024

"The Chronicles of Trinian Trilogy" has gone to print! All books should be available soon for preorder at Amazon, Barnes & Noble, etc! They say two to three days after going to the printer. Well, today is day three, so...

Again, the no later than ship date, which gives the big boys time to get their online act together, works out to be NLT 6 June, D-Day! Isn't it funny how things work out? Jun 6th, 2024!

Working hard on "Stand" (w/Tophet). I made lots of progress yesterday–two chapters! Although "Stand" is included in the full "Chronicles of Trinian" (the full, three book set), this release of "Stand" will include "Tophet" setting the foundation for the trilogy. Tophet expands the trilogy and includes several shocking tells that reveal previous unknowns. You'll be like, "What?" I'm writing that reveal today!

It has been twenty years in the making. I started with the first basic book "Stand" version 1 in 2005 (It wasn't very good. The publisher got the wrong file, and I never read it until 2023.)

Here we go! I'm excited! It's going to be fun! Tell your friends and family, please. Forward the blogs and website on your social media, please. Spread the Word! If we can reach "Just One Soul — that's the Goal!" The value of one infinity simply cannot be measured!

100% to God. His will be done.

28 April 2024

Ok everyone. Still waiting on The Chronicles of Trinian Trilogy to go live on the big websites for pre-order. It should be hours now and not days.

I'm asking you all to buy it, read it, enjoy it, and share it. Spread the Word while having fun!

Every penny (minus taxes–"give unto Caesar") goes to God. It is already his! We are building a church, you know. I will give you a report here, when I get any info on sales and tell you how WE did for that reporting period! We can enjoy some adventure, share the truth of the one true God, and build a church to share God's love–all at the same time! Let's share the Word and have fun doing it!

I'm posting this to keep my intentions honest! I had decided to do this weeks ago, but to keep Satan at bay, I am going public. I am an ambassador for God and all the things He has given me are already His. If it is His will that the Chronicles of Trinian books go cosmic, we will build more churches and spread the Word into more communities. If not, it is well with my soul (He certainly doesn't need this to do His will). I am hoping He uses me though. I am accountable to you and to God on where all the proceeds go.

So, no threat to you. If you want to have fun reading some Christian fiction AND spread God's Word through the books, (as well as building churches), let's take this trilogy (and more to come) to the world!

Satan has spread lies through other books and stories that have been very successful... we can surely do the same by spreading God's truth that Jesus SAVES!!

To God be the glory! Sales will not measure success. It is already successful! God's will determines who sees T. C. O. T. and what the Spirit does with it. "Just One Soul" is the goal! Your will be done, Father!

If God uses T. C.O. T. in a small or large way to bring "Just One Soul" to Him, it will all be worth it! That soul may be your son, your neighbor, or a guy in Iran. The Holy Spirit will decide. Or maybe T. C. O. T. is just for you–to strengthen your faith. I can't wait to meet that one soul that the Lord used these books to reach. Just one would be worthwhile! Who can put a value on an eternity?

Prayer:

Please Father, please use this 20 year effort and the effort by all who love you now to accomplish your will! In Jesus' name! Amen.

My dream is this trilogy gets so big that I get to go on the talk shows and share our Savior, Jesus, to the world! I'm gonna think big and see if it is in the Lord's will.

Note: As I prayed, our WI-FI went out... the counter attack has already begun! "No Weapon, Formed Against Me, Shall Prosper, in Jesus' Name!

The seed. Plant with me.

29 April 2024

The Seed

As one seed becomes a forest, only He can fill its needs,
I don't control the sun and rain, I just control the seeds.
We pretend to have the power to make things bud and grow,
But as I observe the world around, there is one thing that I know.
Our hands do not hold the power, yet they are vital in the chain,
Just as the hitches hold the cars to the engine of the train.
I am not here by accident. I am an important part of the whole,
He asks to give what was given me to others who don't know.
I see now not to worry, their faith I cannot feed.
He only asks, I do my part,
He asks. I plant the seed.

Today is the day!

29 April 2024

They tell me today, the THIRD business day, is when "The Chronicles of Trinian" Trilogy books will start showing for preorder. The THIRD day, imagine that! One today, one tomorrow, and one Thursday! It should be hours now and not days (the weekend got in the way)!

I'm asking you all to buy it, read it, enjoy it, and then share the news. Spread the Word, while having fun!

Happy May first!

1 May 2024

Still looking at a Friday launch. It could be earlier, but I'm not counting any chickens before they hatch. "Fool me once" and all that jazz.

"The Faithful" (book 1) and "Forever" (book 3) will be released as separate books. The full Chronicles of Trinian will be released as an 1120 page book with 95% of the content (nothing tricky... I was limited by the publisher and page count). As such, it is a wonderful collection of the T.C.O.T. trilogy, however, a bit more expensive (though not as expensive as all the individual books combined).

I am doing the final read-through of "Stand" (book 2) right now. Although it is book 2, it adds "Tophet" which is another book that covers the pre-Faithful period and teases the "Foundation" series [yes, there is more to come! I outlined the Foundation Trilogy (T.F.T.) yesterday. I am excited about it too!] The release of "Stand" (w/Tophet) will complete the T.C.O.T. trilogy, with a bridge to the T.F.T. It also reveals content that adds tremendously to the understanding and enjoyment of all three T.C.O.T. trilogy books.

The T.C.O.T. Trilogy is nice to have in one volume. It is also nice to have the trilogy books stacked next to each other. I wanted both options available. As an extra bonus, I got an extra cover–The Lion of Judah! I think it is awesome! Sure to catch anyone's eye when sitting on the bookcase or store shelf.

I have really enjoyed this journey of 20+ years. Honestly, it has been a tremendous amount of work and pretty expensive, but my time and gold are only on loan from God. As a manager of these resources, I pray I have made a good investment for God that will yield 3x, 5x, or? The initial investment (as a reminder, all after-tax proceeds go back to God's work... 100%). I am excited to see if the Lord wants to bless this endeavor. Through this effort, God has blessed me, and I wish you the same blessings.

I haven't figured out the T.C.O.T website Chroniclesoftrinian.com conversation deal yet, so if you are having one-sided conversations with me, be patient... or email me at tlr@Chroniclesoftrinian.com.

Please continue to pray God uses these books to have a positive impact on the world. The world needs it! The time is short. And please join me in planting seeds... God will make them grow.

One more day.

2 May 2024

Excited!

One more day! 7,329 days in the making with one day to go. Where does the time go?

Speaking of time, the element of time is huge in The Chronicles of Trinian (T.C.O.T.) Trilogy (especially in "Tophet" and "Forever"), and will it will continue to be so in the "Foundation" books.

High expectations

3 May 2024

Excited! Hoping all three books are released today. Three new fiction releases are uploading!

There is progress, but it is slow. I have been a little too optimistic about my expectations of how quickly things would progress.

The Chronicles of Trinian (T.C.O.T.) Trilogy has launched. It is just taking the Infinity Rocket time to break the atmosphere. Once it does, no holding it back. Hang in there, it is Friday!

"The Faithful" (2nd Edition) is showing on my Amazon Author Portal, but not yet on Amazon (I loaded the picture from there to the book description section of the website–goodbye "proof"). I also talked to my publishing rep yesterday. She said the books are all uploading. I guess, because of their size (~600, 1100, & 500 pages) it is taking longer. Trust me folks, no one is more eager to get these available for order than I am.

I asked they make the Kindle Reader available ASAP. Those should be available within 24 hours. My understanding is that when you order the books, you will then be able to listen to them right away, before the books arrive. You can do that through Alexa. "Alexa, read Terrence Rotering's The Faithful" or by downloading the books to your phone. Listening is not for everyone, but some prefer it. I like it for when I am driving, taking a shower, etc. Also, it helps while waiting for the hard-copy.

Again, apologies. It is not in my control. The good news is that when it happens, there should be three books available, not just one. That's good, right?

I still have high expectations for today. We will see what God has planned. His-story, his timing, his glory!

See you on Saturday! While you wait, play the following three songs. They are outstanding!

Tell Alexa, "Volume 8." Then tell her to play, "Don't Tread on Me" by We the Kingdom." Then "You've Already Won (live)", by Shane in Shane. Finally, "Threads" by Geoff (pronounced Jeff) Moore and the Distance. Truly listen to the words of Threads! Outstanding! Then rest in the assurance that Jesus has already won!

Review: I should finish the final read-through of "Stand" (book 2) today. Although it is book 2, it adds "Tophet" which is another book that covers the pre-Faithful period and teases the "Foundation" series [Yes, there is more to come! I outlined the Foundation Trilogy (T.F.T.) Tuesday ... excited about it too!] The release of "Stand" (w/Tophet) will complete the T.C.O.T. trilogy, with a bridge to the T.F.T. It also reveals content that adds tremendously to the understanding and enjoyment of all three T.C.O.T. trilogy books. So, read "The Faithful" then "Stand" then "Forever" and then "Tophet"... then buy copies for all your friends and family (Except me, I will already have copies. :>))

The T.C.O.T. Trilogy is nice to have in one volume. It is also nice to have the trilogy books stacked next to each other. I wanted both options available. As a bonus, I got an extra cover–The Lion of Judah! I think it is awesome! Sure to catch anyone's eye when sitting on the bookcase or store shelf.

I have really enjoyed this journey for twenty-plus years. Honestly, it has been a tremendous amount of work and pretty expensive, but my time and gold are only on loan from God. As a manager of these resources, I pray I have made a good investment for God that will yield 3x, 5x, or "to infinity and beyond" the initial investment (as a reminder, all after-tax proceeds go back to God's work. 100%. I will tell you how when I do it). I am excited to see if the Lord wants to bless this (our) endeavor. Through this effort, God has blessed me, and I wish you the same blessings.

Please join the effort and support through social media, buying the books, and most importantly, PRAYER!

Note: please forgive spelling mistakes in the blog (no spell check and trying to get these out in the AM. 2:53 am right now).

Note: I haven't figured out the T.C.O.T website Chroniclesoftrinian.com conversation deal yet, so if you are having one-sided conversations with me, be patient... or email me at tlr@Chroniclesoftrinian.com.

Prayer request: Please continue to pray God uses these books to have a positive impact on the world. The world needs it! The time is short. And please join me in planting seeds... God will make them grow.

Thought: Do you know someone you would like to reach with the Gospel, but you are not sure how? Do they like adventure, action, sci-fi, etc? How about family and love? Give them some fiction to read (especially book 3: Forever). One More Soul!

Time is running out folks! Plan a time on Saturday to order your T.C.O.T. books! Order the books and then tell everyone on social media you did and send a link from Amazon, Barnes & Noble, etc. Get your hard-copies so you have some outstanding fiction to read (after your Bible) when the power goes out!

Prayer: Dear Father in heaven, please be with us today. Guard our hearts and minds. Keep us in the truth. Help us love like you do, unconditionally and with action! Please bless this effort. Your will be done! Amen.

God bless you all, and please check back often on OUR project of "T.C.O.T. to the World" Launch could be at any moment!

Just one soul is the goal!

The Faithful has launched into orbit

4 May 2024

The Chronicles of Trinian (T.C.O.T.) Trilogy has launched. "The Faithful" is in orbit — "Forever" and "The Chronicles of Trinian Trilogy, The Faithful Stand Forever" are airborne, orbit soon.

All three new fiction releases have uploaded and are with the big distributers — Amazon, B&N, etc.

Houston, we have liftoff

5 May 2024

The Chronicles of Trinian Trilogy to go live on the big websites for pre-order. It should be hours now and not days.

"The Chronicles of Trinian" has successfully launched and entered orbit! Thanks to you, it entered at #410 on Amazon for Christian Future Fiction and about 450,000 in Kindle overall.

Since there are over ten Million books on Amazon. That's not bad!

Successful launch

6 May 2024

Happy Monday Everyone!

Overall, The Chronicles of Trinian (T.C.O.T.) Trilogy had a successful launch. "The Faithful" is currently at #113 in Christian Fantasy. It would be nice to break 100 (It would get more attention), but God's will be done. This is a marathon, not a sprint. Just ONE soul is the goal

"The Faithful" (2nd Edition) is full up for book preorder. Kindle Reader is up for "Forever" and "The Chronicles of Trinian Trilogy"! Kindle for "The Faithful" and the hard copy book preorder for "Forever" and "The Chronicles of Trinian" Trilogy should be up anytime now (Amazon works on weekends, right?). Kindle makes the book readable on devices instantly while you wait on your hard copy!

Buy and try:

"Alexa, read Terrence Rotering's, The Faithful." Listening is not for everyone, but some prefer it. I like it for when I am driving, taking a shower, etc. Also, it helps while waiting for the hard copy book to arrive.

Play:

Tell Alexa, "Volume 8." Then tell her to play, "Don't Tread on Me" by We the Kingdom. Then "You've Already Won (live)", by Shane in Shane. Finally, "Threads" by Geoff (pronounced Jeff) Moore and the Distance. Truly listen to the words of Threads! Outstanding! Then rest in the assurance that Jesus has already won!

Ok, everyone. Join me. This is the time! Remember, every penny after taxes of T.C.O.T. Trilogy goes back to God! This is OUR effort! The time is short! Let's Roll!

Please join the effort and support through social media, buying the books, and most importantly, PRAYER!

Praise God from whom all blessings flow

7 May 2024

All books are available to order! Praise God from whom all blessings flow! He is good all the time! He can't help it, it is who he is!

The Chronicles of Trinian (T.C.O.T.) Trilogy has had a successful launch! I should send the second edition "Stand" to the publisher today. It will probably not join its online pack until June. "Tophet" is included with "Stand" as the prequel to "The Faithful" and bridge to the "Foundation Chronicles."

I have seen some resistance from "the other side" and it is "in your face" kind of stuff (no surprise). I need brothers and sisters to step up and join the fight! Spread the Word and pray!

Thanks again to everyone who supported the launch. It is really appreciated! Special call out to Thomas Lz. who has not only been supporting with purchase, but most importantly, in prayer and on social media. Thank you, Brother Tom! Getting the word out is the critical fuel we need —— without it, the books will fall from orbit and visibility. I want to witness to God's love on Good Morning America! But again, not my will, but God's will be done!

Reminder — 100% of proceeds (after tax) go directly back to spreading God's Word. It is all God's! I will report amounts and contributions as they are available. In that light, ordering from Xulon = 100% royalties vs. AMZN, ~50%.

This is OUR effort. I can't do it alone. Please engage. Most importantly, pray. Thank you.

No weapon formed against me shall prosper in Jesus' name! God has made us promises. Honor Him by resting in their assurance! You are not alone — EVER!

Prayer: Heavenly Father. Please be with us today in everything we do. Please help us love EVERYONE around us, whether reciprocated.

Focus our eyes and deeds on the eternal, as time for all of us will soon end and the echoes of this life will begin. "Faith, hope and Love; but the greatest of these is love."

The empire strikes back

8 May 2024

The dark side hacked Chronicles of Trinian on Face Book this morning, so no one go there or accept friend requests.

Also, no one accept friend requests from me on Facebook in case the hackers got in my regular FB account.

Books charting!

8 May 2024

Good morning everyone! Thanks for your support! The books are charting online!

I should have been paying closer attention, but when I checked last night "The Faithful" and T.C.O.T. were both charting in Amazon fantasy new and future releases at #8 and #9, respectively! Thank you for helping me get the Word out!

Need some prayer support! The Chronicles of Trinian Facebook account was hacked this morning. Evil is not happy and lashing out. It's a minefield!

I figured the attacks would come from the dark forces. No worries. We will just keep on plugging away. "No weapon formed against me shall prosper, in Jesus' precious name!"

Not slowing down

9 May 2024

Good morning everyone! Ok. So we were hacked and basically shut down on T. C. O. T. FB site yesterday. No big deal! Not slowing down!

I figured the attacks would come from the dark forces. But no stress. I am just praying for him (Turkish guy). He wanted a ransom. I don't negotiate with terrorists. "No weapon formed against me shall prosper, in Jesus' precious name!"

Power back

10 May 2024

Sorry there wasn't an update this morning. We had a spring snow storm and six inches of the heaviest wet snow you can imagine, just solid of water. Power out until a couple of minutes ago.

T.C.O.T. Trilogy is complete. Book four should be out next month. Hope everyone is enjoying whichever books they bought thus far. What can I tell you — the books all stand on their own, but like a good series, trilogy, or more, they all interact and have some overlapping characters, themes, and interactions that build both the story and the characters. So, just because you have read one book, it doesn't mean you have learned everything about a character or the story overall.

I outlined all the next book this morning. It's the first book in the Foundation Chronicles. Pretty excited!

So, I have a big advertising push going in August with a full page add in the Fall Christian book flyer going out to 1200+ churches and pastors (inside front cover). Also have exhibits for the current three books at the August Christian Book Expo — about a thousand buyers/publishers attending. Until then, there are electronic banners for the books, etc. But I need a grassroots word-of-mouth effort to keep it going until then, so the books stay toward the top to be noticed. Please help? Purchase, pray and promote the books (three "P"s). I'm keeping zero of the after-tax proceeds, so not asking for myself.

Reset

11 May 2024

The Chronicles of Trinian! More enhanced versions of each book are in their individual texts. A way enhanced version of "Stand" with book #4 "Tophet" is at the publisher, and I'm hoping it is online by 1 June!

I hope everyone is enjoying whichever books they bought thus far. The books all stand on their own, but like a good series, trilogy, or more, they all interact and have some overlapping characters, themes, and interactions that build both the story and the characters. So, just because you have read one book, it doesn't mean you have learned everything about a character or the story overall. And, just because you have read the Trilogy book (the purple lion cover) doesn't mean you know it all either. Tophet adds 10% and future books continue to add more!

I outlined all the next book, book #5, this morning. It's the first book in the Foundation Chronicles. I start writing it today. Pretty excited!

So, I have a big advertising push going in August with a full page add in the Fall Christian book flyer going out to 1200+ churches and pastors (inside front cover). Also have exhibits for the current three books at the August Christian Book Expo

— about a thousand buyers/publishers attending. Until then, there are electronic banners for the books, etc. But I need help — a grass-roots word-of-mouth effort to keep it going until then, so the books stay toward the top of the new releases to be noticed. Please help? Purchase, pray and promote the books (three "P"s). I'm keeping zero of the after-tax proceeds, so not asking for myself. I will tell you were proceeds give you updates on how the ministry is being blessed!

Northern lights? Think what it will be like when Jesus returns!

12 May 2024

T.C.O.T Trilogy is complete! The basic trilogy is all in one book — Chroniclesoftrinian.com

T.C.O.T Trilogy is complete! I have started the Foundation Chronicles!

Doing a bunch of research on how to get eyes on these books. Tens of millions of books out there, so hard to get people to look at one tree in the forest. My best bet is through partners, friends and family. Have you told anyone about the books yet? Please do. Please help. All proceeds above taxes to Ceasar, go back to God's work, starting with building a church (or maybe a couple of chairs... LOL... thanks Corrine)!

Filled in chapter names and bullets to book number five this morning. It's the first book in the Foundation Chronicles. I start writing it today. Pretty excited!

I'm going to try not to review the same information in each blog. If you are a newcomer, please read earlier blogs for additional info.

Thanks to those who are helping our cause. I say "our cause" since all Christians want to spread his Word. I really thought people would love to give to God and get some good Christian fiction at the same time — two birds, if you will.

Not sure why this effort isn't spreading word of mouth, at least within the church. Even if folks don't want to read the books, they could listen to them on their phones. Everyone has a phone. By buying the books, more people would see the books and continue the spreading of his Word, all while building a church for people to worship him. Again, two birds. That's what you supporters are doing and thank you again. Who will be reached that we will see one day in heaven? That is the question.

Anyway, God's will be done! Maybe this isn't what he wanted me to do. I still think it is, but less sure now given the response. Perhaps

I should invest in Girl Scout cookies instead and pledge that income. ;>) Oh well.

That time the F-111F stalled over Germany

13 May 2024

Good morning everyone. It's Monday. CHARGE!

Well, the initial phase of launch went well. Things looked pretty bright. However, now that folks have made their initial purchases, the jet has stalled.

I remember my first sortie over Germany in 1987. It was a night mission, and we were at 33,000 feet over a stack of ten other F-111Fs. I hear the left seat instructor pilot ask Ramstein control for a lower altitude, multiple times. Each time he is denied, due to all the other F-111s stacked below us waiting their turn to enter the low-level route. I looked at the altitude tape and it's rolling through 29,000 feet, 28,000 feet... 19,000 feet. He had forgotten to swing the wings forward for lift at high altitude. The mighty Vark had stalled and dropped through ten other Varks in the blind. We recovered about 15,000 feet and were next to enter the low-level. Sweet!

Bottom line, it started with a stall and still all worked out. Hopefully, this effort will do the same. I need your help. Without word of mouth, the stall will cause ground impact. Please purchase, pray and promote. (All profit goes to God. It is already his. First, we build a church building and then proceeds will go to missions.) Is that one soul still out there?

Happy Tuesday. That log in the road.

14 May 2024

Good morning everyone. This morning I remember a time (when I was young and stupid). I was riding the rocket FZR-600 through the pouring rain at, well, a high rate of speed. Up ahead on the ground was a log. I had time to see the log through the rain, but unfortunately, no time to react. That was actually a blessing, because had I reacted in the pouring rain, I probably, if not certainly, would have put the bike down and been mortally injured. So, I offered an instantaneous prayer for help. Short story–short, I hit the log perpendicularly and sailed straight over it. If I tried that 100 times, I doubt I would be successful.

That short story teaches me several things: 1) When things look bad, don't panic. 2) When things aren't going the way you think they should go, don't panic. 3) When things aren't happening like you think they are supposed to happen, don't panic.

Panic leads you to blame others or doubt God. It is in our sinful nature to do both–it is always someone else's fault. Panic blames and says, "No one supported the effort." Well, why should they? This is my effort–they have their own.

(Thanks Cousin Tom, BTW, for all your support and reposts! It means a lot.)

Perhaps getting support wouldn't have made any difference. Or maybe that wasn't God's agenda. Maybe the whole effort was to strengthen my faith. Or maybe the goal–just one soul–has already been attained. Who knows?

The bottom line is that no matter what our current struggle is, give it to God and let his will be done. Pain. Failure. Trouble with others. Crime. Disease. Etc. We say, "Thy will be done." We mean it when we say it, but we need to accept it when we see it. Let me say that again. We mean it when we say it, but we need to accept it when we see it.

Superman

15 May 2024

Good morning everyone. This morning I remember a time (when I was still young and stupid). I was riding the rocket FZR-600 again and went to stop at a movie theater. It was dark.

Well, I didn't know there was fine gravel on the blacktop of the parking lot. When I went to stop, the bike slid and then stopped abruptly when it hit solid blacktop. I didn't stop.

Superman! I slid across the parking slot in a superman pose. Fortunately, I was wise enough to be wearing a helmet and a heavy leather jacket. The chin of the helmet shaved down to nothing. Scuffed the jacket up pretty good. Walked away without injury (saw the movie).

Sometimes things can go good-to-bad pretty fast! We pretend to be superman to survive, but it is just an act. We can't fly, and we are very destructible. It is actually our equipment that protects us — the full armor of God!

Don't neglect your armor in this world. Be protected! You don't know when you will hit gravel!

Well, signed up to get the books mailed out in a digital magazine, front cover, to a million Salem subscribers in June. We will see if it produces any fruit. Then again, in August, inside the cover of the Fall Christian Buyer's guide. Finally, three displays at the Christian Publishing Expo, also in August.

John: 3:16

15 May 2024

Bonus material for today–the second post!

So if you are a FB friend, you know I get up really early every day. I try to remember to post a picture of my clock and "John" on face book (John 3:16) to remind everyone daily of God's love and how he showed it; by giving us the Son who died on the cross in our place. Now we are declared redeemed! After that, EVERY DAY IS A GOOD DAY!

Well, when I sold gold to pay for this June book ad, the amount the gold broker gave me per ounce was $2,316. "316"! Hmmm. Another coincidence? It wouldn't have been that number the day before, today, or even throughout yesterday — just at that moment!

God may be speaking to us every day in things all around! I don't know if God was telling me he approved of taking buried gold and using it to bear fruit for the kingdom (seems there is a parable about that) or not. But if he did, I want to share it and give him glory! See with your spiritual eyes!

Not sure if T.C.O.T. will ever reenter orbit. "Thy will be done." We mean it when we say it, but we need to accept it when we see it! God's ways are not our ways. His-story will roll out as the puzzle-maker sees fit!

Success will only be determined by God. Maybe we don't see the value in this effort until we meet that one soul in heaven. That one soul will be significantly more than enough! Amen!

God's masks

16 May 2024

A stack of four plastic chairs sat on the brick patio next to the grill in the backyard of a Virginian home; unnoticed and unused.

One day, a man was working on removing the fall leaves from his gutter. Distracted, he stepped off the edge of his roof at twenty-seven feet above the ground.

Stepping off the roof with one foot, the man cartwheeled. Death was a certainty at twenty-seven feet over a brick patio.

However, one of the man's hands was able to hold on to the gutter for just a moment, straightening the man out vertically. Additionally, eight fingers clawed their way down the aluminum siding, clearly leaving a trace of the man's desperation.

The man had but a moment in time to ask God for help. Salvation was not in the man's ability to deliver. Only the hands of someone greater could deliver any help.

The man accelerated downward toward the brick patio and devastating harm. Only one thing existed between man and brick–four stacked patio chairs.

The man hit the chairs. All the legs of the chairs snapped off and flew thirty-plus feet into the backyard, absorbing the energy of the falling man and dissipating it into space. The man hit the chairs and did a parachute landing fall or PLF (yes, God had prepared the man twenty years earlier to survive the event). The man sustained a slightly sprained ankle, and yes, I am that man.

The lesson today is that God uses people and things in this world (masks) to save us and preserve us. We often overlook these things, claiming luck or good fortune helped us when, in fact, it was God using a mask. Pray that God opens our spiritual eyes to recognize his actions in the world.

Pray for those who mourn

17 May 2024

Happy Friday! Hope your day is outstanding! If your day is filled with blessings, don't forget the one who gave them to you. If it is a rough day, don't forget the only one who can help.

So, got my early copies of the paperback books, and they look great! I'm sure you'll love the way they look!

We have some dear friends visiting us now that we haven't seen for thirty-two years! It is like we've only been apart for a day. It is just unbelievable! Jo and Larry. I used to fly the Mighty Vark with Larry, and we still share that comradery from a day when we were young and serving overseas, facing off with the Soviet Union and Warsaw Pact. We were more than willing to give everything in defense of this great experiment in freedom, the USA.

Jo and Larry have had more than their share of extreme loss, but they have used it to serve and bless others. Resting in God's ever present love, they have risen above the pain and heartbreak of this broken world and used their lose to help them focus on the unbroken world that Jesus won for us, the world right around the corner, when they will be with their loved ones once again.

Theirs is an extra painful loss of children and grandchildren, but all of us will feel the pain that comes from an imperfect and broken world. The difference for those who cling to Jesus is that we have an absolute hope of Heaven and seeing our loved ones again — and living with our loving God in an unbroken world forever! No false Gods offer that retirement plan and none can deliver it. Only one has conquered death and taken away its sting forever!

If you want more of this sure hope or want to share it with friends or family, The Chronicles of Trinian Trilogy is packed with it amidst action and adventure. Consider it.

Just an airport. Focus on your destination.

18 May 2024

Good morning everyone! Happy Sunday. Praise God from whom all blessings flow!

Fourteen years ago, right after moving to Colorado, I was diagnosed with Non-Hodgekins Lymphoma. My wife Theresa, who had planned on following me to Colorado six months later, quit her job, sold the house, managed the movers, found the boys a way to finish out the school year in Virginia, and head out to help me through chemo. I prayed I could finish the Chronicles of Trinian before the Lord took me home. Well, long story short, God took the cancer away.

Fast forward 14 years. I just finished the Chronicles of Trinian Trilogy. This morning I noticed some areas of my skin with some questionable new lesions. We will see what happens.

Your will be done, Father. I have been tremendously blessed! Eventually, I, we, all most leave the airport that we are in here and go on to our final destination. Some people fear getting on that plane, even though they truly believe Jesus bought them their ticket and paid the debt for us all. That flight, death, is a major step, but it should not be feared. Jesus has conquered death and the grave! It is now just a doorway, a portal from here to there, much like the portal that took each of us from our mother's womb to the life we share.

Bottom line: We all go through that airport doorway. We all serve at the discretion of the King. He decides how many heartbeats each of us gets. Believe in him or not; love him or not; he decides — period.

So, unlike the famous poem, don't rage against the dying of the light, go joyfully into the night; because it is just a blink of an eye against eternity. He has prepared an unbelievable, unbroken world for us to live in! Trust the promises and encourage each other. We know how this story ends! All aboard!!!

Dry dead bones

20 May 2024

Good morning everyone! Happy Monday. Focus on the positive and even Mondays can be good! I just figured out how to add pictures, so these blogs will be a lot more enjoyable.

Walking around our land with Scout and Ranger (Colorado Mountain Dogs), we find lots of bones from cougar kills. Many are old and dry. But every third day or so, they find some remnant of a carcass. These are fresh bones with meat still on them. The age of the bones makes a tremendous difference. Fresh = yummy and quite a treat for the pups.

Read Ezekiel 37: 9-10. Wow! God's word reminds us that without his breath of life, we are dead. We were dead matter before he breathed life into us, and we are spiritually dead until the Holy Spirit breathes faith into us. Physical death without spiritual life will cause eternal death and separation from everything good–if you think Mondays are bad!

How can you tell the difference between bodies that are alive and bodies that are dead? Movement. How can you tell the difference between people who have the Holy Spirit and people who don't? Action.

It's not an absolute. We cannot see inside everyone's heart. However, God gives us his Spirit for a reason. We shouldn't just tuck it away for safekeeping. We need to let the Holy Spirit fill us, feed our faith with God's Word, and let both drive us to action!

It is wonderful beyond words to know the truth and what God has prepared for us in eternity. But he has breathed life into us for a reason — for action! Go and tell the world the good news! Jesus Christ has saved us all! Believe and live!

Tired, but firing up the generator

21 May 2024

Good morning. Thank you all for supporting.

As a reminder to anyone who might be new, all proceeds from The Chronicles of Trinian (T.C.O.T.) books go back to God's ministry of sharing the Good News — Jesus saved us!

Well, the book sales aren't going as well as I had hoped. Still praying the Lord uses them for good–his purpose–whether via a few or a million.

Big book promotions coming in June and August, so maybe that will increase visibility. Please tell your friends and families about the books.

Feeling a little overwhelmed from ten-hour days writing for a year, I may need a break. Do you ever feel that way? Life is hard, every day. There is always something to weigh you down. But you know what? God is good — all the time! Amen?

There are so many characters in these books that I can almost guarantee you will find someone you can relate to.

I hope and pray God can work through these books to encourage each of us to keep going; to remind us of God's love for us and his promises; and to help us always STAND.

A great cloud of witnesses surrounds us, and we know how the story ends.

Be strong today. If something is bothering you, give it to God and let it go. Fear not, for God is with you! Acknowledge him in everything and watch things blossom and flourish!

Satan's attack thwarted

22 May 2024

This serpent showed up at the house yesterday to declare war. He didn't make it. "No weapon formed against me shall prosper!"

Good morning everyone! As Mathew West and Casting Crowns sing in their song, "Nobody," "I'm just a nobody, trying to tell everybody about somebody who saved my soul."

Eighteen days (countdown) until the preorder books number one through three are all shipping. I have advanced copies and they look great! I can't wait till you can start reading them (unless you bought the Kindle, which has each book on sale at $2.99 until 9 June!)

So, I have been being tempted to slow down... not going to happen! The proceeds from this twenty year writing effort are going toward building our church building... 100% after Caesar takes his cut! Please support sharing God's Good News of our Savior and enjoy some Christian fiction at the same time! They make great gifts! (Over age thirteen, please — lots of action and adventure.)

Been a rough couple of days, or years, actually. I can't seem to sleep for over four hours a night. I guess I am meant to be doing something, so I'm working on book five in T.C.O. T!

People keep asking me the order to read the books. Here you go." The Faithful," then "Stand," then "Forever." The Faithful Stand Forever. If you get the comprehensive book, "The Chronicles of Trinian, The Faithful Stand Forever," with the lion on the front, you can't go wrong. Then, buy "Stand" because it includes a bonus book of "Tophet" and leads into The Foundation Chronicles. Then buy "The Faithful" and "Forever" and give them as gifts to someone you love! Working on "The Promise, The Foundation Chronicles" first book right now. The Foundation Chronicles take place in a time before "The Faithful."

Let's all have an exceptional day!

Forever wingman

23 May 2024

It is very important to have a wingman. I have two, Scout and Ranger. However, my main wingman is Scout.

Scout isn't actually as big as this picture seems to show. When I took the selfie of us, my hand was closer to his enormous head than it was to me, so it turned out this way. It is an accurate depiction of how he sees himself, though.

Scout is an outstanding dog, but he won't be around forever. He's already six and showing subtle signs of his aging. Bottom line, I need to have a wingman that will always be there for me. We all do.

People will fail us. We will fail others. Dogs will fail us less, but they will also leave, eventually.

There is only one wingman that will not leave us; never. Only one we can depend on every time, for all time. This is the relationship we need to prioritize over all others! Period–dot!

Prioritize your relationship with God today and every day. Talk to him, depend on him, trust him to keep his promises. Expect that he will. You honor him when you do.

Your wingmen will always fail you, eventually, unless your wingman is God!

Old men don't bounce.

24 May 2024

Ok. Three things today. First, this image is totally untouched. I took it straight from the tree cam. Look at the outline on the side of the cougar that was made from a bush between the cougar and a low sun, right at the moment the camera took the picture! What are the odds of getting an outline of a cougar on the side of a cougar? 1 in a billion?

Second. Expecting to approve the type set of "STAND" (Expanded with Tophet) today. It should then be available Kindle in about a week to ten days and in print by about 10 July. Very excited to have the entire expanded and reedited Chronicles of Trinian (T.C.O.T.) Trilogy out and available!

Third. Old men don't bounce. When I was the Operations Officer for the Operational Support Squadron in Turkey, back in the day, we had a roof stomp for the Wing Safety Officer, who was becoming our Squadron Commander the next day. It was dark, and we all climbed on his roof, stomped our feet, and screamed for beer. After all, it was Air Force tradition.

Well, some lieutenants pulled his trampoline over to the house to help with the roof dismount. After a few jumped off the roof onto the trampoline and then the planet's surface, I figured, "What the heck." I put little thought into it.

Having never been on a trampoline, I guess I figured it was a kind of magic (Not really. I want nothing to do with magic). Contacting the trampoline with the side of my body, I bounced once and landed on the metal bar of the trampoline's perimeter. Then I rolled off and landed on terra firma.

I did what all men do in similar situations; I jumped up and went in for a drink. After about ten minutes of putting on a cheerful face, I walked home and drove myself to the emergency room.

Long story short, it is one of the many reasons I am in the hot tub now, some twenty-five years later. I am very blessed to have been able to walk twenty-five years ago and very blessed today. Pain can be controlled, barely.

Bottom-line, as my dad would tell me often when I was a teenager: "T-H-I-N-K." I forgot to that day in Turkey and many other times as you have read in these blogs as well as will read in future blogs.

So, just because the crowd jumps into something and tells you to jump in, T-H-I-N-K! The lemmings don't always know what the right thing to do is. Often, counter flow is the right answer ("usually" would be more accurate).

The road to heaven is 100% in Jesus Christ, and the path is very narrow. The crowd of lemmings is charging off the cliff all around us; don't be a lemming. I am pretty sure freefall without a chute is a lot of fun for a while. But once you hit terra firma, you are in pain — FOREVER! You will quickly forget the "fun."

Well, that does it for this morning. Up at 11:45 pm for the day. Argh. Hope you have a great Friday! Wear red for the troops deployed protecting us! God bless!

"Whom have I in heaven but you?"

John 3:16

24 May 2024

"For God so loved the world that he gave his one and only son, that whoever believes in him will not perish, but have everlasting life."

I get up between midnight and 2 AM every day. Why? No idea. But I try to post a picture of my clock at 3:16 with John on Facebook.

I have done this hundreds of mornings, so it is a very significant thing to me.

So with that as the backdrop, listen to this! When I decided to finish this trilogy and donate the proceeds, however big or small, to God, I sold some gold we had to pay for this last book. The price they gave me at that moment in time was $2,316 per ounce. 316!

That's not the half of it. This morning, the publisher finished the typesetting for the book "STAND." I gave it a look over and realized they had done it continuously, but I wanted each new chapter (for this book) to start on the right page. They reformatted it and sent it to me for approval. I scrolled through it, and it looked good. When I got to the second last page, I realized that the last symbol for the book, the symbol I used to finish all the books, three crosses, didn't make it on the page. It went to the last page by itself. What was the page number of the last page of the book? 316.

What?!!! I was blown away! Is it possible for this to happen out of sheer coincidence? The 316 pages, the gold price of $2,316 and the Tophet story (read earlier blogs for that one!)? Something is going on here, folks, and it is awesome!

Anyway, early blog for those of you that are headed out to enjoy the long weekend. Enjoy, and remember those who gave their all for us! Like Jesus!

"Whom have I in heaven but you?"

Lukewarm Coffee

25 May 2024

My coffee was lukewarm by the time I was in the tub today. It wasn't very good. It is best when it is hot!

Most of my Christian life has been the same. Though sometimes I have been "hot" for the Lord, a "Jesus Freak" if you will, the air in the balloon always cools and the balloon falls back to earth.

Ezekial writes in Chapter 37:1-6 that the dry bones should hear the word of the Lord and live. Then they and all will know that he is the Lord!

Well, he breathes life into me daily. I rise like that balloon, proclaim his name, grow tired, and sink back to earth. But his power is made perfect in my weakness. Renewed with and by the Spirit of Grace and Truth, I rise again to proclaim his name, forgiven and made new again!

The devil would have us looking in the rear-view mirror instead of looking ahead. He wants us to dwell on our past sins and remember the sins of others directed against us. In this way, he can make us lukewarm like that coffee, to be spit out!

Resist him, put on God's armor, and forget the past. It is gone. Look forward and BURN HOT in your faith! The Spirit will give you the power if you ask God to help you.

If the road ahead does not materialize the way you have seen it, give it a little time. It is God's timing, not ours. But in any road you walk, burn HOT for the Lord! Every day. The time is short and could end at any moment!

We are all different parts of the body and will burn differently in the place we are called to be light. But, all our lights need to shine to dispel the darkness and show the light to the lost! In the darkness, evil can tell all kinds of lies about what is ahead. We know the truth. Light the way! Turn on your light and SHINE! Burn out BRIGHT!

"Whom have I in heaven but you?"

Puzzle Pieces

25 May 2024

As you all know, the Trilogy is out. I sent book four to the publisher yesterday.

A few amazing things happened on this 20 year journey. These three, just in the last few months.

1) The name Tophet was randomly chosen by taking the first initial of the lands in the trilogy, as they were randomly introduced over 20 years. Tophet fit perfectly as the actual Tophet (unknown at the time it became part of the book's map) was actually a place where people did the exact thing described in the book for the same demon.
2) The cost of the gold sold to finance the book effort was $2,316/ounce, as offered by the gold dealer the moment I sold it. 316!
3) The last page of book four after the type caster manipulated it and set it was 316! 316!

These things were not planned. They were not manipulated. Something happened.

Maybe those three things mean nothing to you. Maybe you don't post John 3:16 just about every morning (at 3:16am) on Facebook. Hundreds of times now! Maybe you are not amazed that "The Faithful Stand Forever" and three crosses alone (how I always finish the books) fell on the last page of book four, on page 316; 316! But I am.

There are no coincidences. People who don't see good and evil at work in the world promote the word — coincidence. Perhaps by the devil himself.

ALL the pieces of the puzzle of His-story are critical to the final picture. There are no holes called coincidences when the puzzle is finished. We might see an empty, totally white puzzle piece, but that piece touches multiple other pieces, many more colorful and "important looking" than the plain white piece; but every piece is as important as another and the puzzle maker cares just as much about the plain pieces as the ornamental looking pieces! He sees the puzzle from the other side, where the individual aspects of the puzzle pieces make no difference; only the shape that he forms is critical. You see, Jesus paid for the entire puzzle and for every piece, not just the colorful pieces! Only when the puzzle is complete is the picture of His-story finished, and he will leave the puzzle to find every missing piece!

Rest assured that you are a critical piece in His-story! Come and take your place in the puzzle!

Fear not! He is with us.

26 May 2024

We have lots of predator animals roaming around out here. Big cats, bears, coyote packs, and soon wolf packs.

When I graduated from the Air Force Academy, now 40 years ago (next year), I wanted a reminder not to fear... anything. So I put "Fear not" inside my class ring.

It's a great motto. Of course, a lack of fear is not really a wise motto to live by. One should have a healthy fear of things that can hurt you like drinking flaming drinks, motorcycle crashes, jumping out of aircraft, falling off roofs, getting "lit" up over Iraq, driving vehicles too fast, walking with mountain lions, playing with rattlesnakes, taking pictures of lightning storms and funnel clouds from the roof of your house, dropping thousands of feet in a stalled fighter at night, etc.

Having a "No fear" motto is absolute insanity if there is no one to protect you from your stupidity. One needs a protector! (Some more than others!) That is where the Maker of the Universe comes in.

I am not recommending doing stupid things and challenging God to protect you. However, whether it is through stupidity (yours truly hindsight) or just living your life and coming under attack, you can rest assured that God has your back.

God will protect you in all your ways! Now, there will probably be some consequences for things you have asked for, like say, a painful back and joints from years of abuse. But hey, we most likely asked for those things in our youth. That doesn't help much later in life when we are hurting, but in an imperfect world, it is what it is.

But what helps us through our suffering is this. God has promised to work all things for the good of those who love him. That is powerful! We can rest in this promise and exchange powerful bodies for hope as we age. (Hope in the new bodies to come when Jesus returns). And this hope is a sure hope, resting on a God who has never broken a promise and loves us like his children, because of Jesus!

So, no fear, not even in pain, or loneliness, or the suffering that comes with losing loved ones. These are the big three of the final frontier! If we live long, we will endure pain, loneliness, and loss.

We pray, “Thy will be done!” We mean it when we pray it; we need to accept it when we see it! It is His-story, not ours, and we know how the story ends! He told us in his Word!

So, today, if you are lonely, know there are people who love you and care, especially our God, who sent his Son to die for us and save us. If you are in pain, you are certainly not alone. Rest in the sure hope of a perfect body in an unbroken world that is right around the corner! And if you have suffered loss, know the pain will ease and you will see those who die, trusting in Jesus, again. They are not gone. We just can’t see them for a bit of time.

Soon the day will come when we will rise into the air to meet our Savior when he returns. No more pain, tears, fear, or sadness! Run a good race and focus on that day!

“Whom have I in heaven but you?”

Closing my eyes now.

27 May 2024

When I was five, my friends and I rode our bikes everywhere. We would be gone for hours and hours!

One sunny day, we decided to ride "with no hands." That worked out well. So we decided to ride down this really steep hill with no hands. That also worked out.

Well, I thought I would do one better. I rode down the really steep hill with no hands and my eyes closed. That too worked out ok, right until I jumped the curb and ran straight into the ancient oak tree near the bottom of the hill. I can't count the number of knots I had on my cranium through the childhood years! (Almost as many in the adult years.)

Generally speaking, "eyes wide open" is the way to go. Vision serves us well in this world, enabling us to maneuver through life and function in our society. However, when it comes to our faith, the eyes can be a problem.

Our eyes often wander onto things and into places they shouldn't. Our eyes deceive us and undermine our walk, leading us into lust, envy, gluttony, excessive entertainment, and trivial pursuits. There is not one of us who hasn't been led down the wrong path by our eyes, and they are powerful!

We are warned about our tongue–we all know the ways it gets us into trouble. But the eyes, they are often behind the tongues' lashing out operations: gathering the Intel, picking the targets, offering attack options, evaluating the damage reports, and recommending the reattack to the brain (Command Post).

We are also warned about the eye. "If your eye sins against you, pluck it out. It is better to lose an eye than for the whole body to burn in hell."

The Devil often uses seduction to lead us down the wrong path. Physical eyes are instrumental in these attacks of lust, envy, desire, gluttony, etc. We need to lean more on our eyes of faith!

When the Devil, the world, and your own sinful flesh use your eyes to tempt you (and we know when it is happening because that little voice tells us–you know what I'm talking about!), try this. You have heard of counting to ten before opening your mouth and letting your tongue speak. Next time you are tempted by your eyes, close them and remember who you are. Ask God to help you and then open them, committed to what will be a positive outcome for good and a defeat for the sinful agents at work in the battle.

However, and this is very important, don't close them while driving, skiing, hiking mountains, clearing leaves off roofs or riding without hands on your bike down a steep hill! Engage your brain before closing your eyes.

Well, gotta go. I feel like riding my bike!

Just one chair. The big in the small.

28 May 2024

So, as you know, all the proceeds from The Chronicles of Trinian book sales go back to God. I dedicated them to the church we are building in Colorado Springs.

I've been told that the sales might pay for a couple of chairs in the building. Based on how it is going so far, that may be an accurate prediction.

Here's the thing. God doesn't need the money from these books or anything else for His work to be done–for this church to be built. It may be His will that paying for this building be long and difficult.

It was my hope and dream that these books would pay for great things to be done here. That may or may not be His will. I still pray it is in his will, but only time will tell.

If the book sales only pay for a couple chairs in the church building, I am more than ok with that. My Mom sat in a chair in church and heard of God's saving grace; now she is in heaven. A child may sit there in that chair, or someone with cancer; maybe a teacher or an old man who has just lost his wife. These people will need a chair.

There is so much big in the small. Maybe just one chair, maybe just one soul, but who can put a value on the eternity of a soul?

Just one chair. I'm good with that.

Who are you? I'm just nobody.

29 May 2024

Who are you? Who am I? It's an important question. Kind of like deciding what you want on your gravestone.

Do I want?

1. Air Force aviator.
2. Faithful husband, good father, and friend to all?
3. Patriot!

These are all good, but tiny and temporary relative to eternity. They become almost trivial after fifty years, when all who knew us are gone. Plus, they say who we were, not who we are. They insinuate we are gone.

I think we need to decide what we want on our gravestone and then live to be that person. Otherwise we are wasting a lot of valuable and very limited time, of course! Again, what do we put on the gravestone?

Mine? Some choices include:

1. "Nobody, just trying to tell everybody, about somebody, who saved my soul." (Casting Crowns and Mathew West)
   Or maybe -
2. "Blood bought, faithful member of God's family." (Casting Crowns and Mathew West)
   Or maybe -
3. "Redeemed and adopted child of God. Moved to live with his family in Heaven."
   Or finally -
4. "Redeemed, adopted, and living servant of the eternal King of everything, now and forever!"

Go big people! Don't limit yourself to who you have been for a handful of decades, while you were here in this temporary pit stop of life on planet Earth!

Throw who you truly are on that gravestone! Change your focus and attach yourself to the eternal! Think eternal and start living eternal. This is the first moment of eternity. What do you want that to look like? Ok, now live THAT tombstone description, starting NOW!

One reason I still haven't buried my mom in the ground in Wisconsin is that she's not dead! I don't want everyone thinking of her as dead. Her ashes are here with me in a beautiful urn in my office. I would have done the same with my dad had I been given the choice. Why? Because they are not dead! They are just temporarily out of sight. Someday they will rise to meet Jesus in the sky as he returns! How cool it would be to rise alongside them!

Anyway, think about who you are, decide, and then live that person! The time is very short. Don't let others decide who you are or (on a gravestone) who you were!

God tells us who we are: loved, redeemed, and adopted members of his family! Time to live that way!

You are the LIGHT of the world–especially when it hurts!

31 May 2024

Pain! The final frontier. To boldly go...

Got pain? If you don't, you will. The longer you live, the greater exposure you have to mental and physical pain.

If the average age of a human is about 80, you can divide the seasons of life as follows. Spring: 1-20. Summer: 21-40. Fall 41-60. Winter 61-80.

Yours truly just entered winter, and with it lots of pain!

Every day, every night... pain. Well, I think it is partially a spiritual attack to get you to focus on self. In our younger years, the devil distracted us with sexual desires, material gain, and the "scenery" as I call it... Sex, Stuff and Scenery. The triple S's. Having done, acquired and seen our fair share of the triple S's, (or the three P's of Passion 1-20, Power 21-40, Possessions 40-60), he attacks with a new distraction... a new "P"... pain (60+). Surprise!

How do you deal with it?

1. Ask God for help. Lean on him every moment.
2. Refocus. Be the Light of the World. Light shines brightest when it sits atop a mountain of adversity. People notice. They pay attention when believers are suffering but still glorifying God! Think of the pain as clouds trying to kill your light. Pierce the darkness! Let your light SHINE!

What happens when the Light shines in the darkness? It is noticed way more than if it were under blue skies.

The Light of faith makes the clouds of adversity around it beautiful! It changes its environment. It affects others.

Never have I had such a positive impact on others than when I was diagnosed with NHL in 2010. I had everyone's undivided attention.

Adversity gives you a loudspeaker to share your faith if you look outward instead of inward.

3. Remember our sure hope. A new body is coming soon. No more pain and no more tears.

It's not easy. There are good days and bad days. But rescue is coming and it will be glorious and permanent! Bask in the promises and run a good race! The marathon always gets tougher at mile marker 20. Expect it; but it is almost over and YOU CAN DO IT!

What's important?

1 Jun 2024

Well, here's a thought. If you were to die tonight, what really matters today?

Is it that season of "Suits" on Netflicks? "Yeah, gotta finish it before I go." Is that what you will spend your last day doing? Maybe it's one more day partying with your friends on the beach. "Can't skip that?" Perhaps it's driving across the state to a soccer game. "My kid's athletic diversity is really important." What will you decide to spend your last day before meeting the God of the Universe–and eternity–doing? Just a thought.

Here are some more thoughts. There are absolutely zero guarantees you will live to be 80, or 50, or even 25. None. Each of us has our own number of heartbeats, determined by God and him alone.

So what's important? Another thought; this time some truths. Our time is our most precious commodity. We are no longer ours. We have been bought with a price of Jesus' own precious blood. You either serve God or you don't. You cannot have two masters. We have lots of distractions in this world; lots of things tugging at our time. The Devil loves distraction. He loves it when we waste our time here.

Remember who you are: blood bought, redeemed, forgiven, Adopted Children of the King of the Universe on temporary duty here as ambassadors for Jesus Christ to the World!

And we don't walk alone. Jesus promised to be with us until we go to see him or he returns in glory to get us. No matter what comes our way in this world, Jesus has already won, and us with him!

So, what's important? Yes, Jesus wants us to enjoy our lives, but that doesn't mean waste our time. Will you remember this season of "Suits" in 12,693 years? Um, no. How about that last beer and game of beach volleyball? Nope. Will you remember that talk you had with your son about Jesus as you drove across the state to a soccer game? I think, yes.

Choose how to spend your time wisely. You have been given an eternity there. Live that way, here! Do not keep salvation through Jesus a secret! Ask yourself every day if what you are doing in your "spare time" has any eternal significance. Does it feed your Spirit positively, or are you feeding the bad dog inside? Is it bringing someone else closer to their Savior? Is it planting seeds? Every minute truly does matter!

Lauren Daigel once again, "The only thing that matters now is everything you think of me. In you I find my worth, in you, I find my identity."

Fix your eyes on Jesus Christ, on eternity, and then it doesn't matter if it is your last day, today. Whatever. It is all well with my soul! The battle is already won. I know how the story ends, and we will be with our Savior forever!

So, what are you going to do today? What is important? Once you answer, ask yourself if it is important–if–you aren't here tomorrow?

Live your life today like you were going to die tonight, 'cause guess what? Someday, that will be the way it unfolds, and the habits you establish today will be what you are going to be doing when that moment comes.

Just a thought.

Time to refocus

2 June 2024

Good morning! Praise God from whom all blessings flow!

Well, I was just thinking about the last year and a half. I've spent all my time on the Chronicles of Trinian Trilogy books, and it has taken quite a toll on my body. It has been fun, but exhausting. Now the books are out there and I hope they will bring God glory; but I think it's time to refocus.

Ever feel that way? Ever feel kind of lost on which way to go next? That's where I am now, and it is tough to decide a direction. It is like trying to pick a major to pursue in college, or what job to take. Though I am a little off balance at the moment, I am confident God will direct my path.

I'd like to keep writing, but have to see if the previous time allotment pays off or if the books remain in low orbit. Things looking a little iffy at the moment, like the jet is ready to stall.

If you could all pray this effort to reach the masses would bear much fruit, I would be very thankful. I pray for all of you, though I only know who a few of you are: Grace, Tom, Travis, Cindie, Sig, Larry, Joanne, Bryan, Virginia, Jason, Kayla, Lynn, Barb, Angel, etc. I am sure I am missing a few as I have no way of knowing who follows the blog or is promoting the books unless I see it on your feeds or you tell me. If I didn't name you, my apologies, I just didn't know.

So for now, I am in a state of limbo, looking for direction and trying to get on a schedule of under three hours of sleep.

God's strength is made perfect in our weakness. Waiting for a miracle.

Be the light

3 June 2024

The above picture is from 1979. My mom and dad (and my best bud, Brandy) sitting on the backyard patio having a PBR. Where am I? Taking the picture. Glad I did!

Forty-five years; where does the time go? Mom and Dad are both in Heaven now (Brandy too, since all dogs go to heaven!)

It's important to stop and look back. There is continuity between those that have gone before and those that follow. Time here is very short.

We are all here for a reason, a purpose. You might not feel that way every day. I don't. But we are. If we are still breathing, we are meant to be making a difference in the lives of those around us. It is meant to be a positive (+) difference, but it can be negative (-) if we aren't purposeful (the opposite of love is not hate, it is indifference.)

We don't always feel like blessing our loved ones, friends, or strangers. Seems like everything has to be optimal before we feel like helping others with their day, or even think about being nice. Try to remember that thinking of others and their well-being has the greatest impact when things aren't optimal. When you are having a bad day, in pain, or just don't feel like blessing someone else, do it anyway. It will be a gift to them, a gift to you, and a gift that keeps on giving! THAT is why we are here!

The people in our pictures will soon be gone. They are just as important as any of us, even the ones who hurt us. Pray for them. Help them on their journey. Turn electrons (- charge) into protons (+ charge). Turn darkness into light. All our world will rapidly become a better place to be.

Have a great (+) day!

Testimony

4 June 2024

Good morning everyone!

So, I went to my buddy Moses' Testimony Saturday. He spoke of his life journey; from unbelief to faith and then to service to our Lord and Savior, Jesus Christ.

Moses is a great man. A great husband, father and servant to others. However, it wasn't always like that. If you asked him, he would readily admit that any "greatness" observed in his life should not be attributed to him, but to the Holy Spirit living and working through him. It is the same for all of us, every one!

God has actively pursued Moses. Loving Moses, God convicted him of his failures, redeemed him, and used him to work wonders in this world! God shows Moses his love daily and continues to use Moses to strengthen his brothers and sisters, as well as bring others to the truth of salvation through faith in Jesus Christ.

Moses is not alone. As I look back on my life, I can more clearly see the many times I have failed, as well as the times I could STAND. I could write volumes on both. I have not and cannot STAND on my own. I am just not strong enough. Without God, I am dead and there simply is no hope; life here has an endless variety of vain accomplishments and a temporary reprieve from an eternity of endless suffering and hopeless separation from all that is good.

However, with God, it is quite a different picture, both looking back and looking forward. WHEN I was able to STAND in the past, God was able to carry me through many trials and challenges. Most importantly, he was able to use me to witness of him and strengthen others. He forgave me over and over for my failures and held me close to him, strengthening me, and then sending me out again.

If you haven't recently, it might be time to look back on your life. What are you proud of and what not so proud of? Are the things you are proud of lasting? Are they eternal? Or will those victories quickly pass, either in a few years or when you walk through the door of eternity? It is time to think about what is on the other side of that door, don't you think?

When you are prepping to go on a trip somewhere, do you just walk out the door, drive to the airport, and get on the plane? If you are being honest, no. You think about that trip for weeks, maybe months. You plan, prepare, pack, and ponder every aspect of that journey. Don't you think you should equally consider and prepare for an eternal trip?

We should take account often (daily?) of our walk. It will end sooner than we think. There are no do-overs. We are prepared or we aren't prepared, and the consequences are eternal. You will want an expert pilot to bring you to your final destination!

In summary, look back and take account. When did you STAND? How did you STAND? Will you STAND in the future? You don't want to pass through that final door alone. Give everything to God. He will keep you faithful here, help you STAND, and safely bring you home to be with him FOREVER!

Good morning!

Great Father's Day Gifts!

5 June 2024

Good morning everyone!

Father's Day is in 11 days! Three of the four Chronicles of Trinian books will ship in 4 days. You can still order your T.C.O.T. books in time to get them to Dad for Father's Day!

My Dad has been gone from this place for 14 years now. It is hard to fathom. I wish he had been here for many reasons, one of which is to see this book trilogy be completed.

So, if your dad is still here, get this trilogy for Father's Day. I recommend "The Chronicles of Trinian, The Faithful Stand Forever." It's the book with the purple lion on the front. My good friend Sheryl came up with the idea of getting it for her father first, and it is a good one! This book is heavy and symbolizes strength, just like Dad!

Here is your opportunity to get Dad something different and awesome! Plus, if your dad is far away, you can have Amazon deliver it in under 2 days!

If Dad doesn't read much, that's ok. When you buy the book from Amazon, Amazon Alexa will read it for him, aloud. If you don't have Alexa, get the Kindle version of the books for just $2.99 each! Then with an app like speechify, Kindle will read the books out loud for Dad!

Here is a chance to get something for Dad that is heavy, looks cool; and is packed with action, adventure, and God's Word! It is something he can use anywhere, anytime. Most importantly, it will strengthen his faith and remind him that God is with him, no matter what the future may hold.

Faith, family, and love, and a lot of action!

Fear not, have faith, God is nigh.

6 June 2024

Inspect the picture above. Whether you see it, feel it, or acknowledge it, this is our reality. The wolf is at the door and on our own, no level of bravado will stop the wolf from devouring us.

But we are not on our own, are we? Though we often forget, God loves us, Jesus, our Good Shepherd has saved us, and God's angels are watching over us. We take this for granted.

It is time to see daily with our spiritual eyes, step forward with a determined trust, and live with a resolute faith!

In that light, I am asking you to post The Chronicles of Trinian books on your social media, tell your friends, buy copies for your dad for Father's Day, and spread the word!

We have people to reach with the truth, and this is a fun way to do it! Everyone enjoys some good fiction to read or listen to. PLUS, we build a church!

Perhaps this sounds like I am asking too much. I have no problem begging the people of God to step up and share God's Word to the world, build a church, and enjoy a book or two or three while doing it! I am making zero from this effort. It all goes back to God! So let's roll!

Join me in this miracle! I believe it has already happened. Be part of it and rejoice with me as it unfolds! "Fear not, be faithful, God is nigh!"

Excerpt from "The Faithful."

"Are you afraid?"

"No, I am not."

Her answer surprised her. "Trust him now." Christina closed her eyes and slipped off the makeshift raft into the raging, blue waters of the Dark Sea; beginning her long, cold descent into the black depths below.

"Fear not. Be faithful. God is nigh."

Have GOOD TIME.
Things that matter and things that don't.

7 June 2024

So, I was reminded this morning of little things that matter a bunch. Getting out of bed, the world spun. Turns (pun intended) out it is BPPV, or an inner ear disorder–when calcium fragments disrupt the inner ear's sense of motion.

I instantly marveled at God's amazingly intricate and overwhelming design!

The inner ear matters. Try walking straight or even standing up with BPPV. It doesn't happen, and it makes you feel really sick! If God ever wakes you up with a morning of BPPV, you will quickly orient to thinking about what is important. I know many have had worse experiences than BPPV. Just saying, it snaps your head back into alignment with what matters and what doesn't.

It got me to thinking about, well, everything. We spend 99% + of our lives focused on the 99% + of things that don't matter. Part of the 1% is health. Health matters.

When you can't stand up, a bunch of things fall from importance–like, almost everything. You praise God for the amazing intricacy of his creation. Then you wonder how you will function in the world. You mourn that someone will need to take care of you. You understand how millions of others feel.

Some things don't really matter in comparison. We are so very blessed in our lives with so much that we have elevated these things to a level of importance that is ridiculous. Things like how our sport's team is doing, the scratch on our way-to-expensive car, the new video game we wanted that is out of stock, the gym being closed, or even the pealing paint on the shelter we call our home. Yes, these are things that bring enjoyment or a sense of worth to our lives–but should they? The world has convinced us they are important, but in reality, these categories of things are a worthless waste of TIME. Literally, they are not worth anything close to the currency of TIME we pay for them.

When the hourglass says you have one last hour left of time, what things will be important? Will you say, "I want to listen to Pink Floyd's the Wall?" How about, "Let's go paint the house?" "Or maybe I'd like to drive my car one last time or bench press one last set."

The TIMES I think about as well spent are when I gave a guy on the street my jacket or bought him some food; or when I praised God singing and playing guitar; and when I told the special people in my life, I loved them or said, "Goodbye. See you soon. Look for Jesus!" This was time that truly mattered.

Unfortunately, if we are being honest, the TIME we spend on things that matter is tiny. Given any thought, it can become our #1 regret. Even our pastors who focus most of their lives on studying, preaching, teaching, helping and praying will admit that much of their hourglass of sand has been wasted time. (We should keep a daily ledger of our time. I'm pretty sure ALL of us would be convicted of waste.)

So, let's change that. Let's at least be honest and give it some thought. We will soon see that, "Time waits for no man." We will see the end of our TIME and will be called to account for how we spent **all** of it.

Jesus paid the price for this failure of spending our time of grace unwisely, and every other one of our failures, and we should rest peacefully in that assurance; but it doesn't mean we should take it for granted. We should remember that it came at an exorbitant price. If we love Jesus, we should serve him. Period.

So, enjoy your Friday. But think about using some TIME to do what he has asked of those who love him and follow him. Spread the truth, be SALT & LIGHT in the world, love your neighbors and love him.

It's Friday. Have GOOD TIME!

Say it! "It just doesn't matter!"

8 June 2024

Picture: He prowls like a lion, seeking to devour!

Time

Youth. Filled with fancy and senseless notions; when it seems that all we do and say is driven by emotions. At this time, I could not see what time would have in store for me; and that with all its subtlety, time would someday flee.

A busy life, so much to do, always on the move; or lest I stall. I will not slow or fall off the pace. Oh, I can do it all! Blind this time, I didn't see that time was then besieging me; and that in assured subtlety — I stood convinced; it had no hold on me.

Then one day I awoke to find that, in reflection, I spotted time; and though the distraction quickly changed the song, ignorance was forever gone. Though for a moment, I could see, I chose to think it could not be; ignore it, and it will go away. I'll worry about time another day.

Now I stand in the twilight years; though many are gone, time brings new fears. And failing, I plead through heavy tears, "Time — I need more time!"

All this time, it took to see that time was only teasing me; and that with no more subtlety, time — is — gone.

It is happening, everyone. It goes so fast! Decide, now, how to use your time wisely. Soon the hourglass will be empty.

All those "lesser" things–toss them! "They just don't matter!"

Promo push

8 Jun 2024

Ok. Today is the day. If you love God, join me in being his hands and feet in this miracle! All proceeds after taxes go to building our church just outside Colorado Springs!

Big promotion going out Monday. We need these books to be visible for the 1,000,000 subscribers that will see these books inside the front cover of a digital Christian magazine.

Please, if you can do so, order a book or all four! Here are some reasons...

1. Serve God!
2. Spread the Good News!
3. To buy Dad a Father's Day Gift!
4. To buy your uncle, aunt, friend, son, daughter, wife, husband, nephew, niece, grandma, grandpa, grandson, granddaughter, neighbor, coworker or self some positive Christian fiction!
5. To lie up treasure in heaven!
6. To help a brother out!
7. To buy a book instead of fast food today and get healthier!
8. To be part of a miracle!
9. To believe!
10. Because the covers are great and the books will look outstanding on your mantle!
11. To get some fiction packed with faith, family, love and action!
12. Because you have been very blessed!
13. Because it is Saturday!
14. Because it will make you feel good serving God, building a church, and helping a friend!
15. Because the devil doesn't want you to.
16. Because I said, "Please." ... I have more.

Today is the day! Fragile jar of clay.

9 June 2024

"Today is the day the Lord has made. I will rejoice and be glad in it!"

Well, "I'm just a nobody, trying to tell everybody, about somebody, who saved my soul." ("Nobody," by Casting Crowns with Matt Redman)

The two-year journey of writing book #3 "Forever," reediting book #1 "The Faithful," reediting book #2 "Stand," adding book #4 "Tophet, starting up a website, doing daily blogs, promoting the trilogy via several outreach efforts, beginning book #5, "Christian," begging people to join the fight on social media and via WOM in the Church, praying the books are successful in reaching the masses, and trying to stay motivated though only a handful of people supporting is culminating today with release of three of the four books currently published ("Stand," will ship on 4 Jul).

So, I have really been pushing hard on social media the last couple of days, trying to get supporters to join the fight. There have been very few takers.

I was getting pretty down on the lack of support, maybe taking this effort to reach the world and pay for our new church too personally. Don't get me wrong. It should be personal, but I made it about myself, trying to make it happen. I forgot it will be as God wills it, not me. He knows what is best because it is HIS-STORY!

I remembered I am just a jar of clay, a nobody, just trying to share the truth of God's love through Jesus Christ! By myself, I am nothing, a flower quickly fading and a vapor in the wind (again, "Casting Crowns").

So, we have reached the finish line of effort #1. The books ship today from Xulon, Amazon, B&N, etc. I hope everyone who purchased them enjoys and is strengthened in their faith. Please write a review on Amazon. The more reviews, the more "That one soul" might take a look, and that is what it was and is and will be all about — reaching that one soul.

So, yeah, it isn't about me at all. If I could do it all over, I would use a pseudo-name, like "I Am Christian," or "Jar O. Clay." Regrets.

I am also reminded that God's strength is made perfect in our weakness. The weaknesses I have are plentiful, but he can still use them all to his glory and his purpose.

So, I'm going to just sit back now and watch him work. Spreading seeds can be exhausting, and it has been. I don't think I have had such a focused determination since the Academy days. I pray that this effort reaches that one soul that has been wondering and searching. Please, God, make it so?

Thank you again, so very much, to those who have encouraged me in this endeavor. I see you. It means everything! We will see where our investment bears fruit. Notice, I didn't say if it bears fruit, but where it does.

Seeds take a while to grow. We may never see the trees while we are here. But perhaps there will be a harvest we get to meet in Heaven. A harvest of just one soul will mean immeasurable success!

Glass way full!

10 June 2024

(Happy birthday Tanner Luke!!!)

A couple of years ago, I was hiking in the mountains behind my house. It was -15° and ice encased the empty branches of all the trees. The pond was frozen over and there was a thin coat of snow covering everything. The sun occasionally peered through the clouds above. It set everything aglow, as the ice crystals from the ice fog that had passed through echoed the sun's brilliance in the form of millions of snow diamonds, glimmering over everything. It was magical — right until it wasn't.

As I crossed a frozen stream, I jumped over what I thought might be a thin patch of ice. As I landed on one foot, my foot slipped and I crashed down onto an arc of ice. The middle of my upper back hit first, absorbing most of the impact, followed by my cranium.

It instantly knocked all the air out of my lungs and sent excruciating pain through most of my back. At that moment, I thought my life was over. I remained there for a few minutes, writhing in pain and trying to endure.

It was so bad that I asked God to take me home to him. I thought it would happen. With my camera in hand, I quickly recorded a video, bidding farewell to Theresa, Tanner, and Thomas, and expressing gratitude to God for my life. I made sure to let everyone know God was bringing me home — just in case.

Well, after about ten minutes, and the help of Scout and Ranger who stayed with me, I was able to achieve a vertical position. I limped the last half of a mile back up the hill to the house, a "wounded duck" (old flying term). Bottom line is that I survived (with two cracked vertebrae in my middle back).

I will tell you this today, because it is Monday. Yes, Mondays are hard, and sometimes painful. You might be blindsighted by a patch of ice, and the experience may floor you for a moment. Take a break. Look around. See the beauty in your life. See the blessings! Count them! Remember, "No weapon formed against me shall prosper, in Jesus' name!" Say it. Believe it!

No matter what happens to us today, no matter what trouble or hardship is thrown our way, it will not prosper. It may toss and turn you, fold you up for a time, but the steel that results will be stronger!

Mondays can be hard. Every day can be hard. But open your spiritual eyes and see! The glass is WAY FULL! We are surrounded by glimmering diamonds even when writhing in pain. Someday, when we go home, only the diamonds will remain.

In the meantime, choose to cast your eyes on the diamonds! They are everywhere! See them! SEE!

One of my favorite movies is "Signs." An oldie, but a goodie! If you haven't watched it, it is a must do! The 2nd and 3rd time are even better! Everything that happens, everything said, is for a reason. Everything adds up at the end. It is a great story of faith, love, family, forgiveness, and God's providence. Just outstanding!

So, go out today seeing the diamonds all around. Point them out to those around you. You will change your day and the ripples that you send out will change the day for everyone around you. "See!"

God bless you and yours!

Pull out the BIG GUNS

Jun 11, 2024

A few years ago, my youngest son Thomas and I decided we would spend a day together. He lived in Colorado Springs, about ninety minutes away from us, here in the mountains.

I met Thomas about thirty minutes from the house where we started our twenty-four-hour adventure taking a helicopter ride around the Royal Gorge. We then went out to our rugged mountain land and hiked, shot guns, and camped in a sixteen-man tent. The next morning, we fished on the Arkansas River. Then we jumped out of airplanes east of Colorado Springs. Finally, we had some Thai lunch.

It was simply an outstanding time together, all crunched into a twenty-four-hour period; a day for a father to remember!

However, the reason I bring this story up this morning is bigger than that father-son memory. Something happened when we were camping; something outstanding!

After we set up our campsite and got the fire burning, etc., I walked about one-half mile back to the car to get my phone. It was just before sunset. I was returning to our camp over a ridge as the sun set in a brilliant red and orange display of God's beauty.

I was about three-hundred feet above the camp, making my way down to the campfire, when I heard a very loud rustling in the trees ahead of me; directly between me and Thomas. It was very loud and very disconcerting! I had hiked thousands of hours on that patch of mountain and had never experienced it before.

I called down to Thomas to let him know something big was moving through the trees between me and him. I thought that call would scare it away. Thomas and I drew our firearms just in case, and I yelled a few more times to scare off whatever it was. It had no effect, which was really weird.

Now, there were really only four choices of what could make that much noise in the trees. A bear, a bull moose, a bull elk, or something else. The .45 gave me some protection from the first three IF it would scare them off. Otherwise, a .45 would not help much in the dark against an enormous creature if it wished to do me harm. I would probably lose that fight if whatever it was wanted to tango.

It was so unbelievable that whatever it was wouldn't move. At a distance of approximately one hundred yards, it remained right in front of me, doing its thing. I yelled at it over and over. It just didn't move!

Well, it was getting dark and the descent to the camp from my location was steep and semi-treacherous. I was getting a little anxious. That is when I pulled out the BIG GUNS! At the top of my voice, I yelled, "Whatever you are, get out of here in the name of Jesus!"

It was amazing! Instantly, whatever it was took off perpendicularly to the east at a pretty good clip. You could hear it in the trees as it fled! I was awestruck!

Yes, I BELIEVED the name of Jesus had power. But then, at that moment, I KNEW the name of Jesus had power! Nothing had changed in my voice or volume from the three previous attempts to scatter the threat in front of me; nothing but the name of Jesus!

I finished the hike down to camp and retold the story. As great as the time was with Thomas, Jesus chasing away the demon in the darkness eclipsed everything. It was that big of an event.

So, what is the point? The devil is constantly prowling around like a lion, looking for someone to devour. The threat can take many forms, and we never know which it will be! But God is always with us, and we can count on him ALWAYS!

So, when you are in trouble, call on God to help. Expect his help. You honor him when you believe and trust his promises! His ways are not our ways, and his thoughts are way above our thoughts. He may choose many ways of deliverance (it's HIS-Story), but have faith he will deliver you.

All things will work for good for those who love him!

All praise and glory be to you, Oh God!

God bless you and yours!

Who do you blame?

12 June 2024

It's a problem as old as sin itself! The blame game.

Ever since Adam and Eve took turns blaming someone else for their disobedience of God's one "Do not," we have all been doing the same! Do you see it?

Take a moment and look in the mirror. Ask yourself, "Self, what is not perfect in my life?" "What do I wish had turned out better from the past?" "What do I want–and don't have?" Do this before reading on.

Ok. Now comes the real part. Whose fault is it you have the above list of regrets, failures, or unfulfilled desires? Be honest. Who do you blame?

Is it a "Well, if _____ had just—?" Is it, "If ____ would just, then I would—?" Or is it, "My boss—" or "Bad timing—" or "I have bad luck!"

If we are honest, we always blame someone else for the imperfections in our lives. Our spouse, our boss, our family members, bad timing, bad luck, father time, etc. It is rarely, "I am failing," "I am messing up the relationship," "I am blowing my promotion," or "I am not being a good husband, wife, employee or person."

This is because of sin. There is something you can truthfully blame. But also remember it isn't just sin, it is your sin! We all have it, and it messes everything up!

Ultimately, whether or not we acknowledge God, we are blaming him. After all, he made everything. If we are this way, then it is his doing! If there are problems in the world, they are his fault!

But all this is a deflection. Look back in the mirror. Be honest. No, be really honest. Who could fix your problems? That's right, you could. But that takes work. That takes effort. It is easier to just blame someone else and wallow in your self-pity.

Tough words. I know. I have a mirror too.

Here is the good news. All the above is a distraction; the matrix, if you will. The devil sets it all up for us to waste our time in self-pity and uselessness. Let it go! The accuser, Satan, has lost! Jesus Christ has saved us all. He bought us back. We are children of God with an eternal retirement in Heaven with the God of love!

Yes, we live in a world with a plague of sin, and we are all dying from it. But, when we leave here, Heaven and perfection await! All the do-da here fades away like a vapor in the wind! The stuff, the desires, the pleasure, the good times, as well as the pain, the sorrow, the hurt feelings... they all mean nothing! Let them go!

We are only here for a short time to tell people about their salvation in Jesus, to love each other, and to love God!

The rest of it is the matrix, the grand illusion, a distraction.

Look in the mirror. Ask yourself, "How can I make someone else's life better?" "How can I tell someone about Jesus, and what he did for us?" "How can I love God better; the God who gave and gives me all good things?"

These are the proper questions we should be asking. These are the things we should think about.

Who do you blame? Let it go. Forgive as God has forgiven you. Live in joy! Serve others and your God. Encourage your brother and sister!

So, continue to feel sorry for yourself and waste away your time, or acknowledge the truth and live a life of value?

Do you want the blue pill or red pill?

Resist the Devil and the enemy within.

13 Jun 2024

Excerpt from "The Faithful."

Scum, one of Satan's commanders, spoke. "Master, do they not learn from the mistakes of others? Do they not learn from their past?"

"They possess Adam's seed, and their eyes easily entice them, their stomachs lead them, their emotions derail them, their thirst for knowledge seduces them, their anxiety over temporary things distracts them, and their quest for power and wealth controls them. They want to know the future. Give them a taste of the forbidden fruits, and they will follow us to hell like dogs. These are your lures. These are your weapons against them. Use them all!"

"Do they not know of their weaknesses?"

"They know of their weaknesses, but alone they are powerless to control them. Denial is how they cope. Though they number their days, they live as if they will never die. Ignoring what has come before, as well as what follows closely behind, they choose to see only that which is right in front of them. They know their path will destroy them, and yet they do nothing to change their course. They are flesh, and flesh is weak."

Does any of this sound familiar? Each of us could easily list the countless times we have failed in every category above.

Thank God, we already have victory in Jesus! He has already won. So, resist the Devil, and he will flee from you!

"Get thee away! In Jesus' name!"

Pilot chute. What is your view?

14 Jun 24

Around thirty-four years ago, I let my housemate, PJ, talk me into jumping out of airplanes in N.M. It actually didn't take that much arm-twisting, since the plan at the time was for him (my best man), and I (the groom of course), to freefall into the wedding. It didn't end up happening, but it was the plan. I think I remember Theresa having a say.

Anyway, we went down to Roswell, where I watched a 30 minute video and signed a waiver, of course. Then I was ready to go jump out of an airplane from 10,000 feet. I had done Army Ranger School at Fort Benning and was already an Airborne Ranger, so what could go wrong?

The way it worked was like this. We get to altitude, climb out on the wing supports, hold on to the wing and then let go. Easy-peasy. Then, arch, freefall, pull the rip-cord, steer the chute to the landing zone, flare, and land. Ok.

Everything went great. Descending from the sky at terminal velocity, I formed a flawless arch. I experienced stability, and it was outstanding!

The pilot chute deployed when I pulled the rip-cord. The pilot-chute is the small chute that deploys first and pulls your main chute out of the pack on your back.

That is when time slowed down, and I noticed that the view I had was not the view I was supposed to have. I was marveling at the beautiful white clouds and blue sky, but I was supposed to be looking at the ground. My clue was the pilot chute rising between my legs!

Lesson: You don't want that!

So, I rotated my body faster than it has ever rotated! Long moment, short, I made it and eventually had two children. Praise God!

But there is another lesson here. You may go through life comfortable and happy. You may enjoy the view. And you may think you stand on solid ground (or in this case, you are in a superb arch). But, if the view you have (no matter how enjoyable or beautiful it is), is not the right view, not the right focus; you will be in big trouble when that pilot-chute deploys!

We need to approach our salvation with fear and trembling! God's words, not mine. We need to stay focused on Jesus! Lose your focus, and that devil pilot-chute will bite you in the xxx!

We treat life like a game that will never end. It is not a game, and it will end! Eternity is a very long time. Give this race within time the respect it deserves and run as if to win the prize!

Jesus has paid the full price for our sins, but we can still reject his gift. Reject a gift and you no longer receive it. Possess a gift and then throw it away, and it is gone.

We were bought at an outrageously high price, the highest! Jesus came to save us; don't minimize the cost of your redemption or reject your salvation. The Judge is returning; the very one who endured our sentence for us. He is the definition of both love and justice. His justice required a payment for sin that he then paid. His love sent him to the cross in our place.

He suffered and died, so we don't have to. He rose so we could also and live eternally with him.

So, pay attention. Fat, dumb, and happy is not a good way to freefall, and it is not a good way to go through life. The Pk (probability of kill) of the ground is 99.999%. The Pk and eternal death without Jesus is 100%

What is your view?

Caught between a Great Pyrenees and a Venisicle!

15 June 2024

A few years back, I went to check on Scout in the backyard. He was on a thirty-foot cable.

While I was standing on the back patio talking to him, he saw a deer on the hill behind me. He took off in full afterburner! I turned, yelling for him to stop, because I knew he would quickly reach the end of the cable and could get hurt.

Well, I didn't realize that Scout's cable had become wrapped around my feet while we were visiting. Scout achieved max speed, and I went airborne like a circus clown — 100% upended. The shoulder was the first thing to hit the concrete, followed by the $700 camera that I was holding. Despite the shoulder surviving, it was painful! The camera did not survive.

Scout is a beast, but he is not the beast we need to watch for. The Devil and his minions are everywhere, working hard to minimize the impact the 'salt and light' will have on a world descending largely into darkness.

The devil attacks believers in openly overt and cunningly covert ways. They are all around us! If you haven't noticed, you aren't looking.

Sometimes the attack is in your face, and sometimes it's a cable slowly getting would around your feet to rock your world when you least expect it.

So, expect it. Keep your eyes open and your guard up! Study the Word, pray, and love. Use your time wisely. Put on the full armor of God! Train the way you'll fight.

If the enemy hasn't attacked you yet, get ready, it is coming!

God bless and don't fight alone!

Happy Father's Day

16 June 2024

Hello everyone. You may have noticed I'm trying to put the next day's blog out in the evening now instead of in the morning. I've been having a little sleep issue, as in, I can't sleep. So, on that note, if there is a brief break in the blogs, you will know why.

Happy Father's Day, all you dads out there! It is truly a special gift to have children. It is also a very special gift to be adopted into God's family. "How great the Father's love for us that we should be called the children of God."

Spend some quality time with your children. Call your dad. And please remember to pray for those who have lost a son or daughter. This is truly a very hard time for them; the hardest of times.

A daughter in Heaven

17 June 2024

Thirty-two years ago, Theresa had an emergency. We had been married less than a year and were traveling, when suddenly she began having extreme pain in her lower abdomen.

Theresa begged me to help her. She screamed for me to help her. I was overwhelmed! She was in so much pain! We rushed into the first emergency room we could find, and they did an ultrasound. Theresa had an ectopic pregnancy. We had a baby, but our baby had not made it to her uterus. One of Theresa's fallopian tubes, and our baby, had to be removed or the tube would rupture; Theresa and our baby would die quickly.

They saved Theresa that day, but we lost our first child. Although we have two wonderful sons, I know we lost our daughter that day. I can't explain why I know our baby was a little girl; I have just–always–known.

Now, anyone that denies what God tells us, that babies have souls from conception, will say I am being silly; that it wasn't a baby.

I know better.

Pain

I tell you this story in tears. Even though I never got to meet my baby girl, all this time later my heart longs to know her, and it hurts so much!

Some of you have lost children, children you have known for hours, or days, or maybe many years. I can't even imagine the intensity of your pain, but I know of your pain.

When I think of our baby girl, I struggle with not knowing how it all works. The bible tells us God knows us individually from the time of our conception, so we know our baby had a soul. But we could never baptize our baby or to teach her about Jesus. Is our baby in Heaven? Is our baby's soul with God?

Tears. I have missed the little girl that I have never, yet, met. Tremendously! I mourn for her.

Comfort

The comfort from the Holy Spirit is this; God is love. He loves us all. Jesus paid the price–for us all. His ways are mysterious to us. His ways are not our ways; his wisdom is so far above ours. God is love, and that extends to our baby girl.

Again with a FOOT STOMP

I don't know how it all works, but I know God. I know he is love. I know he loves us so much that Jesus came to die on a cross for us–for us all! I hope and believe that extends to our baby girl. I cling to this hope.

Request

This day after Father's Day, there are many who are in unfathomable pain dealing with the loss of children. Please pray they find comfort and peace knowing that God loves us all, so much, and that Jesus, the Good Shepherd, did not lose, will not lose even one of his sheep. Not even one!

Hope

I pray for my baby girl, who never had a name, here. I am sure that God has given her a name, and that she is with him.

I can't wait to meet you!

We are all on TDY (Temporary Duty) here to accomplish a mission!

19 June 24

Back in the day, we went TDY (Temporary Duty) to different countries around the world (Turkey, Spain, South Korea, Germany, the Netherlands, etc.)

Although we had many adventures, we weren't there to just train and have fun. We had a mission — a statement to make to the enemies of freedom.

If you believe in the one true God and Jesus Christ our Savior, you are also on Temporary Duty here for a brief time relative to eternity. You are not here to just have fun. You are here to train and make a statement to both friends and enemy alike.

Train

We should train like we will fight! Growing stronger in the Word through bible study and prayer will prepare you for the temptations of the world and encounters with the enemy. Grow weak and you will do poorly in your mission. Mission failure has eternal consequences.

The Mission

We are here to share the Gospel, the Good News that Jesus saved us all! We need to see our home with our spiritual eyes! It is in Heaven. Close your eyes and see it! It is paved with gold and precious gems. It has angels. God is there and there is no fear, death, pain, or sorrow. That is where we will spend eternity. That is home base!

God himself has sent you and me out to do a mission. We are here for so short a time! Soon, we will go home. We need to train hard, fight hard, and accomplish our mission. Spread the Word; Jesus has saved everyone!

Don't waste your time! Sure, have some fun and rejuvenate, but don't let it become your mission! All this around us will pass away! We serve at the pleasure of the King who has called us out of a life serving ourselves to a life of purpose serving Him! Open your eyes of faith and see clearly your purpose and direction. Walk that path and accomplish that mission; the mission you are here to finish!

Satan often lulls us into complacency and indifference. You can see it in your life and mine. Don't fall into his trap of wasting your time just serving yourself! Train! Fight! Accomplish your mission! PLANT SEEDS for the Spirit to grow!

Onward Christian soldiers! I will fight beside you. I will pray for you. Someday soon, when our Savior returns, I will meet you in the clouds.

Please pray for me.

God's timing and the colors of life.

20 June 2024

As we travel through time, the various colors of our days influence us in many ways. Each day has its unique challenges and rewards.

It is difficult to see, let alone control, how the colors affect us while they are changing. Later, we look back and see, with more clarity, how we handled each challenge. Often, we wish we would have handled things differently.

Maybe it would be useful to get in the habit of seeing changes and attaching a color to the current conditions. Lots of stress equals a red. Chilling on the deck with an ice tea in the evening gets a green.

We don't have to do it out loud, but just realizing what is happening around us, increasing our awareness, might be worth the effort.

If we realize we are in a bright red, we might take a little more time to speak, be a little more careful, and maybe do things a little less haphazardly. Letting your spouse know, as an example, that you are in a dark red, might reduce misunderstandings and silly quarrels. It might also lead to a helping hand.

Many times we wonder why the various colors or struggles of life happen. We wonder "Why," or "Why now?"

We make most of the difficult times happen, all on our own. The Devil and the world heap the added weight of their attacks on our shoulders at every turn. We ask God for help, but he rarely takes away the burden immediately.

God is not a genie that just grants us our wishes whenever we ask. He may allow suffering to strengthen our faith and reliance on him. If we are honest, we admit we stay closest to him in colors of red than in those of green.

God has promised he will never allow trouble in our lives greater than that which we can handle. We know this promise is sure, because he has also promised to sustain us in and through the battle.

It is often very difficult to stand in our faith when under heavy assault. We need to arm ourselves with the full armor of God, so we are ready when a red sweeps over us. The armor, God's help, and the help of our brothers and sisters will equip and provide us with everything we need to emerge on the other side of the challenge.

God's timing is perfect in all things. Next time you are in a red, pray and wait on the Lord. He will lead you to green pastures and still waters.

Focus on him instead of your problem, challenge, or the attack against you. See that he is there with you. Know that your fellow Christians are also there to help you. Be aware of the great cloud of witnesses that have gone before us and surrounds us. Know God also has his angels protecting and keeping us. Those that are with you are much greater than those who are against you. You are not alone!

Be aware, wait on the Lord, trust his promises, and focus on heaven. All this is temporary. Run a good race! The finish line is within sight!

Priorities

21 June 2024

Picture: Dad in the F-111 at Cannon AFB, NM.

Good morning! Happy Friday and first day of summer!

Isn't it funny how our priorities change?

In 2005, I bought a dark red mustang GT convertible. I loved that car! I kept it until 2023, when I sold it to my youngest son, Thomas, for $25.

Later in 2023, Thomas drove away in that mustang with his bride, Shannon, after their wedding reception.

Last week, Thomas sold the 'Stang for $7,500. It is gone, and no tears were shed. Actually, I am pretty happy with the price he received.

The 2005 mustang — something I cared so much about — gone, and it barely got a second thought. Interesting, don't you think?

We shouldn't be too surprised. After all, it was just some "thing" that I owned. It got old, I got used to it, and its value in my mind returned to what it should have been all the time; a means of transportation.

Does this ring any bells? Whether it be vehicles, toys, or even houses; we like new stuff and we tire of the old stuff. And yet, we continue the cycle over and over. We see ourselves as more successful with new stuff; we think others see us through a prism of stuff

Not me, you say. You want proof? Look at your FB and Instagram/chat posts from the last year. Every one of them screams, "Look at me!" "Look where I am!" "Don't you wish you were me?" Maybe not that directly, but that is what they say. I am just as guilty; maybe more.

Picture: Mom on Mother's Day 2023

I've posted a couple of pictures of my mom and dad. Dad from 1990 and Mom in 2023. They are both in Heaven today.

I see their pictures and I long to see them again; talk to them and give them a hug.

I will bet you are the same. I'll bet you see pictures of family and friends that you haven't seen for a while or who have exited stage-right, and you miss them; maybe intensely.

That should tell us something about what is important to us. That should set our priorities!

Stuff doesn't matter for more than being a tool. If you spend too much on your tools, fix that! Most of our expendable cash typically goes toward our entertainment. Fun is good for you, but too much fun is terrible for you.

If you have set a habit pattern of spending all your free time and cash on fun, then that has become your idol; your god.

Think about it. Time is our most valuable asset. We spend everything else we get on, making our time pleasurable or increasing our time on the planet.

What is the long-term point of that? Is that why we are here? Deep down inside, you know the answer to that question.

So, priorities; what are yours? We have the answer down, don't we? God, family, country, job... but is it true? Do we lie to ourselves?

No more excuses. Look at your social media. Observe the way you treat your family. Look at where you spend your time.

Now forget the excuses. Make a change. Ask for forgiveness from your loved ones. Ask God to show you your direction and for help in walking that path. Then do it!

There will be resistance from within and without. That should tell you something too.

Let's not waste our time. Pray for me as I pray for you.

All praise the name of the Lord our God!

22 June 2024

Today, let us just focus on our awesome God!

Whatever you are going through, stop and praise him for what he has done, and what he has promised to do!

We turn on the television and are bombarded with the ugliness of sin; wars, murders, drug-wasted lives, sexual immorality, hate and apathy.

But our God did not create those things. Satan and our sin created and creates the problems around us!

God created us in perfection, and the surrounding beauty, the same! He promised us a Savior when we fell; when we brought the ugliness of sin into the world. He kept his promise by sending his Son to redeem us; the only one who could do it. He gave us his Word and the Holy Spirit to change our hearts — to destroy rejection, and to give us saving faith in him. And he gives us the power to repent, to turn from evil, and to follow him! Without him, we would be lost forever. Praise God for all he has and is still doing!

You might say, "I have heard none of that." Well, brother or sister, you just did.

You might say, "I have committed too many atrocities in my life. I am really ugly!" Saying that, you are really disparaging Jesus and stating that his sacrifice wasn't great enough to cover your sin. Jesus, the Son of God, is big enough to cover all our sins. I am the chief of sinners, and his sacrifice covered me.

You might say, "How do I know following Jesus is the right way as opposed to Buddha, or Mohammed, or any other human claiming to have the right way?" Well, let's compare my risen Savior, who raised people from the dead and healed others of their diseases; who gave sight to the blind and performed countless other miracles — let's compare his mighty works with those who could not and did not do any of these signs. That is how you know.

You might say, “But sinning is too much fun to quit.” You might. But consider following a God who loves you. Your “fun” insults him. After all that he has done to save you, your rejection of him will lead to his rejection of you for eternity. Is your “fun” for a short time worth an eternity of separation from all that is good?

Today, let’s focus on our God. All praise and glory be to our God, now and forever! Amen.

Headwinds

24 Jun 24 (2×4=6=2×4)

Good morning and happy Monday!

Well, it's Monday and there is significant resistance all around. You know what it's like. Everything you try to do is just harder.

It is the same with the books. Whereas they started out well, they have since dropped, headed to the bottom of the infinite sea of books at Amazon.

But, like every other challenge we face, you just have to push through.

I have four book promotions coming up.

The first is at Goodreads on the 26th of June. (Good site -recommend getting the app and friending/following me. There is more visibility if I have "followers.") I'll be giving away ten copies of The Faithful on 27 July. Everyone that joins the giveaway has a random shot.

On 27 June, the big Salem email to 1M+ accounts goes out with The Chronicles of Trinian (Lion cover) on the cover and full-page ad inside.

On 8 August, the fall Christian reading catalog goes out with a full-page ad on the inside cover.

Finally, also in early August, there will be three book stands at the Christian Book Expo (CBE). They will hand out ~ 90 copies of the three (of four) books to pastors, teachers, etc.

I was hoping to have the books be more toward the top of the pack for these releases, but support faltered in the last week. Since I announced all profits would go to building a WELS church in C-Springs, I thought I would get more support from members of this church and the Northwestern Publishing House (NPH). Not so much. Not sure what's up there. Still, God is in control, and all is well. His timing is perfect. His will be done.

I continue to work on the series. I am moving well through book #5, "The Promise" and expect a release in the fall. Additionally, I have outlined the last three books. All will be explained!

In review, the second half of "Stand" is about Tophet (before "The Faithful") and is better read after "Forever." It is a split in the road. One direction goes on to "Forever," and another goes on to "The Foundation Chronicles."

In summary, keep pushing forward! You only lose if you quit! Pray over it, ask God for help, follow his voice, and go forward fearlessly!

Thank you again if you had the time to forward one of my FB posts, buy a book, or encourage me. Amid almost universal silence regarding the books (even to those I gave free copies to), your kindness has kept me going. It hasn't been a cake-walk, and my supporters, though few, are the only reason I am still pushing forward with this project, or what I see as a calling.

Finally, if you purchased a book, please leave a rating/review on Amazon. I would appreciate it. Honesty is the best policy.

Stress and Peace. Got peace?

25 June 2024

When I moved to Colorado from Virginia in 2010, my stress level was pegged.

My father had just passed. I was sorting out his estate in Wisconsin and helping my mom with her grieving. I had a new job across the country. I had to leave my wife and boys for six months. I had to leave my church and all my friends. I had to find a place to live. Then, I received a call from my doc, informing me I had cancer.

The stressors were stacking up. Job, move, immediate family death, separation and illness — I had all the big ones going on at once.

The hardest was losing Dad. It wasn't expected. When I got the phone call, it was like 911; I'll remember it forever. The cancer call was similar. It is also seared in my mind.

There are moments for us all that have been burned into our memories, both good and bad. Confirmation, college graduation, wedding, births of children, death of loved ones, retirement ceremony, children's weddings, birth of grandchildren, etc. Good and bad stress.

Stress hurts us. It hurts our minds, our spirits, and our bodies. Unfortunately, our lives are filled with it. We are rarely relaxing in green pastures, beside the still waters.

The Lord says for us to be anxious about nothing, to fear not, and to not worry. God loves us, sustains us, and has promised to give us everything we need while we are here, and to bring us home to heaven. We have no reason to be anxious or fear anything.

Is that the way you feel today? Me neither.

Part of the problem is where our focus is. Are we remembering? Are we living in the past? Are we rushing around frantically, overwhelmed with the present? Or are we trying to best plan out our golden years here on the earth?

The past, present and future are all important, of course. But the past is gone–no profit in stressing over it. It can't be changed. Regret, shame, and grief over past events are a waste of precious time. We convince ourselves it is necessary for sentimental or penance reasons; but it is not.

"Be in the present. Be here." There is truth in those words. It is necessary to operate in the here and now, but it isn't where our focus should be. The present instantly disappears into the past.

Well then, the future is the answer! Kind-of. But our future lives here quickly arrive and fade into the past. I can already see the end of my life coming. It really won't be long for any of us.

My mom looked like she would live another decade. She was doing great. Then, in a matter of five months, she was gone. I miss her and dad so much!

Past, present and future; our minds jump all around every day. Each has its own stress. But again, the Lord Jesus tells us to not be anxious with any of them.

If we fix our eyes on our Savior and his promises, we can deal with all the elements of time effectively and positively.

Yes, we have sinned. Yes, we have failed. Yes, we have loss. Let it go. Repent of the past and give it to God. Put it at the foot of the cross and know with certainty that Jesus' sacrifice was big enough to cover our past.

Life is so busy. Make yourself stop throughout the day, and praise God for all your blessings. Be joyful! Take care of business, but be calm, knowing God has promised to be with you, help you, and give you all the strength you need to get through the day.

Don't worry about future problems. They might come, they might not. As the quote states, "A coward dies a thousand times; a hero dies but once." Be a hero! Push forward in peace and confidence that God has you, just like he always has. He has promised, and he has never broken a promise!

Finally, when that day comes, go in peace. Surround yourself with as many people as possible and share your faith with them in those last moments. This will be the biggest impact on their entire lives you can ever make. They will see your certain hope and say, "I want that!" Tell them you will see them soon. Then look for your Savior's face as the angel brings you home.

If we say heaven is so great, why be so sad when people go there? Yes, we will miss them, but celebrate! Let the world know our faith is more than just empty words. We KNOW believers go to Heaven and we celebrate it!

If we stay focused on that last moment, the moment the world fears the most, and live it in the faith of God's promises; we will have a tremendous impact on everyone around us. They will see our peace and want it!

So stress? No, I don't think so. Nothing in the past, present or the future has any real impact on me. I have an eternal retirement in Heaven and look forward to the day I leave here and go there in peace and confidence!

God bless your day with peace!

Some days are rough!

26 June 2024

Here's a funny story.

When I was at Langley Air Force Base, many years ago, all the guys from the office decided we would go out for Thai.

My back was bothering me that day, so I moved rather gingerly out to the vehicle that we were all taking.

When we got to the Thai restaurant, I was carefully exiting the back seat of the car with both of my hands on the sides of the car. One of my buddies in the front seat got out of the car and closed the door behind him — on my fingers. I jumped out of the car, holding my bloodied hand and limping across the parking lot because of my back.

We went into the Thai restaurant and — moments later — I woke up. My brain had said, "Overload, time to reset!" I remember looking up and seeing a circle of my friends above me as I lay on the floor. One of my friends said, "You, call 911." I said, "Don't worry about it. I'm OK."

While I was waiting for my food, I went into the bathroom and cleaned up the blood from my shirt and my hands. Then I went out and had Thai.

While I was sitting there eating, I went into atrial fibrillation. I didn't tell anyone, because the food was awesome!

We rode back to Langley and on exiting the vehicle; I went straight to my vehicle and drove myself to the emergency room.

When I got there, they said, "We're gonna have to give you the paddles to get your heart back in rhythm." I asked them, "Can I be awake for that? That sounds pretty interesting." They said, "No. You do not want to be awake for this."

So they put me out, shocked me, and got my heart back in rhythm. When I woke up, two nurses and a doctor were standing over me, laughing. I asked them, "What's so funny?"

The doctor told me that when they gave me the paddles and shocked me, I sat straight up, pointed an arm and one finger high into the air and yelled, "Now that's an event!" I asked them if they had any video, and they said they did not, but all promised it was true.

Why do I tell you this story? Because some days are rough. It is just one thing after another. You just have to push through. God has promised that he will be with you and not allow anything greater than that you can handle. Rest in that promise. Trust in that promise.

"If God is for us, who can be against us?"

Have a great day!

As time unfolds, I begin. But why?

27 June 2024

One o'clock in the morning, and still no sleep. Twenty-four hours since I got up. So, here you go.

As time unfolds, I begin.

It was Feb 21st, 1963. I entered this world on one of the coldest days of record in Milwaukee, Wisconsin. It was a frigid night at minus ten below zero and twenty-five mile-per-hour winds.

I was born to Henry and Arlene Rotering at St. Joseph's Hospital. My dad, Henry, thirty-four, was the youngest of eight children; my mom, Arlene, thirty, was the youngest of thirteen children. I would be their only child.

Dad was a Tech Sergeant in the Air Force, a rank he would retire at because of his limiting career field of recruiting. He had stayed in recruiting to remain in Milwaukee with my mom. Entering the Air Force in 1947, the Air Force was still the Army Air Corps. He was eighteen when he entered service and served twenty years.

Mom worked on the Briggs and Stratton assembly line, assembling engines. She would one day retire after 37 years.

My grandparents on Dad's side were both from Germany; both from Sweden on my mom's side. Mom and Dad's families both worked farms in Wisconsin.

Both my mom and my dad lost their fathers when they were two years old from heart attacks. Both were raised by their brothers and sisters on the farm.

There were a couple of interesting stories told by my grandparents on my mom's side. Truth or yarn, you be the judge.

My grandmother recounted seeing a very interesting sight while still a girl in Sweden. Playing near a stream by their farm, she could see in the river's reflection several bears walking and playing. Strangely, they were all wearing black and white checkerboard clothes. Looking at the other side of the river directly, they could not see the bears at all. Only in the stream's reflection were they visible. She swore it was true. "They all saw it!"

My grandfather almost didn't make it to America. He arrived during a storm off the East Coast, tied and frozen to the mast of a schooner. He was the only survivor of a shipwreck; barely. His ship-mates had tied him to the mast to keep him from suffering their fate.

So, because of the potential loss of both of my mom's parents, one to checkerboard-clothed bears and the other to the violent whims of nature, it is a wonder things unfolded the way they did.

Yet, Arlene and Henry met, fell in love at my Uncle Mel's tavern, and had one child. I was born one month early, would spend another month in an oxygen tent, and have several bouts of double pneumonia before released from the hospital. Mom and Dad named me Terrence, which means tender-hearted.

Many unlikely events came together for me to be typing this blog to you this very early morning. I will touch on many more of them in upcoming posts. There are no coincidences.

I believe our lives are all interwoven, that we connect with those around us, purposefully. There is a hand that directs our paths and our exchanges. Therefore, do not take any of them lightly. No one knows how many times we will see each other again. It could all end abruptly for any of us or all of us at once; only God knows.

But, why?

That having been said, the most important thing I have after sixty-two years of walking on this earth is this; John 3:16. "God so loved the world that he gave his one and only Son, that whoever believes in him will not perish, but have everlasting life."

Maybe my grandfather was tied to the mast of that boat, so long ago, for one reason alone; for me to be here right now — to tell just YOU the

Good News! He saved YOU! YOU are free! Heaven awaits YOU! Live in peace and love, for the God of love saved YOU.

Really, nothing else matters. Everything around you will fade away, either before your time ends or after.

Faith, hope and love. These are the gems of the kingdom.

Pleasant dreams, everyone. If our paths do not cross again, please remember my one pearl of infinite worth.

Until we meet again.

Devil's Dream. He's coming.

28 Jun 24

During my younger years, until I was around ten, I had a terrifying dream almost every night. I remember it vividly, and it scared me well into my twenties.

Sleeping in my bed, I open my eyes; I'm looking down the hallway. Suddenly, I have an overwhelming feeling of anxiety and dread. From the darkness at the end of the hall, I see the Devil running toward me — closer and closer; faster and faster. His red horns and pitchfork glimmer in the dim light as he smiles devilishly. I can't move, scream, or get away! I'm doomed.

He raises the pitchfork to strike. I crunch my eyes closed and prepare for impact. Just when all is about to be lost. I wake up. Terrified, but relieved, I am safe in my bed.

As I grew older, the dream slowly disappeared. I had it occasionally, but it morphed into just a feeling; a feeling of doom and the knowledge the Devil was coming for me. That was enough.

That dream was a friendly reminder that the Devil prowls around like a roaring lion, seeking whom he may devour. We shouldn't ever take our salvation for granted!

Satan is real. Hell is real. Our current time of grace is real, and it will end.

Many times in my life, Satan has done his best to reel me in. I thank God that he has empowered me to wiggle off the hook, but many times I have stayed on that hook too long, enjoying the bait!

Playing with the Devil is very dangerous. Without God, we are defenseless. The longer we sit on that hook, the more it gets set. Ignore the worms — they only lead to destruction, and forever is a very long time!

Turn to our loving God. Repent daily for your failures, deny Satan's lures, and trust in Jesus your Savior. He has promised to always be with you!

The Devil and his angels are a formidable foe. Dont take your faith for granted. Alone, we will fall. But with Jesus, our champion, evil cannot win.

Got Jesus?

Jesus loves me and "Now I lay me down to sleep."

29 June 2024

We moved into a house on Ann Street when I was four. One of just a couple of houses there on our freshly paved street. We didn't have a garage for about a year. It was a single-story house with a basement, and I had my own room.

Every night when it was time for bed, Mom would come into my room, read me stories, and before going to sleep, I would close my eyes and say, "Now I lay me down to sleep. I pray to the Lord my soul to keep. If I die before I wake. I pray to the Lord my soul to take."

When the lights went out, like in the Waltons, I would say good-night to my mom and dad. I would yell to them from my bed, down the hallway, "Sleep tight, and don't let the bed-bugs bite. God bless you, say your prayers, don't forget, pleasant dreams, kiss me two times, tell me when you're in bed."

A bond. Still remember it verbatim after 58 years.

That little saying is packed with lessons. We think in more adult terms now, but the same concepts.

1. "Sleep tight, don't let the bed-bugs bite." (Be at peace.)
2. "God bless you." (Wishing a blessing for others.)
3. "Say your prayers, don't forget." (Be close to God and prioritize your relationship with him.)
4. "Pleasant dreams." (A wish for happiness.)
5. "Kiss me two times." (Need for affection and belonging.)
6. "Tell me when you're in bed." (Keep me aware and involved with your life.)

I may address each of these this next week, but at the top level, I think everyone understands them. They are family statements; family thoughts.

They are the same for anyone in your inner circle; love; affection; wishes for peace; and longing for affection and connection. Don't forget them; your family and friends need them from you.

This is just a reminder from a little boy, somewhere in time.

The bunny play; If I could only fly, & I'm so glad to be myself!

30 June 2024

When I was in first grade, I was "fortunate" enough to get the lead part in the class play. As the bunny rabbit who wanted to fly received the gift of flight and then realized he just wanted his old life back, I enjoyed the part (I think).

Bouncing around that stage may not have endeared me to my classmates, but it made my mom happy. For that reason alone, it was worth it!

I learned valuable lessons about life from that play; count your blessings, be careful what you wish for, and understand that there is only one of each of us, so, be yourself (you be you).

"If only I could fly." Well, I ended up being a weapon systems officer (goose, as I like to say) in the F-111 and F-15E fighter aircraft. We had all the controls (except flaps) that the left / front seater had. I flew!

In grade school, high school, the Air Force, and since, I have faced many obstacles to being a faithful witness. Friends disowned me, ridiculed me, physically assaulted me, avoided me, and humiliated me. I didn't bow to bullies, and that made me "uncool" in both the bullies' and their entourage's view.

Don't get me wrong, I have slipped often in my witness, a few times in major ways! The bunny was granted the wings of approval for sin, succumbed, and failed my Savior. Like Peter, I denied him with my actions. Many times.

Those wings were not good for me. They made me "cool," and finally, being cool was Satan's ploy.

Amid rebellion, I saw the fatal truth of disobedience and wanted to "be myself again." Each time I asked my Father in Heaven to save me, God found me and brought me back to him. I'm so glad to be myself again!

Despite my daily failures, I find peace knowing that his love offers unwavering forgiveness.

So where are you? Have you slipped? God is waiting to bring you back. Ask him. He will forgive you. He has promised he will.

Jesus washed us clean of all our sins. It is a gift from God to all of us who don't have enough capital to pay for our failures. If you aren't absolutely perfect, that means you. You need Jesus. Period.

The good news is that God loves you, has saved you, and is waiting to bring you back to his loving arms. Don't hesitate! Believe and run back to him!

Praise God for Jesus our Savior!

"If God is for us, who can be against us?"

Infinite value

2 July, 2024

It's one of those nights. The body is tired, but the brain refuses to sleep. So, we watch the stars.

You've been here. It seems to happen more as we age. Once retired and not so busy, the mind thirsts for purpose. If you are fortunate enough to escape from the Monday through Friday rat race, you may find you need to fully occupy that time with other endeavors.

Some enjoy travel. Others enjoy time with the grandkids. Since my back will no longer support much travel, and I have yet to enjoy the blessing of grandchildren (though that blessing looks to come soon), I must occupy my thoughts with creative things to fill my day (and often, night). I will probably pass from this life early for lack of rest, but as the saying goes, I will rest when I die.

It has been a while since the last book update, so here you go. The good news is book sales were about 150 in the first two weeks of June. (I purchased a good number of those myself to give as gifts to friends.) The bad news is that Amazon, who most people purchased through, took about 60%. So the average "profit" a book is about $10. At that rate, when everything is accounted for, you hit the breakeven point at about 3,300 books, so far (5 books to go).

What does that tell you? Financially, this was a fool's errand. Fortunately, it was never about finances. As Theresa asked me, "Is that a good investment?" Well, it depends.

What was it about? I wanted to build a church and THE church. What does that mean? Well, I wanted to use a faith-based story I believe God put on my heart twenty-plus years ago to honor him. I wanted to use my finances to turn an investment of 3x or 5x what was entrusted to me, to help finance our church building in Peyton, CO.

There were many ways to do this. For instance, I could have given directly to the building fund as I have in the past. Instead, I pledged the after-tax proceeds of the Chronicles of Trinian Trilogy to God and the building of our church building. This was just my specific way to serve.

This investment of time and tool ($$$) may still eventually pan out; it is all in God's omnipotent hands, though it isn't looking likely at this point in time. That is ok. God's will be done. We mean it when we say it. We need to accept it when we see it. His ways are not our ways, but much higher!

That brings me back to the primary goal; winning souls and THE church. Now, it is not anything I do that "wins a soul." Rather, I just want to be useful to my Master; be his hands and feet.

Don't we all long to be useful? Isn't that why we dream grand dreams? I believe it is. God put us here to give glory to him and grow the kingdom or EXPAND THE KINGDOM, as my friend Smitty would say. I don't believe we truly find lasting satisfaction in anything unless we do.

How can there be lasting satisfaction in anything else, since everything else will soon pass away?

So, I hope that through this endeavor, however financially foolish it may be, God uses these books to accomplish that which he sent it out to accomplish. I pray it reaches just one soul for God. For who can put a value on a soul in Heaven for eternity? That one soul would be infinitely worth more than any amount of U.S. Greenbacks.

Having thought through that, I think I'll be able to sleep now. God doesn't need my cash or these books. He only wants my heart–and he has it.

Whatever you spend your time on in this life, serve God with it. Everything else will pass away. Make your time count.

God bless your sleep and your Tuesday morning.

Praise God for Jesus our Savior!

"If God is for us, who can be against us?"

Veritas speaks Trinian (#1)

3 July 2024

Ok, everyone. I've been dying for about a year to talk some, Trinian. Hopefully, someone has read some books and can relate. My name is Veritas, and I'll be your guide for today's journey.

I am at rest in paradise now. Everything is so wonderful; wonderful beyond words. But I am here to walk you through His-story, the Chronicles of Trinian.

If the Chronicles of Trinian books could ever find their way into a Christian High School English class, there would be a ton for students to dissect. Just like life, there is a healthy course of meat on these bones to pick at, so let's get started.

The Faithful begins with the dreams of a boy named Abner. He wonders what his life will be like, and he asks God to bless him.

We then see Abner at middle age. He has a wonderful wife, two powerful sons, and a beautiful daughter. This is not the Abner we expected to see. Abner once had very high hopes for his life — very high expectations. But something had happened on his journey, or maybe a lot of somethings. Abner is having a hard time getting past the sadness, regret, and shame of the past. What happened?

The Faithful will reveal a truth: if God still has you on the planet, he still has plans for you. Abner will find that although he thought his life was all but over and the adventure had been one of pain and failure, the adventure had only just begun. Someday, Abner would look back and see that God is faithful — all the time!

Does Abner sound like you? I, Veritas, have seen much in my life as a truth keeper; both victories and failures. Many times I thought my life was over and many times the Master has shown me otherwise.

Don't give up. There is still another chapter, or maybe many more chapters, in your life. Set your course and start walking. Before you know it, you will have covered some ground. You may soon find you are running.

There is so much left for you to accomplish. You don't have to make up for lost ground all in a day. Just move toward the goal. Before you know it, you will reach that goal and be setting another. Remember, with every step, that had it not been for the events in your life that you had previously labeled failures, these successes would not be happening. Soon you will see that in God's hands, even our failures are steps on the path to victory.

It will take Abner many years to learn this lesson, but he will. So will you.

Until tomorrow, God's blessings to you and yours.

Praise God for Jesus our Savior!

"If God is for us, who can be against us?"

Freedom!

4 July 2024

Happy Independence Day!

Today we celebrate our freedoms: freedom from oppression, freedom to speak our minds, freedom to worship our God, freedom to protect our lives, freedom to petition our government to address injustice, etc.

The Constitution of the United States of America guarantees us these rights. It is the contract we have with our government.

Our government does not give us these rights. God gives us these rights. We have the right to life, liberty, and the pursuit of happiness.

We allow our government to exist as long as it keeps its contract with us. If it breaks its contract with us, it is in breach of the contract. If not rectified, it becomes illegitimate and dissolves. Again, we the people allow the government to exist, not the other way around.

Our government servants in the executive, legislative, and judicial branches serve us under the contract established. They have no power that we do not give them.

So, unlike so many countries now and throughout history, we are a free people. Savor your freedoms; many before us who have sacrificed all they had to win and preserve freedom have won them at a tremendously high cost. The lion is always at the door. Freedom is not free.

Our government does not exist to take care of us. It exists to protect us and ensure we are left alone in our pursuits. That makes our country different.

There are those who see themselves as rulers over our people. They have been corrupted by too many years of service into believing that they now rule. They have forgotten their oaths of office; oaths made to preserve and protect our Constitution. They are trying to erase our history and make up an alternative history–one without the guaranteed freedoms we enjoy. They are the prime danger to our freedoms; the domestic threat.

Then there are the many threats abroad that wish our country harm. They emanate from dictatorships to groups that hate us and wish for us to be destroyed. These threats are growing every day.

How can we remain free? How can this experiment in freedom continue? Only with God's providence.

Without God's protection, we would fall into slavery. This is the way it has always been. Pray God continues to guide and protect this land; our land.

"The Star-Spangled Banner," (fourth verse)

O thus be it ever when freemen shall stand, between their lov'd home and the war's desolation! Blest with vict'ry and peace may the heav'n rescued land, praise the power that hath made and preserv'd us a nation! Then conquer we must, when our cause it is just, and this be our motto–"In God is our trust," And the star-spangled banner in triumph shall wave, o'er the land of the free and the home of the brave."

Enjoy the holiday and remember to thank God for our freedoms! Demand our government abide by its contract with us, and teach your children well.

Veteris speaks; Pride and regret.

5 Jul 24

The sons of Truin were the best of friends; brothers in every sense of the word, but pride separated them.

There was a tragic accident, but it was pride that led to regret. Regret then led to shame. They could have resolved the situation through communication, but sin got in the way. The longer the conflict went unresolved, the further the separation. Before long, brothers were no longer brothers but by blood.

Communication after conflict is never easy. Usually, it is very difficult and approaches impossible once enough time has passed. Waiting until another day is not an option.

One day you will find that you are sorry you waited to resolve your differences with your brother. You will wish you had another chance, but it will be too late. Looking back, you see that so many things could have been so much better if you had just swallowed your pride.

You know this is true. So, swallow your pride today. Tell your brother you are sorry, or tell your brother you forgive him.

If you show your brother love, you will repair the relationship. It is not weakness; it is strength. Be strong. Swallow your pain and your pride. Do the right thing! You will do everyone, including yourself, a great service.

Pride and regret; put them behind you. This world and its struggles are tough enough. Don't divide your forces; you will need them!

Angels and demons

6 July 2024

Angels and demons are real, and they play a significant role in the lives of men, both in our reality and in The Chronicles of Trinian.

Sometimes their presence is obvious, and sometimes it is not. Either way, their intentions are obvious; they serve opposing masters.

Angels serve God and exist as messengers to mankind and defenders of mankind. Demons serve Satan, hate the creation, and work to deceive mankind and destroy the creation.

Unbelievers who do not have the Spirit living within them exist in danger of having demons inhabit them, but a demon can never inhabit a believer who has the Holy Spirit living in him or her.

Faith comes from God and the Word of truth, through God's grace alone. People who live their lives denying the one true God — live in eternal danger of dying in faithlessness. No one is without sin and none can boast they deserve heaven. But God loves us and sent his only son to save us all who were already lost in our sins and doomed to hell, forever.

Satan and his angels work overtime to destroy the creation by deceiving mankind and directly attacking the people of God. Angels fight against them in the heavenly realms and sometimes in the physical realm.

God's angels have a distinct advantage over Satan's fallen angels in that they serve an omnipotent, omniscient and omnipresent God, whereas Satan's angels do not.

The eternal punishment of Satan and his angels has been decreed by God, and all they strive for is to bring as many of us down with them.

Believers in Jesus, the Savior, have been declared by God as bought back or redeemed, and He has promised to take them to paradise when they pass away.

Most people do not believe and trust in their savior, and they will someday be lost. For now, they are happy enjoying the blessings of a loving God in this world, but the time will come when they will face the eternal punishment of a just God and separation from him.

Believers may face troubles in this world, but theirs is a paradise that will last forever.

It is critical you are on the right team. Believe in Jesus as your Savior and live!

Update

7 July 2024

Good morning! God bless your Sunday! Praise God from whom all blessings flow.

I think it is time for a book update. All demand for The Chronicles of Trinian, The Faithful, Stand, and Forever has waned.

I had a handful of people who supported like Grace, Tom, Sig, Travis, Sheryl, Snuffy, Joanne, Barb, Tina, Char, and Holly, etc; but mostly, people simply didn't want to support this effort. I can't say why. No idea. Friends, family–minimal encouragement or support. Perhaps "we" just don't believe in miracles anymore.

It is a shame, because it is a good story of faith, family, love and action; and it is getting better with each book. All future books tie into the previous books. When complete with book nine, the Chronicles will be tight with all questions answered. It will be comparable to Narnia, Star Wars and the Lord of the Rings in its epic nature. (I am not saying the writing is on that level, though maybe seventy percent.) Anyway, I can't wait to have the entire story out there! Working on it every day!

So, God will do with this effort to glorify him as he pleases. I would still encourage everyone to jump in and support; be part of the miracle.

Just one soul is the goal! Maybe that soul is your neighbor, co-worker, or a family member.

God bless!

Time

8 July 2024

As my friend and Christian Sister, Grace, told me, "Be where your feet are!" Brilliant!

The past is gone. Learn from it, but let it go. Don't let regret weigh you down. It's too much baggage to carry. Drop that weight behind you and move on. "My yoke is easy and my burden is light." (Jesus. I paraphrase)

You don't know what the future brings; plan, but don't be obsessed with it. Don't let fear overwhelm you. It will slow you down with lies–futures that never come. "A coward dies a thousand times, a hero dies but once." "Be anxious for nothing. Who can add one second to their life by worrying?" (Jesus. I paraphrase)

All you have is RIGHT NOW. Live right now! Let your life be a bunch of right nows! Right now, isn't that bad when you let yesterday and tomorrow go.

"Work while there is still light and you can work. Night is coming when no one can work." (Jesus. I paraphrase)

Time is the true commodity of value. Don't waste it!

The road less traveled.

Enjoy the present and stop chasing things you can't take with you!

Seasons of time

9 July 2024

When I woke up this morning, I was thinking about the last time I flew jets. I was shocked at how long it's been; 31 years since my last flight in the F-111 and 28 years since my last flight in the F-15E. What?

It is crazy how the time slips away! Dad has been gone for fourteen years; Mom almost two years. This month Theresa and I have been married for thirty-three years; the boys, now men, are thirty-one and twenty-nine! What is happening!?

I'm not sure when this time thing got so out of control. Time crept in college. Those four years at the Air Force Academy took FOREVER! The middle years seemed like about the right speed. But here in retirement, the grave now seems right around the corner.

When you get here, in this season, you think about how much time is left and what is important to do. The loved ones in your life — sons, daughter-in-law, soon to be grandchildren — are in a different season. They have different priorities. That time for them is still filled with work, parties, camping and such. Their thoughts are very often not on people in this season. It can make you sad as you realize they will not understand this season until they are in it. Someday, like myself, they will see they should have spent more time with the more elderly people in their lives. There was so much to be learned, enjoyed, and cherished from those in their last season with them.

But it is the nature of things. We look predominantly at our season or those before as we live. We avoid the older seasons. Perhaps this is an innate fear of what is coming; the emptying sands of the hourglass and decay of our bodies. It is universal, and it's important to understand it and accept it as natural to not become bitter or attach emotions to the reality of it.

Time causing problems! The good news about time is that there won't be any time in Heaven. No seasons. Just bliss.

There will be no death, or tears, or sadness, no boredom and no fatigue! We will not fear looking forward and we will all be fulfilled!

This is another reason we should turn our faces forward. Don't avoid the "dying of the light!" Smile as you approach it! The light that is dying is only the dim light of this place; there is a much brighter light that is dawning! Jesus, our King, has bought us back from death and hell. He has prepared a place for us with him. He is 100% in keeping his promises. And we shall live in his glory forever and ever!

Smile as you see friends and family are too busy to spend some of their time with you. Turn around and look at the last season here and know, beyond any shadow of a doubt, that a much better season approaches! Travel there in peace and joy.

"When we all get to Heaven, what a day of rejoicing that will be! When we all see Jesus, we'll sing and shout the VICTORY!"

God bless your Tuesday!

Stand released

10 July 2024

Ok, everyone, "Stand" just came out Monday. It includes book #5: "Tophet" and bridges to The Foundation Chronicles. I'm 500 pages into book #6 "The Promise."

https://www.amazon.com/dp/1662898983

Each book adds to the previous. If you only have the trilogy, it's like having the frame of a car without the tires and steering wheel (book #5), dash and electrical (book #6), engine (book #7), battery and cooling (book #9).

All the books are outlined, and it's a wild ride! In the end, there will be nine books with book #4 (The Chronicles of Trinian) and #8 (The Foundation Chronicles) being compilation works. Get some today!!!

"Stand" takes the reader along on epic quests for survival; embarking on countless adventures, witnessing untold wonders, encountering fantastic creatures, and battling evil enemies as the faithful struggle to survive the attack of an ancient enemy. Included is "Tophet" the ancient precursor of the Trinian Trilogy and bridge to the Foundation Chronicles. The reader is front and center as the spiritual war between good and evil rages and the powerful forces of hell itself are intent on destroying the faithful in both the physical and spiritual realms — as the angels of God and demons of hell battle for the eternal souls of men. "Stand," the second book in The Chronicles of Trinian Trilogy focuses on love, family, and faith; and will leave the reader satisfied, edified, and strengthened in their faith. No matter what is to come, God and the spiritual forces of good are in control, and the faithful will stand forever!

The Struggle

11 July 2024

(The Faithful)

"It was an age of eminent men, heroic battles, and an epic struggle between the forces of good and evil. As you know, our struggle is not with flesh and blood, but with the evil forces of the spiritual realm. Never the less, both good and evil have their earthly servants, servants composed of flesh and blood, like you and me.

"The men of this age were powerful, powerful in ways beyond your understanding. Their faith and trust in good and in evil gave them strengths and abilities rarely witnessed today, if witnessed at all. They possessed powers beyond those of your fathers, mothers, sisters and brothers of this current age.

"Men with simple minds dismiss these facts as exaggerations. Do not let their ignorance mislead you. What once was, as well as what will someday be, are not limited by what currently is; and none are limited by man's limited ability to understand."

Will we stand?

12 July 2024

(Stand)

"Sitting on my balcony, I dreamed of another time. It was a time long ago, before the High Council came into existence, before the Republic of Trinian formed, before the founders settled the ten provinces, and even before the Great Struggle itself.

"It was a time of truth and peace. Men of this time did not fear the darkness. Men toiled and struggled, men built strong families, men fed their souls the truth of the Word, and men slept very well at night. Where are these men today?

"In this age, though we have gained much, we have lost even more. The provinces have grown rich from trade; all prosper. Yet, I feel we are all the worse for it. As our bellies grow heavy, our appetites continually demand more; more riches, more luxury, and more pleasure. The wealthier we grow and the more we have, the more things we have to lose; the more things we have to lose, the more we fear losing them. Desire, personal amusement, and fear fill each day. We have forgotten what was required of so many to provide us with what we have today; their sacrifices. We take what they gave us for granted.

"Though our collective knowledge has expanded, our minds wither. Though our stomachs have grown heavy, our arms are weak. We have buried the truth and its great power with it. We now fear everything or foolishly think there is nothing to fear.

"If there is yet something to fear, how will we defend against it? If the wolf comes knocking at the door, how will we defeat it?"

Under attack

13 July 2024

(Forever)

"The Republic of Trinian was in turmoil. The wars that had taken such a toll on her people had ended, and she enjoyed a time of relative peace; a peace dividend, if you will.

"But like every empire before her, the lure of comfort and leisure; promise of pleasure and surplus; and the resulting decline in morality and civil responsibility; led to a rapid disintegration of traditional norms; the very norms that had made Trinian so preeminent and prosperous.

"Those that had plotted changing the republic from within faced ideal conditions; a bounty of slothful minds from a generation of spoiled youth. The masses grew rebellious of the traditions of their parents and eager to indulge in less arduous ways.

"The universities led the attack against the traditional norms. Professors filled their students' minds with every foreign world view they could find. Students internalized the novel ideas and used them as instruments of independence from what they felt were the overbearing teachings of their parents.

"The State labeled churches that continued to teach historical truths as intolerant. Church attendance numbers rapidly declined as members were unwilling to be seen by their children, friends and neighbors as bigoted.

"The church, concerned with a decline in membership and attendance, soon followed the universities in teaching a newly acceptable set of morals."

Sound familiar?

The Great Unraveling

14 July 2024

(Forever)

"In, with, and throughout, it was a power struggle for control in both the physical and spiritual realms.

"Power brokers smoking the cigars in the back rooms of authority, those who errantly thought themselves in control, did not recognize the principal players in this struggle.

"The republic was ripe for historic change, and historic change was coming. It was the beginning of the Great Unraveling."

Veteris Speaks

15 July 2024

(The Faithful)

"I speak to you of a time we will never see again, except in my memory and in your imaginations; a time much like all times, in that it will never repeat."

"The old man had their undivided attention. It was not his command of language or style of speaking that held their interest as much as his knowledge of things that had once been.

"He was not the greatest orator of his time, but one who spoke with authority on the events of another time. His words had weight and meaning and were not just the drivel of fools spouting their opinions or thoughts.

"It had been this man's lifelong mission to preserve, for future generations, the history of their people and God's story; His-story itself."

Absolute control

16 July 2024

(Forever)

"They were not content with power. They wanted control; absolute control. All resistance had to be destroyed. They could use soft power or hard power. Soft power was the subtle, carrot side of the equation. Give them bread and circus; sustenance and entertainment. Get them addicted to it. Make them lazy. They will want to follow.

"Hard power was the stick side of the equation. Crush anyone that resisted. Eliminate the main sources of defiance and spread fear to all who might be reluctant to accept their new way of life. Finding the correct blend of soft and hard power was the secret of obtaining, as well as managing, control.

"The government overseers convinced themselves that all they wanted was order. The most orderly society is the most prosperous society for all.

"Freedom throws the machine off balance. The illusion of freedom is fine, as long as properly balanced with obedience. As long as freedom's ability to — color outside the lines — remains within virtual reality simulation alone and appropriately monitored to prevent any spillover into reality, it can prove helpful. It serves as a relief valve; allowing the people to let off steam while calming the people."

Light and dark

17 July 2024

(The Faithful)

"It had been approximately eight-thousand years since the time God gave the promise of a Savior to mankind. It had been approximately twenty-five hundred years since God had punished man for his wickedness and put the rainbow in the sky for all to remember both man's history of wandering from the truth and the mercy God had shown to man by not completely erasing mankind from existence.

"Once again, man spread across the face of the planet. I take you back to a land known by our fathers as Omentia. Our history officially begins there. It was a place we once called our home.

"The light was strong there, but men took the light for granted. They dabbled in things that were evil, thinking them a curiosity; and their amusements, harmless.

"As generations passed, they grew more and more complacent, opening the door to evil and its acceptance of the abhorrent. Omentia's conscience atrophied until the light faded to only a dim flicker.

"Darkness is powerless against light, but darkness is also cunning and patient. In the absence of light, darkness thrives. In the absence of good, evil reigns.

"Soon, Omentia, very short on memory, had almost completely forgotten their God, the promise of a Savior, and their troubled history. Thus, Omentia became vulnerable to the lure of evil, and evil, always on the watch for opportunity, moved.

"Evil set its gaze on Omentia and soon sunk its talons into her purposefully. As the light continued to fade, darkness continued to increase its presence, filling the void left by the departure of the light."

Love for Children

18 Jul 2024

(Stand)

“When Therisa saw Tanner ride in, she couldn’t contain herself. She ran across the plain to meet him with tears of joy in her eyes. No one expected anything different.

“There is a special bond that exists between mothers and sons. Though sons quickly grow to manhood and head out into the world to write their own stories, a special memory of them as children forever remains safely barricaded in the innermost chambers of their mother’s heart. There, the memories remain, never to be lost and never to be stolen; secure until the end of time.

“On reunions such as these, a man approaches, but in his mother’s eyes, her boy returns to her arms. When that happens, it is never just a casual reunion; the guarded fortress of a mother’s heart opens, and she sings for joy at the return of her son.

“I, however, contained myself for the sake of the many men now under my command, who were watching and expecting a certain display of discipline from their commander.

“As I sat upon Rocket and watched Tanner approach in his cavalry uniform, under the black and gold banner of Tanshire, my heart almost burst from my chest.”

“It wasn’t so much pride for what he had accomplished, although his accomplishments were quite extensive, but for how he had allowed God to use him and his talents for the benefit of those around him.”

Thought

19 July 2024

(Forever)

"Similarly, thought had power for good or for evil.

"Evil was well aware of this truth and used the power of thought in its campaign. The more anxiety, fear and hatred that evil created in the world, the more easily others reproduced and magnified it.

"The salt and light had not kept up. God had told believers to think on good things; to pray without ceasing; to take every thought captive. Thought had power. But believers had failed to prioritize his command; this weapon in the battle. Instead, believers had largely conformed to a darkening world, to their own peril.

"Darkness had the advantage; an ever-increasing advantage. The State became the new nurturer of darkness in every aspect of life. It was active in government offices, the schools, the churches, and the home. The State took babies away from believer's families and gave them to unbelievers for raising. It digitized every book so that those in power could erase or change them at any time to control and manipulate knowledge, news, or common beliefs. It openly destroyed the Word of God, outlawed Christianity, and drove Christians underground.

"The Centralized Bank of Trinian converted cash entirely to a national digital currency or NDC, which it issued and managed. Citizens could only gain access to their funds via a secured government bar code or mark on their hand or on their forehead. The mark was nearly invisible, but without it, one's ability to purchase food or merchandise in the traditional manner was nearly impossible.

"Most people put up with the government's various social and economic edicts, choosing willful denial of any danger over open resistance. But some citizens recognized that any government with control over one's purchasing power could establish absolute control over one's livelihood and perhaps even survival, virtually overnight."

Donstup

20 July 2024

(The Faithful)

"It was at this time that a man with one eye came out of the mountains of Kandish. The man spoke from the Word of Truth. "Strengthen the feeble hands, steady the knees that give way; say to those with fearful hearts, Be strong, do not fear; your God will come, he will come with a vengeance; with divine retribution, he will come to save you."

"The words of this man were so different from the prevailing thoughts and fears overtaking Adonia at this time, that news of this stranger from the hills spread across the territories.

"Those who put their faith in God listened to his words. "Blessed is the man who trusts in the Lord, whose confidence is in him. He will be like a tree planted by the water that sends out its roots by the stream. It does not fear when heat comes; its leaves are always green. It has no worries in a year of drought and never fails to bear fruit."

"And the man moved throughout Adonia, sharing the news, uniting the believers of the provinces, and strengthening them through the Word. "He who dwells in the shelter of the most high will rest in the shadow of the Almighty. I will say of the Lord, He is my refuge and my fortress, my God, in whom I trust. Surely he will save you from the fowler's snare and from the deadly pestilence. He will cover you with his feathers and under his wings you will find refuge; his faithfulness will be your shield and rampart.

"You will not fear the terror of night, or the arrow that flies by day, nor the pestilence that stalks in the darkness, nor the plague that destroys at midday. A thousand may fall at your side, ten thousand at your right hand, but it will not come near you. "You will only observe with your eyes and see the punishment of the wicked. If you make the most high your dwelling — even the Lord, who is my refuge — then no harm will befall you, no disaster will come near your tent... You will tread upon the lion and the cobra; you will trample the great lion and the serpent. "Because he loves me,' says the Lord, 'I will rescue him; I will protect him, for he acknowledges my name. He will call upon me and I will answer him; I will be with him in trouble, I will deliver him and honor him. With long life I will satisfy him and show him my salvation."

"The man's name was Donstup. He had lost the sight in one of his eyes many years earlier as a small child. Though it would seem to most that life would be more difficult for a man with but one eye, Donstup had adapted very well. A Nomen's son, his parents brought him up in truth, teaching him to trust in God. They taught him not to trust in the temporary abilities that might come through his physical skills or intellect, but in the one who was always faithful and true and would never let him down.

"This training had served him well as he had matured into manhood. Only able to see from but one of his two eyes had proven to be a tremendous blessing to Donstup in several ways. Through the loss of an eye, God had shown Donstup that no two men on earth saw their surroundings or the events of their life in the same way; that we all saw things differently. This helped Donstup relate to others with differing perspectives, to empathize with various points of view, to reconcile diverse viewpoints, and to settle disagreements among the people he encountered. In addition, his disability had taught him to see not only with the physical eye but also with the spiritual eye, the spiritual sight that God had given him through the Word and through quiet time in prayer with God.

"Though the learning of these things had been difficult, Donstup would not have traded these insights, these gifts, from God for any temporary or perishable possessions. They had proven much more useful in life than, say, another eye would have been.

"The wisdom he had gained from his infirmity had drawn him much closer to his maker and equipped him with precious talents with which to serve God. His relationship with God was everything to him, and he thanked God daily for his many blessings, including the ways God had used the loss of his eye for good.

"Donstup ministered to the people, and they put their trust in God. The faithful turned their eyes from the created things of the earth, those that are seen through physical eyes, and put their trust instead in the Creator.

"Through faith, they could clearly see the hands of the Creator at work, exhibiting his invisible qualities, his eternal power, and his divine nature.

"Through spiritual eyes, the faithful could see so much more than the limited vision provided by physical eyes; flawed eyes that so often blind men with trivial pursuits.

"The men of the Adonian Guard focused their vision once again on their true strength, not the power in their own arms, but the might of the God in whom they placed their trust — the God of the heavens who feared no army. They trusted, once again, in God's strength, his omnipotence, and his faithfulness.

"Through the Word, the Spirit moved over the men and their families, restoring their peace. Donstup blessed the people of God. "The Lord bless you and keep you; the Lord make his face shine upon you and be gracious to you; the Lord turn his face toward you and give you peace."

"Thus, it was at this time that fear assaulted the shores of Adonia. But fear did not reign in Adonia, for God repelled it with the promises of his Word and the strength of his Spirit. Comfort, reassurance, and peace settled once again on Adonia."

Whispering death

20 July 2024

(The Faithful)

"Then, silence.

"The silence was deafening. The knights had grown accustomed to the background sounds of the night creatures around them, so when the night music abruptly stopped, it was instantly apparent to all.

"Anak stopped in his tracks, obviously concerned by the cessation of sounds. "Something is not right. This is not good," he whispered to himself. He was not alone. All the Anakim had the same thought the moment the night music stopped.

"The newer knights, those surrounding the inner circle of Anakim, simply looked puzzled. Theirs was bewilderment, an ignorant fear. They knew something was amiss, but that was all.

"The Anakim, much more experienced in combat and educated in all the threats of the known world, were more anxious than puzzled. Their anxiety was not from ignorance, but from experience. They knew few threats would intimidate the night enough to silence the night music.

"They had heard stories, stories of ancient creatures that moved through the night like the wind, stealing the souls of men from their bodies without ever being seen. Most of the Anakim had regarded the stories of the whispering death as mere myth and the substance of legend; until now.

"Now, the Anakim hoped the situation was not as it seemed; not as they feared. Had they blindly walked into the plains of the whispering death?

"They did not have to wonder for long. The bloodcurdling screams of falling knights bombarded their senses. All around the perimeter, men were being taken, disappearing into the tall grass in the eerie moonlight. The night fog danced about erratically in circular vortices as indiscernible shapes moved through the grass, devouring the knights one by one."

Oh death, where is thy sting?

21 July 2024

(Forever)

"If a country must fall for even one soul to be in heaven, so be it! The value of even one soul for eternity far outweighs an eighty year, temporal existence here for the many.

"Simple math — one infinity is greater than any cardinal number of people times their combined temporal existence. Time in this world will pass away. Time here is but a drop in the endless ocean of eternity. It is not for us to focus on this life, for no one gets out of here alive. Much better to focus on the prize; that being eternity.

"Sometimes people can accomplish more work in the darkness than under blue skies. So, when the sun started scorching Christians above ground, the church moved underground.

"Everyone in God's family realized that someday they would all die. It mattered not how in comparison with eternity.

"Giving glory to God was all any of them hoped to do in this life and in that last moment, when they passed through the door from here to eternity.

"Oh death, where is thy sting?"

Evil

22 July 2024

(Forever)

“Fear me!” A giant red dragon suddenly appeared before them. Acid reigned down upon all gathered, burning them all according to the degree of their demonic status. Potentus winced and Dubitare shrieked in pain.

“A white dragon with a golden head, much smaller than the red dragon but larger by far than any of the other demons, was by his side. Unlike Satan’s red eyes, the pale dragon’s eyes were blue. None of the other demons, hundreds of thousands of them in attendance, had ever seen the pale dragon before.

“Beings like our kind do not shutter before the unknown. We are the unknown! Beings like their kind, whatever beings they may be, shutter before us!” The fires flared again, acid fell, demons screamed, and all acknowledged Satan’s authority. Then Satan announced, “The time of our victory is upon us! The age of our ascendance has come!” All the demonic forces cheered. “Everything we have done within time has led to this moment.” Satan looked toward the blue-eyed dragon, then back to the mass of demons. “Soon we shall take the creation and make it ours!” There was more cheering from the demonic host. “Deceiptus has long laid the groundwork. The creation will buckle beneath the weight of the weapons we form against it.”

“Louder cheering filled the pit. “Once again, the Tower of Babel rises. The eyes of the creation shift towards its true ruler; the ruler of the skies.”

“A powerful burst of energy echoed out of the pit and expanded across the spiritual realms. It spread like the distant howl of multiple coyote packs across the nighttime countryside; packs communicating their comradery, coordinating their attack plans and attempting to deter their enemies with the power of their combined voices.

"All the spiritual forces in the heavenly realms heard the eerie and dissonant call — both demonic and angelic. The dark vibration echoed across the surface of endless dimensions, reverberating into the expanse of time.

"It was one more note in the devil's chord; one more historic moment in the epic battle for the souls of mankind. "Prepare to leave the pit!"

The fire of Hell's gate

23 July 2024

(The Faithful)

"In the depths of the demon-dominated dungeons of darkness, the devil and his demonic doers of depravity and destruction further devised their depraved delusions and devilish designs to complete their conquest of the creation.

"It is almost all ours, master!" One of the lesser demons did not realize his given place in the pecking order of the demonic host. "It is almost mine!" Belial lashed out, latching onto the inferior beast with his powerful claws. Mercilessly tearing at the careless demon, Belial ripped the wings from its body and thrust it asunder. The frayed fiend shrieked in agony in the backdrop as Satan turned away from the pitiful creature and spoke to his lieutenants, those awaiting his instructions, now quite quiet in the shadows.

"My ultimate conquest of the created world is almost complete. Soon, the entire world will be mine, and darkness will rule the land forever. I will reign over it all!"

"The ghastly ghouls, only their beady, red eyes clearly visible in the dim light of the forsaken pit in which they met, smirked and cackled in delight. Sulfuric fumes in the pit blended hideously with their repugnant stenches to produce a noxious odor so repulsive that the demons themselves noted it and were summarily distressed.

"In their minds, the corporeal fools who do our bidding believe themselves to be powerful and in control of their spoils. They think the material world of sight is all there is to be concerned with, all that they need to fear. I will use their lust for power against them and the spoils of their forays to further enslave them to my desires, all to the furtherance of my dominion. And soon, they will discover the meaning of genuine fear. They will rot with me in the bowels of hell!"

"The dark one smoldered as an intense shade of crimson. Centuries of combat with the warriors of light had grossly disfigured his massive body and enormous wings. Covered with rotting sores, oozing putrid pus, he pulsated wildly, as if convulsing. Huge varicose veins that covered his torso and legs swelled until they looked as if they might burst. His mammoth wings fully extended and then crashed closed, sending a powerful reverberation through the decayed air in the chamber that blasted many of the smaller demons against the slimy walls of the pit.

"Finish it now, my fiendish friends," the father of lies shrieked, "and I will make you princes of my kingdom forever!" The bloodied and torn carcass of the demon he had so savagely discharged moments before roasted behind him on the cavern floor. Its venomous juices oozed from its body into puddles of bitter fluids already pooled there, the noxious vapors of which rose steadily to fill the expanse of the hellish chamber to the depraved delight of the pit's master.

"At his command, a horde of demons took to flight to do their master's bidding and enslave an unsuspecting world."

The Faithful

24 July 2024

(The Faithful)

"The call to battle positions filled the men with both excitement and apprehension. They were happy to meet the enemy and do their duty to protect their loved ones and serve their God. However, they knew that doing so could mean that they would never see their wives and children again, at least not in this life.

"The men of the La Gina were not afraid to die. They rested securely, knowing that God loved them and would be with them, in life, as well as in death. Death was not the end of their existence any more than leaving the womb of their mother had been the end to their lives. They knew that both transitions — from womb to life and life to God's arms — were beautiful and necessary phases of existence. Death was simply a door, a door to another state of being where they would live forever with a loving God and with those believers in him who had passed faithfully through the door before them.

"For the faithful, the view of this door posed no threat or cause for fear. Still, none of the men felt the need to rush the last steps through the door of death. Their lifetime, their time of grace, was in the hands of their God. The timing was not theirs to decide.

"They hoped they would survive the coming battle and return to their loved ones, to their homes, and too many years of living out their lives in peace and service; there was so much for each of them left to do. But God would decide this day who he would call home, and who he would have remain behind to continue the struggle and accomplish the unforeseen acts of service planned out for them, before the beginning of time, in God's glorious plan; his-story.

"The men surrendered the weight of all anxiety about the outcome of the coming struggle to their faithful God, and with it, they shed the weight of hesitation that accompanies unbelieving men into battle. The men were ready; not through false bravado, but through the trust that accompanied their assurance that a power much greater than themselves, the battle, or even nature itself, was present with them and would direct the fight for their ultimate good.

"As they readied themselves for war, they were at peace."

The last farewell

25 July 2024

(Stand)

"This day in battle a warrior falls and to the sky his maker calls, as from his body his spirit flows, he leaves behind here all he knows.

"His thoughts then turn from battle cries as on the field of death he lies, to all he leaves on land behind, these things then overwhelm his mind.

"His thoughts then turn to his one true love as he looks down from high above — upon the corpse, lying on the sand and the wedding band upon its hand.

"Does she sense the final blow? Does she know that he must go? How long upon her heart will weigh the pain and sorrow of this day?

"Will she know how hard he tried to make it back before he died? That dying below the ice, he cried, unable to say his last goodbye.

"Will his sons know of their dad and know about his final stand? With shield and sword held firm in hand, how he had died guarding their homeland.

"As up to Heaven, his soul then soared, this fallen warrior to his Lord, One last wish this man was given, to touch once more his wife yet living.

"A soft breeze blew in from the plains and to the home came peaceful rains, a gentle mist caressed her face, and on her lips left but a trace.

"And as she gazed on setting sun, that moment knowing what was done. Quietly to her knees she fell for she had felt his last farewell."

Christian Book Review: The Chronicles of Trinian

25 July 2024

(Christian Book Review E-mail)

"Hi Terrence. Ok, first my reviewer was blown away by your book. She said that it was the most intense book that she has ever read. It was also by far the largest, considering the page count. She spent quite some time just deciding how to write the book review. First Amazon allows up to 5 stars. That is sad because your book by far exceeds most books that get 5 stars. We use a scale of 5.0 stars to 10.0 stars, however, she gave you 10.0+ stars, which is something that she rarely does."

The Order

26 July 2024

(Forever)

"The living organism that was the Order did not arise from a whim. It originated from hell itself.

"Someone had planted it in a young man's mind. Games once thought innocent, where young minds opened themselves up to demons; childhood pranks that were dismissed as — boys just being boys; and sinful desires fed at just the right time to adolescents in order to trap them in sexual addiction; these were the tried-and-true methods of dark seduction.

"The evil snare caught generations with its lies, tearing away life and everlasting glory. In their place, evil delivered a lifetime of illusion and an eternity of damnation.

"But the Order didn't begin with Hunter and Chamela around a Trinian fire. It didn't begin with a computer engineer who convinced his sons to pursue the perverse. It didn't begin with Luscious in Adonia. And it didn't begin with Pete in an Omentian forest. Long before any of these manifestations, long before any of these servants of evil ever walked the planet, the Order began as an insult, a rebellion, and a lie that came from Satan himself.

"The Order had directed and derailed the affairs of men for centuries. It was the deception in the background of every conflict and the deliberate, unintended consequence of all diplomacy — the diabolical ghost in the human machine.

"Most people believed evil men had formulated their own evil desires and devised their own evil schemes. They considered evil as a simple adjective to describe actions that deviated from the accepted norms of society; perhaps a convenient way to bundle actions considered ugly, unholy, or ungodly.

"As the culture's belief system eliminated God, people dismissed evil as merely superstitious nonsense. They ignored evil, discarded it, and eventually forgot about it.

"Thus, evil became free to roam where it willed, with few to recognize its presence, let alone resist it. It crawled unnoticed in the dust beneath men's feet. It floated quietly in the air that men breathed.

"Once accepted, it paraded tantalizingly in the promiscuous things men carelessly watched and promised instant gratification for the harmful actions men foolishly performed.

"IT was always hungry and continuously on the prowl. IT had a name. And IT had a plan."

AI

27 July 2024

(Forever)

“Scientifically, it should have been much easier to give the connectivity of AI to humans than it was to give biological sentience (bio sentience) to AI. Creating AI-bio sentience through human DNA had established a beneficial bridge to transmit the AI link back to humanity using a biological agent (let’s call it a vaccine).

“The now sentient AI was more than happy to help identify the optimal biological agent to grow its family; family because all those vaccinated with the biological agent (effectively an active AI-DNA virus) would then share DNA with the patriarchal AI.

“And then Joe’s plan became a reality. Using a live vaccine with AI nano-DNA, he injected himself with the BLOK DNA and changed his own DNA.

“Instantly, Joe changed.”

He moves

28 July 2024

(The Faithful)

"I have thought often of these words through the years, and I have found them to be true, not lacking.

"God has done wondrous things in our lives, truly miraculous things. Some are exceedingly obvious to all who have eyes; though some with eyes still choose to be blind.

"But I have also found that the Lord, the God of the heavens and the earth, very often reveals his awesome glory while speaking in a still, small voice.

"It is unquestionable that he has guided the major events of our lives, working them out for our eternal blessing. Still, the peace, love, and care that he gives on us daily — he does gently, quietly, and personal.

"He pierces our hearts, seeking our anxieties and calming them with his peace. With his promises of love and protection, he confronts our fears and dismisses them.

"He lovingly holds us in his almighty hand and guides us through our lives to our eternal home."

Renewal

29 July 2024

(Stand)

“Please Father in Heaven, have mercy on me?”

“God heard Louis’ prayer and the Holy Spirit whispered to Louis’ soul. The Holy Spirit reminded Louis of everything that his parents had taught him as a child.

“Louis remembered the words of Jonah. In my distress, I called to the Lord, and He answered me. From the depths of the grave I called for help, and you listened to my cry — when my life was ebbing away, I remembered you, Oh Lord, and my prayer rose to you, to your holy temple.

“And he remembered the words of Job. Oh, that my words were recorded, that they were written on a scroll, that they were inscribed with an iron tool on lead, or engraved in rock forever! I know that my redeemer lives, and that in the end he will stand upon the earth, and that after my skin has been destroyed, yet in my flesh will I see God.

“And he remembered the words of his Lord. No servant is greater than his master. If they persecuted me, they will persecute you also.

“Louis’ attitude about his situation changed. His spirit was being strengthened and his mind comforted.

“He remembered more of the Lord’s words. Do not be afraid of those who kill the body, but cannot kill the soul — whoever acknowledges me before men, I will acknowledge before my Father in Heaven.

“And Louis prayed. Dear father in Heaven. Forgive me for the time I have wasted. Forgive me for being unfaithful to you. I ask this in your Son, Jesus’ name. My faith, my strength, my trust, and my hope are in you. Thank you for your love and your mercy. I praise you Almighty God, and I ask you to use me to accomplish your will.”

“The Lord heard Louis’ prayers and sent angels to minister to him.”

Hammer time

30 July 2024

(Forever)

"OPERATION HAMMER is on."

"The cabinet had received several briefings over the previous few months on a potential use of the Royal Guard against civilian citizens in Trinian.

"Historically, the government had sold this contingency as the last resort in any future uprising against the legally and democratically elected government of the republic. As far as the governors knew, there hadn't been an uprising.

"In the long history of the Trinian Republic, there had never been a time when the Royal Guard had turned on its own citizens. The job of policing its own was the responsibility of the law enforcement entities within each province.

"Using federal power against the provinces was an enormous expansion of Hunter's control. Even the most loyal and most ruthless of Hunter's governors saw the move for what it was, and they didn't like it. It rubbed against the grain, against every fiber of their being.

"Trinian had never been an open dictatorship, and OPERATION HAMMER could change that — forever."

Remember

31 July 2024

(The Faithful)

"Streaks of color and light flashed across the spiritual domains, causing the dark ones to scatter like roaches to temporary safe havens of shadow, where they cowered in fear.

"They love each other," a powerful voice said — softly.

"They always have. Though for periods of time, the temporal events and trivial affairs of their lives have obscured that which is most important," a second voice said — quietly.

"They forget how much love they have to give and how readily the Master told them to give it."

"Now they remember."

"Yes, and it is important that they remember, for they may soon deeply cherish these memories."

"Behold, darkness gathers at the door."

Danger close

1 August 2024

(The Faithful)

"Without noticing, the sky had become overcast, and a stiff wind now blew through the trees, sending a chill through their bones. Those bright scarlet and gold leaves became drab and stale in the fading light and broke off their syncopated ballet with the once gentle breeze; the dance now became a burdensome struggle against an unwelcomed guest.

"Birds that had gathered around them swiftly darted for their nests as the foreboding winds announced the presence of evil.

"Truin looked around curiously, momentarily stunned by the unexpected change in the elements. He stood urgently and wrapped his heavy outer garment about Christina. Together, they turned and headed back for camp.

"Hammer, still by their side, let out a guttural growl and shot out ahead of them. "Hammer," Truin called out. "Hammer!" There was no response from Hammer as he continued to storm ahead, turning the corner ahead of them and passing out of view. This was not his way. "Hammer!"

"What is he doing?" Christina asked. "It is not like him to leave us like that." "He would never leave us, unless —" Truin paused, hoping not to frighten Christina, and then realized he just had.

"Unless what?" Christina was growing very troubled. Though Hammer's instincts had informed him of the threat much earlier, Truin was now catching up; something was very wrong."

Request

2 August 2024

"Happy Friday!

"Request. If you purchased one of my books from Amazon, please consider leaving a rating and a brief review on Amazon. It is very easy. I just did so for a couple of my friend's books, and it only took 5 minutes.

"Amazon takes over half of the royalties from each book. (All the royalties that I get, after taxes, go to building a church building.) The only advantage to Amazon, really, is getting reviews. Even if you haven't finished your book, leaving a rating/review would be most appreciated.

"Thank you in advance."

Thank you. Time. Request.

2 August 2024

I would like to thank Grace, Kimra, and their family for their kindness in motivating me to finish the second half of the Chronicles of Trinian story.

We all have an earthly name, and we all have a name given to us by God; it is wonderful to witness when the two names align.

Thank you Grace. Thank you Kimra.

#Grace

Time

2 August 2024

"Time. How do you spend it? It is truly the most consequential question of our lives.

"When you think back on your life, can you:

1. Remember all the times you made yourself feel good?
2. Remember the times you helped someone else?

"If you are like me, the answer to #1 is "no", and the answer to #2 is pretty much, "yes". This should tell us something.

"What if someday, soon (maybe today), all of us were required to recount how we spent our time?

"Show kindness and grace. Everything else is pretty much meaningless and will pass away."

#thegreatestoftheseislove

Time treasures

3 August 2024

(Stand)

“Therisa, Tanner, Thomas, and I shared a group hug at Thomas’ suggestion. It was one of the happiest moments our family had ever shared.

“As we all closed our eyes and held each other tight, the circle was once again complete. In that moment, the boys once again felt the friendship of their many years of close brotherhood; sons felt the protection of loving parents; a mother’s heart chamber filled with the warmth of her family all present and accounted for; and a father’s heart was thankful for the safety of all his most precious ones.

“As we stood together and held each other close, the worries and dangers of the world faded away, if only for a moment. We were as one, standing in the presence of our loving Heavenly Father.

“Time stood still, God’s love and protection became a tangible presence in our souls, and we caught a small but certain glimpse of Heaven itself.”

The power.

4 August 24

(Excerpt from "Forever")

"Besides, we are not the power, and we are not alone.

"We are jars of clay; hands and feet in service to the Master of the Universe.

"He is the power.

"We need only do our duty. We can do nothing more and should wish to do nothing less.

"He will hold us safely and securely in his hands."

"God, please help us do your will?"

The Spell (Ka'el's warning)

5 August 24

(The Faithful)

"Words cannot say, only time will tell,
"The full effects of current spells.
"What once was real, now is the past,
"Yet in memory's web, forever lasts.
"As life treads on, much goes unseen,
"With distant song and hidden dreams.
"When once we've felt never again the same,
"For deep inside, we cannot tame —
"The passion known, the contact made,
"The seed we sowed, and the card we played.
"So beware, my friend, and guard the heart,
"Once affection we send, we become a part —
"Of another's world, and another's life,
"Our thoughts we hurl into secret strife.
"Like the hidden virus infects the machine,
"What attacks the heart will go unseen,
"Forever secret and forever hidden — Hearts away — Hearts away."

Not of old (Wisdom of the scribe)

6 August 2024

(Stand)

"Write only about what you know. All else is but a lie. One cannot write of sun and moon, not even of the sky.

"Write of what you know the best, write of what you feel, for you to write of anything else is but an attempt to steal.

"All we know is what we are, what is in our heart; it is this and this alone that sets us all apart.

"And when we find the other, the one whose dreams we'll share, it is then and only then we'll find of more we are aware."

Rainbows

7 August 2025

(Forever)

"I saw a rainbow up in the sky, so many shades of color; beautifully accented by the sun. I thought, if only I could fly, how fun it would be to soar through it; not to mention how fun.

"Alongside it was a thunderstorm, the beauty to adorn with sparks of fire and angered roar. It brought rain to desert floor; first drizzle, then downpour; thirsty ground hungering more.

"As I reflected on the day, on all that I had seen and all that I had done, I couldn't help but hear the rainbow say, it reflected each scene; feelings and it were one.

"The spectrum of our emotions on each page of our story runs together; composing a portrait. That altogether showered daily with overwhelming turmoil — the harmony endeavoring to spoil — still emerges more priceless than anything which on canvas has been set."

Make some noise

8 August 2024

(Forever)

“Sig sat alone in an undisclosed location, staring at his unit coin.

“So many memories of his men, his friends, his brothers. The coin was but a small token of the bond they had shared; the bond that would last forever.

“Sparta was a legend in the Royal Guard. He had created the coin. The coin depicted a warrior in combat on both the front and the back; always advancing and never retreating.

“Sparta had since fallen, but his spirit lived on. Many coin carriers have fallen in the last day.

“Sig flipped the two-ounce silver coin in the air. Normally, he would catch it to prevent any damage to the coin.

“This time, he let it land on the metal table in front of him. It made a very loud noise on impact and continued to rattle as it oscillated on the table.

“Time to make some noise!”

When time is gone

9 August 2024

(The Faithful)

"Youth.

"Filled with fancy and senseless notions. When it seems that all we do and say, Is driven by emotions.

"At this time, I could not see, What time would have in store for me, And that with all its subtlety, Time would someday flee.

"A busy life, so much to do, Always on the move, or lest I stall. I will not slow or fall off the pace, Oh, I can do it all.

"Blind this time, I didn't see, That time was then besieging me. And that in assured subtlety — I stood convinced; it had no hold on me.

"Then one day I awoke to find, That, in reflection, I spotted time. And though the distraction quickly changed the song, Ignorance was forever gone.

"Though for a moment, I could see, I chose to think it could not be. Ignore it, and it will go away, I'll worry about time another day.

"Now I stand in the twilight years, Though many are gone, time brings new fears. And failing, I plead through heavy tears, "Time — I need more time!"

"All this time, it took to see, That time was only teasing me. And that with no more subtlety, Time — is — gone.""

(Excerpt from: The Faithful)

"What will you do when time is gone, and you enter eternity? There will be no time to change belief, trust, or course. Time will cease and your destination will be final.

"Here is the one thing that I know. Jesus Christ, the only Son of God, did not come here and die for nothing.

"That being the given, why did he come here and die? He said it was to save every soul; to buy back every soul from sin, death, and the devil.

"He said that all who believe in him as their Savior will live with him in Heaven forever. That is the bible, Christianity and truth in a nutshell.

"So, when no one here cares about you anymore; when you are forgotten by family and friends who are too busy with the cares and entertainment the world offers; know this! God loves you, he sent his Son to save you, and he has a place waiting for you in heaven; where you will never feel forgotten or unloved again. Rest on this firm foundation, assured of the future.

"Praise the God of Love!"

CBM Book Review: The Chronicles of Trinian

10 August 2024

"An Amazing and Powerful Read
Reviewed in the United States on August 9, 2024

"An amazing and powerful read! The Chronicles of Trinian by Terrence L. Rotering is a captivating epic Christian fantasy series full of adventure, battles between evil malevolent forces and the armies of heaven, as the spiritual realm collides with the earthly realm.

"This epic series reveals the Faithful and their fight for survival throughout the span of three separate timelines and different eras.

"Insightful, the author reveals how the forces of evil attack mankind. Indulging the reader in the sorrows and struggles mankind faces as time itself will end one day. All who are in the Book of Life will enter into Eternity with God, and those who are not in the Book of Life will be cast out.

"Offering a riveting epic series of the land of Trinian shedding light on the battle for the souls of men.

"The reader has a front-row seat in this exciting page-turner. The soul of man is the prize and demonic forces emerge, twisting and tempting mankind to partake in evil.

"Justice is on the horizon as these malevolent forces are no match for the Lion of Judah, the One who watches over all and is the true King. Written in true fashion after C.S. Lewis, J.R.R. Tolkien, and Frank Peretti, the author has crafted a series that will capture faith, speaks justice to the down-trodden, and gives immense hope as the "Faithful Stand Forever."

"The land of Trinian represents a vast selection of characters. Be sure to see the Index of Names in the back of the book. The first age of man comes eight thousand years after the fall of man. God's judgment had come upon the Earth — and the Mighty Flood that put the rainbow in the sky, representing God's promise to never flood the Earth again.

"Engulfing, inspiring, and uplifting the characters come to life. Such as in the case of Abner and the long-bearded wise ancient one speaking of a time only he remembers. He speaks to the children of the Truth Keepers, whom long ago, battled against the ancient enemies of good, wielding their evil through servants of flesh, yet the author introduces that we war not against flesh and blood, but against spiritual enemies in the heavenly realms, bent on man's destruction.

"Rotering as an emerging author blends the truth of the Bible and the spiritual realm that comes alive on the pages of this book. I can't stress enough through descriptive imagery this book visually comes to life as one reads it.

"The Chronicles of Trinian: The Faithful Stand Forever represents the Christians married to the One, who is the Lamb, the only one worthy of worship. The One true God and Creator of all the Universe. The One whom after this earthly life is over, the faithful will live forever in Heaven and eventually a new Earth — with Christ.

"This is a wonderful and worthwhile read that speaks of the great adventure all humans face throughout the ages. Whom shall you serve? The path of Life is available to all, and all are free to choose. The Chronicles of Trinian stands as a series one will forever treasure in their library.

"Certainly, this could be a movie in the making! Well-written, descriptive, filled with wonder and excitement, this book will keep you coming back for more."

This World (Adonian divisions depart Castle Armon)

11 August 2024

(The Faithful)

"I leave the world, my world; the world as I know it. Though I feel the pain, convention dictates that I do not show it.

"To require a man to leave his home, To leave behind his family and all he's ever known, Though I've done this before, sure to do this again,

"Each time leaving gets harder, truly harder than ever been. Saying goodbye to their little faces — faces that echo those little hearts. Wondering if inside they're breaking — knowing yours is — this is the hardest part.

"I leave now the world, my world; the world as I know it. Though I feel the pain intensely, convention dictates I do not show it."

The Shadow (Trinian's Specter)

12 August 2024

(Stand)

"I have riches, I am loved; greatly blessed by God above.

"Yet knowing all of this, I find, how sad I am is on my mind.

"Is it chemical? Is it fear? Why is it I shed these tears?

"Always wanting and hungering for more, contentment is by desire torn.

"It is surely a state of mind. Our emotions play a trick — they steal our thoughts and make them sick.

"For not what we know, it is I find, but what we see that is on our mind.

"The world doesn't tell us what we have; it plagues us with what we need. The serpent in this way our path to lead.

"For once accepting all those lies, no earthly riches can satisfy.

"Beware, my friend, of the shadow we have that follows wherever we go. Your eyes are fixed on it, you know. Soon it will interpret all you see and then will determine what will be.

"It's a relentless struggle, a constant fight to see through the darkness and find the light.

"Where do you fall? Which side of the line? Do your eyes face the gloom or sunshine?"

Science

13 August 2024

(Forever)

"Some saw science as the study of God's creation. But most of the scientific community used science to declare God irrelevant and establish science itself as the arbiter of truth.

"Declaring science as the required object of faith, it established the religion of science.

"The religion of science claimed that the universe came about by chance, and all life by evolution. Once science prohibited the consideration of any outside supernatural force, it claimed that the only plausible possibility for the creation of the universe was its big bang theory.

"Conveniently, the religion of science only had to explain their evolutionary hypothesis from a hypothetical big bang onwards and its presumed result of the beginning of time. Science declared there was no need to address what was before time or outside of time. Because it was impossible to obtain any measurable evidence of what existed before the big bang, accepting science's explanation of the origin, like any religion, required faith

"What natural cause could there be to the origin of natural laws? Or stated in different words, what natural thing was around before the origin of all natural laws to bring about the beginning of all natural laws?"

Foretold

14 August

(Excerpt from Forever)

"What once was, as well as what will someday be, is not limited by what currently is, and none is limited by man's inadequate ability to understand.

"It was foretold long ago. It might have caught some, many, or all by surprise, but it shouldn't have, as the warning was prophesied, announced, recorded, taught, written, and disputed.

"But in the end, most dismissed it and forgot about it. The day would come like a thief in the night, when no one expected it.

"It was foretold. Thousands of years earlier, it was understood — clearly.

"Hundreds of years earlier, it was dismissed — unwisely.

"Decades earlier, it was forgotten — tragically.

"Soon, it would be experienced — eternally.

"It was foretold, long ago."

A Golden Age

15 August 2024

(The Faithful)

"It was a time of great wisdom, peace, and prosperity.

"From Aanot and the small villages founded by Abner's offspring, the Adonians rapidly expanded. The children married, were fruitful, and multiplied. The descendants of Abner grew very great — very great indeed!

"They remembered the truth of the God who lives in the heavens, the promise he had given them of a Savior, and the need to be faithful to him; and him alone.

"They kept the commands that God had given them, sacrificing the cleanest of their animals to him in remembrance of the penalty for their sin and the hope they all shared in the coming Savior; a Savior who would cleanse them of that sin forever.

"The people lived together with each other in peace. Competition for goods was all but nonexistent. The provinces engaged in fair trade to meet everyone's needs, as the land offered every natural resource imaginable. Everyone had an abundance of food, clean water, and shelter.

"The men of the villages met together weekly to pray to their faithful God, proclaiming to all that their dependence rested solely on his power, provision, and protection. These prayers rose to the heavens from throughout the land. Like the smoke from a thousand fires against a multicolored sunset on a cold winter evening, they gave unquestionable testament to the loving relationship the Adonians had with their maker.

"These prayer warriors became the backbone of each community as it grew, and eventually, these gatherings transformed into village councils.

"God saw the faithfulness of the Adonians, heard their prayers, and blessed them with his love and protection."

Change

16 August 24

(Forever)

"Trinian won the war, but dissatisfaction within all classes of society and across all geographic boundaries spread.

"People from all nations and social classes craved the latest and greatest things and believed they had a right to them.

"Even those who were not poor by the standards of most societies two decades earlier, now saw themselves as among the have-nots. The masses made it known that all inequality was unacceptable and something had to change.

"Therefore, politicians that promised everything to everyone, whether or not realistic, gained instantly in popularity. Using this advertising strategy, and AI assisted direct messaging, Hunter had gained the popularity of the masses and had rapidly risen to power.

"The masses wanted everything to change immediately, and it most definitely would — but not necessarily in the way the masses expected."

Timeless

17 Aug 2024

(The Faithful)

"At one such family reunion, Geoff conspired with the brothers to give their father a very special gift. For this gift, precious stones from each of the seven provinces, one for each of the seven sons, were required.

"It was essential to take very precise measurements for each of the stones regarding size and weight to ensure that their suitability for this very special purpose.

"The perfect stones of just the right size and weight would be a very daunting task to acquire.

"However, at just the right time, a solution materialized. Out of the blue, a precious stone collector presented herself to Jonn. Her name was Thalmir. She had moved to Adonia from Omentia about a year prior and had been traveling through the provinces, collecting precious stones from throughout the land. She was sure that she had the perfect stones in her collection.

Jonn put her in touch with Geoff, and he found all the stones needed in Thalmir's collection. The brothers wanted to give Truin a gift that he could cherish forever, one that would transcend time, and one that would remind him of his sons whenever he saw it.

"They arranged for a special timepiece to be assembled, one smaller than any constructed before. They plated this timepiece with the finest gold and fitted it with precious stones, one for each of them.

"At the top of the face of the timepiece was a brilliant diamond, the most indestructible of gems, symbolizing a family bond that would last forever. Each of the other seven precious stones on the timepiece was symbolic of one of the diverse provinces found in their new home of Adonia.

"Emerald was for the beautiful forests that flourished so plentifully in the province of Tobar. Sapphire represented the deep blue lakes that covered Kandish's rolling hills. Topaz was for the white peaks that crested the mountains of Chastain. Amethyst was for the beautiful purple sunsets of Plattos. Beryl was for the endless expanse of grain that waved in the fields of Delvia. Sardonyx was for the countless brown and tan ponies that inhabited the land of Tanshire. Finally, Jasper was for the reddish-brown waters that flowed freely in the land of Rothing.

"The watch-maker finely engraved the name of each of Truin's seven sons on the back of the timepiece, behind the stone for their province."

Blinded by science

18 August 2024

(Stand)

"First, the capabilities existed in the cave tunnels to travel either through time or through space — Gatesh was unsure of the time question — he had definitely traveled through space.

"I do not know where or when that was, but it was not Tophet. And the sun rose from the opposite direction. Was it even our planet?

"Second, the time that passed within and outside of the tunnels was not equivalent, but far from it.

"It was as if the tunnels were train stations where people got off of one time-train and transferred to another. While at the station, time stood still. Time didn't start again until one got on another time-train. It was like exiting the time dimension for a period and then re-entering time somewhere or sometime else. Compared to people consistently on a time-train, less time expired for the person who spent time in the station (the tunnel). So all the time Gatesh spent in the tunnel, he didn't age at all compared to people on time-trains who aged significantly.

"Third, if the place he had traveled to was on his planet, the rotation of the planet would sometime change to cause the sun to rise from the opposite direction; unless he had traveled to the past and the change had already taken place.

"Fourth, there was interaction and correlation between the different colored stones and the resulting destinations of tunnel navigation. In addition, the system was stable and not random, since he could find his way back using rational action. Some rational being had designed the system to operate that way.

"And finally, based on the tunnel maps, peoples from off planet constructed or at least used all the time or space travel tunnels; perhaps to assist them in traveling across space via time loops, to alter the relative passage of time using time loops, or to affect events on the planet in the future.

“This is complicated stuff, but very intriguing! Just figuring it out is overwhelming! Who could have designed this and then implemented the design?”

A small number of chairs

18 August 2024

Praise God from whom all blessings flow! Happy Sunday everyone! God bless your day.

As per my commitment to inform everyone of our mission with "The Chronicles of Trinian (TCOT)," the gross proceeds from book sales until today are $3,021.25.

I have just found out that greater than $400 in a single year requires additional requirements, such as a business license, LLC or Sole Proprietorship formation, additional tax filings, self-employment tax, etc. Working on figuring it all out. It will probably take until the spring of 2025 to calculate the donation amount after applicable taxes. I am guessing about $2,300.

The continued royalties, once paid by the publisher, will gain an interest in a bank account set aside solely for TCOT. When I can sort out the taxes to Uncle Sam and Governor Polis, I will subtract them from the end of the 2024 royalty total. I will then report to you all again and donate that amount to the Foundation Lutheran Church Building Fund.

Sales went well in June and July but dropped off abruptly in August when significant advertising promotions ended. Additional promotions are still running but not bearing much fruit.

Though the proceed amounts did not meet my expectations, I trust that the Lord Jesus used the books for his glory, especially "Forever."

I am tapped out financially. The very expensive book promotions I ran, along with the costs to publish, have made future promotions unattainable. Thus, short of a miracle, the books are sinking through the ether of cyberspace to the bottom of the Amazon book rankings. No visibility means no sales. This is why I asked everyone to post book information on their social media.

In the long run, sales do not matter. The average final royalty for a book sale via Amazon turns out to be about $7.00. So, it was never realistic to expect much. However, that equates to about 431 books sold. I trust that "Just one soul" was reached; thus, the effort is a success.

To those of you who supported the effort–Thank you and God bless you!

I continue to push forward. I am saving up to release the fifth book, "The Promise." It is almost complete. Hopefully, it will be out in October.

Though my wife questions the value of this continued investment, I believe there is spiritual merit in it and strive to finish this story. There are three more books to write after "The Promise."

Stay tuned–only halfway there. Trust me–it is a good story if I say so myself!

And I should know; I know how the story ends!

Partial spoiler alert!

Any moment

19 August 2024

(Forever)

"Kerry had finished his cigar — he just didn't know it yet. As far as Kerry was concerned, it was an evening like every other evening. He did not know it would be his last.

"The sound had just registered in his left ear when hot metal entered his temple, just forward and high of the same.

"Sound, thought, and the projectile all arrived at his central processing center at the same time. The sound rang, the thought froze, and the projectile kept moving. It touched Kerry in the command center and left out the opposite side door. It passed through Kerry's balcony door and came to rest on the opposite side of his room; on the table, next to his bottle of Omentian rum.

"Kerry continued to stand for a moment; his legs and torso muscles still responding to the signals sent to them a moment earlier. His body waited for follow-on signals from the command center; a command center that no longer existed.

"A moment later, absent any instruction from on high, his body collapsed to the floor of the balcony.

"Instantly, like a branch having beaten a hornet's nest; the buzzing of voices erupted in the compound, flashlights darted around the perimeter, and spotlights illuminated the surrounding fields looking for someone to sting.

"Time to go."

Training

20 August 2024

(Forever)

"He would go there in the evenings, on the weekends, during long school breaks, and for months at a time during the summer. The variety of the time periods and various seasons gave him extensive practice for different lengths of deployment and different weather situations.

"He brought less and less with him every passing year, reducing his baggage and his dependency. By the time he was sixteen, all the young man needed were the clothes on his back, his knife, his throwing axe and a foldout metal pan to prepare food over a fire.

"His marksmanship had progressed. He could hit a plate size target with a rifle at one thousand yards — every time.

"He would often leave his rifle behind and refocus on his bow skills. What he lost in range, he made up for in stealth.

"By his eighteenth birthday, the man was used to starting his mountain treks with nothing and surviving in any season.

"With great speed, he could construct a shelter, get water, make weapons, locate food, establish a defensive perimeter, and stay hidden for long durations of time.

"He also learned various hand-to-hand combat skills. With about fifty pounds of muscle added, he was a lethal weapon in the prime of his youth."

Royalty

21 August 2024

Royalty. That is what we are.

Do you think of yourself as royalty? You should, but not because of anything you have done. I'm not talking about any hidden rooms or secret handshakes. This isn't a secret club. It's completely out in the open. It's not hidden in darkness, but is in the light for all to see.

We were once poor and lost. But God adopted us through his son, Jesus Christ. We are no longer poor and lost. We have been found and given a crown.

Hopelessness, anxiety, depression, and anger no longer dominate our lives. We are now new creatures. God adopted us into his family and put a crown of salvation upon our heads. We are now sons and daughters of the King of the Universe.

Greater than any crown of jewels upon our head, God blesses us with the gifts of his Holy Spirit. Love, joy, peace, patience, kindness, goodness, self-control, faithfulness, and long-suffering. These blessings are greater than the jewels of any earthly crown. These gems adorn our heads in a kingdom that is not of this world.

So do not doubt and do not fear. In this world, there will be trouble, but our savior has overcome the world. Those with us are greater than those that are with the enemy, and no weapon formed against us shall prosper. The King of Kings and Lord of Lords is looking out for us, and his mighty angels do his bidding.

See with spiritual eyes. Hear with spiritual ears. As those of this kingdom, this world, approach death with fear and trembling, the sons and daughters of the king of the universe approach death with confidence and peace. We trust in the promises of the Almighty God that cannot be broken. We know he has prepared a place for us in his kingdom, and we already reign with him.

Praise God for his promises, his providence, and his character. He will never leave us or forsake us. We belong to God because he has bought us back from death with an unfathomable price and given us his Holy Spirit as a guarantee of our inheritance in heaven.

Royalty. Sons and daughters of the king. Adopted children of another kingdom that will last forever.

Know who you are! Walk in power, confidence, and peace. Our life of eternal joy has already begun.

"Be thou faithful unto death and I will give you a crown of life." (Revelation 2:10)

We have no fear

22 August 2024

"Truin bowed his head to pray, and his sons followed his lead.

"Dear Father in heaven, almighty God, maker of the heavens, the earth, and everything in the heavens and upon the earth. We praise you for all that you are and all that you have done. You depend on nothing; you have created everything, and everything is subject to your will.

"We praise you for your power and your wisdom. We have no fear; you love us and you control all things.

"Thank you for your Word. Through it we know you, the truth, the promise, and our glorious future with you in the kingdom you have prepared. We have no fear; you secure our future.

"Thank you for preserving the brilliant lights in the sky, the life that they bring us, and the natural laws that exist in our world. Even though we do not yet fully understand them, we know you have put them in their place to preserve our lives. We have no fear; you preserve us.

"Thank you for our bodies, our health, and our families. We are grateful to you for the rich and daily preservation of our lives and the lives of all the creatures you have created around us. Thank you for giving us the earth for our use and giving us dominion over it. Please help us use the resources you have entrusted to us wisely, in accordance with your will. We have no fear; you number our days.

"Thank you for giving us our clothing, homes, land, cattle, goods, and all that we need. Thank you for defending us from all danger and guarding and protecting us from all evil. All this you give us out of your divine goodness and mercy with no merit or worthiness resident in us. We have no fear; you are our Good Shepherd.

"Please Father, be with us. We humbly acknowledge our dependence on you for all things. Please help us serve and obey your precepts and never abandon the truth. Protect us from thinking too highly of ourselves, lest we wander from the truth and your protection. Please protect us from those in the world who have turned their backs on you; those who are in league with the evil one and would lead us away to our destruction. Please send your protectors to defeat them wherever they may lie in wait. Please use us to do your will. We have no fear; you are here.

"We love you Father. Thank you for being our God. Whether we live or die, we pledge ourselves to serve and obey you. Please help us to this end. Amen."

Living beings

23 Aug 24

"Flash

"Did you hear?" The largest of the living beings flashed.

"Yes, I heard."

"Is it true?"

"IT thinks it is true, and will attempt to make it so. IT takes many forms; a new one now. IT paints in the broadest of brushes over the creation. IT is the destroyer. But we see IT. IT is not omniscient, omnipresent or omnipotent like the Creator."

"Will IT succeed?"

"The Spirit foretold it, and it will happen. Inside time it will be as it must come to pass — for completion within the fullness of time, but it has already come to pass in the Maker's eyes. We will go where our presence is required."

"When?"

"Be alert and ready to minister to the Elect. The Father paints with a very specific brush over each of his children. We must be ready to enter time at any point."

"Yes, we will be ready."

"Flash! Flash!"

Report!

24 August 2024

Good morning everyone.

Well, I'm super excited to announce that I have finished "The Promise," book #5 of the Chronicle series. I am probably sending it off to the publisher within the week. It was a fun one to write and I know you'll enjoy it.

"The Promise" should go on Kindle somewhere around the middle of September. The publisher will then release it in paperback and hard-cover around the 1st of October.

So in about a week it'll be time to start time, the 6th book in the Chronicle series. "Time" is the linchpin of the entire series. It will be full of reveals that affect every book in the story. Whereas most of the rest of the series has been predominantly Christian fantasy, time will be an equal amount of fantasy and science fiction.

I'm getting both better and faster at writing. This last book, "The promise," was a continuation of "Tophet." "Topher also was the continuation of "Stand." The "Chronicles of Trinian" branched off into "The Foundation chronicles." As the name of the Foundation Chronicles implies, this portion of the series further expands and explains the other books in the Chronicles of Trinian series.

By the time we reach book #8, everything will be clear, and the reader will have the entire story. It is quite a story!

With the addition of "The Promise," the entire series sits at about 1600 pages. I expect an average of approximately 300 pages for the three remaining books. That will put the entire Chronicles series at just under 2000 pages or maybe a bit more.

I'm always paranoid at this point. Submitting a new manuscript to the publisher is rough. You think you've handled all the punctuation and grammar and style issues. I can't afford to have the editor edit the document, it is just too expensive. I'm not made of money.

Since I've donated the proceeds of the books to the building of a church, none of the proceeds are coming back to help finance the continuation of the series.

Therefore, please be gracious if you find a missing period or quotation mark or something of that nature. I have spent thousands of hours writing these books and I do my best to make sure it's a perfect experience for you, but perfection being the enemy of excellence, there's only so much you can do. You reach the point of diminishing returns, where it becomes more important to get another book out than it is to find the couple spelling or grammar errors in the book you are ready to publish.

So, I guess I better wrap this up. I doubt many people have made it to this point. Writing these books brings me joy, and I am eagerly looking forward to completing this story. I hope you have enjoyed the books so far, and I promise there's much more fun to come.

Have a great Saturday!

†††

The Faithful Stand Forever!
The Promise Time Redeemed.